A Magnificent Crime

AB&T Novels by Kim Foster

A Beautiful Heist

A Magnificent Crime

Published by Kensington Publishing Corporation

A Magnificent Crime

Crime

KIM FOSTER

Kensington Publishing Corp.

http://www.kensingtonbooks.com

KENSINGTON BOOKS are published by

Kensington Publishing Corp.
119 West 40th Street
New York, NY 10018

All Kensington titles, imprints, and distributed lines are available at special quantity discounts for bulk purchases for sales promotion, premiums, fund-raising, educational, or institutional use.

Special book excerpts or customized printings can also be created to fit specific needs. For details, write or phone the office of the Kensington Special Sales Manager: Kensington Publishing Corp., 119 West 40th Street, New York, NY 10018. Attn. Special Sales Department. Phone: 1-800-221-2647.

Kensington and the K logo Reg. U.S. Pat. & TM Off.

ISBN-13: 978-1-60183-065-4
ISBN-10: 1-60183-065-3
First Kensington Electronic Edition: June 2014

ISBN-13: 978-1-60183-227-6
ISBN-10: 1-60183-227-3
First Print Edition: June 2014

Printed in the United States of America

For my mother,
who sat me down many years ago and
informed me I could do whatever I put my mind to.

Chapter 1

Five minutes before everything fell apart, the job was going smoothly on a number of fronts. Specifically, the forty-seven-story hotel was proving easier to scale than its glass and concrete exterior had otherwise suggested. Also, it was a clear evening, which was a rare treat for springtime in Seattle. Best of all, scarcely any people were around. In my mind this meant one thing: fewer potential witnesses to a crime.

A situation that warmed my crooked little heart.

Halfway to the top, I paused on a ledge to readjust my footing. A breeze rose up and ruffled my hair. I gazed down at the twinkling lights of the city below and took a deep breath. This was going to be good.

I was climbing this building with one clear objective: to steal a particular set of emerald earrings I happened to know was, at that moment, tucked away in the penthouse suite.

I'd been casing the hotel for two weeks. I knew when the cleaning staff polished the floors and when they took their coffee breaks. I knew when the security guards ran their cross-checks and when they chatted with the cute delivery girl who pulled their eyes from the CCTV screens.

I also knew that the couple from New York who had arrived this Thursday would be attending the opera tonight. They had tickets to Verdi's *Rigoletto* and the reception that followed. I knew Mr. Peabody would be ordering the lamb shanks for his supper, and I knew Mrs. Peabody would not be wearing her emerald earrings tonight, because she'd worn them to the symphony the night before. Besides, they clashed with the orange gown she'd selected for the evening's affairs.

Ordinarily, I might have chosen an easier route to the penthouse. Something from the inside, specifically. But this couple had insisted on a security detail, a guard posted twenty-four-seven outside their suite. When planning a job, I always preferred the option that didn't involve contact with other people. Physical barriers and technology could always be overcome; hero security guards who decided to get all suspicious about your chambermaid disguise were a far trickier matter.

Tonight was my last opportunity for this job, as this was a mere stopover for the Peabodys on their way from New York to Kuala Lumpur. They were headed to Malaysia to check on the Asian headquarters of their mom-and-pop business, a highly profitable human trafficking operation.

The thought made my stomach curdle. This job tonight was merely an assignment from my Agency, but I had to admit a certain vigilante pleasure at robbing such a repulsive pair.

My muscles burned as I climbed higher, breathing chilly air that smelled faintly of car exhaust and coffee. I was in my element. I was doing what I was born to do. Everyone's got a talent, right? Mine happened to be a prescription-strength case of sticky fingers.

I didn't view it as pathology; I was simply playing out my role in society. Every well-functioning civilization has its leaders and its followers. Its spenders and its savers. Its cops and its robbers.

My particular calling had revealed itself at a young age. I was stealthy, I had quick hands, and I was quiet. It didn't take me long to put my skills to profitable use—something beyond the artful smuggling of a tampon to the girls' room in junior high.

I was genetically destined to be a thief, but for me it was more than that. There was nothing I'd rather be doing.

I continued climbing the hotel. And then, about three-quarters of the way to the top, I began to feel the telltale signs of a highly unwelcome emotion. My pulse quickened, and my mouth grew dry.

I took a deep breath and tried to slow my heart rate. *Not now.* Ever since the London incident the previous year, strange things had been happening to me on the job.

During a minor jewelry shop heist two months ago, an uneasy chill had settled between my shoulder blades, and then I'd had difficulty breathing. I'd chalked it up to early springtime allergies. On the next job—while safecracking at a private estate—I'd experienced heart palpitations. I'd attributed that to too many lattes that day.

I focused on my breathing. Focused on the job at hand, visualizing the penthouse and the emerald earrings patiently awaiting my arrival up there. I swallowed and tried to quash the growing fear that was curling into the edges of my consciousness.

It was ridiculous. I'd done this kind of thing a hundred times. I had been a professional jewel thief for hire for my Agency for the past six years. I'd scaled buildings, leaped off moving trains, crawled through air vents countless times. There was always a tense edge, an awareness that my job was more dangerous than, say, a tax accountant's. But it had never been a problem before.

And I would be damned if I was going to let it be a problem now.

I gritted my molars together and continued climbing the hotel, clutching on to cold concrete. I pushed myself up to reach for a handhold, and suddenly the memory of the last time I was clinging to the stone of a building came flooding back. It was London, and I was at the top of Big Ben, struggling with a bad guy named Sandor, grappling over a Fabergé egg.

Back to reality in Seattle, I squeezed my eyes tight and waited for the vision to subside. When it did, I forced myself onward.

The higher I climbed toward the penthouse, the more my arms and legs shook. I pushed through it. I was a professional, and I had a job to do. Somehow, I arrived at the top. I pulled my glass cutter out of my pack and made the dire mistake of looking down.

Visions of Sandor falling and screaming filled my mind. Images flickered, and for a moment, it was me plummeting instead. Smashing on the ground below, limbs twisted and broken. Head cracked open like a cantaloupe.

Something snapped. I couldn't breathe. My heart galloped and threatened to punch through my chest wall. My head spun, and I clung to the wall.

I was having a full-blown panic attack.

I was suffocating. There wasn't nearly enough air. I needed to get out of here, get off this ledge. I felt an irresistible urge to escape; my head filled with a commandment to get to safety. The earth tilted, and I felt like I was going to black out.

It will pass. I squeezed my eyes tight and pressed myself back against the cold concrete of the building. I waited, unable to move. . . .

And then my phone rang. Or at least the wireless earpiece in my left ear did. After several rings I managed to reach a shaky hand to the small unit strapped to my hip to answer it. I knew this had to be important, because the Agency patched through only the most crucial calls when I was on the job.

"Catherine?" said a shrill voice, piercing through the pea-soup fog of my panic attack. "Are you there?"

My mother.

"I'm here," I said weakly, the waves of terror slowly subsiding.

"Are you working? It sounds very loud there. Am I hearing traffic?" She didn't bother waiting for an answer but continued with an exasperated sigh. "Do not tell me you are on the job. You know full well about your uncle's retirement party. You are supposed to be here, and you are very late." The *young lady* in that sentence was unspoken, but understood.

As supremely irritating as it was to have my mother call me while I was on a job—and Lord knows how she managed to convince them to put her through—there was a small piece of me that was thankful for the momentary distraction. It appeared to have helped drag me out of the well of my panic attack.

"I'm not going to make it to the retirement party, Mom."

"Yes, well, I gathered that. I hope you at least had a decent meal before you left. You know how I feel about you working on an empty stomach. How you can *possibly* do the things you need to do on a few pieces of sushi and three cups of coffee, I have no idea. . . ."

I breathed deeply while she continued. The wind whistled around me, and I swallowed. It was time to get off this ledge and inside the hotel suite.

"I really have to go now, Mom. I'm not in a good spot—"

"And what does *that* mean? Has Templeton got you doing something dangerous? I hope they're paying you enough. I'm sure I've mentioned it before, but I just don't think they value your work enough. Maybe if you got paid a little more, you could take fewer jobs, and that would give you more time to live like a regular human being. . . . Maybe you'd even clean your apartment once in a while and have time for family commitments, like retirement parties—"

"*Mom!* Hanging up now." I disconnected the call. I would deal with the repercussions of that at a later time. I turned my attention to the task at hand, breaking into the penthouse.

I reached down for my gear and, unfortunately, discovered a whole new problem. In the throes of panic, I had dropped my glass cutter.

I had no way of getting inside this window. I was good and trapped forty-seven stories up.

Chapter 2

The wind stirred, and I pressed myself to the window.

At this height, hotel windows don't open. Smashing the glass was not an option; that would set off an alarm. Breaking glass has its own distinctive sound frequency, and intruder alarms are set to detect that frequency.

And I certainly wasn't going to climb back down. I looked at the glass, trying to assess my options, working to suppress the panicky feeling crawling up my throat again.

I concentrated on studying the windows themselves. They were divided into two, with a smaller panel on the bottom and a larger picture-window viewing panel on top.

I pulled out my penknife and set about removing the rubber strip around the lower panel.

It took longer than I would have liked, but eventually, I got the stripping off and then, with just the right amount of pressure— more than required to open a jar of pickles, less than necessary to remove the plastic wrapping of a CD—pushed the glass forward into the room.

I clambered through the open window and collapsed on the floor. I breathed and reminded myself I was safe. For now.

I had never had a panic attack before. It was an entirely new experience, and it was one I did not relish. But I had to stop thinking about it. I needed to get my head in the game.

Fear is a luxury a professional thief cannot afford. Especially a fear of death. Yes, I'd been in tight spots before. And I'd been afraid, sure. But it had never been the kind of fear that paralyzed me. It had never stopped me from doing what I needed to do.

I exhaled and pushed the ledge out of my mind. I beelined for the bedroom in the suite. There were only a few places a pair of emerald earrings would be kept.

One, locked away in the room's safe. Two, hidden in a jewelry box tucked in a drawer. But more likely? Option three, sitting in plain view right on the dresser.

Sure enough, on the mahogany dresser top, a diamond bracelet winked at me. A jade brooch beckoned. A lustrous black pearl necklace summoned me over. And as appealing as each of these jewels seemed, they were not on my list.

So I left them alone.

Instead, I reached for the earrings that lay beside them. Briolette-shaped gems, they were a vivid green, sparkling like the Emerald City, glimmering like magically frozen teardrops of the Wicked Witch of the West.

I snatched the earrings in one fluid swoop and stuffed them into my small velvet sack.

But now I had to get out. I went to the window and looked outside. I had climbed up, so surely I could climb back down. But I felt forced away from the edge, like there was a big hand on my chest pushing me back.

Still, I had to try. I crawled through the open window onto the ledge. I got halfway out. My heart galloped, and my head started spinning. Terror shredded the edges of my mind like a combine harvester. I lunged back inside and lay on the floor, breathing heavily.

This was bad. Very, very bad.

I knew I could do it. I knew I had the skills to do it. But that head knowledge didn't seem to make any difference. It didn't seem to hold any stock in the rest of my being, the one that was screaming with every fiber that I was going. To. Die.

I needed to find another way down.

I forced myself to stand and walk over to the hotel room door.

And this was where things were going to get tricky. Because there was almost certainly a security system built into the hotel room door.

So now I was faced with the less common task of not breaking *into* a room, but needing to break *out*. Without drawing attention or being stopped by the security guard.

I checked my watch. Not much time. The Peabodys would be returning from the opera any minute.

I glanced at my outfit. Head-to-toe black Lycra. Great for staying hidden in the shadows when scaling buildings but a little too "jewel thief" in the elevator and the lobby of the Westin.

I returned to the bedroom and slipped over to Mrs. Peabody's closet. Inside were gowns in every hideous color imaginable. And about six sizes too large. It would be very challenging to be inconspicuous like that. Didn't the woman ever wear jeans? My kingdom for a nice, subtle pair of yoga pants.

And then, stuffed in the corner, I spotted a robe. A white, fluffy, otherwise nondescript hotel robe. Perfect.

Ostensibly, I could go down for a late-night swim. I grabbed the guest handbook from the desk and quickly scanned it. Pool opening hours: 7:00 a.m.–11:00 p.m. It was ten minutes before eleven.

Okay, a swim it was. But I didn't have long.

I threw on the robe, pulled the black Lycra out of view on my arms and legs, and tucked all my hair inside a swim cap I found in the bathroom. I exchanged my sneakers for the hotel slippers at the bottom of the wardrobe. I found a small tote bag—which could easily double as a pool bag—and stuffed my sneakers in there, along with my climbing gear. And the earrings, of course, tucked safely inside their velvet sack.

So far so good. But things would get sticky from here. I needed to get out the hotel room door and down the elevator—ideally without being seen. Less optimally, observed but not suspected of doing anything amiss.

I inspected the door security panel. There was a touch pad for a key code, and buttons that controlled the settings. I needed to hack in and disable the whole thing.

The first task was identifying the numbers. Fortunately, I had a complete bag of tricks with me—the tools I brought with me on every job. Girl Scouts aren't the only ones who know the value of being prepared. I pulled out my mini UV wand and illuminated the touch pad. Fingerprints smudged four of the numbers: one, three, eight, and nine. Now it was a matter of entering the various combinations. It took me a few long minutes, during which I imagined the Peabodys strolling through the door. At last, the panel emitted a polite double beep and clicked off.

I glanced back at the window through which I'd entered. It would be so easy. It was the best option for a clean escape. But the mere thought of climbing through that empty sky made me feel like I was going to vomit. Nope, I would have to go down the hard way.

And my next task was dealing with the security guard.

In casing the hotel, I had learned who was staying in the Governor Suite, the other accomodations on this floor. Paisley Shaw was a television personality, a notorious early riser. Surely she'd be in bed by now.

I encrypted my cell phone to conceal the originating number, then called the hotel front desk.

"I think something has been stolen from my room," I said, making my voice suitably shrill. "This is Paisley Shaw, and I'm in the Governor Suite. I'm in my closet, and my laptop is not where I left it. I need you to send security in here right away. Tell him not to bother knocking, to just come right in. I'm searching the drawers now to see if anything else is missing."

I squinted through the peephole in the door. The security guard was there, trying not to fall asleep on the chair in the corridor. I held my breath and crossed my fingers.

Then his walkie-talkie crackled to life. He picked it up, listened, and nodded. "I'll check it out."

As he disappeared down the corridor, I waited several seconds, then slipped out the door. Both Paisley Shaw and the guard were in for an unpleasant surprise shortly, but it couldn't be helped.

I darted to the stairwell door. I raced down one flight, then left the stairwell to grab the elevator the rest of the way.

The exposure made my skin crawl more than conversations with insurance salesmen did.

Security cameras I could take care to avoid. Less predictable were witnesses. At this hour it was unlikely anyone would be in the corridors or the elevator. But I wasn't taking any chances. I forced myself to stroll toward the elevators.

When sneaking around in a public place, there are two ways to go. One, you can skulk along quietly and sneakily. But this must be attempted only when you are absolutely positive you will not be seen. Because if you *are* caught, nothing looks more guilty.

The other way to go is walking purposefully, casually, like you're doing absolutely nothing wrong. This, generally, is my preferred way to move about. It's much easier to cover if someone asks you where you're going. But it's also far less likely that anyone will ask you in the first place.

If you keep yourself as non-memorable, as non-noteworthy as possible, you can slip through this life doing just about anything you please.

Inside the empty elevator, I pressed the CLOSE DOOR button and kept pressing it. Then I pressed the LOWER LEVEL button and did not let go until the elevator started to move downward. It's an old police trick, commandeering an elevator. The elevator wouldn't stop now until it reached the lower level.

The car glided all the way down, motor humming, a vanilla instrumental version of Van Halen tinkling softly.

The doors opened, and a dimly lit, blue paisley carpeted corridor stretched out ahead. A small sign pointed the way to the pool and exercise gym.

My escape from this hotel was getting closer; I could taste it.

The pool door led directly onto a deck, into a viewing area. I pushed the glass door open and walked into a powerful cloud of chlorine. The air echoed with the sound of a solo swimmer's arms slapping rhythmically on the water's surface. I ducked into the changing room. My plan was simple at this point. Lose the robe, escape out the window, and we'd be all done here.

And it was a good strategy. Except for one small issue. As I looked around, I noticed a distinct shortage of windows. Specifically, there were none. I did a quick mental review of the blueprint. *Shit.* The changing room was smack in the middle of the hotel. Solid walls all around.

Memo to self:

Next time, mentally review blueprint before *patching together impromptu escape plan.*

Fine. I'd have to walk out through the lobby. First, I needed a costume change; I couldn't walk out wearing this robe. I looked immediately at the lockers. *Perfect.* I'd just take the clothes of the unlucky person who had come down to do a few laps.

I found the locker with the missing key. And picked the lock in approximately the time it takes to file my nails. I opened the door. I was going to be out of here in less than five—

Robe.

I stared at the sole item hanging in the locker. A white, fluffy hotel robe, the exact same one I was already wearing.

Crap. Not helpful. Not even a little bit.

Okay, I couldn't exit the hotel in my robe. I couldn't exit in my black Lycra. I couldn't sneak out a window in the changing room. What was my next move here? I thought of the emerald earrings on my person, imagined being caught with them. I couldn't let that happen.

Then I heard a faint clanging coming from the far side of the changing room. And the soft whirring of a machine. A treadmill?

The gym. There was a gym on the other side of these changing-room walls, and somebody was in there. Maybe, just maybe, *that* person had come down to the gym and changed out of regular clothes.

I entered the gym changing room, preparing to crack another locker. Instead, I was rewarded by the sight of a hoodie and sweats hanging from a hook.

I grabbed them. They were too big, but they would work fine. I replaced them with my robe.

I hesitated a second, then pulled out a wad of cash—the getaway funds I always carried. I separated several bills and slipped them into the pocket of the robe. It would be bad enough getting out of the shower after the gym with nothing to change into. The cash was my way of softening the blow.

I took the elevator up to the main floor—no rushing, no hijacking this time. The doors glided open onto a lobby that gleamed under glittering chandeliers. It smelled of floor polish and lavender. I strolled across the marble floor, past potted palm trees and plush lounge chairs, eyes pinned on the revolving doors. I was almost clear.

At that moment, a couple entered the hotel lobby, emerging through the revolving doors: a middle-aged, blowsy woman in a bright orange, flouncy gown and a gentleman who looked like he'd been stuffed into his suit. I'm not sure whose face was more pinched and sour. I recognized them instantly as Mr. and Mrs. Peabody. They were returning from the opera.

I stepped out of their path as they strode into the hotel, oblivious to anyone else. A faint smile played on my face. In two more steps I was inside the revolving doors, spinning my way to freedom.

As I stepped into the cool night air, I knew I was clear. I walked farther, putting distance between myself and the hotel. Relief washed over me like surf on a beach.

But it didn't last long. In spite of the success, I had a much bigger problem. I had put myself in a highly compromising position because of fear. Because of a terror I had allowed to control me. And that was not okay.

Paralyzing fear was a major liability for a thief. And it wasn't particularly compatible with a life of crime.

I'd become spooked. I'd heard other thieves talk about this. But I'd never imagined it would happen to me.

So what was I going to do? I could barely execute the most straightforward of jobs. How would I fare doing something more complicated? And dangerous?

I kept walking, past glowing shop windows and banks with their locked-down entrances. A cab honked somewhere behind me, and a crosswalk sign uttered its chipper bleep.

No need to overreact, Cat. Surely it was just a passing phase. Maybe I just needed a little time. A short break.

I nodded. *Fine.* That was what I'd do. I would talk to my handler, Templeton, and tell him I needed a brief hiatus—some time to rest and clear my head. No heists, no jobs for a short while. A few weeks should do it. Enjoy a nice, easy life for a bit, specifically with no life-threatening scenarios. I'd be ready to come back to work after that.

I stood at a corner, waiting for the crosswalk light to turn. A cool breeze kicked up; it smelled of rain. A storm was coming.

And then someone gripped my upper left arm with a hold as tight as a pit bull's jaws. Someone else grabbed my right. The hands belonged to two men the approximate size of Kodiak bears.

"Cat Montgomery," the one on my right said in my ear, his voice low and threatening. "We need you to come with us."

Chapter 3

Panic flooded over me, and alarm bells clanged in my ears. Had I been less distracted, I might have been quicker with an evasive maneuver. But it was too late for that—these men had grips of iron. There was nowhere for me to go.

As they marched me quickly down a side street, I clenched my teeth, mostly with anger at myself for not being on my guard immediately after a job. I looked sideways at them. These guys did not look like cops. Were not acting like cops.

I needed to get out of here. I didn't know who these men were, and I didn't want to know.

Then, before I could do anything, a black Lexus limousine pulled up to the curb.

This might be my only chance to get away. The one thing I had to my advantage was that people usually underestimated me. Especially men. Especially steroid monster-type men. I began to execute a Krav Maga escape maneuver to break free—and found my move immediately anticipated, eliciting a counter-maneuver from the man on my left.

I barely had a second to register shock at this as the door to the Lexus flung open and I was roughly stuffed into the backseat.

This was bad.

I struggled upright. A man sat opposite me, and the two thugs lowered themselves in on either side of me. My every nerve screamed at the entrapment, but I stayed quiet, rapidly making calculations and observations. The interior was lined with buff-colored leather, and there was a lit crystal bar at one end. The air smelled of cigars and single malt.

The limo began to move, gliding quietly away from the curb. I quickly glanced out the window; to stay oriented, I needed to keep track of the direction we were headed in.

I turned my attention to the barrel-chested man sitting opposite me. He looked to be in his late sixties. His watch, a Patek Philippe, was worth more than my condo. He watched me coldly from behind gold-rimmed glasses. The downturned, taut set of his mouth betrayed a misanthropic son of a bitch.

I looked closer at his face, and recognition clicked.

Icy cold water poured down my spine. I was in trouble. Very big trouble.

Albert Faulkner III had been the victim two years ago of a high-profile theft: the Caesar Diamond. The jewel was a sixty-four-carat, cognac-colored stone, one of the largest in private ownership. It had been ripped from the famous Kimberley mine in South Africa in 1982, cut into a cushion shape, and sold at auction for six hundred thousand dollars. It was considered a deal at the time—brown diamonds were not as fashionable then as they are now. In today's market, its value would be much more than that. The Caesar had been the pride of Faulkner's substantial collection.

Until two years ago, that is, when it was stolen from his private safe in Palm Springs, California. The perpetrator was never caught.

Faulkner had been quite public about the fact that if he ever caught the thief, he would have his revenge. His threats were highly un-pleasant but rather creative, with a . . . shall we say, *medieval* flavor. Fortunately, he never discovered the identity of the bandit.

Until now, it would seem.

I tried to still my nerves, to not show visible shaking, as he leveled his viper gaze at me.

"Miss Catherine Montgomery. We have some business to attend to, you and I."

"Oh?"

"I believe you took something of mine."

My stomach curdled. I needed a way out of this vehicle. "What do you mean?" I decided to stall. Stalling was always a safe tactic.

Faulkner gave an infinitesimal nod. In a heartbeat, the thug on my left grabbed me by my throat and gripped firmly. Panic bounced inside my skull as crushing pain seared into my throat from his grip. I raked at his hand. I couldn't move it.

"Miss Montgomery, perhaps you don't realize this, but I do have other business to attend to besides yours. So cut the shit," Faulkner hissed.

"Okay," I choked out.

The thug released me. I breathed hungrily and rubbed my bruised throat.

Memo to self:

Stalling can, in fact, be a very poor *choice in certain circumstances.*

I realized the only way to get out of this car alive was to play along, play nice. My next move was straight-up honesty.

"You're talking about the Caesar Diamond," I said.

"Very good, Catherine. Now we're going to get somewhere."

"It was nothing personal. It was just my assignment." I tried to strike an innocent lamb expression. This also happened to be the truth. I worked for an organization—AB&T, the Agency of Burglary & Theft—as one of their roster of professional thieves. They assigned us heists whenever they were hired by an outside client in need of a job done. Much like an advertising agency, but with a little less pinstriping.

"Oh, yes. I'm sure it was just your assignment," Faulkner said. "Nonetheless, you were the one responsible. And you cost me dearly."

I frowned for a minute, thinking. "But didn't your insurance cover the theft?" The idea that I'd done a job that violated one of my rules made me very uncomfortable.

You see, I have three policies, my Thief's Credo.

Never steal from anyone who would go hungry.

Never steal anything that's not insured.

Never steal frivolously.

Stealing was my job. But I decided long ago that this didn't give me a license for bad behavior in the rest of my life.

Faulkner looked at me with impatience. "Yes, of course my insurance covered it. That's not the point. I lost something special. Something no amount of money can replace. And now I want it back."

I studied Faulkner carefully. There was something heartfelt in what he was saying. Two years ago, when I'd been casing his home and planning the Caesar theft, I did some background research. I had encountered stories about Albert Faulkner III. His family had been wealthy and powerful before the stock market crash in 1929. But that was fifteen years before Faulkner was born. He had grown up the hungry youngest child in a house full of kids who remembered what life was like before, and with a father embittered by the loss of wealth, status, everything. They had been raised to fight for everything they had lost, taught to claw and battle back to the top, trained to possess and hold on to every scrap that was their own.

I sat silently, not sure what he wanted me to say at this point. I actually sympathized with his plight. But did he really expect me to hunt down the Caesar and steal it back for him?

I didn't have to come up with any sort of response, however, because he kept talking. "Trouble is," he said, "I've had my people look into it. And here's the tricky bit. There is no Caesar anymore. It was broken up into three pieces and sold off. The pieces are scattered all over the place now."

I winced at the very idea. It was repellent. How could they do it? The Caesar had been spectacular. I remembered holding it in my hand, admiring the fire that smoldered inside the ice. How could they break up such a rare gem? At the same time, I knew why it had been done. The Caesar was such a recognizable diamond, even though it was worth more as a whole stone, intact it was, essentially, worthless. You wouldn't be able to sell it, wouldn't be able to move it. The only way to gain financially from stealing the Caesar would be to break it up and sell off what would still be decently large diamonds.

But where did all this leave me?

"So . . . you want me to, um, retrieve the pieces for you?" I said, guessing.

His mouth twisted, and he laughed scornfully. "No. Those pieces are meaningless now. The Caesar was special to me, but it's gone."

I found myself of the same opinion as Faulkner. But if he didn't want me to steal the pieces, why had I been brought here? My skills were of no use to him.

My skin cooled. Perhaps he just wanted revenge. I had an image of my throat cut, my body dumped in a ditch somewhere. I shuddered. I had to get out of this car.

I gripped the leather seat and tried to slow my breathing. I couldn't have a panic attack in this car. I needed to keep a clear head. My glance flicked to the doors again. No handles.

"It's not about the money," Faulkner was saying. "I want the jewel. But I can't have my precious Caesar back. So here's what we're going to do. Since you're so clever at stealing things, I want you to get *this* for me."

The thug on my right handed me a newspaper clipping.

I held the smooth paper and stared at a black-and-white picture of a diamond. A full-page article spread beneath it. INFAMOUS CURSED DIAMOND BLAMED FOR DEATH AND DISASTER THROUGHOUT THE AGES read the headline. I didn't need to read the article to identify the diamond.

It was the Hope Diamond.

I choked again—not from a thug's hand gripped about my throat this time, but from pure disbelief.

"What? *The Hope?* It's impossible," I sputtered. I studied Faulkner's face. Was he serious? "The Smithsonian is a fortress. Nobody has ever stolen anything from the Smithsonian."

"Read closer, my dear. The Hope is taking a little vacation from the Smithsonian. I know you can get it for me then."

I looked down at the page. The paper crinkled in my hand as I scanned the article.

The Hope Diamond is scheduled to be loaned out on a rare tour. The legendary gem has not left the Smithsonian since 1996, when it was sent to Harry Winston, Inc., in New York for cleaning. The last time the Hope traveled overseas was in 1965, when it journeyed to Johannesburg, South Africa, on loan to De Beers for the Rand Easter Show. "We're excited to announce that in ten days, the Hope Diamond will be winging its way to Paris," said Madeleine York, Director of the National Museum of Natural History, "to be the centerpiece of a special exhibit dedicated to Marie Antoinette at the Louvre."

The Louvre? If I wasn't so terrified, I might have laughed. The Louvre was even more ridiculous than the Smithsonian. Sure, people had successfully taken things from the Louvre in the past, in contrast to the Smithsonian. But after the Louvre had been embarrassed by the truly sloppy—but, nonetheless, successful—theft of eighteenth-century silver candlesticks in 2002, they had totally overhauled their security. And then, last year, they'd upgraded everything again. The Louvre would be impossible now.

Although, maybe there were chinks. New systems often contained bugs, little quirks they hadn't quite ironed out. Moreover, visiting displays with temporary security systems were often more vulnerable than the permanent, well-seasoned installations in a museum. There was a good chance there would be gaps and cracks. The sort of things an enterprising young crook like myself could take advantage of.

In spite of myself, I felt a glimmer of excitement, a ripple of possibility. My fingers twitched.

But no. It was ridiculous. I couldn't possibly pull it off.

Besides, this was how I'd landed in trouble with my Agency last time, with the Fabergé egg job. Taking assignments outside of AB&T was the quickest route to getting fired. It was also risky—I would be safer with the resources and backup of my Agency.

The limo took a slow turn around a corner, and I realized I had lost track of where we were headed. Raindrops began to splatter against the windows. Fat splotches of water blurred the streetlights outside, serving to further disorient me.

I needed more time. I needed to think. I glanced down at the newspaper article again. It was dated three weeks ago, which meant the Hope Diamond was already in Paris.

Farther down the page there was a small photo of a woman in her sixties—impeccably groomed, with flinty eyes and a square jaw. "Madeleine York," read the caption. "Director of the Smithsonian Institution National Museum of Natural History."

"She looks tough," I said.

Faulkner gave a grunt. "She is. We belong to the same private club in Palm Springs. I've met her many times." I glanced at him in surprise. "And she's tough as nails. Relentless and sharp. Which is why it will be easier for you to procure the diamond when it is not under her eagle eye."

I nodded, thinking.

"It's interesting, Mr. Faulkner, but I still don't believe it can be done. The security around the Hope will be ridiculous. There won't be any getting near it."

He examined the cuffs of his shirt. "I'm sure it won't be easy, Miss Montgomery. But, to be honest, I don't really give a shit about the degree of difficulty here." He fixed me with a hard stare. "You're going to do this for me. And, by the way, I don't want to wait forever. You have one week. Do not forget that you owe me. And I intend to collect on that debt." Faulkner's mouth grew even harder and thinner than before.

"Okay, but—"

He stopped my protest before it even started. "Let me be clear," he said. "If you do not do this for me, if you do not acquire the Hope for me, I will have my satisfaction in another way. I cannot have a thief who has stolen from me—who may yet steal from me again, in the future—walking around. I do not have any degree of squeamishness, Miss Montgomery. I have seen a lot of violence in my life.

Torture means very little to me." His voice was flat. He was stating plain fact. I could tell that much. "It has been pointed out that I do not seem to be afflicted by any degree of empathy when it comes to human pain or suffering."

My mouth went dry.

"The punishment for a thief," he continued, "in ancient times was cutting off his—or her—hands." At this, Faulkner caressed my bare wrists, sending unpleasant prickles up and down my spine. "I do believe this to be a fitting sentence and will happily mete it out." He glanced at the man on my left. "This is something that is still done in certain countries, yes?" The thug grunted his assent.

It was true. Under strict Islamic law, this was still the punishment for theft, as dictated by the Koran.

The man on my right produced an envelope, withdrew a photograph, and showed it to me. "This was the last thief who crossed me," Faulkner said. It was a black-and-white photograph of a blindfolded man tied to a chair, with both arms severed at the wrist.

My head spun, and my vision went fuzzy at the edges. I remembered hearing about that incident in the news a couple of years ago. It had stuck in my memory because the thief had been one of ours, in AB&T. Nobody had known at the time who had performed the horrific deed.

There had to be a way out of this nightmare. I needed a bargaining chip.

And then I thought of something. I scrabbled in my tote bag and pulled out the emerald earrings. "Here. Why don't you take these? I just, um, acquired them. You don't have to wait for me to get the Hope. You don't have to risk that I'll fail. Just take them, and we'll call it even."

Of course, I would have to explain this to Templeton, and I'd have AB&T to answer to. But at least I knew my Agency wouldn't cut my hands off.

Faulkner sat back and narrowed his eyes. His lips curled back. "This is no gentleman's game, Miss Montgomery," he hissed. "I am not pissing around." He leaned far forward, right in my face. I could feel his hot, sour breath on my cheek. "You get me that diamond. Or you will never steal again. Actually, you will never eat a bowl of corn flakes again, for that matter."

My palms were sweating, and I felt a wave of queasiness. A panic attack started to brew deep inside.

"You should know," Faulkner said, "I am well aware of your FBI . . . *connections,* shall we say?" His voice carried an unpleasant sneer. "If there is any indication you are attempting to have me investigated or charged, the retribution for you will be the same."

He inclined his head at the photograph held by the gentleman on my right.

"Trust me," Faulkner continued. "The FBI has been attempting to arrest me for quite some time. There is nothing you could provide or do that would make a difference in their wasted efforts."

I shifted uncomfortably in my seat. The rain was falling steadily now. Our tires hissed on the wet road.

"Furthermore, there will be no running away. I imagine all you thieves have various escape hatches and emergency plans," Faulkner said. "You will be watched. If you attempt to run away, know that you will eventually be caught and brought to me. And then you know what will happen next."

He inclined his head, studying me like a bird of prey would study a mouse in its talons. "But really, why would you want to run away? Why wouldn't you want to steal the Hope? Surely this job is a jewel thief's dream."

He was right, of course. And any other time, I would have loved the mere idea of this. But I had only just promised myself that I would take a hiatus until I was back to normal. How could I possibly steal the Hope while I was crippled with panic attacks?

It was something I'd have to work out on my own. Right now the only thing that mattered was getting out of this car, in whatever way I had available to me. I'd have to figure out the rest later.

"Okay, Mr. Faulkner, you have a deal. I will get the Hope Diamond for you, and then we'll be square. You'll leave me alone. Yes?"

His face rearranged itself into something that resembled a smile. "Very good, Miss Montgomery. Very good."

He was satisfied. For now.

As the car pulled away from the curb where they left me, rain poured down on my head, but I barely felt it.

I had made a pact with the devil.

Chapter 4

Jack Barlow strolled casually along the downtown Seattle street, keeping his gaze pinned on the man in the Mariners cap in the small cluster of people ahead of him. The hat was funny, a good joke. Jack figured the guy hoped it would make him blend in. It did anything but.

It was about eleven-thirty at night, and in spite of the light rain that had just started, many businesses were still open. Jack walked past a restaurant with an open door, laughter and the sounds of glassware clinking spilling out. It was springtime, which meant more or less continuous rain and drizzle. But the residents of Seattle never let a little precipitation stop them.

Tailing this man effectively in public like this meant Jack was not sticking to shadows. He couldn't look like he was doing anything furtive. He was simply out for a walk.

He strolled along the broad sidewalks, past the brightly lit shop windows. As he walked past a café, the door opened and a rich coffee aroma swirled out. Dampness was starting to seep in at the bottom of his pant legs, but Jack barely noticed. His purpose tonight was singular, and he was not going to lose this guy.

Jack was an FBI agent stationed at the Seattle branch in the organized crime division. He'd transferred departments a couple of times within the past year—mostly because of a personal conflict of interest—and was now working closely with the organized crime section in DC headquarters.

But Jack was the low man on the totem pole and had only recently been given field duty. Up to now he'd been pushing a shitload of paper.

Now he had an assignment: to follow this guy. Jack had precious little information on the man. Just a slim file with a name (Ned Snyder), a photograph (a grainy shot of a pale man with a nonexistent chin), and a brief description of activities (Internet gaming, casino slot machines, and comic book collecting).

And a warning that the guy tended to be slippery, and very good at eluding a tail.

Jack's assignment was to follow Snyder and arrest him if he did anything illegal. Ned Snyder had landed in Seattle only two days ago from his last known address in Philadelphia. Apparently, Snyder had some important information on a crime ring. He'd made first contact via e-mail when he was in Philly. Seemed he'd gotten spooked after that, and the FBI had heard nothing more.

Snyder had clearly thought he was being anonymous. But e-mail is never anonymous.

The FBI needed a reason to bring him in. Arrest would be the best way of doing that. So they'd been tracking him ever since. Snyder surfacing in Seattle had brought the case into Jack's lap.

Jack wanted badly to complete this assignment. If he could, it would garner him major kudos with his supervisor. If he failed, it might mean back to filling out goddamned forms. Who knew when he would get his next field assignment?

Jack approached the curb to cross Pine Street; on the other side, Snyder had just entered a convenience store. As Jack stepped onto the street, a stretch Lexus limo slid by, making a right turn, almost rolling over Jack's toes in the process. He jumped back to avoid getting his toes crushed but didn't break his gaze with the doorway of the store.

He crossed the street and paused at the hot dog stand just outside the store entrance. He wouldn't go in—it would be a rookie move to be spotted by his target in such a small shop. The smell of frying onions and sizzling hot dogs made Jack's mouth water. When was the last time he had eaten, anyway?

The rain was falling heavier now, landing in larger drops on the top of Jack's head and sliding down the back of his neck. Jack shivered and turned up the collar of his jacket.

What was this guy doing? So far, he'd stopped at a coffee shop, gone to City Target, and bought chips. And beer. And now he was checking out magazines. It seemed like he was killing time.

Jack shifted his feet restlessly. When was this guy going to make a move? When was he going to do something illegal? He was supposed to be a small-time criminal, but he sure wasn't acting like it.

Jack had seen opportunities for at least three different criminal moves in the time he'd been following the man. Pickpocketing that oblivious guy they'd passed on the street a couple of blocks ago, whose wallet was hanging out of his pocket. Reaching over the counter at the coffee shop when the cash register was open and the barista was distracted with an unruly coffee grinder. Shoplifting that magazine, instead of waiting patiently in line, like he was doing right now.

It would be so easy. A piece of cake to just tuck the magazine under your arm, like it was already yours, stroll right out . . .

Not that Jack was into that kind of thing. It was just an occupational hazard when you were in law enforcement. Well, truth be told, for Jack it was probably more than that.

Fact was, Jack's father had been a crook. Hell, *Jack* had been a crook unwittingly, growing up. An accomplice, sure, but he'd made crimes possible.

Jack had spent a lot of years struggling with that guilt. And the resentment toward the man who'd led him down that path. He'd more than atoned for it, though, by becoming an FBI agent. What he hadn't figured out yet was how to excise the part of his brain that still ran to criminal-type thoughts.

Ned Snyder walked out of the convenience store. Jack gave him several beats and then mobilized. He followed the man along the sidewalk, heading north along Pine. Snyder strode with somewhat more purpose now. Jack wondered, What had changed?

And then Jack noticed that someone else was observing Snyder, too.

There was a man standing at a bus stop, wearing a gray overcoat, whose gaze flicked down just a little too quickly as Snyder walked past. And who, after a few seconds, turned away from the bus stop and started walking in the same direction as Snyder.

Jack clenched his teeth. A complication. Yet there was something about the man that was familiar. Then the man removed his hat to shake off drops of rain. At the sight of the man's deep red hair, Jack's memory was jogged. He'd seen him in the coffee shop. He'd been lingering by the milk and sugar stand.

Now Jack just needed to figure out if the other man was friend or foe.

Car tires slid on the wet road, and a van honked in the intersection. As Snyder paused at a streetlight, Jack snapped a photograph with his phone of the red-haired man and sent it to the staff at FBI headquarters.

He typed a message: Identify.

Jack rubbed his face and thought back. Was the new tail aware of Jack's presence? He mentally mapped out the last few switches and moves and didn't think he would have made his intentions obvious to a third party.

But these were the sorts of decisions that were life and death for a field officer. Until he knew otherwise, he had to assume that both men were a potential mortal threat.

The light turned, and Snyder was on the move again, crossing the street.

Jack hesitated a second. There was only one way to do this now—he'd have to wait for the other tail to go first. And then he would follow suit. There was a greater risk of losing his target, doing it this way, because he counted on the other shadow being proficient at the task. But there was no other way. Until he knew what side of the law the red-haired man fell on, Jack couldn't be caught doing surveillance.

A message from FBI headquarters pinged on Jack's phone: Not identifiable. Subject unknown.

Jack frowned. That was odd. He looked up. Both men were still in view, for now. But tailing by proxy was shit. There was too great a chance of losing Snyder. He tightened a fist. He had to find out who the other shadow was.

There was one other way.

He sent the photograph to a different number, an encrypted one. A number his superiors knew nothing about.

After Jack pressed SEND, Snyder made a quick turn toward an alley. But the red-haired man's attention had been diverted for a second. He'd missed Snyder's direction change.

Jack crossed the street to close the distance, his gaze pinned on the mark. He had to get to that alley as soon as possible.

At that moment, an elderly gentleman crossing the street ahead of Jack stumbled on the curb and fell on the slick sidewalk. He went down right in front of Jack. The gentleman tried to break his fall, but his hand glanced off the wet curb and he landed face-first in a large puddle.

Jack was at the man's side in a second. "Are you all right, sir?" Jack said, bending to help him up. He broke his gaze on Snyder just for a moment.

Jack helped the man off the ground and then looked up quickly, holding the man under the arm. No sign of Snyder. The red-haired man was just ahead, by the alley, turning his head frantically. Jack quickly helped the dripping and embarrassed—but otherwise not injured—gentleman to a bench, scanning the area nonstop.

Damn. The red-haired man had lost Snyder. Which meant *Jack* had lost Snyder, too.

He strode to the alley, but it was deserted, apart from half a dozen closed doors. There was no way of knowing which one Snyder had gone through. It was over. His target was gone.

Well, maybe it wouldn't be a total loss. Jack could always follow the red-haired man now—see what he could learn about him. Maybe he was a partner in crime. Maybe he would lead somewhere interesting.

He turned back to face the spot where the red-haired man had been. But there was nobody there. He, too, had disappeared into thin air.

Shit.

Jack scanned the area, trying to be casual in case he was being watched now. He rapidly skimmed the spots where one might tuck oneself and hide—alleys and doorway alcoves. Nothing.

Worse than losing both men, however, was the fact that Jack didn't know if he'd tapped himself with that last frantic grasp at locating Snyder.

This was a double fail. Jack felt like the dog who dropped a bone in the water to retrieve the one in the reflection, losing them both.

But at least he had the photograph of the red-haired man. A new suspect perhaps. A new lead to give his supervisor. He wouldn't be returning entirely empty-handed.

And then his phone bleeped. A message from his covert contact came through.

Subject identified: Ludolf Hendrickx. Interpol agent. Interpol?

Jack's heart sank. The red-haired man was on the same side as Jack. So much for the new lead he could give his supervisor.

Jack turned and headed for home, stuffing his hands in his pockets. Rain streamed down now, soaking him thoroughly. Maybe that goddamned Mariners cap hadn't been such a ridiculous idea, after all.

But as Jack walked, he frowned. Why the hell was Interpol involved in this case, anyway? Since when had this become an international investigation? And why hadn't Jack been briefed about Interpol's involvement? Usually in the case of international crime operations, the FBI and Interpol worked together. So why the secrecy this time?

This was a bad beat, and Jack wondered if he'd been destined for failure before he'd even begun. But there was something else going on here. And Jack was going to find out what.

Chapter 5

When I got home, soaking wet, I burst through the door to my apartment and collapsed on the floor. I had walked numbly through the rain, away from the terrifying meeting in Faulkner's car. I was happy to be safe. All I wanted was to be safe.

I sat there, shivering, wondering what I was going to do.

My mind was wheeling. I had agreed to the job. I was in bed with Mephistopheles now, and there was no way I'd be able to live up to my side of the bargain. There had to be a way out of this. I couldn't do the Hope job. I wasn't up to it. But if I didn't do it . . .

I looked down at my hands and tucked them protectively under my arms.

Maybe AB&T could help me. They had a security desk, I seemed to remember, a department that protected their assets.

I needed to talk to my handler, Templeton. Yes, that was what I'd do. But first, I needed a drink. And to get out of these cold, miserable clothes.

I peeled off my soaking shoes and dripped my way into the bedroom. I stripped out of the filthy, sopping sweats I was still wearing—the hotel locker room incident now felt like a week ago—and crawled into a warm cashmere robe.

I slid into soft slippers and padded to the kitchen. I reached directly for the whiskey and poured myself three fingers, neat. I grabbed my phone on the way to the living room and flopped down on the couch, cradling my glass like a security blanket.

I dialed Templeton's direct number. I sipped my drink as I waited. The whiskey was burning, smoky syrup going down—smoldering my insides, heating me and soothing me at the same time.

Templeton picked up after two rings. "Petal," he said in his rich British timbre. "Always a pleasure. You have good news for me?"

I decided to tackle first things first. "I have the emerald earrings," I said, confident this line was encrypted and totally secure.

"Fabulous, my dear," he said. "Everything went well, then? No hitches?"

I fidgeted with the edge of my robe. "Everything went smoothly with the job. More or less." I did not want to confess my paralyzing panic or that I'd had to improvise my escape.

"Excellent," he said. "Meet me tomorrow morning at Pike Place Fish Market, nine-fifteen sharp, for the handover."

"No problem. I'll be there." I swallowed, not sure how to proceed. Partly, I didn't want to admit I'd been caught by Faulkner. More than that, I found myself hesitating to get into the real reason I couldn't possibly do the Hope job—because of my newfound, crippling fear.

But I needed Templeton's help. I needed him to tell me that AB&T would take care of this, and that I wouldn't have to worry about Faulkner or try to do the Hope job or anything.

"Templeton, I ran into a little trouble . . . *after* the job."

Silence. Then a worried "Go on."

"It seems I've been tracked down by a previous mark. Someone who is not too happy with me."

His voice became low, ominous. "Who?"

At that moment, the front door of the apartment opened. And in walked a tall, sopping figure. Jack. He didn't look up, just tossed the keys to our front door into the dish on the front hall table.

The blue Chinese porcelain dish we'd bought together at an auction this summer, that is, and the antique Pembroke table we'd found at a garage sale together a couple of months ago.

Jack was my boyfriend, and this was our apartment.

I took one look at Jack's face and knew he'd had a bad night.

My conversation with Templeton could wait. Besides, I was always more comfortable talking to my handler without my boyfriend, an FBI officer, listening to the conversation.

"Um, look, Templeton . . . I have to go, actually—"

"No, Catherine. Tell me who confronted you."

"We'll talk about it tomorrow, okay?" Before he could protest further, I disconnected the call.

"Hey, hon," Jack said as he closed the door behind him. "You didn't have to get off the phone."

"I know. It's okay. It can wait." I walked over to him and put my hands on his face. "You okay? You look like you had a rough time out there."

Yes, my boyfriend was an FBI agent. I know. It sounds crazy to me, too. But we'd been over all this territory so many times before, and this was just how it was.

We had full disclosure about our respective professions. He knew about my line of work, and I knew what he did, of course. We had so many other things in common. Truth be told, we had *this* in common, too. It was just that when it came to the line in the sand— what was legal, what was not—we happened to fall on opposite sides of that line.

Couples with other differences figure out a way, don't they? Take politics. She's a Republican, and he's a Democrat. It doesn't have to be a deal breaker. Or, say, she's a vegetarian and PETA evangelist. He hunts ducks on the weekend and likes nothing more than blue-rare steak with blood pooling all over the plate.

People make it work, right?

Well, we were going to make it work. Sure, we'd had our bumpy times. We'd split up for several months last year, when he went through a thing. Specifically, he wasn't sure he could handle my criminal tendencies.

But then, or so he tells me, he realized that was crazy. And that no matter our differences of opinion on this topic, we belonged together.

And I'd agreed. Although, to be honest, while we'd been apart, I had explored the option of a more logical relationship—one with a fellow criminal. Ethan Jones was his name, an art thief with AB&T, and a charmer to boot. It had been . . . pretty fun, actually. Well, much more than just fun. But that was in the past.

Jack was the man I belonged with. In spite of our differences, that had to be the truth. Or at least that was what I was counting on.

I scanned Jack's body, head to toe. "Are you hurt anywhere?" I knew he'd been out in the field. One of his first field assignments after so long being a desk jockey. What he'd been doing out in the field, I had no idea. And frankly, I didn't want to know.

I knew he wouldn't really tell me, though. Just like I wouldn't tell him the details of what I'd been doing that night. We had a no-ask, no-tell policy. And that's how we made it work.

It's a common bit of advice given to couples, to leave your job at the office. So that's what we did. He knew I was doing stuff that would get me arrested. I knew he was arresting people for a living. As long as we didn't give each other the grisly details, it was all good.

Nobody wants to hear the boring details of their partner's job, right? Don't every woman's eyes glaze over when her spouse starts regaling her with details of his meeting? Doesn't every man surreptitiously watch the game on TV when his girlfriend starts recounting the various office dramas she's embroiled in?

"Nope, no injuries," he said, peeling off his wet coat and shoes. "Could do with a shower, though." His gaze focused on me. He moved closer.

Even though he'd just come in from outside, his body radiated heat. He put his arms around my waist. I got warm. Very warm.

Jack was a tall man, six-foot-three. He would have been a perfect cast for one of those extremely attractive werewolves on TV—great hair, dark and glossy, broad shoulders, and long, muscular legs. He did well as an agent because he was smart. But his physical capabilities alone might have assured his climb within the ranks.

Jack stood out in a crowd. I had never understood why he didn't have more trouble doing the covert part of his job—he was too noticeable. Women's heads turned when he entered a room. Hell, men's heads turned, too. He had an electric presence that was undeniable.

And he was all mine.

His hands slid up my arms to my hair. He smelled of rain and leather. He pushed my hair aside and leaned down to kiss my neck. Shivers traveled the length of my spine.

"Care to join me?" he asked suggestively.

I closed my eyes and felt his warm mouth meet mine.

As he led me down the hall to the shower, all my worries about Templeton, the Hope Diamond, and Albert Faulkner grew blunted and fuzzy. As he slid the robe off my shoulders and kissed my bare skin, I forgot about everything else entirely.

Chapter 6

Rome, Italy

Ethan Jones sipped an espresso at an outdoor café in Piazza Navona. Ancient buildings in shades of ocher and vanilla fringed the pedestrian square; fountains glittered and splashed in the piazza's center. Couples strolled with gelato, surrounded by the sounds of children laughing and kicking a soccer ball. Pure Italian sunlight warmed the side of Ethan's face.

Behind his Ray-Bans, Ethan kept a careful watch on the doorway of the palazzo across the square. He mostly maintained a peripheral gaze as he sipped his coffee and read the newspaper. He didn't need anyone noticing he was casing the house. And as soon as his targets left, he'd be going in.

Ethan shifted in his chair and felt the weight of his lock-picking kit inside the breast pocket of his Zegna jacket.

People liked to compare Ethan to James Bond. But Ethan knew he wasn't anything like James Bond. He had no interest in killing people. All he wanted to do was steal things, have a shitload of fun doing it, and make a little money. Well, okay, a lot of money.

For a moment, Ethan thought about how much more pleasurable this would be if he had a certain other career criminal working with him today. Which was unusual—he normally loved nothing more than working alone. Sleeping alone was another matter, of course. But working alone had always been his preference.

Except today.

Cat Montgomery had certainly gotten under his skin, as much as Ethan hated to admit it. The girl was unbelievably compelling. Cute, sexy, fun, and a highly competent thief. A very appealing package. And the best part: she had no idea just how incredible she actually was.

Not in a head-case, inferiority-complex kind of way. She just was who she was.

He flicked a page in his newspaper and checked the time on his TAG Heuer. He swept his gaze around the piazza, doing a scan to ensure he wasn't being watched. A group of tourists on a guided walk, led by a docent with a small red flag, entered the piazza. A woman crossed the piazza in front of the group, and for a second, Ethan thought it was Cat.

He did a double take—no, his mistake.

The last time he'd seen Cat Montgomery had been on Blackfriars Bridge in London in the early hours of the morning. They'd just made their escape from the Palace of Westminster after stealing a Fabergé egg. It had been a difficult, dangerous job, and the victory had felt incredible.

On the bridge, however, after all was said and done, Cat had celebrated their escape in the arms of Jack Barlow. An FBI agent, for Christ's sake. The thought of it set Ethan's teeth on edge. He'd been so sure he and Cat had a major connection. But then Jack had shown up like the goddamned hero—even though he hadn't actually done anything. Ethan had been the one risking his neck for her, for the job that was so important to her. Served him right for doing such a ridiculous thing.

After Ethan had returned to Seattle, he'd requested an overseas transfer within AB&T. They had branches all over the world and had found him a great position in Rome.

So from his home base there, he did jobs all over the Italian peninsula. Which was pretty sweet work. There was a lot of art in Italy.

Not to mention the great food. Exquisite coffee. La dolce vita.

Throwing himself into his work was Ethan's primary strategy for forgetting the jewel thief who had worked her way under his skin.

Ethan refocused on the palazzo across the square just as the owners of the house were walking out. Middle-aged Italians with deep tans and plenty of old money. And no compunction about flashing it around. They both wore a lot of bling. Montgomery would like that.

They were going out for lunch. Ethan knew this was their routine. Like many Italians, they enjoyed dinner at home, but they almost always went out for lunch, and they were usually gone for about an hour.

Which should give Ethan just enough time.

Once they had strolled out of the piazza, out of view, Ethan tossed back the last sip of his *caffè* and sauntered across the square. Italians never ran anywhere. They drove like lightning, sure. But once they arrived at their destination, there was no hurry any longer.

Ethan used the key he'd pickpocketed from the owner ten days ago. Ten days was the perfect length of time. It was just enough time for the owner to replace the key and to feel relieved that no trouble was going to come from having lost it.

The door was heavy oak, painted a dark green that had faded a little in the Roman sun, framed by the arching stone of the palazzo. An old iron knocker occupied the center of the door like the big ring under a bull's nose.

Ethan unlocked the latch in an unhurried manner. The trick was acting like he absolutely belonged, like he was doing something perfectly natural. He gave himself an imaginary role. He was a visiting cousin from overseas. He'd been loaned a key, assured that he should go inside and make himself comfortable while they were out. *Help yourself to a Peroni, cousin. Sit out on the terrace.*

The entrance was dark and cool and smelled of garlic and olives and fresh paint. Ethan climbed the steep stairs and arrived at the first floor, his heart beating rapidly with eager anticipation.

The house was beautifully appointed. High ceilings soared above gleaming polished floors, and every window was surrounded by ornate moldings. It was hushed and quiet: the rich furnishings, heavy curtains, and plush carpets absorbed almost all sounds. Only the ticking of a clock penetrated.

Ethan knew exactly where he was headed. He'd been in this apartment once before. Disguised as an artisan, he'd come to provide a quote on replastering their ceiling. He'd been shown around. As a result, he knew exactly where the Caravaggio was located.

Ethan spoke Italian very well, but it wasn't perfect and carried a slight accent. He sounded a bit like an immigrant, he knew. Which was why, he was sure, he didn't get the job replastering the ceiling. Italians trusted other Italians the most.

And—to be fair—they would have been quite right not trusting him.

Ethan crept along the corridor, confident in his ability to evade the few security cameras. This was just too much fun. And too easy. It's not that he wasn't afraid of being caught—he was. Ethan just happened to be willing to do things most people wouldn't, in spite of the fear.

Anyway, if he wasn't doing this, what else would he do? Return to being a schoolteacher?

Not in a million years.

Ethan hadn't always been a thief. In fact, while he was growing up in LA, his friends had once considered him to be the last existing good guy. They would always razz him, saying, "Nice guys finish last, Jones."

He hadn't believed that. Until everything came crumbling down.

Ethan had majored in art history in college. Not because of any particular career aspiration, but just because he enjoyed it. He was moderately overweight in those days and didn't spend time or money or effort on a good haircut or great clothes.

The only thing Ethan had going for him was his fiancée. He was engaged to his high school sweetheart, a pretty thing, sweet and supportive. He was lucky to have her, and he knew it.

When he graduated with an art history degree, he found he was qualified to do . . . well, jack shit.

He started taking work as a substitute art teacher, making next to nothing, eating baked beans on toast every night because he couldn't afford better.

It was frustrating. He wanted much more out of life. He wanted more for his wife-to-be and the family they hoped for. He'd always had the feeling he was destined for something bigger. He just didn't know what.

All around him, men who were willing to sell out, fight dirty, look out for number one—they were all getting ahead. His best friend, for example, was a master of industry. He made tons of money as a stockbroker and lived a glamorous life. And Ethan couldn't help being envious of that. He was only human.

He'd been teaching for a year when everything changed.

It happened in an instant. It was the moment he walked in on his best friend—yes, the master of industry—with his fiancée.

Things got worse from there, though. After the shouting and the pleading and the gnashing, they decided they might as well inform Ethan that they were, in fact, in love.

And just like that, his sweetheart left him. Ba-da-boom, nice guy loses. Looks like everyone *did* have it right, after all.

Life got pretty ugly after that for Ethan. Depression affected his work performance, and he soon lost his position as a substitute teacher. He had to move to a crummier apartment because he couldn't afford the rent. But after a while, after he was on a first-name basis with rock bottom, that was when he discovered his own particular talent.

It was all because of a painting.

There was a painting—a little neo-Expressionist work by a twentieth-century artist named Colby Wallace—that he wanted back from his fiancée. They'd bought it when they first moved in together. Ethan had saved up for a year beforehand. He knew she'd never appreciated it, but that hadn't stopped her from taking it with her when she moved into Ethan's former best friend's massive house.

Ethan had tried to be nice about it. He'd asked politely. And she'd refused to give it to him. She'd just kept on blathering about how much *dickhead* liked it—possibly Ethan's term, not hers—and how well it matched the decor in their library.

Something snapped inside Ethan. And there was only one thing for him to do. He broke into his former best friend's house and stole the painting back.

But the most interesting aspect of that deed was that Ethan pulled it off with very little difficulty. In fact, it was one of the most successful things he'd ever done. And the most satisfying.

The seed was planted. No more Mr. Nice Guy.

He cashed in all his savings, left California, and moved up the coast to Seattle for a fresh start.

He started working out and lost seventy-three pounds. He dropped five inches around his waist and went up two shirt sizes in his chest. Good haircuts became a ritual for him, and he began paying attention to his clothes—dressing like he meant it. Soon, Ethan started feeling really good about himself. And it wasn't hard to notice the effect all that confidence was having on women.

Eventually, he knew he had to figure out a career. When he sat down to think about it, there was one glaring possibility. He'd been so good at stealing back his Colby Wallace. . . . What if he just *expanded* that enterprise a little?

He knew plenty about it. Could tell a real from a fake. Knew what was valuable and what was worth taking. Whether he found himself in an art gallery or a private collection, he'd be able to home in on the money.

He started off fencing his own stuff, but it wasn't long before he was approached by an agency, AB&T. Once he entered that world, there was no turning back. Life was too good. It's like when a tiger gets its first taste of human flesh and forevermore becomes a man-eater.

Becoming an art thief was how Ethan had achieved his potential. It was the only way he'd found of being able to be part of the art world and enjoy a comfortable lifestyle at the same time. That was eight years ago.

Nice guys finish last? You bet they do.

Ethan moved silently through the lush rooms of the Piazza Navona house, past potted palms and velvet draperies, making his way to the room he knew contained the Caravaggio.

But when he got there, he came to an abrupt stop. He stared at the wall, at an empty square of dark ocher amid the sun-bleached butter-colored surface.

The Caravaggio was gone.

Ethan frowned with irritation. *Okay.* It was fine. They'd probably just taken it down to dust or something. *Wait.* The smell of fresh paint. They were having the walls repainted, in addition to having the ceiling replastered. The Caravaggio had to be in the house somewhere.

He went upstairs to the next level and crept from room to room. Ethan was sweating a little now. A jittery feeling jumped under his skin. Time was ticking.

At last, he went into an empty bedroom. The shutters were closed in this room, and only knifelike cracks of light peeked between the slats. A row of paintings in large, ornate frames rested against the papered walls, waiting to be replaced on the freshly painted surfaces below.

The job was on again.

He spotted the Caravaggio. Flipping the frame over, he cut the canvas from its frame in a matter of seconds, rolled it carefully, and tucked it into a cardboard mailing tube.

The average person would take a good thirty minutes to properly remove a canvas from a frame. For an art thief, this was the sort of thing that could be accomplished in twelve seconds flat. It was the fruit of lots of practice.

Now for the tricky bit. The exit.

Ethan went to a front room and tucked himself beside the window frame. The glass was open, so he could hear outside, as well as see. He scanned the piazza, looking for anything out of place. People were sitting at sun-soaked café tables, nibbling pastries, drinking cappuccino. Afternoon crowds now lingered by the fountain's edge, taking photographs of one another with the stone river gods of the Fontana dei Quattro Fiumi in the background.

And then he saw it. A man sitting stiffly at a café, with his face turned toward the front door of the palazzo Ethan was in. Unmistakably an undercover member of the *polizia*. Ethan scanned for another and saw him perched on the fountain's north edge.

Did they know he was inside? Would they have let him just walk in? Sure they would. And let him hang himself by his own rope.

Would they let him walk away with the painting? Of course not.

Ethan sat back to think. There were a few options. He could go out in disguise. Or go out an entirely different way.

He needed to do something creative. Something that would distract the undercover officers.

For starters, he had to do something about the painting. It was rolled up in the mailing tube and strapped to his back. But that wouldn't do at all. He removed it from the tube and curled it around his body, underneath his jacket.

Now he needed a way to get to the church belfry two rooftops over. Saint Agnes Church had an open belfry at the top that was accessible from the red-tiled roofs.

A distraction in the piazza would be exceedingly useful right about now. *Think, Ethan.*

He crouched there a minute. Then pulled out his phone.

Twenty minutes later, he was ready. Hunkering down, waiting for his moment. He looked out the window at the piazza. Everything was the same: couples strolling hand in hand by the splashing fountains, a child playing with a yellow balloon, a bent old woman feeding pigeons from a jar of seed.

He glanced at the first officer, sitting at a café, on a metal chair, pretending to read a book. He was on an outside chair. Perfect. And the other perched on the stone fountain's edge. They were forming a zone defense. But Ethan had a trick play that didn't exist in the playbook.

Suddenly, a small blue Fiat burst into the crowded piazza, right beside the café where the first *poliziotto* was sitting. An angry cry rose up. And then a second car burst into the piazza—a black Renault—heading straight toward the fountain where the second *poliziotto* was seated.

Ethan smiled. *Right on time.*

The cars had rental plates and carried bewildered tourists. For a hacker, it was a piece of cake to commandeer the GPS of a rental car and send it in the wrong direction. In this case, into the pedestrian zone of Piazza Navona.

It was a task particularly easy for Ethan's hacker Gladys. Gladys was Cat's favorite hacker, and she'd happily shared her contact info with Ethan.

"No problem," Gladys had said when Ethan made the request. "Give me about twenty minutes."

"Actually, can you take about thirty-five?" He looked at his watch. That would time the event to minutes before the church service ended. It was a wedding, and Ethan knew exactly when the ceremony would wrap up. All part of being a thorough professional thief.

The instant the cars were in the piazza, pigeons took to the air in a loud flurry and people scattered. The unfortunate tourists in their rental cars were enduring extremely passionate insults from the Romans whose afternoon *caffè* had been so rudely interrupted. Desperate to get out of the piazza, the drivers of the rental cars swerved through the crowds.

Ethan watched it all with a weather eye. And the instant he saw the *poliziotti* leaping to their feet—both to get out of the path of the errant vehicles and also to intervene with the crowds—Ethan was out the far corner window. Next second, he was up on the roof.

He bolted across the rippled clay-tiled roof, keeping the church belfry in view.

There was a small gap, which he leaped like a jackrabbit. In a flash, he clambered through the open gaps in the stone of the belfry. Once tucked inside, he glanced down at the piazza. The cars had been redirected, and the two officers had resumed their positions. The distraction had lasted a matter of moments. As far as the *poliziotti* appeared to be concerned, they hadn't missed a thing.

Ethan smiled. But his escape wasn't complete yet. He had to get out of the church. Down below he heard the final strains of the organ and the general rustle of the congregation shuffling about, rising to leave the service. Ethan had no idea if the officers had his description, if they knew what he looked like. He had to assume they did.

He clambered down the iron ladder from the belfry and gripped the cold, smooth stone handrails of the twisting marble stairs to the church itself. The smells of incense and flowers and the perfume of the ladies attending the wedding wafted up. Arriving on the main floor, he scanned the church and the people milling about. He spotted a gray fedora on a pew, not yet picked up by its owner.

He slipped over and casually plucked it from its spot.

Then he scrutinized the faces in the crowd, strolling to the entrance doors, looking for a particular type. *Ah, there.*

He homed in on his target, sidled up beside the young woman. She was attractive, in her mid-twenties, with dark, wavy hair and Italian coloring. She wore a yellow sundress, but more significant to Ethan was what she was missing. There was no wedding band on her hand, no attentive male in evidence. She watched the bride wistfully. Ethan picked out her family members, who were paying her very little mind.

The crowd jostled, and Ethan lifted a pair of white gloves sticking out of the purse swinging at her hip.

"*Buongiorno, senorita,*" Ethan said smoothly. "Are these yours?"

She froze and looked down, startled at the sight of her gloves, confused a moment. Then she looked up at Ethan's face. Dots of pink bloomed in her cheeks. Ethan flashed his most disarming smile.

The hook sank.

A minute later, Ethan strolled out of the church, an attractive young woman on his arm. He popped the fedora on his head, putting most of his face in shadow.

In the piazza he could see the undercover officers gazing at the exiting congregation. They made a halfhearted effort to study the people in the crowd but shortly thereafter returned their steely gaze to the Caravaggio house.

As Ethan strolled out of the piazza, he wondered—with a grin— how long the *poliziotti* would stay in their positions. He put a hand to his side, felt the crinkle of canvas against his flank. He took a deep breath and savored a moment of triumph.

Which was quickly soured by a new line of thinking. Question was, how had they known about Ethan in the first place? Who had tipped them off?

Chapter 7

Seattle

I walked into the cool, damp air of Pike Place Fish Market. I wondered if people who worked there ever got the smell of fish out of their clothes, their hair, their skin. Pike Place is mostly open to the outdoors, with a freshening breeze coming off Puget Sound. I strolled past piles of farm vegetables, gleaming and ripe. I caught glimpses of the sky over the waterfront, the gray, waterlogged clouds. My shoes slipped a little on the concrete floor, slick with damp and grime and fish oil.

I stopped near the central fish market, where the fishmongers hurl enormous king salmon that are the length of a man's arm and must weigh at least thirty pounds. Slippery fish flashed silvery scales as they flew through the air in a display that was part entertainment, part workout, part efficient teamwork. The air sang with the fishermen's jokes and calls to one another.

I scanned the crowd—roughly thirty people or so, loitering and watching the show. I reflexively sized up those nearest me. It was an occupational hazard, I knew, continuously assessing strangers' physical attributes. Their weaknesses, any limps or favored joints—anything that would give me an advantage, should things come down to a physical fight. It sounds exhausting, but at this point in my career it came as naturally as breathing.

I saw him standing there, observing the performance. Templeton. Templeton could do print ads for orthopedic surgeons, his spine was so straight and so long. Fine-boned hands ended in long, tapered fingers. He watched the flying fish with penetrating blue eyes that had faded to a steely gray over the years, under eyebrows that looked like they would become terribly bushy were he anyone else. As it were, they were impeccably tidy. You had the impression he owned an eyebrow-grooming kit, with one of those itty-bitty combs.

I approached him. My professed purpose here, meeting with Templeton, was the earring handover. But I was also desperate for his help with Faulkner and the Hope Diamond issue. I needed Templeton to find me a way out of this. I needed him to make it all better for me.

I maneuvered myself to stand beside him. "The fish looks excellent today, doesn't it?" I said. I carried a shopping bag from Williams-Sonoma. Buried inside mounds of tissue paper were the earrings.

"I'm not sure the fish would agree. But it's a fine kettle they've got themselves into, haven't they?" He chuckled lightly. "I wonder, do you think we might witness someone getting flattened by an errant flying fish? I've always had a devilish wish to see that."

"Templeton, please! That's not a very gentlemanly thing to say."

"Darling, I may look like a gentleman on the outside, but I am a knave through and through." His British accent grew even plummier.

I smiled. "I know it."

Templeton had been my handler ever since I joined AB&T over six years ago. I trusted him implicitly. We almost always met in public places like this; it was our most reliable way of protecting ourselves and Agency secrets.

I placed the Williams-Sonoma bag on the ground and waited a few beats for him to pick it up.

That business taken care of, I said, "Listen, I have to tell you about my problem."

"Something besides an unusual penchant for pilfering things that don't belong to you, my dear?"

"Yes, besides that one."

"I know. I've been waiting for you to tell me about it. So, who smoked you out?"

I felt a moment's hesitation. My gut clenched. I wished I didn't have to tell him what I did. Was I sure it was a good idea? I glanced around. Was I being watched by Faulkner's men right now? Would they consider this a breach? My skin prickled.

"It's Albert Faulkner the Third. Two of his men grabbed me right off the street." I described being forced into the meeting with Faulkner in his Lexus.

Templeton's face grew stonier than usual and his mouth grew very thin, his concern for me evident.

I kept talking. "He found out somehow that I was the thief who stole the Caesar Diamond from him."

Templeton made a choking sound. "He found out?"

I nodded. "And he's pissed."

"How did that happen, exactly?" Templeton demanded. All humor had left his voice; his tone was hard-edged and drum tight. "That job was two years ago, if I'm remembering correctly. If you'd made a mistake at the time or left some kind of clue, he'd have tracked you down far sooner than this. Something must have happened—somebody must have talked."

It was the conclusion I'd come to, also. Most of the career criminals in AB&T were pretty tight-lipped, but there were always weak, vulnerable people. People likely to be successfully blackmailed or otherwise coerced. A few names sprang to mind, Brooke Sinclair in particular.

"So . . . doesn't AB&T have some sort of ability to do something about this?" I asked. "Don't they have some kind of obligation to protect us?"

Here Templeton's expression changed from one of anger to one of discomfort. He winced slightly and looked away, toward the fish market. "Well, yes, in a manner of speaking, we do have a department of asset protection." He looked back at me then, meeting my gaze. "But I have to be honest with you, Catherine. It's a bureaucratic nightmare. The man in charge is worse than useless. And he loves paperwork. They don't lift a finger without a thoroughly completed form. In triplicate. I've been fighting for an overhaul of the department for years. But the chairman doesn't agree it's a priority."

This was a punch in the stomach. "What? Not a priority? How could they possibly justify that?" I spluttered.

"He feels it's part of the risk of the job. Thieves know about the inherent risks going in. He sees part of our job at AB&T as doing what we can to keep your identities safe. But if there's a breach in the system, there's not a lot we can do."

"Templeton, that's crap, and you know it."

"Of course I do, Petal." He looked at me sympathetically. "But I also know about Albert Faulkner. And as despicable as he is, he happens to be a man of his word. If he says the Hope will call things square, my suggestion to you is this. You should do it."

"Steal the Hope?" I couldn't believe what I was hearing.

"Just listen. It could be a fantastic opportunity. An excellent chance to prove to AB&T how much you can handle." I knew what he was getting at. My status in the organization had been a little shaky ever since last year, when I went a little . . . shall we say, rogue from the Agency.

"They wouldn't consider it moonlighting?" That was what had got me in trouble last time.

"Not if it's doing something they should be doing themselves— protecting your fanny. And if we get preapproval . . ."

I nodded. It all sounded reasonable. Except for one small problem.

I couldn't possibly do it.

But how was I going to tell Templeton that? I chewed the inside of my cheek. I had no choice. I had to tell him. I wasn't going to keep secrets from him. I'd done that before. Never again.

I glanced around, ritually checking the crowd, ensuring we weren't being watched. A pair of tourists was haggling over the price of lettuce at a vegetable stall. Kids were climbing onto the bronze piggy bank statue at the entrance to the market, smiling for photographs.

"Templeton, I have to confess something. When I was at the top of the hotel, at the penthouse, for the emerald job . . . I had a little problem."

He narrowed his eyes. "What? Were you seen?"

"Not that," I said, shaking my head. "It's . . . I was terrified. Of the height. I couldn't stop imagining falling."

Templeton frowned. But he said nothing, allowing me to continue.

"I basically had a panic attack. I couldn't go back down the outside of the building. I had to improvise and find a way out from the inside. It wasn't pretty."

He watched me carefully. "Well, that's new. Isn't it?"

I nodded. "I mean, I was never fearless. I always knew somewhere in the back of my brain that bad things could happen. But it never took over. It never owned me or stopped me from doing what needed doing."

"Is it just a fear of heights, though? Not every assignment requires heights—"

I shook my head. "It's more like a fear of . . . *death.* I can't stop thinking of all the ways my job puts me in danger. And that's what triggers the panic attack."

He arched an eyebrow. "Catherine, my love, danger is not exactly a new thing for you. Why now?"

I hesitated a moment. "I think it's because of Sandor."

Templeton's face went the color of gunpowder. This was a verboten subject. "So what you're saying is that you can't do the Hope job because you're afraid?" When he put it like that, it sounded terrible. Maybe I shouldn't have mentioned anything.

This was not going the way I wanted it to. I needed Templeton to make this go away. My shoulders slumped as dark clouds gathered inside.

Templeton watched me carefully. "Speaking of Sandor . . . you're not getting involved in all that again, are you?" he asked.

"Getting involved in what, exactly? The egg is gone." I looked at Templeton, who fidgeted with his watch. I narrowed my eyes. "Is Caliga up to something?"

Templeton shook his head. "We haven't picked up any activity from them lately."

That was good. I did not enjoy my last brush with Caliga Rapio, a nasty organization of violent thieves and underworld types, and I did not relish the idea of a repeat encounter.

"But the fact is, this egg has resurfaced in the past," Templeton said. "Twice before it has appeared to have been destroyed. And both times it turned up again, the contents of the egg unharmed."

Ah, yes. The *contents*.

"But, Templeton, I dropped it. I saw it fall from the top of Big Ben. I wouldn't hold my breath that it's going to come back after that."

"Ah, but, Catherine, did you see it *land?*"

We both knew I hadn't seen that. The egg had been swallowed up in thick fog and darkness before I could witness it smashing on the ground far below. As Agency superiors had told me at the time, nothing had been recovered. There was no evidence the egg had even landed on the ground.

Which didn't make any more sense now than it did then.

But I really couldn't think about the Fabergé and Caliga and all that right now. Not like this, not when I had Faulkner hanging over me.

Faulkner. The Hope Diamond. How was I going to get over this goddamned fear?

Templeton seemed to read my thoughts. "Never mind about the Fabergé," he said soothingly. "You've got much more pressing issues on your plate. As for what happened to you last night on that building, don't even think about it. You will be fine, my dear. Shake it off."

I looked at him with doubt.

He studied me carefully. "Don't be afraid of fear. It shows only that you value your life above all else. Which is as it should be."

I was disappointed Templeton didn't have a clearer way of helping me. But even still, I began to feel a glimmer of hope. If I could wrestle the fear thing—if I could figure out how to prevent a panic attack—well, the Hope Diamond certainly represented a tantalizing target. It would be the job of a lifetime.

Chapter 8

As I walked away from Templeton, my stomach grumbled. I walked a direct line from the fish market to the Chinese restaurant in Pike Place. I was going to be right on time for lunch with my girls.

I walked into the tiny, one-aisled Chinese restaurant and saw Mel and Sophie sitting there. The delicious smells of onions and beef and bean sprouts frying in hot oil and steaming rice curled into my nose. Misted, grimy windows offered a fuzzy view of the working harbor of Seattle. This place had cracked vinyl booths and aluminum-lined tables, but the best Chinese food in the city.

I slid into the booth, and once we'd caught up on gossip, I told them about my adventures last night. And, in particular, about the panic attack.

"I'm not surprised," Mel said, picking up rice with her chopsticks over the sounds of clattering dishware and orders barked in Cantonese from the kitchen right behind our backs. "In my opinion, it's about time. Your job is terrifying. I'm surprised it's taken this long."

Sophie nodded in agreement, crunching into an egg roll.

My girls knew all about my line of work. They weren't thieves or con artists or any other brand of criminals themselves. Mel was a pediatrician, and Sophie a computer engineer. We'd been best friends since the days of sticker collections and soccer practice and friendship beads.

Sophie chewed thoughtfully and then said, "Maybe it would help if you remembered how you felt about the danger before. How did you deal with fear on past jobs?"

It was a good question. "I don't know. It was never really an issue." I squinted out the hazy window, trying to come up with some way of explaining. "It's like when you're driving. You're not sitting there thinking about the two tons of steel you're encased in, hurtling down the road at top speed. . . . You're just doing it," I said. "You're listening to music, thinking about what you're going to make for dinner. Driving itself is a truly dangerous act statistically, but you're not *feeling* it. That's what it's like for me, doing my job. Yes, it's dangerous, but because it's what I do, I don't feel the fear constantly." I paused. "Until now, I guess."

They watched me closely. Then Mel nodded. "That actually makes sense," she said, sounding mildly surprised.

"What? I don't usually say things that make sense?"

"Not typically."

I gave her a wry look. I went on then to describe my most pressing trouble, the Albert Faulkner situation and my conundrum over the Hope Diamond.

At the mention of the Hope, Sophie gasped. "Oh my God, Cat, you can't go anywhere near that thing," she said, eyes wide.

Mel and I exchanged a glance.

"You know," Sophie continued, lowering her voice and fidgeting with the boho wrap bracelets on her wrists. "*The curse,*" she hissed.

Ah. I laughed. "The curse of the Hope Diamond?" I said. "Soph, that's a bunch of baloney. Nobody believes that anymore. They discredited all that a while ago."

"Well, that could just be propaganda. That's what they *want* you to believe," Sophie said.

Mel put her chopsticks down with a loud clatter on her plate. "What are you two talking about? Curse?" she demanded.

"You know," Sophie said impatiently. "The curse of the Hope Diamond. It goes way back." She lifted her soup bowl and took a sip of the steaming broth. "All kinds of people who have had contact with the Hope Diamond had terrible things happen to them. Like, they were killed. Or their kids were killed. Torn apart by wild dogs, that sort of thing."

"Well, *that* one is totally untrue," I said. "You're talking about the guy who first found the Hope in India and brought it back to France, Tavernier. But it was just a rumor, that wild dog thing. He lived well into old age and died in his bed."

"So you *have* looked into the curse," Sophie said wryly, eyebrow raised over the edge of her soup bowl.

Okay, so she was right. I had looked into it, late last night. It was fascinating stuff, truth be told. You know, ghost tales for the most part. But I had to admit, there did seem to be some weird coincidences.

Like the postman James Todd. He was the one who delivered the package to the Smithsonian in 1958 from Harry Winston in New York. His leg was crushed by a truck, his wife had a heart attack and died, then he was in a second car accident, his dog was strangled by its leash, and finally, his home burned down. All within a year following his fateful delivery of the Hope Diamond.

Even I had to admit that was strange . . . and disconcerting.

"What about Marie Antoinette?" Sophie said. "And King Louis . . . the Fifteenth or Fourteenth . . . whatever. Anyway, they were the Hope's most famous owners. And how did things turn out for them?" She made a slashing motion across her throat. "Not so good, right?"

Okay, so yes. This was true, too. Having your head chopped off at the hands of the peasants revolting and throwing over your rule certainly fell in the category of "bad fortune."

"And that socialite? Evalyn something, I think," Sophie continued. She was really working up a steam here, and I knew exactly who she was talking about. Evalyn Walsh McLean. "There was a whole PBS special on her. She didn't believe there was a curse, either, when she bought the Hope from Cartier. Her son died in a car crash, her daughter committed suicide, and her husband went insane and was committed to an asylum. How about all that?"

Mel's eyebrows went up. "That's true? That all happened?" She looked at me for confirmation. I shrugged, conceding the truth.

"Okay, Sophie, okay," I said. "I get your point. It's weird, and I'm not sure I can explain it all. But what am I supposed to do about it? I can't refuse because of that. Faulkner is serious," I said, taking care to lower my voice. "When he says he's going to sever my hands . . . well, I *believe* him."

Sophie said nothing.

"If I have to choose between a possible threat of some mysterious curse that may result in me getting my head cut off like Marie Antoinette . . . and the very real threat of a flesh-and-blood bad guy who will remove my hands? I'm taking my chances with that curse. I have to. It's the only thing I can do."

At that moment, a waitress came by to clear our dishes. We watched in awkward silence as she stacked the plates and left.

"Besides," I continued, lifting my coffee cup, "nothing bad has happened in recent years. People freaked out when the Hope was donated to the Smithsonian." I smiled and took a sip of hot coffee, thinking of the self-righteous and panicky letters I'd read last night, written to newspaper editors with outrage. One began,

If the Smithsonian accepts the diamond, the whole country will suffer.

"But nothing has happened lately. In fact, most people feel the Hope has been nothing but good luck for the Smithsonian, bringing in millions of visitors."

I hoped my voice sounded firmer and more confident than I felt. And that my friends could not tell that a creepy, cold fear twisted my gut.

They were right. It was a crazy thing to do. It was impossible, curse notwithstanding. I needed a way out of this mess. But so far, there didn't seem to be one.

The curse? That was the least of my worries.

It was actually the Louvre I was more concerned about. The guards at the Louvre carried semiautomatic weapons, for one thing. And then there was just the matter of being a thief in general.

Things went wrong sometimes. You had to escape through the roof sometimes. You had to crawl through vents sometimes. Places where there was little ventilation. Places where you could fall from.

There were infinite ways a thief could be injured or killed. I had no illusions about this.

And even if nothing went wrong . . . there was still that pesky issue of my own fears. Was I going to have a panic attack at a critical moment, say, and ruin everything?

We left the restaurant and walked through the underground labyrinth called Down Under, a jumble of merchants, comic book stores, and antiques dealers. Our heels clicked on the polished wooden floors. The air down here smelled of incense and patchouli tinged with the faint smell of urine coming from the truly terrifying public washroom down the corridor and around the corner.

We passed a shop, a tiny wedge-shaped nook of a store, with a sign that read: WORLD-FAMOUS "ROMANY ROSA," SOOTHSAYER, FORTUNE-TELLER, GYPSY. FORTUNES TOLD. PALMS AND CARDS READ.

"Oh, perfect!" Sophie said. "Let's go in."

I hesitated, hanging back. This was not the kind of thing I went in for. Mel flat out refused as a first reaction.

"Come on," Sophie said, goading us. "I missed my appointment with my psychic last week. Ridiculous meeting at work ran late," she grumbled.

"Um, *your* psychic, Soph? That's not normal. You know that, right?" I said.

She ignored me. "I just want to go in for a sec and get caught up."

I glanced at Mel, and she just shrugged. Reluctantly, we walked into the fortune-teller's shop, parting a jangling curtain of beads. The air was heavy with the perfumes of tea and sandalwood. Soft flamenco music played from an old radio in the corner.

As soon as we walked into the room, the fortune-teller looked up. She gazed at the three of us in turn, but her stare fixed upon me. "You, dear. I shall read your cards, no?"

She looked to be about fifty, but a hard, haggard fifty. Her weathered face bore lines and creases that came only from a lifetime of heavy smoking. Above her small eyes arched very thin eyebrows, overplucked and drawn on to creepy effect. Gauzy scarves surrounded her like an aura.

"Thank you, but no," I said. "I'm just here with my friend. She's the one who needs her cards read."

The fortune-teller slid her beady glance to Sophie, who was standing beside me. "No, you can wait." She looked back at me. "You must allow me. I will charge no fee."

Sophie urged me forward. "It's okay, Cat. I can wait. You should do this."

"Hey, Cat, you might as well," Mel said flatly, but I could see the laughter in her eyes. She wasn't buying into the hocus-pocus act for one second.

I wished I could be as dispassionate as Mel, but I couldn't deny the chilled feeling that crept up my scalp.

I sat down on a stool upholstered with threadbare gypsy fabric in faded, peculiar swirls and flowers. Romany Rosa lit a candle, then shuffled the large, old cards, brown around the edges, with her eyes closed. She opened her eyes then and laid the cards out reverently.

I was prepared to scoff, to dismiss this whole thing. But, strangely, as I watched her work, a peculiar coldness came over me.

She laid the cards in a cross formation, with a column to her right. As she set each card down carefully, she spent just a moment looking at each one. When she had spread ten cards on the table, she paused and looked at the entire display.

I was reading upside down, but I could see the names printed on the bottoms of the cards. The Star. Wheel of Fortune. King of Coins. The Empress.

Rosa frowned and tilted her head. She touched each card in turn.

"You are on the doorstep of fire," she said, gazing at the cards. "There is much danger, but also much reward at stake. But you have little choice. Your hand is being forced."

An interesting choice of words. I rubbed my wrist, happy that it was still intact.

The gypsy continued. "However, although it is hard to see, there is always a choice. There is always an alternative path," she said. "You are too close to the venom. You need protection."

At this, Sophie gasped. "Oh my God, Cat, the *curse,*" she whispered loudly.

In spite of myself, I was hanging on the fortune-teller's every word. The things she was saying were just too close to the truth to be ignored.

I shook my head. No, fortune-tellers were just like the rest of us con artists, I staunchly reminded myself. They told people what they wanted to hear. They read nuances in reactions and modified their responses moment by moment as they went along.

That was what I told myself, and that was what I had to believe.

There was no curse of the Hope Diamond. There was no such thing.

"Much harm will come to you if you touch the object," Rosa said, still gazing at the cards. "It is too deep. The magic too old. You must not come close to it or possess it." Even Mel stiffened at this, standing beside me. "You are talented, and you are strong," said the gypsy. "But you cannot outwit magic this old."

Then Rosa reached forward and plucked a card from the table. She held it out to me. "Here. You must take this. This will keep you safe." Printed on the bottom were the words *The Star.* The card pictured a naked woman kneeling by a pool of water, pouring liquid from a jug. A large star sparkled above her head. I took the smooth card into my hands and looked at the gypsy with surprise. She nodded her head. "Take it."

Sophie whispered in my ear, "The Star. That's the card of hope and tranquility."

As I walked home, thoughts of the fortune-teller's warning swirled inside my head.

Death. That was what this was all about, wasn't it?

I remembered when I was a kid and first beginning to grapple with the issue of my own mortality. I would lie in bed late at night, thinking about the fact that I was going to die someday. It scared the hell out of me. It almost made me wish I'd never been born. Because if I'd never been born, I would never have to die. It was like I was on a horrible runaway train, heading inexorably in one direction and totally powerless to stop it.

There was nothing I could do. One day I was going to die. For a little while, I attempted to convince myself that I was special—that I was the one person in the world who wasn't actually going to die. People would study me and write about me and wonder how I'd done it . . . but I was going to be the girl who lived. The one who would never have to face that threshold. The one who would never have to cross over and feel terrified, not knowing what was on the other side.

But although I wanted to believe that fantasy, I never fully did, of course. I knew I wasn't special. I wasn't immortal. I was going to die. And there was nothing I could do.

I became terrified then of dying. Every day I'd wonder if this was my last day. My last day had to be someday, so why not today?

I think it was becoming a thief, ultimately, that helped me get over my fear of dying. When I discovered and honed my skills, I began feeling special. And powerful. And . . . perhaps just a little bit invincible.

So what was I going to do now? Now that the full terror of death had returned to me, stopping me from doing the one thing that made me feel indestructible.

Chapter 9

Jack walked into the office at FBI headquarters with a feeling of dread. The office was buzzing, phones were ringing, and file cabinets were clanging. It smelled of stale coffee and printer toner. Fluorescent lighting glowed reluctantly against the dull white walls and industrial-grade blinds and carpets.

He was not looking forward to having to admit to his boss he'd lost the guy from last night. Special Agent Victoria Sullivan was a real ball breaker.

Somehow Jack needed to convince her that he was still worthy of being out on field duty. But he also wanted to know what the hell was going on with this case and why Interpol was involved.

Jack hated office work. He much preferred to be out in the field. He shuddered, thinking of his recent jailbreak from the world of paper and computers and watercoolers. He couldn't go back to that.

Jack walked into Victoria Sullivan's office. He pressed his mouth into a line and closed the door behind him, shutting out the chaos of the outer offices.

Her office was quiet and very still, as if the very air was afraid to disturb her.

"Barlow. They tell me you lost him," she said.

Jack cleared his throat and shifted. "I did." He lifted his chin. There was no point denying it. "But the main reason was because of Ludolf Hendrickx."

"Who?" she asked, narrowing her eyes. "I don't know that name."

"He works for Interpol and he was following Snyder, my mark. I think there's something more going on."

"I doubt that. Snyder is just a small-time criminal. Part of a larger network, sure, but not worth the attention of Interpol. You must be mistaken. What's your source for that intel, anyway?"

He couldn't tell her. That was because he'd used a less than strictly licit source. And Victoria Sullivan was a stickler for doing things by the book. But Jack knew the best information often came from the underworld itself. And the number he'd sent the photograph of Hendrickx to was a source of Cat's.

He shrugged and tried to change the subject. He writhed inside under the familiar conflict of interest that's part of the territory when you're dating a career criminal.

Even to him, it sounded ridiculous. On the surface, of course, it seemed like cops should stay on their side, criminals on theirs. But Jack knew that reality was complicated. The law and lawbreakers were intimately involved. There were many cops and FBI agents who had working relationships of various types with criminals.

It was like that old Bugs Bunny cartoon, the one with the sheep-dog and the wolf punching their time clocks and greeting each other. *Morning, Ralph. Morning, Sam.*

But even given those pseudo working relationships, not many FBI officers were actually dating criminals. Much less living with them.

God knows he'd tried to end it. Last year he couldn't handle it. Decided they were just too different. But then he'd been shown just how wrong he was. He couldn't live without Cat. She meant too much to him.

His boss was still standing there, waiting for an answer as to where he'd come by the information that Hendrickx was Interpol— even though Interpol didn't have an official record of him.

"Well, it doesn't matter," she blurted before Jack could start explaining. "Write it up in your report. Then here are the cases I want you to work on. An audit of the department's performance that needs analysis—"

Jack closed his eyes and groaned silently. Paperwork. She was pulling him out of the field already.

Jack stepped closer to Victoria's desk. "Listen, I know I screwed up last night. But I need another chance. And I really believe there's something more to this than we know."

"Yes, you said that. And like I said, put it in your report. Then get to work. You're off this case."

At that moment, the page on Victoria's desk phone beeped. "Special Agent Sullivan?" said a tinny, plaintive voice. "They called up to tell you the computer forensics meeting has started."

"Get to work, Barlow," she said, throwing on her jacket and striding out of the office.

Jack turned to leave and then spotted the file folder sitting on the edge of her desk. The file that contained details of this case. The one he was not privy to see.

He hesitated a moment. Victoria was way down the corridor now, nowhere in sight. He looked up to see if anyone else was watching.

And then Jack slid his hand under the smooth folder to flip it open and take a brief look inside.

The top page was an e-mail that had been printed out. He scanned the page like lightning. Some words stuck out, like *Snyder* and *Washington* and *Interpol* and *the Gargoyle.*

Gargoyle. Now, where had he heard that name before?

And Interpol. Fuck. He knew they were involved. Why would his supervisor deny it? He read the document through more carefully. And a gnawing feeling developed in his gut.

He should leave it. He should walk away and forget what he had seen.

Jack closed the file and strode from the office at medium speed, nothing furtive or guilty or rushed. But his brain was churning.

Sitting down in his cubicle, he turned on his computer and watched the lights flicker and heard the CPU fan start to hum.

What he should really do here was forget all about this.

His supervisor was not going to be impressed with him doing his own little side detective work. He was not some amateur sleuth in a cozy mystery. He was a professional. He was FBI. There were rules and regulations. Protocol. He needed to operate within those bounds, and that was the way to get ahead.

But he was not convinced they were doing this right. He leaned back in his desk chair, the springs bouncing gently under him. He scrubbed his hand through his hair. The file suggested they were barking up the wrong tree.

Interpol involvement—initially suspected, now ruled out.
Involvement with the Gargoyle—unlikely.

If the Gargoyle was the bigger fish and Interpol was truly involved like Jack suspected they were, why *wouldn't* this involve the Gargoyle?

There was something important about this investigation. Jack could feel it in his gut. He knew criminals. He knew them from the inside out.

It was Jack's bane . . . but it was perhaps also his advantage. Something he possessed that his supervisor did not.

Maybe he could keep investigating this case on the side. No fanfare, just surreptitiously. No matter what Victoria Sullivan had told him or not told him to do.

As long as he could keep it a secret. Of course, he had no idea what he'd do if he actually learned anything of value. He'd have to call an audible on that play, if it happened. But maybe it wouldn't come to that.

And then Jack's phone buzzed. Wesley Smith's number flashed onto the screen.

Jack's eyebrows lifted in surprise.

"It's been awhile, Jack," came Wesley's voice, relaxed and friendly, when Jack answered the phone.

"What's up, Wes?" Jack said cautiously.

"I need to talk to you. Can you meet me?"

Jack hesitated. He did not need more criminal involvement. But . . . Wesley was different. He was a crook, true, but somehow he was also one of the good guys. He didn't play mind games with Jack. He was a straight shooter.

Truth was, if Jack had a choice between working with someone like Wesley and working with someone like Victoria Sullivan, he'd take Wesley anytime.

But this was not a request to work together. This was just a meeting. There was nothing illegal about that. Out of respect, he could go and hear what Wesley had to say. But his involvement would stop there.

Jack rubbed the side of his face and exhaled. "Sure, Wesley. Where?"

Half an hour later, Jack strolled into Pioneer Square. He spotted Wesley on a bench on the far side, beside the ornate Edwardian streetcar shelter. Old brick and stone buildings, refurbished into bookstores and coffee shops, surrounded the square.

Jack turned up the collar of his jacket against the chilly mist.

Wesley was a lean, wiry man, and when he grinned, he showed far too many teeth. But he wasn't grinning now. He was looking away, holding a paper Starbucks cup, pretending not to recognize Jack.

Jack sat down on the bench and pulled out a newspaper. "So what's this about?" he asked, keeping his eyes on the paper and flipping through to the sports section.

"We need your help. It's the Fabergé."

Jack said nothing for a moment. His hand froze midair, about to turn a page. The Fabergé? But that was impossible.

"What are you talking about? The egg was destroyed," he said finally. He lowered his voice. "The Gifts are gone."

Wesley shook his head. "No, they're not." He took a sip of his coffee. "Jack, this has happened before. The egg always resurfaces."

Jack sighed. "If you're going to go all weird on me, bro, and start talking about mystical powers—"

"No. It's not that." Wesley paused as a mother with a baby in a carriage strolled by. "There are rumors about a clandestine group of people who protect objects of extreme importance."

"Just protect?"

"Apparently, they're not concerned with ownership. They watch and wait, and if there is a need, they intervene to prevent an object's destruction."

"You're saying they were in London when we were there? They saved the Fabergé when it fell?"

Wesley shrugged. "It's possible."

Jack looked away, across the square. It sounded pretty far-fetched. They didn't care about ownership? But they were willing to go to extreme lengths to protect valuable objects?

But if there were such a group, this particular Fabergé egg and what it contained would certainly fall under the heading of extreme importance. The Gifts of the Magi, the original gold, frankincense, and myrrh that had been given to Jesus long ago—and then stolen, an act that had spurred the creation of thieves' guilds—were immeasurably significant.

The quest to recover the Gifts and return them to their rightful owner was the only honorable thing Jack's father, a career criminal, had been involved in. It had been a mantle Jack himself had taken up.

Until he'd believed the Gifts had been destroyed.

"We've been searching for the Fabergé egg nonstop since it disappeared in London last year," Wesley said. "And now it's been tracked to Dubai. I need you to come with me and help me find it."

"Isn't there an overseas team?" Jack could still taste the bitterness of being left out of things last time, at the last minute, for just this reason.

"Yes. But you're the one I trust the most."

Trust. That was ironic. Here was a professional crook talking to a federal agent about trust. Jack looked sideways at Wesley.

Jack had no doubt the man did, indeed, trust him. Jack had the ability to make things difficult for Wesley officially, but here the man was asking for help. Likewise, Wesley could screw Jack if he wanted to. He had more than enough material for blackmail, if he chose to go that route.

But Jack knew he wouldn't. There was definitely mutual trust here. And that was a very rare thing.

Jack felt the same pull as before when it came to the Fabergé and the Gifts. Last year it had become more than just fulfilling his father's wishes, and it was a hell of a lot more than just a treasure hunt. It had meaning.

But Jack was on the edge of something else that had meaning now. Finding the Gargoyle.

And while there was a team in place to hunt for the Fabergé with Wesley, there was no such team searching for the Gargoyle. At least none that Jack knew of.

Then there was the small issue of Jack's career, his tentative position within the FBI. He just couldn't get involved with the criminal side right now. He had to focus on staying on the right side of the law.

Something else occurred to Jack. "Have you talked to Cat about this?"

"Not yet."

"Why not?" As far as Jack could see, Cat was the perfect choice. She'd been heavily involved last year—in fact, she'd been the only one to successfully capture the egg. It was a short-lived possession, sure, but it was closer than the rest of them had come.

"The Agency says Cat is tied up with another big case right now. She's not at liberty to join us. We're going to try to keep her out of it for now."

Jack frowned. *A big case?* He wanted to know, yet he didn't want to know. A familiar struggle.

For a second, Jack thought how much easier it would be if he just left the FBI. If he joined the dark side. No more secrets.

But he just couldn't do it.

Still, how many different ways was he going to blur the lines before he lost sight of who he truly was?

"Jack, come on," Wesley said. "I'm flying to Dubai tomorrow. Why don't you join me? We've been a great team in the past. Let's do it again."

Jack folded the newspaper and held it tightly in his hand, not saying anything for a moment. It would be easy. He was valued by Wesley and his team. It was something he could do and do well.

"I can't," Jack said at last and shoved the paper under his arm.

Wesley nodded, accepting defeat. "Okay. But if you change your mind, you know how to get in touch with me."

Jack stood. "I do. Good luck."

Chapter 10

It was a foggy spring day, and mist clung to the old stone buildings on campus. The damp seeped into my bones. I still hadn't decided what to do about the Hope. The tarot card the fortune-teller had given me, the Star, was tucked into my pocket. It was silly, I know, but somehow it made me feel just a little safer.

At any rate, I had something else I needed to do this afternoon: get myself to the library and pick up an essential book so I could finish my French lit paper on *le mal du siècle*.

I was getting my master's degree in nineteenth-century French literature at the University of Washington and, admittedly, taking a long time about it. I worried constantly that my supervisor would kick me out, but so far I was hanging on by my fingernails.

I intended to finish my degree. Besides being excellent cover for a professional thief, it was smart to have a career to fall back on. Once my burgling days were over.

Which, given what was happening with me lately, seemed like a closer possibility than ever.

I strode through the leafy campus, along cherry blossom–lined pathways, thankful I had avoided seeing Professor Atworthy when I passed the campus coffee shop—a regular hangout of his. Atworthy was my thesis supervisor, and I had blown off a loosely arranged meeting during his office hours earlier today, and I didn't have a ready explanation for why my assignment was late.

I didn't think "Needed time to plan an emerald heist at the Westin penthouse" would be a particularly acceptable excuse.

I made it to the Suzzallo Library, an imposing Gothic stone building, and climbed the steps to the cathedral-like edifice. I loved this building. Oak bookshelves adorned the walls, and carved friezes and vaulted ceilings decorated the reading rooms. I breathed in the smell of books and ink and a faint note of sweaty student. As much as I would have loved to linger here, I made my way quickly to the graduate desk and signed out my book.

On my way out, down the grand staircase, there was a crush of people entering and climbing upward. As I jostled through the crowd, somebody reached out to catch hold of my arm.

"Catherine, there you are! I missed you at my office hours this morning," said a pointed voice. I looked up into Professor Atworthy's face.

Crap.

Memo to self:

When attempting to avoid university professors, add campus library *to the list of locations to stay away from, for Christ's sake.*

So there I was, standing on the central staircase of the library, trying to produce an excuse, muttering various old standbys about dogs and computer crashes and lost files and the like.

I could tell he was as convinced as I usually am when the computer sales guy does a pitch for the extended warranty.

Considering Atworthy was one of my younger profs, he certainly had a finely tuned bullshit meter. He looked at me over his sharp nose with extreme skepticism. He seemed tired, pushing a lock of muddy brown hair back from his forehead, glancing out the window, and sighing as I rambled on. Doubtless I was headed toward probation of some sort.

Just then a voice boomed right next to us. "Andre, my goodness!" The man spoke with a heavy French accent. He was standing beside Atworthy, staring directly at him. "I haven't seen you in ages! How have you been? *Comment ça va?*"

Atworthy looked at the man blankly. "I'm sorry, but I don't know you," he said. "You've got me mistaken for someone else."

The Frenchman laughed. "Andre, that's ridiculous."

But Atworthy insisted he didn't know the man. Eventually, the Frenchman gave up and walked angrily away.

"Well, that was weird," I said, laughing lightly, which I hoped hid the fact that my every hair was standing on end. Coincidences like that always mean something. My every alarm bell was jangling.

I forced a smile as I excused myself and descended the stairs to leave the library.

All the other strange incidents involving Atworthy began stacking up in my mind.

There was the time I'd found a handgun in his desk drawer. And we're not talking about some charming antique professor-ish pistol. This was a Smith & Wesson model 945, a .45 caliber semiautomatic. What I was doing snooping in his desk drawer was another story, of course, but it didn't change the fact that Atworthy, my leather and tweed professor, had been in possession of a concealed weapon.

There was the moment I'd spotted Atworthy in London. He was on a boat on the Thames, watching me silently as I stood on Blackfriars Bridge after the Fabergé job. It was the middle of the night, sure, and the sky was foggy, but I'd been sure it was him.

Then a horrible thought occurred to me. Could he possibly be an undercover cop?

The truly paranoid part of myself then asked, Could he possibly be investigating *me?* Had he been under deep cover all this time? A cold fist gripped my stomach.

Somehow, I was going to have to find out.

I arrived at 125 Bay Street and ducked behind the back of Atworthy's house—a two-story clad in cedar shingles. It was twilight, and darkness was closing in all around me. It was a comforting feeling for a thief.

I needed to be very fast. I knew Atworthy was at an evening lecture. Of course, I was supposed to be at that lecture myself, but this was a much more pressing task.

I could count on at least another thirty minutes, but beyond that, anything could happen. I hadn't had much chance to plan this break-in, so it wasn't ideal, but I had to figure this out right away. I picked the doorknob lock with little difficulty. The doorknob turned, I pushed, but the door held fast. *Fine.* There had to be another lock. I got through that in another few seconds.

But then there was another latch. And a lock at the top of the door. *Jesus.* This was not a high break-in neighborhood. Atworthy had to be hiding some secrets. Finally, I opened the door.

An alarm wailed like a banshee.

Shit. My heart was in my throat as I located the security panel just inside the door. I identified the manufacturer in an instant and knew it was one I could hack into and disable. After several seconds of manipulating the circuits, there was a sudden, single beep and the siren cut abruptly. I exhaled steadily into the silence. I hoped I could count on neighborly apathy—that tendency to assume everything was fine once an alarm shut off by itself—and that nobody would come to investigate.

Now to find what I needed.

This, typically, was a task made easier by knowing what one was looking for. Which I didn't. I began skulking through the darkness of Atworthy's creaky old house. The small bright circle of my pen-light bobbed ahead of me and slid over walls, carpeted floors, the TV. An office or den might be useful, if I could locate such a thing. Or a bedroom. Typically full of personal information.

Wait. There was the kitchen. Beyond a doorway I saw dishes piled in the sink and smelled the faint aroma of burnt food. The kitchen could be useful—maybe I'd find some phone messages or bills. I tiptoed that way. I was relaxing into the job now. And I was pleased because, if nothing else, I was giving my new soft-soled black shoes a dry run. So far, they were definitely working well. Except for one irritating little spot by my left heel—

Just then, the cold blade of a sizable knife pressed against my throat.

Chapter 11

The hand holding the knife was Atworthy's. I knew because a sharp voice in my ear said, "Do not move," and it was unmistakably his. I'd heard it in the lecture hall often enough.

I was frozen, mentally calculating my chances of getting out of this ambush with my carotid arteries still intact.

Then there was a sharp intake of breath, and Atworthy said, "Catherine? Is that you?" He withdrew the blade and spun me around. "Jesus, Catherine, I could have killed you." He was angry but clearly relieved. "What are you doing here?"

As he flipped the knife closed, I stared at it. The weapon was a balisong, which was no kitchen knife. A balisong is an illegal blade, a classic choice for crooks.

My professor. With the weapon of a criminal.

"Well . . . I . . ." I struggled to find a suitable pretext. I decided to lob the ball back to him and buy a little time. I planted a hand on my hip.

"You know, Professor, I might ask you what you're doing with a balisong. And how did you learn how to subdue an intruder like that?"

"That does not answer the question, my dear."

"Right. Well, I really wanted to know my grade on my last paper . . . and I thought you might have it here. . . ."

"Catherine," he said, holding up a hand, "just stop. I know you're a thief. I've known for a long time, in fact."

My heart stopped for a second. He knew? Did he think I was breaking in to steal from him? His tone suggested he wasn't about to clap handcuffs on my wrists or place an imminent 911 call. It also suggested that denying things, at this stage, would be pointless.

"I wasn't robbing your house," I blurted.

"I believe you."

"Are you a cop?" I asked. Truthfully, I didn't want to hear the answer to this question. I was getting ready to bolt. I'd already assessed the exits. The answer to this question was going to dictate a lot.

"No."

"No?" I squinted at his face in the darkened kitchen, trying to read his expression and figure out what was going on. Was he lying? I had an uneasy, fun-house feeling of standing on an unsteady floor that was about to tip at an awkward angle. "Let's say I believe you. How do you know about me, then?"

He scrubbed his face, looking at me uncertainly. Then he sighed and took a seat at the round oak kitchen table.

"Catherine, I think it's time I told you the full story."

"Please do."

"Atworthy isn't my real name," he began, loosening the navy rep stripe tie he'd worn to class that day. "It's Andre Gaston. I've been using Atworthy as an alias. It's a name that was given to me for protection."

I scraped a chair out from under the table and joined him. "Protection from what?"

I leaned my arms on the table, and a few sharp crumbs stuck into my elbows. A clock on the wall ticked softly, and the refrigerator gave a click and began humming in the corner.

"My old life."

"And that was?"

He hesitated. He raked a hand through his thick hair peppered with several strands of gray. "I was a hired killer, Catherine. An assassin."

My mouth dropped open in full cartoon style.

"I grew up in Paris," he continued. "And that's where I trained to be a killer."

I leaned back in the seat with a thud. Atworthy then spun the tale of how this all came to be. A shadowy agency, in the business of seeking out promising subjects, had recruited him at a young age. He came to their attention when he showed an early skill at sport shooting while out hunting every Sunday with his father. He was shipped off to boarding school—which turned out to be a school in the covert arts, training contract killers. After graduating, the agency took him on as an assassin.

I looked down, shaking my head slowly in disbelief. "I had no idea." I looked up at him again. "So, you actually killed people?"

He suddenly looked very old, like he'd lived a thousand lives. His shoulders sloped under an invisible burden.

"Catherine, you need to understand that the people I killed were marked men. They were dead, anyway. Whether I pulled the trigger or someone else. It's not an excuse, but—"

"So what happened? Why did you stop?"

He spread his hands out on the table before him. "I had doubts. As I grew older and saw more of the world, I started to see things differently. And then I got an assignment that changed everything."

"In what way?"

"It was something I just couldn't do. The target was a woman. And . . . she was pregnant."

"Oh. So you refused."

Atworthy's face was grim and pale. "There is no turning down an assignment. No, I did it." I stared at him in horror. "After that I couldn't live with myself anymore. I wasn't sleeping. I wasn't eating. I couldn't go on." His eyes looked haunted. It was an expression I'd never seen on my professor's face before. Streetlights shone in through the window of the breakfast nook, illuminating a row of kitchen knives hanging on the wall.

"So you quit?" I asked.

He laughed without humor. "Quitting wasn't an option. People *own* you. Instead, I turned myself in."

"To the police?" I asked slowly, the very idea of this causing an involuntary physical repulsion in the pit of my stomach.

"I struck a deal. I provided names. And I was placed into witness protection. The only skill I had other than killing was in French literature. Strings were pulled, calls were made, and I ended up being placed as a professor in this little corner of the Pacific Northwest, here at the University of Washington."

"Okay, but how did you find out what *I* do for a living?" I asked, leaning forward. Crumbs crunched under my forearms again.

"I still retain some underground connections, and they told me when a professional thief enrolled in my department. Criminals under protection need to know about the movements of other professionals in the area. It wasn't an accident that I became your academic advisor. I specifically requested it. I thought . . . maybe the time would come when I could help you."

"Help me? In what way?"

"Oh, I don't know. Maybe I could help you understand the choice ahead of you. Maybe help you choose a less illegal life. Or help you deal with the emotional repercussions of the path you've chosen."

I was quiet a moment. I thought of the Star tarot card I had tucked into the waistband of my black Lycra pants before coming here.

"And was that you . . . in London? Did you follow me there?" I asked.

"I thought you might be in over your head."

He was right about that. I had been in over my head. And I still was—just now with Faulkner and the Hope Diamond.

"All this time, why didn't you tell me?" I asked.

"I've been afraid of openly mingling the two sides of my life. It's one thing when it's all covert, but quite another when they mix. I was afraid of falling back into—"

"The dark side?"

He smiled. "I guess you could put it like that."

I squirmed in the uncomfortable kitchen chair, thinking about whether I should bring it up.

"Well, since you mentioned helping me," I said at length, "maybe you're in the mood for providing some advice? I'm in the market a little bit."

"Go on."

This was familiar territory. Since he was my thesis supervisor, I often consulted with him about thorny problems. In the past they'd revolved a little more around Alexandre Dumas and Victor Hugo, and somewhat less around committing major felonies, but this might work, too.

I told him about my trouble with Faulkner. I told him about the deal I'd made about the Hope Diamond. And I told him about my panic attacks, the fear that would make it impossible for me to actually do the job.

Throughout, he listened intently, frowning.

"So, can you help me?" I asked. I held my breath.

Atworthy sat back in his chair. "No."

I stared. "No? Just no?" I stammered with disappointment. That was it?

"I can't help you, Cat. Only *you* can help you. And the way you can do it? You have to do this job. You have to take the Hope Diamond job. If you want to get over this fear, that's the only way to do it."

"But I thought maybe it would be better to lay low for a bit. Stay safe. No?"

"That is the opposite of what you need to do," Atworthy said. "Running away from fear is the quickest route straight into its arms."

I said nothing.

"Your brain will, over time, figure out that you can do this, that you'll be fine," he said. "And the panic attacks will subside."

Now that it was said, that it was out there, I knew he was right. I'd been tossed to sea from a sailboat, knocked overboard by a flailing boom. If I didn't get back in the boat now, I would never be able to.

"Catherine, I have every confidence you will find your way. But right now you need to embrace the fear. You need to do exactly what your instincts are telling you not to."

Chapter 12

The next day I sat at my desk, staring at a plane ticket to Paris. One traveler. Solo. Leaving tonight.

Earlier today I had told Jack I was going to Paris, and I had tried to convince him to come with me. I thought maybe he'd be able to get away for a few days. Spending a little time together in Paris— the most romantic city in the world—would be wonderful. Of course, me casing the Louvre might not be the most romantic thing ever. But I figured we could spend an hour sitting at a sidewalk café or nuzzling in the park, like everyone else in Paris.

But when I brought it up, he was evasive. Said he had some important stuff he was working on. He started running his hands through his hair and looking away, out the window. Then he began muttering things about making a difference. That this was his chance.

It was one of the things I found most fascinating about Jack. He truly wanted to make the world a better place.

But even if he couldn't go to Paris, I still needed to. I told him I needed to head out of town for a couple of weeks for business.

When I said those words . . . well, I could see what it did to him. He hesitated a second, during which I knew he was processing the fact I'd said, "For business," and he knew I meant "To do something illegal, which most likely involves stealing something."

I could see the conflict on his face. He was simultaneously re-pulsed by what I did and fascinated by it. And, at the same time, schooling himself to not ask a lot of questions.

But of course he was fascinated. Jack came from a long line of lawbreakers. His father, in fact, was one of the legendary jewel thieves of all time—John Robie, the man who'd been the inspiration for Hitchcock's *To Catch a Thief*, the Cary Grant and Grace Kelly film.

To Jack's credit, he merely nodded with my news. There were no follow-up questions. We both knew we did what we had to do.

I have to confess, sometimes it bothered me that there was so much we didn't talk about. We tiptoed around these taboo subjects, and it had become a habit. Sometimes we even tiptoed when we didn't need to.

I looked at my ticket again, read the details for the hundredth time. The flight time, the baggage limitations, the departure date, April 20. Today.

My heart dropped into my stomach. How could I have forgotten?

There was somewhere I needed to be.

Twenty minutes later I pulled up to Lake View Cemetery in my black Mini Cooper and parked in the lot.

I still wasn't sure I wanted to be here. Actually, I was quite confident I did not want to be here. Being in a place like this was terrifying for me. Death occupied way too many of my thoughts these days.

But I couldn't *not* be here. So I forced myself to put my hand on the door handle and step out.

It was okay, I told myself. I'd just make a quick visit. The cellophane crinkled as I clutched the flowers by my side. I'd do this thing, then get out of here.

I padded across the thick grass of the cemetery. Past some graves that were well tended, some that were ancient and crumbling and looked like everyone who had ever loved that person was now in a grave, too.

I passed some familiar headstones. The looming tomb-like one. The pretty one in pink granite with engraved roses—I'd liked looking at that one when I was a kid. Then, a few steps away, the scary one with the face carved into it.

I tried not to think about what it meant, this place. And what each of the stones represented. People who had all faced their final moment, had stood before death, and had gone through to the other side. It was something that was occupying my dreams, my nightmares, my waking thoughts.

And then, as I grew closer, I took a sharp breath of surprise. Crouched by the side of the grave, hand touching the headstone, was my father.

"Dad?"

He turned, startled. His eyes were red-rimmed. This was a jolt for me. I rarely, if ever, had seen my father cry.

"Ah, Cat. I wondered if you'd be here today."

"Of course I'm here today. I always come on this day." Today was the anniversary of my sister's death.

It was fourteen years ago that Penny had died. On her bike, by herself, a hit-and-run. And it had been my fault.

She had wanted me to—no, she had needed, had *begged* me to—steal something for her. Her lucky ring. She'd asked me to get it back from the mean girl who'd taken it and stashed it in her locker.

I had refused.

And Penny had taken matters into her own childlike hands.

If I'd just done it, she'd be fine. But I had tried to fight my true nature, the gifts given to me.

And that was one of the reasons I kept doing it. Being a thief, I mean. To honor Penny. At one time I'd thought I might find atonement by doing this. That maybe there was a job out there to release me. I now knew that wasn't going to happen. This was too much a part of who I was.

Of course, it might be the end of me, too. And this was something I didn't know how to handle in the least. Not anymore.

I looked at my dad and wondered what it meant that he had started coming to Penny's grave again. Also, where was my mom?

Truth was, I really didn't have time for a whole family reunion. I had to get on a flight.

Both my parents knew about my real job. My mom had known

for a few years, and she was on board. Actually, more than that—
she considered herself my business manager. This was an opinion
we did not share.

My dad was another story. He had learned the truth only a few
months ago. And he had taken it very hard. "I feel like I've lost two
daughters now," was what he'd said.

I placed my cellophane-wrapped tulips on Penny's grave. My dad
and I stood silently for a few minutes. But I didn't need to look at
my watch to feel the time ticking.

"Dad, I know I just got here. But I really have to go."

I wanted to cry in his arms. I ached to tell him how scared I was.
Tell him about the bad guy threatening me. To stand in this place of
death and tell him I was terrified of dying. I wanted to stay there
longer. I wanted to give him a hug.

But the time wasn't right yet for all that.

I desperately hoped he'd come around someday. When I got back
from Paris, reconnecting with my dad would be the first thing I'd do.

As long as I got back in one piece.

Several hours later, the plane roared beneath me as we lifted off
the runway. I'd made my connection in Washington, DC, with no
problem, and now there was nothing standing in the way of this mission except a lot of open sky.

En route to the airport in Seattle, I had sent Faulkner a message
on the encrypted cell phone he'd given me to communicate with him.
"Mission accepted. En route to Paris."

The message had come off far more confident than I felt.

At least I was flying business class; that perk came courtesy of
Templeton's campaign with AB&T. It was the least they could do,
he'd said.

As the overhead compartments rattled during takeoff and my
torso pressed back into the seat, I felt fresh doubt. There was the
fear thing, of course. But also, did I really have the chops for this
job, anyway? Faulkner hadn't commissioned me because I was

the best. He'd commissioned me because I was the one he could blackmail.

As we bumped through a turbulent patch and passed through thick clouds, I gripped the arms of my seat.

The plane banked to the right as the pilot adjusted his course for Paris.

I needed a distraction, so I turned to the woman sitting beside me. "So what takes you to Paris?" I asked.

She didn't look up from her book right away. Yes, that's my favorite. Trying to strike up perky small talk with someone who utterly ignores you. Nothing awkward about that.

At length, she raised her head and turned to me.

"Business," she said, fixing me with a cold gaze. She didn't volunteer anything further and went straight back to her book.

"Ah. Me too," I said.

I looked at her a little more carefully then. And as I did, I realized she was familiar. She had brown hair, chopped short at the back and longer on top and in the front, in the sort of stylish cut I imagined I'd get when I was her age—which I guessed was about sixty. Her fingernails were perfectly manicured. She had a strong jawline. And the sort of smooth, plump skin that is the fruit of good genes and much attentive care from a skilled facialist.

But I definitely recognized her from somewhere.

"Do I know you?" I asked. "You seem familiar."

After a few beats she looked at me again. "I don't know. But you are not familiar to me."

I furrowed my eyebrows, trying to place her. "What's your line of business?"

"Museum curation," she said. Clearly, she was growing extremely impatient with me.

Fine. I would leave her alone. I turned to stare out the window.

And then it dropped. Oh my God, I could not believe it. This was Madeleine York, the director of the Smithsonian's National Museum of Natural History.

What were the chances? And then I became suspicious. What *were* the chances?

Was this pure coincidence? Or was there something more going on?

I shifted in my seat, uncomfortable now. *Think it through, Cat.* How could she possibly know about me? The only people who knew what I was doing were underworld types. Not established pillars of society and directors of national museums.

After the flight was well under way, Madeleine ordered a whiskey sour. I did the same. I needed her to open up a little, and I knew the best way to do that was to play the mirror game. People tend to trust people who look and act the same as they do. It's a dirty trick, really.

But it works.

I channeled my inner culture snob, called up everything I knew about fine art, and after another round of drinks, Madeleine started to relax.

Somewhere over the Atlantic, after the dessert had been served, Madeleine became downright chatty. "I mean, can you imagine such a thing?" she was saying, pausing in her story to take a spoonful of crème brûlée. "All of us at the Smithsonian thought that was simply ridiculous. . . ."

I jumped on that like a five-time bridesmaid on a bouquet. "Oh, you work at the Smithsonian?" I tried to maintain a casual tone, drinking my wine.

She looked at me and nodded. "Yes, I do."

I wondered if I could press this advantage a little. Could I get some useful information out of her?

"I love museums," I said with a smile. "I can't wait to see the Louvre."

"Well, that's where I'm going, too."

"Ah! Comparing notes?"

"In fact, they are holding an exhibit that will feature some of our pieces on loan. You've heard of the Hope Diamond?"

"Oh, um, yes. Hasn't everyone?" I said noncommittally. "Not that I follow that stuff much." On second thought, this was heading into uncomfortable territory. But Madeleine York was warming to her subject now, and I didn't want to come off peculiar at this point.

"It's quite a fascinating undertaking, you know, transporting precious objects overseas," she said, swirling the ice in her drink. "The last time the Hope went to the Louvre, it did so in the hands of one man. Or, more specifically, in the secret pocket hand sewn by his wife, inside his trousers." She leaned in conspiratorially.

I knew about this, of course. No armored vehicles. No high-tech security systems. No guards with M16s.

And, when you think about it, it's the perfect way to transport a priceless gem. Flying absolutely under the radar. A single person would be invisible, slipping in and out of the system exactly like one of the three million people traveling that day.

As long as nobody knew who was carrying it and when. Nobody with a willingness to murder, namely.

Because, of course, that one man with the secret pocket would be at terrible risk. The flesh-and-bone obstacle to somebody's multi-billion-dollar fortune. I can think of many people who would be sorely tempted to cut that flesh and break that bone to get to that fortune.

That's the thing about jewels: although they can lift you to the heights of inspiration, they can also blind you with their brilliance. And they can drive you to your knees with greed and want.

Truth is, every time the Hope Diamond has been transported, it's happened under extremely low-tech, sneaky security. Which, to the public, seems crazy. Where is the platoon of security guards? Where is the iris-scanning technology? To a thief, however, it's absolutely brilliant. And infuriating.

One man with a diamond sewn into his trousers is a far more effective security barrier—simple, elegant—than an entire army. With an army, there must be communication. There has to be a plan and various moving parts. And when there is a complex plan, there are seams. There are weaknesses. And those are the opportunities a thief can use to his—or her—advantage.

"Well, I must say, it's very Jackie O. of you to loan the Hope to the Louvre," I said, taking another slurp of my drink. Madeleine tilted her head quizzically. I continued. "You know, wasn't she the one who arranged for it to travel there in the sixties for the 'Ten Centuries of French Jewelry' exhibit?"

Madeleine looked at me with a peculiar expression, then said, "I thought you didn't know much about things like this?" A smile curled her lips.

Jesus, Cat. Too much wine. At altitude. Rookie mistake, to say the least.

I laughed and waved my hand. "Oh, I was reading a newspaper in the airport. A feature on Paris, things to do and see."

It was time for me to smile and shrug and turn my attention to the freaking movie. No more incriminating slipups please. I settled back in my seat and attempted to enjoy the rest of the flight.

And tried not to think about the varied sticky situations I might find myself in when we landed in Paris and I started plotting to rob the Louvre.

Chapter 13

Rome, Italy

Inside the Vatican Museums, Ethan entered the first of four Raphael Rooms. He strolled easily among the crowd of tourists who snapped photographs with their pocket cameras. Their sneakers squeaked on the intricately lain marble tiles while they gawked at art Ethan knew they could not even begin to fully appreciate. The galleries smelled of window cleaner and wood polish and the coconut sunscreen some visitor must be wearing.

Sun filtered in from high windows, making streaks through the colonies of dust motes.

Ethan walked through exquisitely decorated rooms, ceilings and walls lush with frescoes by Raphael and his pupils, depicting allegorical tales and biblical stories from the Old Testament.

At last he reached the room that contained *The School of Athens* fresco.

He stood before it for a few moments, until a finely dressed British man in a gray Ralph Lauren suit began to speak to him in a low tone. "Enjoying your visit?"

"Well, it's certainly educational," Ethan replied.

"Mm, wonderful art."

"I meant the security systems. It's eye-opening, the old-fashioned systems they use here. I'm taking plenty of notes. Should I ever receive an assignment here, I think I would quite enjoy myself."

Templeton snorted. In the most dignified way possible, naturally.

"So what's up, Templeton?" Ethan asked. "You flew all the way over here. What's the emergency?"

"Well, for one thing, I was coming to Italy, anyway. I always make a spring shopping trip to Milan. But you're right. There is something I want to talk to you about." They strolled toward the next Raphael Room. "It's about someone who occupies a special place in both our hearts."

Ethan paused and gave Templeton a sideways glance. "Are you talking about Montgomery?"

Templeton smiled and opened his hands. "Of course."

"What about her?" Ethan frowned. Something was wrong.

"It seems she might be in a bit of trouble. I'm afraid she's found herself on the receiving end of a little blackmail."

"At whose hand?"

"Albert Faulkner the Third."

Ethan sucked air through his teeth. "That's not good." The guy was a son of a bitch.

Templeton explained the situation as they walked through the museum. It happened very rarely, thankfully, a mark hunting down a thief from a previous job. It was one of the advantages of having a layer of removal, the Agency. But the idea of it happening to Montgomery made Ethan snarl.

"So what is he threatening her with, exactly?" Ethan asked.

"The oldest punishment for a thief you can think of."

Ethan knew exactly what Templeton was referring to. The idea of severing a person's hands turned his stomach inside out with revulsion. "What is AB&T doing to help her?"

"Very little. Which is why I'm here."

Ethan clenched his jaw and walked on. They reached the Braccio Nuovo, a neoclassical gallery bathed in light from the row of skylights in the soaring coffered ceiling. Alcoves lined the long gallery, filled with larger-than-life statues of Greek heroes and Roman emperors.

Ethan stopped in front of a marble Augustus, and Templeton walked up and stood beside him. "I know it's not your nature to stick your neck out, Jones, but I would think you might make an exception here."

Ethan gazed down at the mosaic tile floor. "What does she need?" he said.

"Well, she's going after the Hope Diamond."

Ethan's head snapped up. "Are you fucking kidding me? The Smithsonian?"

"Worse than that, actually. The Louvre."

Ethan was speechless for a minute. His gears started churning. In fact, the Louvre might be easier in some ways, more difficult in others. It was interesting—

No.

He was not getting involved with Cat Montgomery again. He was not in the market for getting his emotions spanked again.

Normally, women were easy for Ethan to get over. But not this one. And it wasn't just the thrill of the chase, because he'd already gotten her in bed several months ago. Had turned out to be a very good idea, that.

Sure, Ethan knew Cat had just been rebounding from her breakup with Barlow. But it had been more than that for Ethan. And if it were up to him, that wouldn't have been the end of it.

"There's something else," Templeton said. "It seems she's become spooked."

Ethan studied Templeton carefully. "Really?"

"It's not a surprise, I suppose. After what happened to you two in London. After what she saw. She certainly isn't the only thief this has happened to. Trouble is, she seems to be more or less paralyzed by fear now. I'm worried, frankly, that she's going to get herself into a sticky situation and not be able to get herself out."

Ethan rubbed his face. *Shit.* He could feel himself getting sucked in.

"Also, if you do this, Ethan, you'll get major brownie points with AB&T. And you know you need that right now."

Ethan looked down at his shoes. *Ah.* He figured this would come up sooner or later.

A couple of months ago, after Ethan's requested transfer to Italy, his knuckles had been rapped when he refused a job. He'd never refused a job before. But that one was not cool.

It was taking a painting from someone who couldn't afford it. He'd never had a problem with that before. And it was very rare that AB&T had that kind of assignment. But Cat Montgomery seemed to have influenced him. It was one of her rules.

Once he'd started casing the job in a small village outside Florence, he soon discovered that a little old woman who had nothing owned the painting. This was the one thing she possessed. She was otherwise a pensioner, scratching out an existence, and she had inherited this heirloom from her family. It was a small sketch only. But it was significant because of the artist who had sketched it: Leonardo da Vinci.

If only she had sold it, she would have been able to afford a much more comfortable life for herself. Warm house, better food on her table. But she wouldn't let it go; it meant too much to her. On one level Ethan couldn't understand that at all. On the other hand, it made perfect sense.

Once he started to realize her true situation, he just couldn't do the job. He'd refused AB&T, something he'd never done before.

And, boy, had they been pissed.

"You are a thief, Jones," his handler had said. "Not a charity worker."

Ethan's handler was not as enlightened as Cat's. Templeton would never have given her an assignment like this.

Ethan had shrugged. His handler puffed with exasperation. "They're not going to be happy with you, Jones," he said.

So be it, Ethan had thought at the time.

Suffice it to say, Ethan was not the favored thief at AB&T at the moment. Which meant he was left scrounging for the shit jobs. Not that the Rome job had been shit, exactly. It had been fun, for sure. But, for whatever reason, it had not paid well. It just wasn't that important a job. Other thieves had turned it down because of that.

Trouble was, Ethan didn't have much choice these days.

Templeton stood beside him in front of the Augustus sculpture, the Italian sun beaming down on his steel-gray hair. "AB&T is not keen to spend additional money and resources on their asset protection department," Templeton said. "If they can outsource it, great. You'll be back in the good books, my boy, if you do this for them. All you have to do is help her with this job. Help her, and do what you can to keep her safe."

Ethan was torn. He was no hero. He was no knight in shining armor. At least, he never had been before. He needed to look out for himself, first and foremost. That had been his philosophy for the past several years. And it had worked out pretty well for him so far.

But Montgomery was in a mess of trouble. Could he leave her out to dry like that?

Chapter 14

Jack sat down in seat eight, row nineteen, section 328 at Safeco Field. He wondered if this meeting would actually go ahead, if the guy would even show. A loud crack echoed through the stadium as the batter made contact with the ball. A roar rose up from the crowd. The field spread out below, a broad swath of emerald green dotted with players in their bleached white uniforms. The roof was open, as it was a rare clear day in Seattle, and the air was filled with the smell of hot dogs and beer and popcorn.

Jack glanced around at the people sitting in his section. He'd selected seats way up near the back, well away from anyone else. Nobody was in earshot.

Then someone entered the row, carrying a steaming cup of coffee. The man sat down two seats over from Jack, leaving an empty seat between them. It was Hendrickx, the red-haired Interpol agent Jack had seen tailing Snyder the other night.

It hadn't been easy setting up this meeting. Jack had been forced to use some illicit channels. Mostly this was because the licit ones weren't open to him anymore.

They watched the game in silence for a couple of minutes. It was the second inning. The Mariners had another out. The Rangers jogged into the dugout. Jack shifted in his plastic seat.

And then Jack spoke. "Pitcher is looking good, hey?" he said casually to Hendrickx.

Hendrickx kept his gaze on the field. "Sure is." Everything about the guy was ice—the opposite of what Jack expected due to his flaming hair.

After a couple more batters went up to the plate, they started talking business.

"What do you know about the Gargoyle?" Jack asked.

Hendrickx turned stiffly to Jack and stared him down. Jack didn't blink. At last, Hendrickx said, "I thought the FBI wasn't getting involved in this one. They've stonewalled us after multiple attempts. Why are you coming to me now?"

Should Jack tell him the truth? That he was operating on his own?

As Jack debated the merits of full disclosure, organ music and bright flashing lights emanated from the Jumbotron. Jack could pretend he was still operating within the bounds of his organization. But that would be a tricky charade to pull off. And would likely end in a heap of trouble.

"The FBI isn't coming to you," Jack said. "I'm coming to you. Nonofficially."

Hendrickx sipped his coffee and then smiled. It was the first exhibit of emotion. And it was a truly creepy sight. "Ah. I see. You think it's worth investigating. They want you to leave it alone."

Jack gave a brisk nod.

"So why should I tell you anything?" Hendrickx asked. "What are you bringing to the table?"

It was a good question. "I can help."

"We don't need your help. Our investigation is going just fine."

"That's not how it looked the other night."

Jack knew, of course, this was not how to make friends. The other man's face immediately darkened. He looked ready to stand and walk out of the stadium.

Jack decided to change his approach. "I can bring the FBI around. You need our manpower. If I get involved and start gathering evidence, I'll be able to convince my supervisors that we need to work together on this."

Hendrickx seemed to be considering this. Jack assumed the man had checked him out, verified his identity and his claims, before agreeing to meet him.

"Also," Jack continued, pressing his advantage, "I know how to get the Gargoyle. I saw in the file that he frequently uses theft—art, valuables—to fund his operations. That's how we can get him. And that just so happens to be my area of expertise."

Hendrickx sipped his coffee stiffly and watched the field. Another batter struck out.

Finally Hendrickx spoke. "Here's what we know. Gargoyle is the big fish. The man you—and I—were tailing the other night, he is just a peon for a much bigger operation."

"And the term *Gargoyle,* is that Interpol's code name for him?" Jack asked.

"No, that's the name he likes to call himself."

"Oh. Well, that's affected."

Hendrickx ignored Jack and continued talking. A sense of humor wasn't his strongest feature, Jack realized. He also realized they were not going to be friends; the guy was stone.

But that was fine. Jack didn't need friends.

"The Gargoyle has tentacles all over the place," Hendrickx said. "And he's into everything. Drug trade, weapons trafficking, smuggling, theft . . ."

"Where is he based?"

"Here in the United States somewhere. He operates under a legitimate front, we believe."

"Do we have an ID? Photo?"

Hendrickx's mouth hardened into a line. He shook his head once.

Jack's gears spun, as he was thinking about how they were going to find this guy and nail him. Although, there was something about it he didn't quite like. Something that tickled a cluster of neurons at the back of his brain.

There was a sudden outcry from the crowd, an angry roar and a hiss of outrage. Jack glanced at the field. A Mariner had been called out and was arguing passionately with the first base umpire.

"So what now?" Jack asked.

"Now we wait for Snyder to make a move. Currently, he's our only solid lead. We monitor the Gargoyle. We wait for one of them to get caught up in their own webs," Hendrickx said. "And you wait for me to contact you. I will call for your assistance when I need it."

"In other words, don't call me? I'll call you?" Jack asked with a wry grin.

Again, nothing from Hendrickx. He stared at Jack with the steely look of a highway cop.

Jack bristled with irritation. He had a feeling he wasn't getting the full story. Jack didn't know if it was because of a security issue or because he was being manipulated, or something else. Sometimes he felt like the criminals in his life were more up front than the supposed good guys.

Not for the first time, Jack questioned if he was doing the right thing. Sure, he'd succeeded in getting Hendrickx to trust him with some details. But that meant he was involved now. It would be hard to go back from here.

And more than that. Was this icy, cyborg-type guy really the person Jack wanted to be joining forces with?

Chapter 15

Paris

I stood in front of the entrance to the Louvre. Carved stone palace walls rose up all around me, framing the broad cobblestone square whose center was occupied by the sharp glass and steel angles of the pyramid. I breathed crisp morning air that still held the coolness of April in Paris. A low, lemony sun gleamed off the pyramid.

Traffic hummed just a few blocks away. Tourists waited in line to enter the museum, snapping photographs of the cheesy, yet somehow compelling, human statues. One, a woman painted white down to her eyelashes and dressed like Marie Antoinette, held a pose for an impossible length of time.

The pyramid was the public entrance to the museum. And it was how I, a jewel thief, was going to walk in. The first time, anyway.

I polished off the last bite of the *pain au chocolat* I'd bought on my walk: it was crisp, buttery, and warm, with dark, melty chocolate. I crinkled up the paper bag and tossed it away in the trash.

Today I was casing the Louvre.

Just those words gave me a shiver. I had always wanted to say them.

I wouldn't be the first thief to attempt it, of course. The Louvre had been robbed many times. It's a huge building and a mighty tempting target. In the past, the Louvre has come under fire for not having sufficient security. It's been called lax, outdated, and insufficiently staffed.

Once, there was a theft of a Renoir, and while they were investigating that, they discovered a bunch of jewelry was missing, too—but they had no idea when those pieces had been taken. It could have been months prior.

These were the sorts of stories that soothed the career criminal in me. They gave me an inkling this job might actually be possible. I might actually pull it off. If everything went exactly right.

I entered through the pyramid. I was scrutinized, like everyone, at the security checkpoint. Guards rifled through day packs. Metal detectors bleeped as people walked through. I wasn't worried; I didn't have anything suspicious on me.

Not today, anyway.

There was a faint smell of cheese and garbage coming from the bin beside the guards, where people were dumping their food and trash. No outside food was allowed inside.

As I rode the escalator down into the heart of the entrance, the spacious atrium beneath the pyramid, my senses fired on full alert. My fingertips tingled. The Hope was in here somewhere.

I moved through the museum, down endless corridors of artwork and treasures, scribbling mental notes on the guards, the exit points, the physical space, the surveillance systems, the burglar alarms, the sensors on the windows and doors . . . everything.

Gladys, of course, had furnished me with a whole file on the security specs and architectural drawings of the Louvre. I knew this building inside out. But I still needed to flesh everything out with some on-site details.

Because I was a tourist, I could take as many photos as I wanted. And take notes on my iPhone, under the guise of texting someone.

When I saw the first sign pointing the way to the Hope Diamond, my heart fluttered. It was time to get a good look at the jewel itself.

I was in the eleventh grade when I first saw the Hope. Our big class trip for the year was to Washington, D.C., and one of the stops on our itinerary was the Smithsonian National Museum of Natural History. It was meant to be educational.

And it was.

But perhaps not in the ways my teachers had intended.

Seeing that gem had solidified my fascination with jewels and had pushed me further down my path. It was the first truly world-class piece of jewelry I had ever seen. And I'd felt drawn to it like nothing else.

My favorite part of *Snow White* was the dwarves' diamond mine. My favorite part of *Cinderella* was the sparkling glass slipper.

What was it about bright, shiny things that made my heart beat faster? Was it that something so unworldly, so gorgeous, so magical in appearance was also so earthy and natural? Or was it more about what jewels represented: freedom, financial independence? Jewels were a prize. They carried the lore of a treasure chest. Maybe my ancestors had been pirates. Or maybe it was just a magpie tendency.

Whatever it was, I loved everything about jewels. Especially diamonds. And especially this one.

But I needed to knuckle down here, because I had arrived at the exhibit. Banners announced the subject of the exhibit, Marie Antoinette.

Marie Antoinette was, of course, the controversial queen of France who was one of the more famous victims of the curse of the Hope. She wore the Hope—when it was called the French Blue—before it was stolen during the French Revolution and cut down in size.

This was a woman who had met a grisly end. I tried to ignore the chill that touched the base of my neck.

Throngs of people milled about, mostly tourists in shorts and sneakers and white socks. The exhibit was filled with glass display cabinets and freestanding cases. Natural light filled the high-ceilinged gallery. I inhaled a strong, powdery cloud of perfume from the clutch of ladies fresh off the tour bus, standing next to me.

I wandered the gallery, looking at the gowns and the letters and the paintings of Marie Antoinette. She had had everything. And none of it had saved her.

When it came right down to it, what would save me? And . . . why was I assuming I would be saved at all?

The centerpiece of this particular portion of the Marie Antoinette exhibit was the Hope Diamond itself. I gazed about the room. Besides the uniformed security staff, I spotted a plainclothes security officer by the water fountain. And another, pretending to read a plaque about the history of the Hope Diamond. They were as obvious to me as if they had been wearing uniforms.

I'd expected heavy security personnel to be surrounding the Hope Diamond, much as I expect public restrooms to run out of toilet paper. It was annoying when it happened, but inevitable.

I took the sight as a good reminder. I had to be cautious here of appearing to be anything other than an innocent tourist, an interested visitor. So I started snapping some carefully framed photographs.

After a few minutes a uniformed guard appeared at my elbow. *"Mademoiselle, qu'est-ce que vous photographiez?"*

This was where being a grad student in French lit would come most in handy for this job. I was fluent in French. He had asked what I was photographing.

"The painting, of course," I said, taking care to produce an authentic Parisian accent.

"It looked like you were taking a picture of the door."

I looked at him with a bewildered expression. "Why would I do that?"

"I don't know."

"Well, I wasn't."

He looked at me carefully, the tissues around his eyes as tense as a first date. He didn't seem convinced.

"I mean, I didn't mean to. Okay, you got me. This is a new phone, and I don't really have the feel for it yet. I'm not much of a photographer. . . ."

Frick. These guards were a little more on the ball than I had expected them to be. I needed to step up my game a little.

But also, I needed to see the security in operation.

After the security guard walked away, I strolled up behind a tourist in khaki slacks. I casually bumped into him without breaking my stride, which pushed him forward into a display, breaching the ribboned barrier.

I kept my gaze pinned on the panel by the doorway—lights flashed frantically. A silent alarm. Two guards in navy uniforms immediately descended.

They started questioning the man who was standing closest. And then called into their walkie-talkies to get the director of security down there to reset the system. Which struck me as odd. Why would they need the director?

Then I overheard one of the guards saying to another guard that if anything happened on the first day of the exhibit, Monsieur Pierre Severin wanted to know about it.

This was fortuitous. I already knew Pierre Severin was the director of security for the Louvre.

I watched as Severin arrived on the scene. He bustled in, an intense-looking man with a small mustache, wide-set eyes, and deep frown lines between his eyebrows. His hair was brown with a lot of gray on the sides and was thinning on top. He listened carefully to the two guards, then removed his gloves and reset the system with his fingerprints—first all the fingers and thumb of his left hand, then all the digits of his right.

Now, that was interesting.

Memo to self:

Obtain Severin's fingerprints, if at all possible.

I wondered how much of the Louvre's security was hooked up to Severin's fingerprints. I'd have to find out. With them, a whole lot of doors could be opened for me. Literally.

But how to get them? His office at the Louvre, surely, would have his fingerprints. Could I get an appointment with him there? Maybe. But dusting for prints while chatting to him would be . . . awkward.

Breaking into his home would be much more up my alley.

So I needed to find out his home address. Gladys could hunt it down, I'd be willing to bet.

I continued my stroll through the Marie Antoinette exhibit and at long last arrived at the gallery of the Hope.

I waited patiently for my turn to view the Hope itself. I reminded myself to *blend*. Tourists read the plaques lining the queue. Tourists spent very little time looking at the actual gem. I needed to do the same.

I gazed at a plaque called THE HOPE DIAMOND IN FULL COLOR. It described the Hope's unique property of glowing a deep bloody red when exposed to ultraviolet light. Most blue diamonds phosphoresce a blue-white light, but not the Hope. . . .

"That's why everyone thinks it's cursed, you know," the tourist standing next to me said with a South African accent. "They say that red glow is the devil inside."

"Mmm," I said absently, reading on.

"Did you know it was stolen from an idol? It was the eye of the Hindu idol Sita in India," the South African man said.

I rolled my eyes, on the inside. You could always count on at least one of this type of know-it-all at every museum exhibit. I was willing to bet this guy had applied at some point to be a contestant on *Jeopardy.*

"An explorer stole it in the seventeenth century, and that's what started the curse," he continued. *Here we go again. The curse.* Why did everyone need to talk about the curse?

"It was all because of that original theft that people think it's cursed," he said.

I did my best to ignore him. But he wasn't to be deterred. He continued chattering at me about all the trivia he'd learned about the Hope from various programs on TV.

At that moment I spotted another plainclothes security guy. Over by the Hope display case. I kept an eye on him without being obvious.

We moved farther ahead in the queue, inexorably.

And at last, it was my turn to view the Hope. I walked up to the display. The diamond rested in its impenetrable case. The stone was as blue as salt water. It was walnut size, surrounded by white diamonds and suspended on a diamond chain. Under the bright lights of the display, perfectly arranged, it glittered like a Fourth of July sparkler.

Nobody knew for sure if this stone had been an idol's eye. Those were just rumors. But standing here just for a moment, I found myself believing it. It seemed to look straight through me with that deep blue gaze. Time slowed down, and I could hear the blood pounding in my ears.

But that's the deceptive thing about jewels. Precious stones, like thieves, are sly and artful. Diamonds appear to be full of life, but they have no life in them whatsoever.

I was dazzled by the sheer beauty of the Hope, of course. And this stone was truly a thief's diamond. Many crooks throughout history had laid their crafty hands on it. The original thief, Tavernier, if you believed the stories. The thieves who stole it during the French Revolution. And who knows how many others as it wound its way through Europe, intermittently disappearing and resurfacing.

It occurred to me that the curse was particularly strong when it came to people who had stolen and held the diamond, those to whom it hadn't truly belonged.

And now I was about to be next in line to steal it. A cold chill centered between my shoulder blades.

Enough, Cat. I could not give in to the sensationalism. I had a job to do.

I looked at the faces in the crowd, glanced at the security staff to make sure they weren't overly attentive to my presence. And they weren't. I was just like any other person there.

As my eyes slid away from the Hope to look casually around the room, my gaze landed on a man's face on the other side of the gallery. We locked eye contact just for a moment before I looked away.

My heart skipped a beat. And not in a good way.

I didn't know his face. I had no idea what his name was. But I recognized the look in his eyes. I glanced back and watched him for several seconds to confirm my suspicions. I can't explain it exactly, but there was something about the way he moved, the way he was looking at the displays but not really looking. The facial expression indicated that he was trying to appear casual and perhaps a little bored . . . but was anything but. I didn't know this man, but I knew exactly what he did for a living.

A tour group passed through my sight line, blocking my view for a moment. When the group cleared away, the man I'd been watching was gone. I scanned the room uneasily, looking everywhere. Where had he gone? It was like he had disappeared into thin air.

So that's what that felt like.

It didn't change anything. I knew what I had seen. The expression on his face had been one that I knew myself to possess. Alert, vigilant, paying attention to every small detail. And a certain hunger. It was the face of a fellow thief.

Somebody else was casing the Hope Diamond.

Chapter 16

I suppose it wasn't entirely unexpected that another thief was planning to snatch the Hope. The Louvre had its share of circling wolves, no doubt.

But had this rival thief recognized me for what I was?

I returned to the sun-filled atrium under the glittering pyramid. The escalator swept me up toward the glass, and I walked out into the fresh, crisp air of Paris.

I held my phone to my ear as I crossed the roundabout, heading away from the Louvre, and walked toward the grand stone archway to the Tuileries Garden.

Templeton picked up after two rings.

I skipped the small talk. "Templeton, there was another pro at the Louvre," I said. "I saw him in the Hope gallery."

There was a pause. "How did you know he was a thief?"

"I just knew."

It was difficult to hear over the traffic sounds on the street. I walked more quickly and passed under the archway into the garden. With each step, the city noises of cars and cabs grew farther away, replaced by the soothing sounds of birds and fountains.

"Okay, describe him," Templeton said.

"Dark hair, lean face. About five-seven. Wiry. Pale eyes. He looked a little like . . . What's that actor's name? Um, Jonathan Rhys Meyers . . . that Irish guy. Like a slightly bigger version of him."

"Hmm. Sounds familiar. Let me check the database, and I'll get back to you."

I disconnected the call and kept moving through the garden. Fine white gravel crunched underfoot, and I took a deep breath, attempting to calm down. As I passed a crepe stand that filled the air with the smell of sugar and hot frying butter, I could barely think of food. The garden was rich with the kaleidoscopic colors of blooming flowers, but I couldn't enjoy it.

I had one further phone call to make.

"Hello, Gladys. Listen, I need some info on the man who is the director of security at the Louvre. His home address, specifically."

Through the line I could hear the sounds of water sloshing and china clinking. She must have been washing dishes. "No problem, dear," Gladys said. "I'll get that to you right away. Give me a few minutes."

I disconnected and kept walking. I passed deep green hedge mazes and women in day dresses and white gloves taking their tiny yapping dogs out for walks. Calliope music wafted on the breeze from an old-fashioned carousel tucked in a corner of the garden. The soothing beauty of Paris began to work its magic on my nerves. And then everything changed.

It's difficult to explain how I knew I was being followed. Except that I was always aware on a subconscious level of what was around me. So I could immediately tell when someone was not moving like they should.

It's like watching a dance performance. If someone suddenly misses a step, your eyes go to them immediately. Even if you don't know the steps, it doesn't matter. It just messes with the overall movement of the performance, and it jars you into noticing.

Something was wrong. My breath quickened as I ran through the options in my mind.

The best way to shake a tail is the 180. A complete turnaround. It's virtually impossible for a tail to continue following without utterly revealing himself.

But, although highly effective, it's also aggressive. And risky. The tail will know you're aware of their presence, and you may be forcing their hand. Their next move would depend on how desperate they were.

So I preferred to leave that tactic as a last resort. Besides, I didn't want to just shake the tail. I wanted to know who exactly was following me. If I'd been busted or spotted in the Louvre, I needed to know.

I headed for the garden exit. A street with shops and cafés would offer more opportunities for stopping and changing directions as necessary.

I stepped out onto the Champs-Élysées, the bustling avenue of wide sidewalks and loud traffic and the smell of car exhaust. I walked a few blocks and paused in front of a bookstore.

As I gazed at the window display, I stretched my peripheral vision as much as possible. I spotted a figure stopping more abruptly than seemed natural and pausing at a shop window half a block back.

The figure was female, unmistakably. Something about the frame, the movements. I held my phone and pretended to check a message but instead snapped a photograph of her.

Okay, good. Now time to shake her. I could work on the ID later, but for now I was satisfied this wasn't the thief I'd spotted in the Louvre.

I walked half a block farther, then quickly ducked into the next store I came to, a perfume store. I knew some of these stores had entrances at the front and the back. I hoped this was one of them.

The musky, flowery smells had a thickness I could taste. Glass bottles glittered on shelves; a handful of women browsed the shop, dressed in the finest couture. I, on the other hand, was not. Which was unfortunate. I preferred to blend in a little better when out in public, especially when attempting to dissolve into a crowd. I suspected my tourist garb wasn't going to help me in that endeavor. Neither was the aroma of the dog poop that, I now realized, was stuck on my shoe from the garden.

Damn it. How was it that everyone in Paris didn't have dog shit on their shoes? The city was practically paved with it. I had a fairly high degree of agility, I liked to think, but I obviously had nothing on the ninja-like poop-dodging skills of Parisian women.

Fashionless outfit and the aroma of feces notwithstanding, I beelined to the back of the store. I estimated ten seconds' lead time on the tail before she entered the store herself. As I reached the back of the store, I heard the chime of the front door opening. I tucked around a freestanding display of perfume and . . . yes. There was a back entrance. I slipped outside.

I found myself in a courtyard with nowhere to go. The air was quiet, and plain buildings formed a stark square. I'd just entered a world of black and white and gray, like a reverse *Wizard of Oz* scene. A clutch of pigeons suddenly flew up toward the square of sky above. I was trapped. I needed another doorway back into civilization.

I darted along, hugging the buildings closely, and grabbed on to the next door I encountered. My hand closed around the brass knob, and I pulled. Locked.

Panic fluttered in my chest. I could pick the lock, but I wasn't sure I had the time. I raced to the next door. The handle turned, mercifully. I slipped through the door and into the shop.

I repeated this process a couple of times, weaving my way through various shops—a shoe store, a china shop—and after a while, I knew I'd shaken the tail. It was over. At least for now.

I needed to get out of the First Arrondissement. I strode to the first Metro stop I spotted and darted underground. I stayed vigilant as I waited on the platform, but there was no sign of anyone following me anymore. The train arrived in a screech of engines and a whoosh of air. I rode it to the other side of town, to the Marais.

On the streets of the Marais, cobbled and narrow, in stark contrast to the Champs-Élysées, I walked to an area of market stalls. The stalls were piled high with vegetables, fruit, soft ripe cheeses, sausages, and golden loaves of bread.

And then my phone rang. *Ah, good.* Gladys must be getting back to me with that intel. I took the call, but unfortunately, instead of Gladys's voice, I heard my mother's.

"Catherine, my dear, where are you?"

"Um, I'm at a market, Mom," I said, closing my eyes and pinching the bridge of my nose. I took a calming breath.

"You know what I mean," she said with an impatient tone. "What city?"

"Well, er, Paris."

She gave an annoyed sniff. "Yes, I thought it was something like that. Your father said you were rushing off to an airport. Don't you think this is the sort of detail I, as your business manager, should know?"

"Mom? *Not* my business manager."

She launched into a tirade about keeping communication lines open and then asked if I brought appropriate footwear with me on this trip. "You know how you always manage to bring the wrong shoes."

While she carried on, I caught the attention of the vegetable merchant, requested three tomatoes, an eggplant, and a handful of mushrooms. My mother didn't even notice the interruption.

As she talked, though, I started wondering something.

I wandered farther along the row of market stalls and stopped by a fresh baker's stand, the heavenly scent swirling into my brain.

"Mom," I said, interrupting her stream of consciousness. "Mom, have you ever had a panic attack?"

"What? Of course not," she said, laughing. "What a question. Why?"

"Well, because I—"

"Are you having panic attacks, Catherine?"

"Well, it's just that lately, I've been feeling off my game. When I'm working, specifically, my fear seems to be getting a little out of hand—"

"Fear? You have nothing to be afraid of. You put yourself on top of tall buildings all the time, yes? Regular people, of course, they would fall—horrible way to die, wouldn't you think?—but you don't have to worry about that. I mean, yes, you might encounter people with guns and weapons and the like. The rest of us might have trouble with that, get shot or stabbed or arrested or whatnot, but you've always told me you don't have to worry about that. Isn't that what you've trained to avoid?" She laughed dismissively here. "Of course, I know you don't have superhuman skills or anything, but don't they teach you at AB&T how to avoid bullets and that sort of thing? I mean, that's what I've always told myself."

I felt queasy.

"Darling, are you all right? You're not saying anything."

"Well, it's just that I think you might be giving me a bit too much credit."

Pause. "Are you saying you don't have special skills? What are you saying, sweetheart? You could get killed in your line of work? Or maimed or blinded or other such things? Good heavens, I've never thought about it, but now that I'm thinking about it, I do *not* like the sound of all that . . . not one little bit."

At that moment the baker handed me a baguette. I let my mom rant a little longer as I pointed to a few other items from the baker's stall.

"Mom, I have to go," I finally said. "I'll call you later."

"All right, dear. Well, stay safe. Don't forget to double-check your knots. Oh, and carry an extra sweater, would you? I heard the weather is chilly in the spring, and I don't want you to catch a cold."

Admittedly, it was odd that my mom was so accepting of my chosen profession. Sometimes it made me wonder about her. Did she have secrets in her family she was keeping from me? Had someone in her family been a thief, too?

I'd wondered about these things before. Surely I wasn't the only one in my gene pool who had actually discovered these talents and put them to good—or, more accurately, bad—use. I mean, I got these skills from somewhere. Maybe I came by them more honestly than I realized.

I paid the baker and tore off a piece of baguette. I was hungry. I bit into the crisp, chewy bread, and it hit the spot. My shoulders relaxed immediately.

And then someone came up to stand right behind me. A warning prickled my neck. I had dropped my guard while on the phone with my mother.

"Hello, Cat. Didn't think you could lose me that easily, did you? You're slipping, sweetheart."

I knew the voice right away. I closed my eyes. *Damn.*

Chapter 17

I turned, and there was Brooke Sinclair standing behind me. "Brooke, what the hell? Why were you tailing me?"

She gave me a wicked grin. It was one of the trademark expressions of her deceptively angelic face. Brooke looked the same: long raven hair and slender, curvy figure. Not only was Brooke highly competent in everything she did, but she was also drop-dead gorgeous.

And, I must say, irritating perfection is a quality one does not typically want in a rival. Tends to trash one's self-esteem.

My relationship with Brooke Sinclair was, in a word, complicated. She was a jewel thief, too. She had, many years ago, been my mentor. Until she started to feel threatened by my growing skill. And then she'd stabbed me in the back. Rather skillfully, too. I had to give her credit even for that.

"Just messing with you, Cat," she said, shrugging, as we stood in the street market. "Maybe testing you a little. Seeing where you are in terms of skills. And I gotta say, I'm noticing some spots that need polishing."

"Okay, great. Well, thanks for that. I'll be sure to read all about it in my report card," I snapped.

"Hey, no need to get defensive. Just trying to help out a fellow professional."

I regretted my reaction. She was right. Better to make mistakes with her than with somebody who truly meant me harm. "I know. Sorry."

There had been many years when we'd been rivals and arch-enemies. That status was clinched when she ended up in prison, in part because of me.

The hatred was solidly mutual at that point. When she got out of prison, there were a lot of other unhappy emotions thrown into the mix, revenge being among the most fiery.

And it stayed that way for a while. Until I needed the sort of help only she could provide last fall, with the Fabergé job. Shockingly, she stepped up. It was a tough job, but we made it through together.

Of course, on the other side of that, I wasn't completely sure where I stood with her. And I don't think she knew, either. I mean, we were still rivals in the same industry, right?

After learning about our success with the Fabergé, her old agency, Larceny New York, offered her a job again. I hadn't seen her in months. Until now.

I respected Brooke as a thief, and I was extremely grateful for the help she provided me in London. But I still didn't know if I could fully trust her, because Brooke was who she was. She would always, I suspected, look out for herself first.

Or maybe not. Maybe I wasn't giving her enough credit. Maybe she was different now. I'd always been somewhat skeptical about the idea of people truly changing. But maybe that was wrong of me.

We walked away from the market, and a cool breeze rustled the trees in the square. I pulled my sweater tighter.

I wasn't sure I bought her story about just testing me. It was an awful lot of effort just for that. I'd watch carefully, reveal very little, and see what Brooke's game was.

We sat on a park bench in the square, and I asked her what had brought her to Paris.

"I just did a big job in New York," she said. "A close shave in the end. So LNY wanted me to get out of the country for a bit—so did

I, to be honest—and Paris seemed like the perfect place. April in Paris, after all. Isn't that what Sinatra sang?"

"So you're just here laying low and killing time?"

"Can you think of a better place?"

"Fair enough."

I hesitated, wondering how much I should tell her. I fiddled with the edge of my sweater and gazed around the square. People lounged on benches, reading books and nibbling sandwiches, while pigeons pecked at crumbs on the basalt cobbles. "So how did you know I was here, in Paris? And how did you find me, exactly?"

"I didn't know you were in Paris. But I saw you when you were in the Louvre."

"You just happened to be there, too?" How had I not seen her?

"Like moths to a flame, sugar. You think it's weird for two professional thieves to happen to be in the Louvre at the same time?"

She had a point. "I guess not."

Why was I being so edgy? I guess old habits are hard to crush. I'd had many years of feeling much worse than edgy around Brooke.

"Okay, so?" she asked. "What's up with you being here in Paris, Cat? Were you casing the Louvre? Got a little something in mind?" She inspected her fingernails—a glossy dark red manicure—then looked up at me innocently.

I chewed the inside of my cheek. Maybe Brooke could help me. Maybe she could assist with this job. We could be partners again, like we were in London. She really had pulled through for me then, at great risk to herself. Maybe I could trust her.

"Yes. I was casing it," I said.

Her eyes glittered at this. "Good girl," she said. "Big job, though."

"Yes. And, well, that's maybe where you could help me. It's not a regular job."

"No?"

"There's a little more riding on it than usual. And I'm not going to be making any money off this one."

"This is another pro bono job? Cat, you're going to go broke, doing all these good deeds."

"This time it's not a good deed. I'm saving my skin. My hands, more specifically." I told her all about Faulkner and the deal we'd struck.

Her face clouded at the idea of a past mark coming to find a thief and demanding retribution. And she visibly recoiled at the hand-severing bit.

"So, obviously," I said, "it's a big job. And I could use some help."

Brooke was quiet a moment. "You've really got yourself in a pickle this time around."

"I know."

She pulled out a MAC tube and touched up her lipstick. "And, although I'd really like to join in," she said between swipes, "I'm going to have to politely decline this time around."

"What? Why?"

"I work for LNY now," she said. "And they are very clear in their contract. I am not to take on any outside work."

"They don't need to know," I said. I hoped my voice didn't carry any of the desperation I was starting to feel.

"They know I'm here. I can't do it. They would find out. And then my professional life would be in ruins again. I can't risk that."

"AB&T knows I'm here, doing this. Maybe LNY would be fine with it."

"Your Agency is not giving you a hard time, because they know it's their fault you're facing this problem. If they took the time to get their heads out of their asses, they would realize they should have prevented this from happening, or at the very least, should be making this problem go away." She shook her head in disgust. "What ever happened to protecting your assets? Anyway, they're not kicking up a fuss, because they figure the easiest thing to do is just let you do the damn job and end the case. LNY doesn't have the same motivation. They wouldn't support me helping you."

She was making sense. The baguette sat like a hard lump in my stomach. Brooke would have been a great asset. But I was asking her to put her career in jeopardy just to save me. Well, me . . . and my hands.

I shouldn't have been surprised. Brooke had made it no secret that her philosophy was every woman for herself.

I dropped it. It had been a good idea. I just needed to come up with a different good idea.

Brooke wished me luck, and we parted ways. As I left the square, I passed a *fromagerie* with an open door. The ripe smells of Brie and Camembert wafted out. At that moment my phone bleeped: a message was waiting.

It was from Templeton. He'd sent me a file of possible suspects. I scrolled through the images of faces on my iPhone. And then I stopped. *Yes, that one.* That was the guy. Those same icy eyes looked through me, giving me that same cold feeling.

I called Templeton and confirmed the guy's identity. He went silent after I told him who it was. "This isn't good, Catherine," he said at length.

"It's not?"

"No. The name of that thief is Sean Reilly. And he's good. Really good. And . . . not very nice."

"Templeton, I hate to break it to you, but we're all crooks. Generally not considered to be the nice people of the world."

"Yes, but there's bad and then there's *bad*. And this guy, well, he's the second type."

"Can you be more specific?" I asked, swallowing hard. This didn't sound good.

"Sneaky, underhanded, rotten, unscrupulous. Not afraid to use violence, unconcerned if people get hurt. And people, in this scenario, could include you."

Well, I didn't like the sound of that. But it didn't change much. A vague threat from another thief versus the very concrete threat coming from Albert Faulkner? I'd just have to take my chances with the vague threats.

I was just about to hail a cab back to my hotel when my phone bleeped again with another incoming message, this time from Gladys.

Pierre Severin's home address: 3782 rue Dauphine, Paris.

Chapter 18

At daybreak the next morning, I sat beneath the red awning of a sidewalk café in the leafy neighborhood of Saint-Germain-des-Prés. A weak sun was just starting to break through the misty chill, and the street sweepers were out, whisking away the previous night's litter with their green-bristled brooms. Bakers had fired up their ovens long ago, and now the irresistible smells of brioches and croissants filled the narrow streets.

Right across from the café was Monsieur Severin's home. I was waiting for him to leave for work. I knew I wouldn't be able to get anywhere near the Hope without one key thing. Severin's finger-prints.

My café au lait rested atop a tiny round table. Waiters in long white aprons moved between the tables, looking very bored and annoyed. The café was surrounded by the gracious architecture of five-story Haussmann buildings of honey-colored stone and ornate black Juliet balconies.

I flipped a page of the newspaper *Le Monde* and took my first sip. Hot, frothy foam and an exquisite blend of rich, bittersweet espresso were the perfect balm to soothe my jumpy nerves.

I adjusted my oversize sunglasses and moved the long blond ponytail of my wig off my shoulder. Hair is a key component of a woman's disguise, of course. It's amazing how dependent people are on hair color and style when describing someone, particularly someone suspected of shifty business. My disguise was complete with a stone-colored trench coat. As a career criminal, I'm delighted at the return of trench coats to the fashion table. Makes it even easier for me to blend in.

Butterflies of apprehension flitted in my stomach. Actually, not so lovely as butterflies, exactly. More like crickets and grasshoppers.

I glanced at his front door. Still nothing. Fortunately, it was completely expected for a person to occupy a seat in a sidewalk café in Paris for the better part of the morning. Even the majority of the afternoon was totally acceptable.

As the waiter brought me another café, sliding it deftly onto my table, my phone rang.

I frowned at the number—Mel, one of my girlfriends in Seattle. *Odd.*

"Hi, Mel. Everything okay?"

"Cat, I have some news I think you need to know."

I took a peek over my newspaper at Monsieur Severin's door. Still no sign of him. But it could be any minute now. "Actually, I'm a little busy right now. Any chance this can wait?"

"No. Listen, this is important. A woman named Sandra Appleton just died in a car accident outside Baltimore."

If this was supposed to mean anything to me, it didn't. "Okay, well, that's sad. Someone you knew?"

"No. But it's important because she was the woman who won a contest to have an up close and personal encounter with the Hope Diamond last month at the Smithsonian."

I frowned. "That's a shame. But you're telling me because . . . ?"

"The *curse,* Cat."

I rolled my eyes. "Oh no. Not you too?"

"I know. It's ridiculous. But I'm really starting to think there's something to this. And it's not just Sophie making this connection. Listen to the newspaper headline. "THE CURSE OF THE HOPE DIAMOND STRIKES AGAIN, AFTER ALL THIS TIME."

"You know they're just trying to sell newspapers, right?"

"Maybe. But that doesn't make it any less true."

I pinched the bridge of my nose and sat back in the chair. "Okay, I have to admit, it's odd. But it's just a bizarre coincidence. The curse is fiction, Mel. But you know what's real? What will happen to me if I don't do this job."

"Cat, just listen. I think you're making a big mistake—"

At that moment, the glossy black door at 3782 rue Dauphine opened, and Monsieur Severin walked out his front door. My stomach lurched. Go time.

"Listen, Mel, sorry, but I'm going to have to talk to you later." I hung up. I waited until Severin had walked a block and disappeared down the Metro staircase. Then I left money on the café table and strolled toward his apartment. But instead of going straight to the door of his apartment, I made a quick stop at the silver WC pod, the public restroom, on the corner.

Inside the pod, I removed my trench coat, revealing a house cleaner's outfit: a pale blue uniform dress, knee length with short sleeves with a white cuff, an apron, and flat white sneakers. Tidy and tasteful, just like all the housemaids with Eclat, the company Severin's building used. Another little tidbit courtesy of Gladys, who had hacked in and found his bills.

Severin didn't use Eclat for his own apartment. Evidently, he was too distrustful for that. But it would be enough to get me in the building.

As I zipped up the uniform, I reminded myself that I had simple goals here. Get into Severin's apartment, get his fingerprints, and get out.

I walked up to the small alcove of the front door and buzzed the panel. It took me two tries to find someone who would answer.

"Bonjour," I said and continued to speak in French. "Package delivery for Monsieur LeMarc." I read the name from the small label beside the button. A brief pause, and then I heard the buzzer. The door clicked, and I walked in.

Much like you can always count on two ice cubes refusing to pop out of the tray, you can always count on someone buzzing you through a secure entrance with only the scantiest information.

The staircase was dark and cool and smelled of the breakfasts being cooked behind apartment doors. It was an old building, and there was no elevator. The steps were made of old stone with smooth, weathered treads in the center. I climbed to the top floor, four stories up. I stood outside Severin's door and made sure nobody was in sight as I withdrew my lock-pick set.

My hands were stock-still, the hands of a surgeon. Or a professional burglar. So far so good. But would I have a panic attack while in here? What if something went wrong? My brain started spinning out images of the various ways this could go wrong. I had to push that all down and focus.

It took me a little longer than usual, but at last I had unlocked the door.

I crept inside. All the extra adrenaline racing around my system gave me heightened vigilance, widened peripheral vision, and a faint buzz. Severin's apartment was brightened by morning sun beaming through tall windows. The place was pin tidy. If I kept my apartment this shipshape, my mother would put an announcement in the local papers. Or have a stroke.

I pulled out a duster and started sweeping for prints. Doorknobs are usually the best place to begin.

But these were clean.

I swept the brush over the smooth surfaces of the door, the door-jamb, adjacent walls . . . then into the kitchen. I tried the fridge door handle. The faucet handle.

All spotless. No prints.

How could this be? Did the guy wear gloves around his own house?

And then, thinking about it, I realized that each time I'd seen him, he had been wearing gloves. At the Louvre. And just now, outside his apartment door, he'd been wearing a pair of fine leather gloves.

Shit. He was a security guru. How paranoid was he about his own security? Maybe he protected his fingerprints every chance he got.

Okay, fine. Where would it be impossible for him to keep gloves on?

I quickly made my way to the en suite. The room was a gleam of sparkling white tile, chrome, and glass shower doors. And clean as a new car.

Even still, there had to be a set of prints somewhere in here.

The drawer handle of the vanity caught on my maid's uniform skirt, and I turned, opening the drawer a crack. A pistol rested in the drawer.

Okay, we were moving from fastidious about security into the fanatical category. Why would you need a weapon in the bathroom?

I closed the drawer and kept dusting, sweat breaking out between my shoulder blades. My maid's uniform started sticking to my back. Time was ticking.

After several minutes, I'd lifted a complete right hand. But for the left hand, I'd found only the fingers. The thumb was missing. I dusted everything I could find in the vicinity.

Okay, I needed another brilliant idea. What would he be sure to use his left thumb for—

I heard a key in the lock of the front door.

My heart slammed into my rib cage. I needed a way out. But there was only one door. And although there were plenty of windows, I wasn't prepared for climbing. I hadn't brought any ropes or a harness. I could slip out the window, but . . . we were four stories up. Right on the borderline of a guaranteed fatal fall.

Fuck. This was exactly why I needed to get over this fear thing. It was going to be the end of me.

Well, if I couldn't escape, I'd have to hide. I moved soundlessly to the bedroom, opened the door, and slipped inside.

And then I saw it. Too late. A tiny strip of paper resting on the wooden parquet floor.

It was a trap Severin had left—a classic trick. A tiny strip of paper stuck in a doorjamb will silently flutter to the floor if the door is opened. But far worse than this, I realized if there was such a trap on the bedroom door, there was likely such a trap on every door. Including the front door.

I then realized things had gone extremely silent in the front hall. Which meant one thing. Severin knew someone was in his apartment.

I immediately thought of the gun in the bathroom. Unlikely it was his only one.

I raced to the bedroom window as fast and silently as I could, expecting the entire time to receive a bullet in my spine.

Where was he? I mapped how far he could possibly have gotten in the time since opening the door and discovering I was there.

I made it to the other side of the bed without being shot or otherwise killed. The window was huge, reaching up to the ceiling, and I pulled up hard on the sash, trying to be silent. It stuck for a heart-stopping moment, then gave way.

A black wrought-iron balcony ledge beckoned just outside the window. Unfortunately, this was the worst possible spot: a window on the street side. I would never go this way if I had another option.

I scanned for something helpful, like restoration scaffolding. No such luck. Still, the building was ornate and very belle epoque, with plenty of balconies and carved bits of stone, which meant lots of handholds and footholds.

It would have to do.

I climbed out onto the balcony, my fingers curling around cold iron. A cool breeze ruffled my housemaid's apron, and my ears filled with the clatter and hum from the street. The morning bustle had reached its zenith, but I was high enough that the bustling business-people and swerving cabdrivers paid me no attention. There was no sign anyone had noticed me clambering out.

I started to climb down. And then I heard the gendarmes. The sirens wailing, coming this direction. Of course. Severin had called them.

Over my shoulder I saw flashing lights heading toward the building. If I climbed down now, there was a good chance I would land on the ground the exact moment they pulled up to the curb.

I had to go up to the roof.

My head spun and my breathing came faster, but I began climbing. And then, just before I reached the top, I heard a sound behind me. I glanced back in time to see the face of Severin peering around the open window glass. With a Glock 17 in his hand.

I heaved myself onto the roof and flattened myself down on the zinc roof sheeting. I glanced over the edge to see Severin clambering out the window himself with a determined grit to his mouth.

I stood, willing myself to get out of there. But I couldn't move normally. I tried to run across the roof, but my normally fluid movements were stiff and halting. It was like those nightmares where you can't move, can't get away, like you're trying to run through water. If I could just sprint across the rooftops here, I could get away. But I was picking my way across, instead of racing and leaping.

My eyes filled with visions of my body lying broken in the streets of Paris. My rational thinking began to crumble. My legs felt like pudding.

And then things got so much worse.

Chapter 19

Ethan swept at a particularly stubborn patch of sidewalk litter, gripping the green street broom tightly in his hands and trying to ignore the massive internal battle waging inside his head. He adjusted the coveralls, which were two sizes too big for him.

He was disguised as a Parisian street cleaner on rue Dauphine. He'd seen Cat slip into Severin's apartment building fifteen minutes ago.

The smell of garbage rose up and made his eyes water. As far as jobs went, this had to be the worst. But it did provide excellent cover. Nobody spared him a glance.

Cat had no idea he was here, which was exactly how Ethan wanted it . . . for now. He really wasn't sure he wanted to reveal his presence to Cat just yet.

In fact, he wasn't sure this was the right decision at all, coming to Paris.

At first, Ethan had refused Templeton's request. He'd assured Templeton that Cat would be fine. She didn't need him. And—more importantly—he didn't need Cat.

But it turned out he couldn't get her out of his mind. So he'd decided he might as well come and see for himself, see how much trouble she was in. Maybe Templeton had been exaggerating.

Ethan glanced at his watch. Montgomery should be exiting by now. No matter what she was up to, she'd been in there too long.

While he swept the sidewalk, Ethan scouted the building. If it came to it, he'd be able to climb the exterior. There was window-washing scaffolding just around the corner. However, it was a full block away. It would give him access only to the roof. He'd have to make his way from there.

But he wasn't going to do any such thing.

No matter what Templeton said, Cat was an extremely capable and resourceful thief. She would be fine.

And then Ethan saw Severin return to his apartment, looking flustered, like a man who'd forgotten something at home.

He knew Cat was in trouble.

Come on, Montgomery. Get a move on. Get out of there.

Ethan kept sweeping, thinking hard about his next move. The minutes ticked by. Then he saw a window slide open right at the top of the building. Cat, dressed in a pale blue housemaid's uniform, clambered out. Her face was pale and grim.

Good. She was making an escape. She'd be fine now. Except why had she gone out on the street side? What the hell had made her do that? It was so exposed.

It was still early in the morning, and people weren't paying much attention to the rooftops of buildings. Generally, they were looking down or toward the nearest café. Ethan seemed to be the only person who'd noticed what was going on. For now.

But . . . there was something wrong with Cat. Instead of her normal agile self, she was awkward and shaky.

A pit opened in Ethan's stomach as he realized Templeton had not been exaggerating. She really was in trouble.

And then he saw Severin look out the window. He'd spotted Cat. Without hesitation, Severin tucked a semiautomatic pistol into his waistband and began to clamber out.

Ethan's vision focused to a laser and his muscles contracted as he immediately went into action.

In three strides he was at the Vespa he'd parked on the street beside the apartment building, and he slid the key into the ignition, leaving it there. On foot still, he turned the corner and climbed up the scaffolding just as he heard the sirens of the gendarmes barreling down the street.

He climbed all the way up to the roof and leaped parkour-style across the rooftops. This was familiar territory for Ethan. He experienced a momentary flashback to his recent escape in Rome and briefly wondered how often art history teachers were required to execute rooftop escapes in their line of work. He smiled to himself. *Definitely the right career move.*

But although this was a thrill for him, the edges of that bright feeling were clouded with dark worry for Montgomery.

And then he spotted her. She was clinging to the roof, looking utterly paralyzed. She glanced up, startled at first, and then recognized him. Her face changed to a look of hope.

Effectively causing his heart to burst open. He was going to rescue her if it killed him.

In a few more strides he reached her. "Come on, Montgomery. Let's get you out of here."

"Sounds good, but . . . I can't move."

"I know. That's why I'm here."

"How did you know—"

"No talking. Later."

Ethan helped her, keeping her steady, as they made their way across the rooftops. He glanced over his shoulder and saw Severin climbing up and over the roof's edge. They were out of range of his Glock, but not for long. Sirens blared from the street below; the gendarmes had arrived at the curb. Ethan knew they were out of sight from the street below, up on the roof like this, and he imagined the gendarmes spilling out of their cars into the building.

Which might give them the slice of opportunity they needed. He looked ahead—the scaffolding was too far away. They needed to get off the roof now.

"We're getting down from this roof," he said. "Now."

"How?" Her voice wavered.

Ethan pointed down to the red café awning they were directly over.

Cat lost the last bit of color in her face. "No way. That just happens in the movies. And even then, it doesn't usually work."

Ethan nodded. "This time it will. That awning is new. I checked it out while I was sweeping the streets. The canvas is strong, and it's reinforced with steel. It will function like a trampoline. It will support us. Well, one at a time, anyway." He looked at her and gripped her shoulders, locked onto her blue eyes. "You can do this, Montgomery."

She looked back at Severin, who was growing closer to them. "Okay."

"See that black Vespa? That's where you're headed. Now go."

Ethan waited. *She's not going to do it.* She was shaking like a meth addict. And then she nodded grimly. And jumped.

She free-fell down to the awning, then slid and bounced. And then just kept sliding right off the end of the canvas.

Her body must have gone into automatic pilot, because she tucked and curled before hitting the ground. Ethan couldn't help a victorious grin. He knew she had it in her. She just had to get out of her own head.

But there was no time to stand around admiring her skills. Once Montgomery was clear, he jumped, too. Ethan's stomach flipped into his chest as he fell, and then everything jolted when he hit the canvas. Sky and trees blurred as he slid and then flew off the end feetfirst, to land on the sidewalk.

Ethan raced a few feet to the waiting Vespa and got there a second after Cat. He leaped on, and Cat jumped behind him. She clamped her arms around him, he twisted the key, and they were instantly flying across cobbled streets.

In the rearview mirror Ethan saw a police car—bright royal blue with a red and white stripe on the hood—suddenly mobilize, lights flashing, racing after them.

The chase was on.

He felt Cat's arms tighten around him as they took a sharp turn and zipped and veered between cars. Paris traffic was the fifth circle of Hell at the best of times. And this was something he could use to his advantage, because he was able to slip through unmoving lines of cars, instead of being caught up by them.

The task at hand was to lose the single police car that was chasing them, because undoubtedly, that car was calling for backup, and then they'd be screwed.

And where was the best place to lose someone in a chase? Ethan needed a broad street, where he could get some speed, with lots of traffic, into which he could vanish.

Boulevard Saint-Germain would be perfect. He sped toward the big artery, leaning forward, feeling the engine vibrate underneath him.

Then he heard another siren coming toward them. Now there were two cars chasing them. It was only a matter of time before there would be many. And then getting away would be impossible.

The police car behind him was keeping pace. But the minute they got to the bigger road, Ethan would be away. He just needed to get there.

The other siren was getting closer.

Ethan's heart rate sped up. The idea of getting caught was barely conceivable. French prisons had a brutal rep.

He was not rescuing Montgomery for both of them to get caught. No way.

The engine gave a subtle chug. Ethan glanced down and saw the gas gauge was dangerously low.

He could see the intersection for boulevard Saint-Germain just ahead. It was their salvation, with four lanes of traffic and endless options for ditching this pursuit.

He squinted into the side-view. The other police car was going to catch up with them before they got there.

And then there was another slight pull of the engine.

Ethan made a decision. "Hang on," he said to Montgomery. She clutched tighter.

He pointed the wheels up and onto the curb, onto the sidewalk, and zipped through pedestrians the last half block to Saint-Germain. Shocked, angry faces turned to them, but Ethan ignored them all.

In the mirror he caught a glimpse of the police car behind them getting tangled in traffic. They were powerless to follow.

At last, the Vespa burst onto Saint-Germain, with its blissfully broad lanes and numerous intersections. Ethan glided the moped through, weaving among cars, and putting a lot of distance between the Vespa and the two gendarmes chasing them.

The big artery took them straight into the heart of the Latin Quarter, and Ethan steered the bike abruptly off Saint-Germain. They entered a rabbit warren of ancient streets around the Sorbonne, the university, and bumped across old cobblestone roads and lanes.

He took a zigzag route, and then, in a small side alley, Cat leaped off. Ethan ditched the Vespa and filed it in the middle of a row of similar vehicles parked at the curb. Cat quickly removed her wig and pulled a long coat—swiftly liberated from a sidewalk vendor— around her maid's uniform. Ethan climbed out of his coveralls, revealing a T-shirt and jeans underneath. Then they strolled out of the alley casually, joining the crowds of students and tourists in the maze of streets around the Sorbonne.

They were clear. It was over. He glanced at Cat, whose cheeks were flushed. She was beaming gratitude at him.

The thrill of the victory sent exhilarated ripples through his chest. He felt amazing. He grinned back at her.

And immediately regretted everything he'd just done.

One of the reasons he'd decided to come to Paris was to prove to himself he was over Cat Montgomery. That she was just like any other female in his life—a brief interest. Fun but, ultimately, a throw-away.

Now he knew he was really in trouble.

Chapter 20

Once you've made a getaway, and once you're clear, the key is to blend into the crowd. You need to keep putting distance between yourself and the scene of the crime, but not in a rushed way. You don't want to draw anyone's attention.

I strolled with Ethan in the Latin Quarter, moving at a good pace but not hurriedly. We walked with a purpose, like we were on our way to lunch and had a decent appetite. Not like we were late for a train. Or escaping the police.

Ethan steered me toward an entrance to the Metro. We passed underneath the ornate art nouveau Metropolitan sign, headed down the staircase, and bought tickets for zone 1. The platform smelled of grease and three-day-old urine.

Once on the train, seated on worn brown vinyl, I breathed a sigh of relief as the train accelerated away from the platform. We were safe.

I turned to Ethan. "What the hell are you doing here in Paris?"

He grinned. "Rescuing you. What does it look like?"

"Okay, but . . . how did you know?"

He hesitated a beat. It didn't matter. I knew the answer.

"Templeton told you, didn't he?"

Ethan nodded.

My cheeks burned with shame. What kind of thief was I, needing to be rescued? My insides squirmed with discomfort, like they were wearing Spanx that were two sizes too small.

The train flew into the next station, paused for a minute, then continued on.

Ethan watched me closely. "Montgomery, don't sweat it. It's *Albert Faulkner.* There's no shame in that. Any of us would need help if we were dealing with him."

I smiled. Ethan coming here to help me was incredible. And that escape had been truly awesome, let's face it. A warm spark ignited in my chest.

"So, anyway," he said, "what were you in there for?"

"Fingerprints."

His eyebrows rose. "And did you get them?"

"I did get them."

"Great."

"But I didn't get *all* of them. I only got nine. I'm missing the left thumb."

He winced. "Oh."

My shiny feeling over our victorious escape was now tinged with rust. I exhaled. "The problem is, now Severin will be on even more heightened alert. As if he wasn't wound tightly enough as it was. I don't know if I'm going to get another chance." The train lurched to the left, and my body jostled against Ethan's.

"Don't worry about it, Montgomery. We'll figure it out."

I looked at him carefully. "We?"

"You don't think I'm just going to leave you hanging like this?"

A glimmer of hope. On an otherwise bleak landscape.

Ethan insisted on escorting me back to my hotel, an extra pair of eyes. I was staying at the Four Seasons George V in the Eighth Arrondissement. I invited him up to my suite so we could discuss the job in more detail and figure out the next move.

As I unlocked the door for us, I felt a twinge of doubt. Was this inappropriate? But it was ridiculous. We were colleagues. And we had important private matters to discuss.

I flopped down in an armchair, cracked open a bottle of water, and took a long sip. The morning's exertions had left me mighty dehydrated. Meanwhile, Ethan went into the bathroom to shower and scrub off the grime from his stint as a street sweeper.

The phone on the nightstand rang.

"Hey, hon. How is the City of Lights?" Jack's voice came down the phone, warm and comforting, like hot chocolate for my soul.

"Jack! I'm so happy to hear your voice." And then my eyes slid to the bathroom door. A twist of guilt centered in my stomach. "Yes, Paris is amazing, of course. As always. But it would be so much better if you were here."

"I know," he said. "And I'm hoping, actually, that things wrap up here soon and maybe I can fly over for a couple days. We can walk by the Seine, get crepes, have coffee at Les Deux Magots, drink wine, and poke into bookshops in the Latin Quarter. . . . How does that sound?"

It sounded amazing. It sounded perfect. And if I didn't have this impossible job to do, there was nothing I'd love more.

"Jack, I—"

At that moment Ethan emerged from the bathroom, wet and shirtless, with only a towel around his waist. "Montgomery, have you got any Band-Aids?" he asked, his voice loud over the sound of the bathroom fan. He was examining a scrape on his left knuckles, presumably from the roof tiles.

I stopped breathing. There was silence on the line for a second.

"Cat, who's that?" Jack asked. "Is that Ethan Jones? Is Ethan there with you?"

Shit.

"Ethan's here just helping me a little with this job," I said brightly. I wanted to sound casual. I wanted to sound like I wasn't doing anything wrong. Which I wasn't, of course. Unfortunately, my voice came too stridently to meet either of those goals.

The tension down the phone line was audible. I could hear his struggle. I could feel him wanting to say something, yet not wanting to say something.

Ethan was still standing there, flexing and examining his knuckles, waiting for me to locate the Band-Aids. I sent out a brief prayer of thanks that this wasn't a video call, and silently pointed to a small first-aid kit on the desk.

"Oh. Well, I'm sure he's being helpful," Jack said. I couldn't tell if he was being sarcastic. Either way, there was a little too much emphasis on the "helpful."

"He's staying at the Ritz, you know. Not even staying at the Four Seasons," I added hastily and then realized how ridiculous and defensive that sounded.

Just shut up, Cat. You have nothing to feel guilty about. Nothing.

I just didn't want Jack to get the wrong idea.

"Uh-huh. Whatever, Cat. Listen, I gotta go."

He got off the line quickly after that. Which was like a punch in the stomach.

Chapter 21

You are an ass, Jack thought.

Acting like a jealous fishwife was the last thing he wanted to do when Cat was so far away. Of course Ethan was there. Why wouldn't he be? They were both in the same profession. They had a working relationship. Jack was going to have to find a way to come to terms with that.

He stood outside in the grungy darkness of an airport motel parking lot. Airplanes roared overhead, and the smell of jet fuel filled the air. It was late—close to midnight—and he'd gone to the lobby to get a coffee from the complimentary carafe next to the check-in desk. He took a sip. Unfortunately, it was stale and bitter—barely worth the effort of walking down from the room. The room where he and Hendrickx were interrogating a suspect.

While walking to the lobby, he'd spontaneously decided to call Cat. The time zone difference made it challenging to catch her at a moment when they were both awake. So he'd taken the opportunity when he'd glanced at his watch and realized it was nine in the morning in Paris.

Big mistake.

Why was this bothering Jack so much? Didn't he trust Cat?

Trust. *Ha.* Funny. Cat, a professional liar, thief, and cheat.

He stopped himself. Those were ungenerous, unkind thoughts.

Where had they come from? *Okay, enough.* Right now was not the time for this. Right now, he needed to get back to the interrogation.

Jack walked along the second-level outdoor corridor and knocked on door 209.

At least they were making headway on their case, he and Hendrickx. Jack had finally hunted Snyder down at this motel just outside town. So he'd called Hendrickx to come in and interrogate with him.

This was not exactly proper police procedure, and Jack knew it. But he also knew they didn't have a lot of choice. He wasn't ready to make this official with his supervisor, not yet.

The motel room smelled like stale cigarettes and three-week-old pizza. Every surface was covered with sticky garbage—old take-out containers, half-finished soda cups. The carpet was industrial, the bedspread polyester, and the armchair vinyl. The whole place would go up in an instant fireball if anyone lit a match.

"Why am I here?" Snyder demanded. "You can't hold me. I haven't done anything wrong."

"We're not holding you. We're just having a chat," Jack said.

"What can you tell us about the Gargoyle?" Hendrickx said.

Snyder went white as milk. "I don't know who that is."

"What makes you think the Gargoyle is a person?" said Henrickx, with a curl of a smile. "We didn't say that, did we, Jack?" He looked at Jack innocently.

"Nope. Nothing about a person." Jack crossed his arms and shrugged. "Could have been a place. Name of a boat. But thank you for supplying that bit of information."

"So now that we know *you know* the Gargoyle, why don't you just make this easy and tell us everything?" Hendrickx said.

Snyder sat silently.

"We can protect you," Jack said. "If you help us. Don't you think the Gargoyle is going to find out you were brought in here? Don't you think he's going to assume you cooperated, anyway? You're protecting someone who is going to remove your internal organs one by one."

Snyder's face went slack.

Jack kept pressing. "Face it, you're blown, Snyder. Don't you think the Gargoyle deals with loose ends like you in a highly professional manner, first chance?"

Snyder was breaking; Jack could tell. He estimated two, three minutes tops, and the guy would talk.

They pushed and probed. And finally, Snyder's face crumpled and his shoulders slumped.

"I've never met him," Snyder said, blurting it out. With that, Jack knew he was theirs. Now they could really dig in and get some solid intel. "I don't even know what he looks like. Or what he sounds like. He calls me on the phone, but his voice is changed, all warped and everything with one of those voice-altering software things."

"That's good. That's a start," Hendrickx said. "Now, you must be able to tell us something else. What's he involved with? What's he into right now?"

"A lot of shit. He's involved in everything. And he doesn't care. He's ruthless. His ambition knows no bounds. You don't understand. You won't be able to get to him."

Something still wasn't sitting right with Jack every time they mentioned the Gargoyle. But they were getting major traction now. So they kept going.

"Why don't you tell us what you were working on for him?"

Snyder looked like he was going to start blubbering. "Don't make me tell you. I'd be incriminating myself. I can't go to prison."

Hendrickx sat back, unmoved. "Right. Well, like we said, we could protect you. But it's take your chances with that or take your chances with the Gargoyle. Would you have the ability to cut off your own arm to survive if you had to, like that kid who got stuck in those rocks? Think of yourself as that kid, Snyder." He looked at Jack and grabbed a handful of pretzels. "What was that guy's name?"

Jack shrugged. "Aaron something maybe?"

Hendrickx crunched loudly on the pretzels. "That's right. Aaron something. He cut his own arm off to survive. You're like that. So, are you going to take your chances with us or with the Gargoyle?"

Snyder looked like he was going to throw up.

After that, he fell apart like a dime watch. He told them every-thing he knew. Which, unfortunately, was not a lot.

"He's planning a job. A big job. Stealing something big. Some-thing that is going to fund a lot of operations. There are a lot of people who the Gargoyle owes money to, and they're getting restless. If this job goes through, he's in business. If it fails, the Gargoyle could be in trouble."

"Okay, so where is this job happening?" Jack asked.

"I don't know for sure, but I did hear something about the Gargoyle going to Paris. I think that's where the job is happening."

At the mention of Paris, Jack recoiled.

No.

Paris? What were the chances? But it was a big city. Plenty of stuff went down there, he was sure. It didn't necessarily follow that Cat was involved in this. But . . . could it really be a coincidence?

Jack and Hendrickx left the motel room, reviewing the scanty bits of information they'd learned, and walked to their respective cars.

"So what next?" Jack asked.

Hendrickx unlocked his door. "I'm going to Paris," he said dis-passionately. "To hunt down the Gargoyle."

Jack raked a hand through his hair. "Oh," he said. "Okay, well, I guess I can put in for a short leave at headquarters—"

"No, Jack. Not you. Just me."

Jack folded his arms across his chest. "What are you talking about?"

"You know you can't come," Hendrickx said. "You have no juris-diction overseas. And you're not on Interpol's payroll. We will continue this investigation without you. You were helpful when this was an American investigation. But no longer."

Hendrickx stated this with indifference, like the cold fish Jack had come to realize he was. Jack protested, more or less gnashing his teeth as he did so, but Hendrickx remained unmoved.

"Barlow, forget it. Just go back to doing whatever it was you were doing for the FBI."

And just like that, Jack was cut out of things. Again.

After Hendrickx drove away, Jack thrust his hands in his pockets and walked to his car in the deserted parking lot. Underneath a lone flickering streetlight, he passed a Dumpster that emanated foul smells of garbage.

He slid into the driver's seat and was about to put the key in the ignition when his phone vibrated. He pulled it out. Wesley again, on an encrypted line.

Jack pressed the answer button. "So, how's the weather in Dubai?"

"Actually, Jack, I'm in Amsterdam now," Wesley said. "The Fabergé didn't stay long in the Middle East. We're back to Europe."

Jack said nothing.

"And remember that underground group I talked to you about? The one protecting the Gifts all along?"

"Sure."

"They're real. They've been around for centuries. In fact, it appears they were the ones who brought the Gifts to Peter Carl Fabergé a hundred years ago and concealed them within the Aurora egg."

Jack nodded. That piece of the puzzle had always been a mystery to him.

Wesley continued. "The modern name they use for themselves is the DOA."

"Dead on Arrival?"

"Nope. The Department of Antiquities."

Jack thought for a moment. "It sounds like we have similar ideals. Maybe they'd be open to working together. Have you approached them?"

"Nope. They don't see us as much different from Caliga. We're thieves, criminals. They will try to protect the egg from us as much as from Caliga."

It was frustrating, but Jack understood the urge to draw that line in the sand. He worked with many people in the FBI who needed to think in terms of *us* and *them*. Good and bad.

Jack was beginning to realize it was much more complicated

than that. Not everyone who bent or broke the rules of the law was inherently evil.

Caliga was a different case, though. They were cut from a different cloth than other thief guilds. They wanted the Fabergé, and the Gifts of the Magi hidden inside, for the power. And what made Caliga dangerous—whether you believed in the mystical power allegedly contained within the Gifts or not—was their willingness to hurt a lot of people to unlock that power.

"We're getting close, Jack. You ready to reconsider? It could be just a matter of days before we have it pinpointed."

Jack tightened a hand around the steering wheel. The timing was fortuitous. The Gargoyle case was drying up. Jack was being cut out by Interpol, and the FBI had forbidden him to follow his leads. He was out. He had nothing to do but paperwork. Flying overseas to join Wesley would get him back in the game. It would be something he could contribute to, be a part of.

But if he crossed over this line right now, if he flew to Amsterdam, could he even still consider himself a cop? Could he even say any small part of him was legitimate?

"Wes, you're making a good case," he said at last. "But the thing is, I'm right in the middle of something big here. They really need me." Jack caught a glimpse of his lying eyes in the rearview mirror.

Wesley was a good sport about the rejection. But he didn't make the same offer as before, to call if Jack changed his mind.

Message received. He wouldn't be calling Jack again.

After hanging up, Jack sat in his car and stared through the windshield into the dark sky. He threw a question out to the darkness. *What now?*

No answers came.

Chapter 22

When I got off the phone with Jack, I cringed. That had not gone well.

But it was ridiculous. Because I wasn't doing anything wrong. *Right?* I was just doing my job. And Ethan was simply a colleague.

Okay, so *yes,* technically, we had slept together that one time. But Jack and I weren't together at that time. We were on a break. You're allowed to sleep with other people when you're on a break, right? Plus, it was under circumstances of extreme stress . . . and a lot of alcohol. Not entirely my fault.

So why had I never told Jack about that? If there was nothing to hide, why was I hiding it?

Automatically, reflexively, the memory of that night with Ethan flooded back. A warm flush rose up my neck.

Ethan looked at me as I sat on the bed with my hand still on the hotel phone. He was applying one of my Band-Aids to his left hand. "Everything all right, Montgomery?"

"Yes, of course," I said brightly. "That was Jack. He, um, says hello."

He raised an eyebrow. "I'm sure he does."

I stood and busied myself straightening things on the desk. The awkward silence was interrupted when my stomach let out a great groan of hunger. I cringed.

"Good idea, Montgomery," Ethan said, responding to my stomach's comments. "Let's grab a bite to eat. Come on. My treat."

Embarrassment notwithstanding, it was a great idea. When was the last time I'd eaten, anyway? Of course, I immediately felt a pang of guilt. Was it a date if I went to a café with Ethan? *Don't be silly, Cat. You have to eat.*

Ethan got dressed, and I gathered my things. A few minutes later we strolled along the sunny, gracious streets of Paris.

We found a sidewalk café just a block from the hotel. Traffic hummed nearby. Waiters bustled deftly among three-deep rows of tables.

I sipped a frosty Kronenbourg and ate an omelet that melted in my mouth.

"What are the chances they have our faces?" I asked. I'd been thinking about this ever since our escape.

"Zero."

"How do you know?"

"There's not a lot of CCTV in Paris. It's nothing compared to a lot of big cities, like London. They keep talking about installing more cameras, but it keeps getting caught up in the bureaucracy. Most of the cameras they do have are clustered around the high-crime areas and the tourist traps. Not where we were today."

That made sense. And made me feel much better.

I cast a sidelong glance at Ethan as he swallowed a sip of beer. He looked effortlessly cool in his khakis and Tom Ford sunglasses and linen shirt rolled up at the sleeves, revealing tanned, strong forearms. He was the picture of laid back. And he was, noticeably, not sitting there, being all jealous or making me feel guilty about a thing.

Not fair, Cat. I knew where my head was going with that line of thinking, and it was undeserved.

I turned my attention to my food and the rather large leaf of lettuce confronting me on my plate. If I wasn't so hungry, I'd leave it alone. But I had scarfed down my omelet in record time, and I was still starving. I was self-conscious at the idea of ordering a second lunch in front of Ethan, so lettuce it was.

I wasn't entirely sure if the lettuce leaf was part of the meal or merely garnish, but I didn't care. I needed to eat it. Trouble was, how to tackle such a large leaf? Cut it with a knife and fork, and look like a ridiculous princess, or just stuff it right in? Also, why was I even giving this so much thought? It was not like this was a date.

I opted to simply fold it a bit and shove it in my mouth. Unfortunately, it was even bigger than I'd thought, and it partially sprang back into its unfolded state as it reached my mouth, so little bits stuck out as I tried to chew a very full mouthful in the most ladylike manner possible.

It was at that moment that the waiter returned, asking if we'd like another Kronenbourg. Really? He'd largely ignored us up to this point, but this was the moment he decided to come back?

I smiled and tried to indicate that I was still chewing. He stared at me with a sour, snobby twist to his mouth. I didn't know if he didn't understand or just didn't care, but either way, he wasn't leaving, so I tried to chew faster, my cheeks warming with embarrassment.

But then a bit of vinegar from the salad dressing—Aha! It *was* supposed to be salad—shot down my throat, which promptly closed with a burning spasm.

Both Ethan and the snooty waiter were staring at me, waiting for a response. But my throat had seized. Not only could I not talk, but I knew exactly what was going to happen next. I scrabbled for a napkin, but I was too late. I coughed suddenly, loudly, and an enormous masticated lettuce leaf flew out of my mouth and plopped in Ethan's water glass.

Memo to self:

Next time, order the second lunch.

After the waiter hurriedly, and with a show of great disdain, tidied our table and removed the offending water glass, I sat there in awkward silence with Ethan.

Ethan was trying very, very hard not to laugh.

I lifted my glass to take a casual sip of Kronenbourg, except it was empty, given that I'd never actually gotten around to answering the waiter's question. I sighed. *I give up.*

After a moment, Ethan sat back and said, "Okay, so what's next with the Louvre plan?"

I nodded. *Right. Back to business.*

We had selected a table that was off to the side, with a cushion of confidential air between the nearest patrons and us. Besides, we were speaking English, and although Paris was a cosmopolitan city, it was surprising how little English the locals spoke. Especially if we spoke quickly and at a low volume, it made eavesdropping virtually impossible.

"I need security schematics," I said. "Blueprints, details. All of it. I'm waiting on a bunch of that stuff from Gladys. But I'm not sure it'll be enough."

He nodded and raised his glass to take a sip. Then paused midair. "You know what's interesting, Montgomery?"

"What?"

I watched him sit there with his wheels spinning. He sipped his beer, and a mischievous look took over his gorgeous chiseled face.

"Severin doesn't know that you didn't get all his fingerprints, does he?"

"No."

"That's a little fact that could be used to our advantage. I'm going to have to think about that. It could be leaked to him that the thief in his apartment was stealing copies of his fingerprints to use in a theft."

Hmm. Now that *was* interesting.

Later that night, my heels clicked on the cobblestones of Montmartre as darkness cloaked my movements and a gloomy mist swirled around me. Montmartre is the home of the Moulin Rouge. It's a spiderweb network of narrow cobbled streets, layered with the now-invisible stains of blood and absinthe and sweat, topped by the pristine cathedral of Sacré-Coeur on high, like a white wedding cake looming over it all.

I looked at the scrap of paper I held tightly in my hand and peered at faded house numbers on buildings, looking for a specific address. I was searching for a fortune-teller's shop.

And then I stopped myself. What was I doing? This was absurd. A waste of time.

And yet . . . I felt strangely compelled. I didn't seem to be getting over my fear on my own. Nobody else had said anything to help me yet. So who knew? Maybe a fortune-teller would pick up on something the rest of us hadn't. Maybe there was something else I could do to get out of this pickle. I hadn't been able to come up with it on my own. Templeton couldn't. Atworthy couldn't. But perhaps . . . someone who saw things in a different way could.

Worst-case scenario, a trip to a fortune-teller would serve as a brief distraction. I certainly needed one—I was stalled on planning the Louvre job, waiting to hear back from Gladys with more security details.

Before heading out of my hotel, I'd called Sophie for advice.

"Montmartre!" she'd said with excitement. "That's exactly where you need to go. Oh, Cat, I'm so happy—"

"Just slow down, Soph, and don't get too excited. I'm not a convert or anything. Just . . . looking for a little guidance."

She'd given me the address of a French gypsy fortune-teller she knew in Montmartre, which I'd scribbled on this paper. Of course, the street name had now blurred on my paper, soaked through with mist, but I knew it started with *P,* and I remembered it had been the name of some kind of food.

I stuffed a hand in my pocket to keep it warm, and I felt the tarot card Romany Rosa had given me. I seemed to be carrying it everywhere with me now. It was superstitious, I knew, and I scolded myself for being so silly.

And then I spotted a road sign: RUE POULET. Chicken. Yes, this must be it. Streetlights punctuated the narrow street, each one forming a small glowing nimbus against the cold gloom.

I turned down rue Poulet and found the spot I was looking for. Underneath a falafel restaurant crammed between a bistro and a souvenir shop, steps led down to a lower level. A small hand-painted sign leaning against a grimy lower-floor window was the only confirmation I was in the right place.

LA CARTOMANCIENNE. DISEUR DE BONNE AVENTURE.

I walked down the steps and into the fortune-teller's den. It was dark and smelled of bergamot and cardamom. Beads clicked softly as I pushed the curtain aside and entered an inner room. A chill rose up my arms.

Did I buy into any of this? I hadn't thought so. I'd always believed fortune-tellers were basically people like me. Or, more specifically, people like my friends in the con department. People who could read people. People with supremely honed powers of human observation. They saw things, all right, but not from some otherworldly plane. They saw people's reactions, their body language, their involuntary facial expressions.

The fortune-teller emerged from a back room behind a green velvet curtain with tassels.

The bangles on her wrists clinked and jangled as she moved the curtain aside. She was younger than the fortune-teller at Pike Place. I would have put her age at thirty maybe, although it was difficult to say. Her face was heavily made up, with smoky kohl-rimmed eyes and deep red lipstick. She was petite, maybe five-two, and had masses of curly brown hair. A faint linear one-inch scar marked her upper left cheekbone.

"Bonjour, mademoiselle," she said to me. She indicated a chair; I took a seat at the scarf-covered table. "You are here because you have a question?" she asked in French.

"Well . . . not exactly," I replied in French. "I just need to know . . . if I'm doing the right thing. If there is some other way."

She nodded and silently placed an old wooden box on the table. She released the brass latch and swung the lid open on its hinges. From the box she removed a tarot card deck.

They looked different from the cards at Pike Place—much older, more worn around the edges. And the pictures were somewhat different. The illustrations looked ancient, primitive.

She arranged the cards on the table in the same cross pattern Romany Rosa had used, then stared at them for a long time.

"You are in great danger," she said at last. "You are playing a game that will end badly. There is an old power held in a charm of some sort, an amulet perhaps. You would do well to stay away."

I stiffened in spite of myself. How could she know that? Either she was incredibly good at reading people or . . .

"What if I don't have a choice? What if I need it?"

The fortune-teller frowned and tilted her head at the cards, bird-like. She turned over three more.

"But there is something else," she said. "You are torn. You have a choice to make."

Of course. Was there any other reason to come see a fortune-teller besides struggling with a choice? She must say those exact words to every single person. The spell began to break down as I felt renewed skepticism for this whole idea.

"It has to do with love. With a man," she said. I could see her watching me carefully and gauging my reactions. "*Two* men," she added, correcting herself.

She was good, I had to admit. But I wondered what my tell was. What had made her say that?

Then she pointed to a specific card facing up on the table. "One is the Knight." Her finger rested on the card with the name *Le Cavalier d'Épée*. The Knight of Swords.

"The other is the Trickster." She pointed to a card that carried the label *Le Bateleur*. "In other tarot suits, this is often called the Mountebank. It means 'a swindler.' Or 'a sleight of hand artist.'"

I had to admit that was strange. It almost sounded like she was talking about Jack and Ethan.

"What's this one?" I asked, pointing to an unlabeled card that contained a golden disk in the center. It was the card she'd been staring at when she'd talked of an old power within an amulet.

"That is the Ace of Coins," she said. "But it goes by other names. Ace of Pentacles. Ace of Deniers. Or . . . in more modern suits, Ace of Diamonds."

Diamond? Like the Hope Diamond?

The back of my neck tingled, as though spidery fingers were tracing a path down it. This was too close again. Too accurate. How could she possibly know all this just by reading my face?

And then I remembered. Sophie was the one who had arranged this. *Ah, right.* She'd set this up. She'd probably put the fortune-teller up to it. Told her what I needed warning about.

I felt mildly annoyed, but mostly I knew Sophie's heart was in the right place. She was just trying to keep me safe.

I thanked the fortune-teller for her time, paid her, and walked out of the incense-filled haven to the cool air outside. I retraced my steps along the dark, shadowy street, past people up to varying degrees of mischief.

I pulled out my cell phone and called Sophie. "That was fun, Soph. Thanks for playing. Just what I needed, actually, a little diversion for an hour."

"What are you talking about? My fortune-teller called me. She said you never came."

I frowned into the phone. "What? I was just there. I literally just left the shop. I'm walking along rue Poulet as we speak."

There was a pause on the line. "Rue Poulet? Why are you there? No, I said rue Poisson. My fortune-teller is on rue Poisson." She laughed, understanding dawning. *Poulet* was French for chicken, and *poisson* was French for fish.

"Well, I knew it was a word that started with *P* and it was a food name," I said, starting to laugh too.

"Oh, there are a million fortune-tellers in Montmartre," Sophie said. "You just went to the wrong one."

Then I stopped laughing. "Wait, so I went to see a fortune-teller you *hadn't* spoken to first?"

"I guess so," she said blithely.

I felt anything but blithe. A creeping shiver covered every inch of me.

I went back to my hotel. I needed a hot bath, and I needed it now. I still hadn't heard from Gladys, and it was making me crazy.

The fortune-teller as a distraction strategy—even as an alternative problem-solving strategy—had utterly backfired.

I opened the closet to retrieve a robe . . . and knew something was off. Where was my navy cashmere cardigan? I was sure I'd hung it up there earlier.

Frowning, I opened drawers and checked the armchair. By the time I crouched down to look under the bed, I had a very bad feeling.

Now, everyone misplaces things from time to time. And people don't typically panic over a missing sweater.

But as a thief, I notice when things are missing. I pay attention to these things. Because in my world it's hardly ever a coincidence.

I checked if anything else was missing. All my valuables, my purse, my passport, my iPod, everything was where it should be. Nothing else was gone.

Just my cardigan?

I lived a pretty messy existence, I admit. But I always had a sense of where I'd left things. It was like a constant mental inventory, like a big game of Memory, and I always knew when something was gone.

And there was no doubt in my mind that my cardigan was definitely gone. Which meant it had been taken.

My mouth felt dry. I began searching for signs of entry. As a pro, I could spot when someone had busted in, even if they were also a pro. But there was nothing. No scratches on the door handle. No sign that things had been moved about or overturned.

I started doubting myself. And laughing at my own ridiculousness. Why on earth would a thief break in here and steal *a cardigan?* Cold evening? Feeling a little chilly and couldn't be bothered to go back to his own place?

I must have left it somewhere. At a café maybe.

I guess I needed that bath more than I'd realized. The cardigan would turn up. I went into the bathroom and turned on the hot water. And tried to ignore the uneasiness between my shoulders that just wouldn't go away.

Chapter 23

Ethan tried not to shudder as he walked through the doors to La Santé Prison in the Fourteenth Arrondissement. It wasn't the morning chill that made him feel cold as he entered the concrete and steel structure. Everywhere he looked, all he could see were steel bars, moldy concrete, locks and alarms. It was a building designed to contain people like him. Was it any wonder the very sight of it made him want to turn and walk very quickly in the opposite direction? Instead, though, he was voluntarily strolling in.

Ethan had been working all day on this lead. Now it was time to see if he could pull it off.

He knew they needed an insider's view of breaking into the Louvre. It wasn't something that currently occupied a spot on his own résumé, sadly. He'd done jobs in Paris, of course. You couldn't call yourself an art thief otherwise. But only from smaller galleries and private collections.

The Louvre was his white whale.

A buzzer sounded in the prison—harsh and jolting—as the security guards buzzed him through to the inner layers. To hide his discomfort, he straightened his suit, tugged on the starched cuffs of his shirt. He wore a sharp pin-striped three-piece and a Zegna silk tie that alone cost more than the guards' weekly wage. Ethan knew he looked good. Which was important. He had to play the part here.

Because although he'd never hit the Louvre himself, he did know someone who had. And today Ethan was posing as his lawyer.

The thief was an old acquaintance, a man named Bruno Murphy. Ethan had succeeded in tracking him down. For the most part. With just one catch.

The man was in prison.

Last night he'd called Montgomery to tell her about his plan. When she'd answered the phone, a smile had come over his face at the very sound of her voice. Which he quickly shook off. What the hell was he? A fifth grader with a crush? *Jesus.*

"I'm going to go talk to this guy named Bruno Murphy," he'd said.

"Okay. Why?"

"Because he's the only person I know who has successfully broken into the Louvre."

"*No,*" she breathed. "That's perfect."

It was slightly less perfect when he told her where the guy was currently located.

"But . . . how are you going to get any useful information?" she asked. "If you visit, won't your conversation be recorded?"

"That's why I'm going posed as his lawyer. It'll be a confidential conversation that way."

There was a pause. "Isn't that kind of risky? Going to the enemy's nest that way?"

Ethan heard the worried edge in Montgomery's voice. And in spite of himself, he could feel a smile growing again. *She's concerned about me.*

"Yes, there's a risk. But I think I can pull it off. Don't worry, Montgomery. I'll be fine."

The smell of the prison as he walked in was the thing he was least prepared for, in spite of the notoriously bad reputation French prisons maintained. No amount of industrial cleaner would ever kill the smell of urine. Or tobacco. Prisoners—especially French prisoners—did little else other than smoke all day long.

Ethan had never been to prison, which was unusual for a career criminal, to be sure. Most crooks ended up in the pen from time to time. Usually just short stints, if they were lucky. It never seemed to stop them from falling back into old ways when they got out, of course.

But Ethan had never been caught.

So walking into this prison now, and being shown into a small concrete room featuring a door with steel bars, was not high on his wish list for Paris sightseeing. That he was obliged to leave his phone outside with the desk clerk served only to increase his discomfort. He was cut off from the outside world.

The door closed, and he waited.

And did his best to maintain his composure. Inside he felt like scaling the walls. Outside he hoped he looked cool. He knew he had a pretty good ability to appear unflappable—he'd been told this many times—but that didn't mean he never got stressed. He did. He just had a better poker face than most.

Something he was counting on today.

At last, the doors made a loud clunk as they were unlocked, and a prisoner was shown in.

Bruno was a tall, lanky man, much taller than Ethan. He had a long horse face and slightly asymmetric eyes: the left was just a little higher than the right. It was the face of a Picasso painting. Appropriate for an art thief, truly.

Ethan knew Bruno to be an agency man. He had worked for an American agency with a French branch. Bruno sat down and looked up at him with dead eyes. He pushed back a curtain of lanky hair, and then recognition dawned. A bitter fire kindled in Bruno's eyes.

The guard left, closing them inside the room. The room Ethan was trying his best not to think of as a cell.

Bruno gave a snort. "You've got balls, man. Showing up here, pretending to be legal counsel."

Ethan smiled and gave a slight shrug. "It's good to see you again, Bruno."

"Right. So, what do you want?"

Ethan nodded. The sooner they got down to business, the sooner he could get out of there. "I want to talk to you about the Louvre. You broke into it."

Bruno nodded.

"How did you do it?" Ethan asked.

Bruno laughed, an unpleasant noise that sounded like he was coughing up a fur ball. "You want me to just describe it? Why?" He narrowed his eyes. "You planning to try the same thing?"

Ethan shrugged.

Bruno's mouth twisted angrily. "Did that son of a bitch Lafayette send you? Are you working with him now? Bastard. Fucking double-crosser." He spat with rage.

Ethan had no idea who Lafayette was, but decided to play along. "Are you saying I shouldn't trust him?"

Bruno laughed again. "Sure. Trust him. Be my guest. He'll give you everything you need. Then fuck you up the ass if it suits him."

"Okay, maybe you're right," Ethan said. "Yeah, I'd had a feeling he wasn't a good partner. So can you help me instead?"

Bruno just stared at him a moment, studying Ethan's face. And then his expression went from merely unpleasant to downright hostile. His lips curled back. "You don't remember, do you?" Bruno said, eyes flashing with a vaguely psychotic spark. "That makes it even worse."

Ethan's brain started spinning, trying to figure out what the man was talking about. He scanned through memories, anything that involved Bruno. And then—

Oh, shit. Many, many years ago—like, maybe seven—Ethan had slept with Bruno's girlfriend. He'd totally forgotten about that. She'd been a bookings clerk at the Agency. It had meant very little to Ethan—obviously. He'd never figured it would come back to bite him in the ass now.

Ethan held his hands outward in a gesture of supplication. "Dude, I can explain—"

"Are you for real? Are you fucking kidding?" Bruno was getting increasingly agitated. Ethan started sweating.

"I should *out* you right now," Bruno said. And then laughed. It was the short, barking laugh of someone who is seriously pissed and right on the edge of five-alarm crazy. "Of course I can't, though. How's that for irony? I pled not guilty. So how would I know another professional thief? I'd be incriminating myself." He was rambling to himself, a very concerning sight.

"I appreciate that," Ethan said.

"Don't. I might decide to take a chance, after all. You need to get the fuck out. Before I do change my mind."

Ethan could tell he was serious. It was time to fold his hand.

"Much obliged, Bruno. Good luck to you." He called for the guard and exited quickly.

Well, that sucked. The encounter had proved way less helpful than he'd hoped. Except for one piece of information.

A name: *Lafayette.*

Chapter 24

Stone saints glared down at me as I walked through the great oak doors into Notre-Dame Cathedral in Paris. A gloomy drizzle filled the sky outside. The inside somehow managed to be even more gloomy.

Perhaps it was the smell of burning candles with a faint undertone of sweat—people who prayed were nervous, evidently. Tall Gothic windows surrounded a black-and-white chessboard floor. Honey-colored stone archways and columns soared to the heavens. Wooden chairs, arranged in perfect rows, appeared to have been lined up by a worker wielding a ruler. And a bad case of OCD.

I shivered; the air was drafty and cold.

Faulkner had wanted this meeting. He had more or less demanded it, saying he required a progress update. I wiped my hands on my pants and tried to get some saliva into my mouth.

Of course, this could be a trap. Maybe he'd changed his mind. Maybe he was growing tired of all this and would simply decide to get his satisfaction.

But I couldn't have refused to meet him. And I couldn't find anyone to come with me. Ethan wasn't answering his phone. I tried not to think about the fact that he was going to La Santé Prison today.

One thing was for sure. I needed to convince Faulkner to give me some more time. Because there was no way I was going to get the Hope before the week was up, like he'd wanted.

Maybe if I had been able to retrieve all Severin's fingerprints.

Maybe. But not now. And there was no way I was going into the Louvre anything less than spectacularly well prepared.

So I would just have to ask Faulkner for a short extension.

I spotted him by a side alcove, standing in a trench coat, holding a drippy umbrella. I walked to the alcove, stopping to pick up a small votive candle from a table and to drop a coin in the box, and stood beside him in front of an oil painting of Saint Peter.

"The stained-glass windows are spectacular, aren't they?" I said casually, as though talking to a stranger.

There was silence. And then, "I prefer to look at the gravestones. They're people I've never heard of, and that fascinates me."

There weren't many people in this corner of the cathedral. The one nearby woman wandered off to examine the organ pipes farther away.

After another pause, Faulkner said, "You are on schedule, I trust?"

"Er, well, that's something I wanted to talk to you about."

He said nothing.

So I kept talking. "I know you wanted me to do this job before the end of the week. But it's impossible." I had to make him understand the intricacies involved. "There are a lot of things at play here. It's not a simple job."

"Miss Montgomery, the details are of no interest to me. I do not care how you do it. Only that you do it. And soon."

Sweat trickled between my shoulder blades. Maybe hoping he was going to be reasonable was too much to ask. What was I going to do if he refused to give me more time?

"I will, however, consider your request," he said.

I exhaled the air I'd been holding in.

"Now, there's one other thing you need to know," Faulkner said. "You appear to have popped up on the radar of an Interpol agent. Or, at least, the idea that a thief is targeting the Louvre has."

This was a punch in the stomach.

"What? How do you know?"

He shrugged, disinterested. "What you need to understand is that if you go down for this, I am not going down with you. Shake Interpol, or I will cut you loose. There will be no connection between you and me. The name of the Interpol agent is Ludolf Hendrickx. And, evidently, he has just turned up in town." He shook out his umbrella, readying to leave.

"Here in Paris?"

Faulkner pulled up the collar to his trench coat and opened his umbrella, heedless of any superstitions about opening umbrellas indoors. "Take care of it, Miss Montgomery."

"I'll do my best," I said.

I swallowed. I had no idea how I was going to do that.

Chapter 25

I got off the phone with Gladys and sat back in the chair in my hotel suite. Fresh from the shower, I rubbed my wet hair with a towel and thought hard. This was not good.

Gladys had learned a little more about the Interpol agent Faulkner had mentioned. She'd hacked into Interpol e-mail accounts and learned that Hendrickx was indeed in Paris. He was investigating the Gargoyle—whoever or whatever that was—and had a high-grade suspicion that a Louvre theft was an imminent part of the Gargoyle's plans.

Which made about as much sense to me as the hieroglyphic laundry instructions on my clothes.

And what made even less sense was what Gladys said next.

"You should know, Cat, that Jack asked me a similar question last week. He sent me a photograph of Hendrickx on a street in downtown Seattle and asked me to identify him."

"He what?"

"Maybe you two should compare notes. Hendrickx is obviously a party of interest for both of you."

I sat there dumbfounded. Jack had spotted Hendrickx? He needed to identify him and went through my hacker to do it? Why?

Gladys was right. In an ideal world, I should talk to Jack about it. Maybe we could help each other out.

But that would mean telling Jack way too much about my situation. And I wasn't ready to do that.

No, I'd have to leave that alone for now. The whole thing left me feeling uneasy, though.

Even if Interpol wasn't investigating me, per se, Hendrickx's radar was up about the Louvre and the Hope, and he was going to start poking around.

I fiddled with the pencil on the desk and gazed out the window. The view of Paris was misted over with sheets of rain pouring down the plate glass.

If only I had someone who could get close to this guy, find out what he knew, find out how much he knew about me, specifically. Someone who could gain his confidence, then maybe slip something into his drink, check his private files, his private notes . . . that kind of thing.

I could do it in disguise, but the risk was insane. If he was already on the lookout for me, it would be a foolish thing to do. But I knew someone who could do it for me.

Brooke Sinclair.

This was absolutely her area of expertise. Getting men to trust her and tell her everything? That was her superpower.

Playing the femme fatale was not my strength. Not like Brooke, anyway. If I tried it, I'd probably say something stupid. I'd probably say something incriminating. No. This was definitely Brooke's domain.

I had to convince her.

Later that afternoon, I watched as a bent little Frenchwoman spun batter clockwise on a hot circular plate. She waited patiently for it to cook fully, then brushed the crepe with butter, dusted it with sugar, and folded it like a piece of origami.

She slid the hot crepe into a paper envelope and handed it to me. It matched the one I held in my other hand.

As far as bribery went, I thought it was pretty good.

The rain had stopped, and the sun was out now. The Luxembourg Gardens were blossoming, the colors fresher because of the recent showers, the air crisp and lush with the scents of iris and lily.

I walked farther into the park and spotted her. I had tracked Brooke down, finding her sunning herself in one of the Luxembourg's numerous olive-green metal chairs and trying to attract the attention of local French businessmen on their lunch breaks.

I handed her one of the crepes.

"What's this?"

"I passed a crepe stand on my way over. They smelled irresistible."

She looked at me suspiciously. But took my offering and bit into the steaming, crispy crepe, nonetheless.

I bit into mine and melted just as much as the butter. Parisian crepes are a miracle of hot, crisp, soft buttery sweetness. I took a seat next to Brooke.

Sunlight glinted off the octagonal pond where small children played with wooden sailboats, pushing them with sticks, watching as the crayon-colored sails floated serenely in front of the grand palace of Luxembourg.

"Brooke, listen. There's this Interpol agent who is, apparently, crawling all over this case. It would be really helpful for me if I knew what he knew. And, ideally, if he could be directed to sniff elsewhere."

She chewed her crepe slowly and swallowed a mouthful. "Like a false trail. Good idea."

"So I was thinking," I said, "who would be great at this? Who would be perfect for a job that involves gaining a man's trust, getting him to let his guard down, getting information out of him?"

Brooke barely paused a beat. "Cat, darling, flattery is not going to help you here."

"Come on, Brooke. This has nothing to do with the actual Louvre job. Your agency can't object, even if they were to find out. It's not moonlighting. It's not anything, actually. Come on, you'd just be flexing your skills."

And, let's be honest, she'd probably enjoy it, too.

I received nothing by way of a response.

"You know, it's not without benefit to you," I pointed out. "If this guy is investigating a potential theft of the Hope, it means he may have a beat on jewel theft in general. Finding out his deal could benefit you at some point down the road."

"And you can't do this why, exactly?" she asked me.

I tilted my head and gave her a look suggesting that she knew full well the answer to that.

"Good point," she said.

She paused, thinking, and took another bite of crepe. She chewed thoughtfully. And then looked at me levelly. "All right. I'll do it. You're right. It would be useful to know what an Interpol agent investigating jewel theft is thinking." A wicked grin escaped her lips. "Might be fun, actually."

"Thanks, Brooke. I really owe you one."

She popped the final bite of crepe into her mouth. "Me helping you has nothing to do with this crepe, by the way."

I grinned. I still had to figure out how to get Hendrickx off the trail. And the small matter of planning to rob the Louvre, of course. One step at a time, though.

Chapter 26

I walked back to my hotel, lost in thoughts and plans. As I walked, the sky grew dark and muddy. One thing about Paris springtime weather, you could never count on anything for long. A chilled breeze kicked up.

Then cold fingers prickled the back of my neck. But this wasn't because of the change in weather—I was being followed again.

I rolled my eyes. It must be Brooke again. Testing my skills, seeing if I'd brushed up since her little sport on the Champs-Élysées.

Surely she would grow bored of this, though, if I ignored her. I kept walking.

And then my phone rang. I fished it out of my purse and looked at the display. Templeton.

"Feeling okay, love?" he asked when I answered the call.

"Templeton, why don't you come right out and ask me? You want to know if I'm still afraid of dying. If I'm still having panic attacks."

There was a pause. "I'm attempting to be sensitive."

"And I appreciate that. Still, the answer is yes."

"Yes, you're okay? Or yes, you're still afraid?"

"Well, I had a panic attack the other day, when I was on a rooftop, if that helps you."

Silence. "Well, in that case I've got a little good news."

"That, I could use."

"Your professor Atworthy will be in Paris this weekend," Templeton said. I had told Templeton about Atworthy's past. I had told him he'd helped me in deciding to come to Paris to confront my fears. "It might be good to talk to him again, get some advice on dealing with this fear. It's obviously a forte of his."

"How do you know he's going to be here?"

"Tsk, tsk. What little faith, Flower. I know *everything*," he said. I laughed.

"He's coming to the City of Lights for his niece's wedding," Templeton said. "You could see him then somehow."

"Templeton, I've got so many things I have to do to prep for this job—"

"Stop. Catherine, this is not a suggestion. You are going. His assistant said he is going to be in Paris for only twenty-four hours, and his schedule is packed. But surely you two can find a little time. Call him and set it up."

He was right. There was no way I would be able to get through what I needed to without a little more help.

I hung up and walked several more blocks, getting closer to the Four Seasons. I turned down an alley, a shortcut to the hotel.

But as soon as I made the turn, I realized I'd chosen the wrong alley. This one was a dead end. It was shadow filled, littered with garbage bins, and cut off from the surrounding streets.

Then I heard footsteps behind me.

I exhaled through my nose. *Not in the mood, Brooke.* I turned to face her and send her on her way.

But when I turned, there was no Brooke. Instead, blocking the entrance to the alley stood Sean Reilly. The other thief who had been casing the Hope.

All my blood drained through my legs to my toes.

He stood there staring at me, observing me with a clinical detachment. I became acutely aware of how alone I was.

"So, Cat Montgomery," he said with a clipped voice. "It looks like we've got a problem. You and I seem to want the same thing."

It took every ounce of intestinal fortitude not to step back. I had to stand my ground. "I don't know what you mean," I said, willing my voice to stay strong. Everything Templeton had told me about

Reilly was surfacing in my brain, crumbling my nerve. *Rotten, unscrupulous, not afraid to use violence . . .*

"Don't treat me like I'm stupid, *Cat.*" There was something creepy about the way he used my name in such a familiar way. I felt violated somehow. "I know what you're doing here in Paris. And I know you know who *I* am. I know you accessed my file."

My brain was churning. Who did he work for? How did he know about me?

He took a few slow steps toward me. An immediate adrenaline blast helped me locate escape options—through a door near the back, which might be unlocked, or maybe up the wall somehow—and sent a surge of blood to the muscles of my legs. Ready to run. Or fight.

"You cannot get the Hope," he said. "And you can only interfere with the plans of people who can. So leave it alone." His lips were tight as he spoke. "I'm trying to be nice about it. But you will soon find out . . . *I'm not all that nice.*"

When I returned to my hotel a while later, Ethan was waiting for me in the lobby. He was seated in an armchair, looking at his phone.

"Good timing," he said cheerfully as I walked in. Then he really looked at me. "What's wrong?" he asked, serious now. He stood and moved toward me.

"I just had an encounter with Sean Reilly."

Ethan knew exactly who I was talking about. He raked me with his eyes. "Are you okay? What happened?"

"I'm fine. I'm not hurt," I said. "He didn't touch me. He just warned me to stay away from the Hope and then walked away."

His shoulders relaxed. "Well, that's good . . . that you're not hurt, anyway."

I looked up at him. "What am I going to do about Reilly?"

"Are you going to back off?" he asked, gazing into my eyes.

"You know I can't."

Ethan shrugged. "Then don't worry about him. Just keep moving forward."

I nodded. "I need a drink."

"Coming right up."

We walked through the lounge to take a seat at the bar. Once I had a vodka martini in front of me, and once Ethan knew I was okay, he started grinning again. I could tell he had something good to tell me. He could barely contain himself.

I sucked on a vodka-soaked olive as Ethan described visiting the prison. And shared the only piece of useful information he'd gleaned: a name, Lafayette.

"Lafayette? Who is it?"

"Well, I didn't know at first," Ethan said, leaning toward me on his bar stool. "But then I started looking into it, doing some digging. And I found that Lafayette was the name of a security guard at the Louvre who was instrumental in busting Bruno."

"But in prison Bruno said he was a backstabber," I said as the pieces began to fall together. I shifted in my seat and did my best to ignore the incredibly appealing scent of Ethan's cologne.

"Yes. So I'm thinking, this prison guard was helping him out. Up to a certain point, anyway."

"Maybe he was a plant. Someone setting Bruno up, like an entrapment sting."

Ice cubes clinked in the glass as Ethan took a sip of his whiskey and narrowed his eyes, thinking. "Possible. But the thing is, Lafayette still works at the Louvre. If he had any kind of official capacity, wouldn't he have been reassigned if he had been undercover? I had Gladys pull up some of his performance reviews as an employee of the Louvre. Seems to be a fairly disgruntled employee. Bad attitude, frequently late, that kind of thing."

"So, if he's a disgruntled guard, he may be motivated to help a thief."

"He did it once before, it seems. I think something must have gone wrong, and he panicked and blew the whistle on the guy."

I drained my martini glass. "So this is someone we could not trust."

"Trust? No. Get information from? Maybe." Ethan beamed and raised an eyebrow.

"Hmm. Interesting."

* * *

The next day, Ethan went off to see what he could make of the lead, and I got ready to attend a wedding.

Or, more specifically, to crash a wedding.

When I'd called Professor Atworthy, he'd said it would be impossible for me to see him while he was in Paris the next day.

"I'm sorry, Cat. I just won't have time. My niece is—what is that term?—a bridezilla. She has booked out every minute with various family activities."

My only option? To crash the wedding and try to speak to him there. I was in trouble, I needed help, and I needed it fast.

I dressed in my best wedding-crashing outfit: a navy silk Alexander McQueen, cocktail length. Not so much swagger to draw undue attention, and just enough swank to blend in.

I hired a car to take me to Vaux-le-Vicomte, a seventeenth-century château just outside Paris. A fairly opulent venue for a wedding, but evidently, this was a bride who would settle for nothing less.

Fortunately, I wasn't totally inexperienced when it came to crashing weddings. Receptions were traditionally a fabulous opportunity for a little pickpocketing work. I'd had many assignments at weddings. It was refreshing to be able to use my skills for less directly nefarious purposes.

Walking in, all I could see was jewelry. Bling this, sparkly that, it was enough to throw my concentration. The air rippled with the sound of a string quartet and the lush scent of white peonies by the thousands. An ice sculpture shimmered beneath a glittering chandelier.

Crashing a wedding requires a few things. You have to look the part, of course. You need to know the dress code. Furthermore, you need to behave naturally. No furtive behavior, no hiding from people. And under no circumstances should you attempt to sneak in. Just stroll in like you were invited.

Of course, nobody will recognize you, but how different is that from many of the weddings you attend? Don't be unnerved by people wondering who you are. Just smile with an expression that suggests you're wondering who *they* are.

And this approach was working for me today at Vaux-le-Vicomte. Right until I encountered the wedding planner.

The bride might be bridezilla, but the planner was equal parts drill sergeant, gestapo, and inner-city vice principal.

I was standing among a group of people signing the guest book when I got yanked out of the crowd and interrogated in a caustic rain of French. A rough translation of her words went something like this: "Who are you? I do not know you. Are you an invited guest? I do not think so. Wait here. I am going to find out exactly who you are."

Waiting was not going to work for me. Because waiting wouldn't get me any closer to talking with Atworthy.

So I watched the wedding planner disappear through an arching doorway into the Grand Salon. And then, when nobody was looking, I slipped along the foyer and through side doors into the ballroom. Guests dressed in Valentino and Versace were mingling, sipping champagne. Waiters wove through the crowd, offering lacquered trays of hors d'oeuvres.

Now I was doing a trickier maneuver. I had to keep one eye searching for my target—Atworthy—and one eye on the lookout for the wedding planner.

I programmed my brain to register green—the color the wedding planner was wearing. Anything green in my peripheral or direct vision would trigger an alarm. Likewise, I needed a quick change of outfit. There was a sky-blue pashmina resting on the back of a chair. I casually swiped it as I walked by and wrapped it over my shoulders.

That should help a little.

As I walked, I surreptitiously tugged at the pins holding my bun together and let my hair fall down. Good. Another little change. Each of these should buy me a few minutes, anyway.

I saw the wedding planner speaking urgently to the father of the bride, and the two of them angrily looking about the room. I assumed they were looking for me.

And I must say, this was a lot more hostility than I typically received during a party-crashing effort. But I soon figured it out.

In the meantime, I needed to attach myself to a group. I scanned for appropriate candidates. There was a small clutch of women nearby—not my first choice. I usually had a little more luck with men, but I didn't have many options at the moment. I needed to join a herd, where I could safely look around the room for Atworthy, while avoiding the hunting gaze of the wedding planner.

I approached the women, plucking an unattended glass of wine off the table as I went. I had no intention of drinking it; I just needed something to hold in my hand.

Now, if I were actually looking to make friends, I'd perhaps introduce myself. As it was, I just wanted to gather into the circle unobtrusively. So I sidled up to them and smiled politely, as though we were distant acquaintances. They were in the middle of an animated conversation, in rapid French, about babies.

This was somewhat unfortunate, as it was a topic I knew nothing about. I caught a few fragments on sleep-training techniques and then a little something about toilet training. Was parenting just a series of training exercises? Some of the women had passionate viewpoints on both topics, which I found fascinating, because I was sweating with the effort to seem even mildly interested.

I grew increasingly uncomfortable as it became obvious I was not contributing in any way to this conversation. One or two of the women looked my way with curiosity, and perhaps mild suspicion. I had to join in. I had to say something, or this was not going to work.

Glancing at the woman beside me, I grasped at an opener. "So when is *your* baby due?" I asked in French, smiling brightly.

At this point, all conversation in the group ceased. Hell, I think maybe the string quartet even stopped playing.

I knew in an instant, by the woman's offended expression, that I had selected the worst possible thing to say.

"I am not pregnant," she said through her teeth.

The smile remained frozen on my face as I struggled for damage control. But what could I possibly say? My eyes flicked down to her belly again—I couldn't resist—and, *damn it,* she really did look pregnant. I felt awful, but this was an innocent mistake. Anyone could make it. I glanced at the other women to see they were not on board with this.

I took a big gulp of wine and scanned my brain for damage-control strategies. The instant I swallowed, I remembered a key point: *not my wine.*

Oh God. I raised my hand to cover my mouth as a wave of queasiness pulsed over me.

At that moment, someone across the circle said, "Hey! Is that my pashmina?" She was staring directly at the pashmina I was wearing draped across my shoulders, one that I had most definitely swiped.

"Hmm? No, I don't think so . . . ," was all I could say, feigning confusion.

She reached across and grabbed the bottom corner. "It *is*," she said. "Here's where I spilled red wine earlier." Sure enough, she held up the pashmina to reveal two telltale drops of red wine, like the blood on Lady Macbeth's hands.

"Oh, ha-ha," I said weakly. "I suppose I did grab it by mistake. I have one just like it." I promptly removed the pashmina and handed it to her.

At this, the women turned on me like bad cheese.

It was time to exit stage left. See what I mean about having better luck with a group of men?

I slunk off to the side under disgusted glares of contempt. French women, I might point out, have no natural urges to hide such emotions out of politeness.

But now I was exposed again. Fortunately, the wedding planner was on the other side of the room. For now.

At that moment, I spotted Atworthy. I headed straight for him, keeping one eye locked on the wedding planner. I walked up behind him and tapped him on the shoulder.

He turned, his expression a mixture of surprise and confusion, and then a smile played over his face.

"Catherine," he said. He turned to place his empty glass on the bar. "Good girl."

We slipped away and found a corner of the lobby lounge.

"I probably have only a few minutes," he said. "I'll be required back in the dining hall for the speeches and all that. I'm the emcee."

He looked at me carefully and began to smirk.

"You probably don't have long, either," he said. "Has anyone here told you who you're a dead ringer for?"

And then I learned about the one thing guaranteed to interfere with a successful wedding-crashing effort: if you resemble too closely the groom's mistress.

Awkward.

So that was it. I got straight to the point after hearing that. I described everything that had been going on. I needed some strategies for dealing with the panic attacks.

"I need to know. How do I get over this fear?"

"I don't know if I can tell you that, Catherine. I'm not a psychiatrist."

"But what strategies did you use when you were afraid?"

"Well, do you feel like you're floating away? Like you're going to disappear? Hold on to something tangible, something real. Like keys. Or a door frame."

I thought of the tarot card I carried everywhere with me now. Maybe that was what I was attempting to do with that card.

"What if I'm already doing that and it's not working?"

"You need to make sure you're breathing. You know, diaphragmatic breathing. And maybe you need to work on some meditation." I was taking mental notes. This was good stuff.

"But you know what I think is going to help you the most, Catherine?"

I waited.

"I think you need to embrace the fear. I think you need to dance with the black beast, instead of running away from it."

It wasn't the first time I'd heard this piece of advice. I just didn't know how to begin to do it. Atworthy watched me struggle with that, and then he said, "Listen, maybe the words of Victor Hugo will help."

"Hugo?" I said, looking up sharply. As my professor, he was striking a chord, of course. My field of study was nineteenth-century French literature, after all. Hugo was a demigod in that world. In any world, really, but especially in the particular field Atworthy and I had in common.

Atworthy nodded. "In *Les Misérables* he wrote, 'Diamonds are to be found only in the darkness of the earth, and truth in the darkness of the mind.'"

I sat there, stunned, for a moment. Hugo had said that? I'd read *Les Misérables* many times. How was it possible I'd forgotten that passage? It was like he was speaking right to me.

At that moment the bride and her wedding planner were marching over to where we were sitting.

With homicidal expressions.

I needed to get out of there posthaste. I thanked Atworthy and made a quick exit. I slipped out the side door and climbed into one of the hired cars waiting in line. As the car pulled smoothly away from the curb, my phone rang.

"We've got a meeting with Lafayette," Ethan said when I answered the call.

"Excellent!"

"There's a catch. He won't meet with me. He'll meet only with a woman. It's got to be you."

"What? Okay, well, it is my job, so that's fine."

"Um, don't say that just yet. You might want to hear where the meeting is taking place, first."

"Where?" An uncomfortable feeling crept up my neck and over my scalp.

"The Eiffel Tower. The top."

Chapter 27

Sunshine illuminated the emerald-green lawn that spread out behind the Eiffel Tower like the train of a formal gown. People lounged everywhere, picnicking and taking pictures of one another, using the tower in the background as a prop: jumping onto it, biting off the top of it, leaning on it.

The air smelled of popcorn and fresh cut grass. Sounds of laughter rose up everywhere as kids chased each other in circles and begged their parents for an ice cream cone.

The tower itself speared the sky, its curly iron fashioned like lace. And it drove no small amount of terror into my heart.

I hoped this would be worth it. Ethan had learned Lafayette was still a guard at the Louvre, still very much of the disgruntled variety, which I hoped meant he would be willing to share a little insider info.

He'd done it before, after all. The fact that he had subsequently double-crossed that person was a detail I needed to put out of my mind. Knowing the mistake of trusting this guy, I wouldn't be providing any information, of course. This was an exercise in information gathering only.

My disguise for today was a little bit librarian. I wore a mop of black, curly hair in the form of a wig, heavy-framed tortoiseshell glasses, and a floral-print dress with a light spring coat and flat shoes.

He'd never know who I was, never know what I was up to. If I could help it.

Now, I just needed to get over my paralyzing horror of this damn structure, and everything would be fine.

I just had to keep in mind everything Atworthy had told me yesterday.

Besides, Ethan would be right there on the tower with me, in a tourist's disguise of walking shorts, sandals, hat, guidebook, and camera around the neck. He'd never be far away, and he'd be in my ear the whole time.

I slid a hand into my coat pocket and rubbed my thumb over the smooth tarot card I had tucked in there.

At the bottom of the tower I watched people in long snaking lines, and I knew I was putting off the inevitable. Elevators moved up and down, and hordes of people marched up the open stairs that zigzagged through each leg, climbing like ants in an ant farm. Surely some of these people were afraid to go up. Not everyone was so keen. Right?

I took a deep breath, attempting to slow my racing heart. I stared at the open-lattice staircases and elevator shafts and wondered: did Gustave Eiffel have something against people with a fear of heights? *Damn you, Gustave.*

It wasn't the first time I'd seen the Eiffel Tower, however. Jack had brought me here two years ago. It was our first romantic trip, taken when we'd first fallen in love, and the memory clutched at my heart.

And a twinge of guilt immediately followed. Here I was in Paris again, this time practically joined at the hip to Ethan Jones.

But I couldn't think about that stuff right now. I needed to gather my nerve to go up. I couldn't afford to have a panic attack and show that degree of weakness to Lafayette. It was time to deal with this fear. Today was the day.

"Ethan, are you there?" I said discreetly, knowing my voice was being picked up by the micro-receiver in my ear. "I'm going up."

"I'm here, Montgomery. You're looking good."

I approached the tower and elected to take the elevator. Neither the elevator nor the stairs were particularly appealing options, to be honest, but at least the elevator would be quicker, like ripping off a Band-Aid. Besides, the staircase was open, like a rather elaborate fire escape, so you could clearly see through the grating of the steps to the ground below. I didn't trust my knees to carry me the entire height.

I waited to get into the elevator. My hands were clammy, and I wiped them on my printed dress. This was so ridiculous. How was I going to do this job if I couldn't even go up a goddamned elevator?

Calm down, Cat. I took three deep breaths, which helped a little.

I stepped onto the elevator, and once it was jammed full of people, we started our climb. We were shoehorned in there, and the tween girl standing next to me was chomping grape-flavored bubble gum with a smell so strong, it made my eyes water. The tracks slanted with the changing angles of the tower, contributing to the strangest elevator experience you can imagine. I tried to ignore the hiss and groan of the hydraulics and cables.

The elevator stopped briefly on the first floor and continued on to the second floor, where I exited. Once I focused on the task at hand, my nerves quickly settled. As I walked around, taking pictures, I blended right in. There were young couples and students and small clutches of retirees and families, all enjoying the views and posing by the guardrail for photos with the city of Paris sprawling in the backdrop.

The wind whistled through the open tower, fluttering my dress. I tried to stay well away from the outer edges.

I hadn't even circuited the second floor once before I spotted Lafayette. I recognized him from the photograph Ethan had supplied.

"Got him," I said to Ethan through the micro-communicator. "South pillar."

I walked up beside Lafayette to stand at the edge, looking out over the city. I pulled out my camera and started taking pictures. Up here on the second level there weren't quite so many tourists. There was nobody in the immediate vicinity to eavesdrop. Even so, I used the code phrase.

"The cherry blossoms are lovely this time of year, aren't they?" I said.

"Yes, but they make a mess of the sidewalks," he said, the expected reply.

After speaking, he looked at me sharply, somewhat negating the whole purpose of our clandestine code phrase. Hmm. Clearly, the man was not a professional.

"So. What you want to know?" Lafayette grunted in French, looking away, out over the city.

"Did you bring the Louvre schematics?" I asked.

Gladys had furnished me with most of the security detail of the Louvre. The only part she couldn't obtain specs on was the newly renovated wing. This was what I was hoping Lafayette would give me.

"Yep, got 'em right here," he said.

I was about to give him instructions to fold them inside an Eiffel Tower guidebook and leave the book on the bench behind us so I could pick it up after he walked away. Instead, he simply pulled them out and stuffed them into my hand.

"Here ya go."

I cringed. Well, there was nothing clandestine about that. The guy was about as effective as the tiny red string in Band-Aid packages. I glanced around at the people within view; nobody seemed to be paying attention, thankfully.

I asked him about the security measures for a few of the Louvre's treasures, leading him on a bit of a wild-goose chase, hoping to throw him off the scent, before asking him what I really wanted to know.

"So what can you tell me about the security involving the Hope?"

Lafayette laughed. "The *Hope?* That's what this is about?"

I said nothing, simply waited.

"Well, you can't get near it in the display case. It's too public, too exposed. The security is in layers. Vibration sensor in the glass, temperature sensor inside the case, three-inch bulletproof glass."

I stared straight ahead, my mind churning.

"But at night it often goes into the vault."

"The vault?"

"Yeah, but that's impossible, too."

"Why?"

"Because it was modeled after the Geneva Freeport vault. Severin has a total hard-on for that vault and made pretty much an exact replica of it, installed in the basement of the Louvre."

I knew all about the Geneva Freeport vault.

It was a private, super-high-tech secure site where the billionaires of the world stored their priceless art and wine . . . and various things they weren't supposed to have. Drug lords and royalty alike used freeports like the one in Geneva.

This job was looking increasingly difficult. Not impossible, though. There was almost always a way.

"Of course, there's also the issue of drowning to death if you try to breach the vault," Lafayette said.

"I'm sorry. What?"

"Well, there's this rumor that Severin is so psychotic and takes the idea of someone stealing something so personally that he made the engineers create a booby trap. If the vault chamber is tampered with, it instantly fills with water directly from the Seine. Or so the story goes."

"What? That's ridiculous," I said.

Lafayette shrugged, that classic French gesture. "It's an underground vault. It's possible."

There were so many rumors about the underground world of Paris, like the secret lake underneath the Palais Garnier—supposedly the inspiration for *The Phantom of the Opera*—and the bands of people who allegedly lived in the catacombs. Not to mention the giant rats and mutant fish.

But as for a vault chamber that would fill with water . . . Could that possibly be true? This job just went from difficult to impossible.

And then I noticed we were being watched.

Well, not so much me as Lafayette. A man lingered by the souvenir shop, and his gaze was pinned on the Louvre guard. He was average height, with red hair, and perfectly matched the photograph Gladys had supplied of the Interpol agent Ludolf Hendrickx, who, Faulkner had said, was on the case.

My mouth went dry. I had to get out of there. Although it looked like Hendrickx was primarily interested in Lafayette, I couldn't be sure he wasn't following me, too.

Question was, did I warn Lafayette? I felt tempted to just go and leave Lafayette to his own devices. But he was so useless and helpless, I just couldn't do it.

"I think we need to end this conversation," I said to Lafayette. "We're being watched."

Lafayette's eyes went wide. The guy was a terrible actor and a very unprofessional operative—his reaction told me in a minute, he knew nothing about Hendrickx.

"Just be casual," I said. "If he knows we've spotted him, he may be more tempted to act. Whatever you do, don't run. We'll separate. You casually stroll around to the east side, take a few pictures, and then go down. I'll go the opposite way, weave my way through the gift shop, and go down after that."

Lafayette nodded, his eyes darting. How the hell did this guy get a job as a security guard, anyway?

And then, just as I turned to do my part, I saw rapid movement in the corner of my eye. I turned and saw Lafayette disappearing into an elevator just before the doors closed. He was off like a prom dress.

Shit.

My gaze went immediately to Hendrickx. Frustration and anger flashed on his face as he saw Lafayette disappearing. Then he rapidly looked back at me, and we locked eyes.

I was the new target.

Chapter 28

"Ethan, I've got a problem," I said in a low voice, moving quickly toward the elevator.

"I see that," he said.

As I approached the elevator, Ethan cut in. "No. Not that way, Montgomery. There are no elevator cars approaching the second floor quickly enough. Get to the south staircase. That's your best bet. *Go.* I'll run interference."

I darted to the entrance of the staircase. The grated floor was completely open, and I could see far below.

Memo to self:

Refuse all future requests for risky meetings on top of freestanding towers.

I felt a swell of nausea, and my head spun in a way that threatened to knock me over. I did not need a panic attack right now.

Okay, breathe. Slowly.

Except I needed to move fast. I had to get the hell out of here. At the top of the stairs I glanced back. I saw Ethan attempting to stall Hendrickx by asking him to take his photograph. Hendrickx just glared and pushed past him.

I clamped my jaw and stepped onto the top step. I knew a full-blown panic attack was not far away, but I had to get off the tower.

For one thing, I had the security schematics of the Louvre in my possession. It would be extremely incriminating to be caught with these. It would guarantee my arrest. I could get rid of them . . . but I desperately needed them.

And even if I managed to explain the schematics somehow, Hendrickx would start questioning me about Lafayette. He would run my prints. He would see my real face. After that, it wouldn't be too tricky for him to figure out who I actually was and what I did for a living.

No, getting caught was not an option.

I willed my legs to keep moving down the stairs in spite of my worsening tunnel vision.

I made it several flights down before I heard "Stop that woman!" behind me. Hendrickx was shouting.

Shit. He would choose the most complicated option. What now? He was hollering for people to grab me.

Fact is, that didn't often work. People never clued in to what was going on fast enough. And bystanders rarely wanted to get involved, anyway. Besides, I was a woman. They would always let me through, especially when a non-uniformed man was chasing me.

A few faces looked like they were considering it, though. These were the people I gave my most pitiful look to, my most scared look. "Please help me," I said. I let them draw their own conclusions. They let me through.

The scared expression on my face wasn't much of a stretch. I made it down several more flights. I was getting closer to the ground. I could see my way to freedom.

And then a group of guards started thundering their way up. Hendrickx must have had a way of communicating with them. I was trapped from both sides.

"Ethan, where the hell are you?" I hissed into my earpiece. "I'm trapped on the south staircase," I said.

"I'm coming. I'll be there . . . in about five minutes. . . ."

It was too long to wait. Besides, did he have a plan? *Think, Cat.*

I had to count on the guards not knowing exactly who they were looking for. I could see they weren't looking closely at people as they thundered their way up. But what I did notice, peering through the grated steps, was that they stopped a couple of women with black hair. Just like the wig I was wearing.

There was only one thing to do.

I would have to remove my disguise. It was a risky maneuver. If I was caught at this point, it would mean my true appearance would be seen.

On the other hand, if I was caught, my wig and the rest of my disguise would be removed, anyway, so what difference did it make? Still, I felt naked without my disguise.

I whipped off my glasses and wig and stuffed them in my handbag. I figured Hendrickx had given a pretty cursory description to the guards. I slipped out of my coat and wrapped that around my waist.

But I knew that wouldn't be enough. I needed to attach myself to another party; I didn't want to be seen as a solo woman. A quick glance around revealed limited options. And then I saw a little girl trailing several steps behind her mother, gazing away at the view of the city.

The guards thundered up. They were on the flight below me now.

I crouched down to the girl. "Hi, sweetie. Do you like the view?" I asked. She turned and smiled at me. The barrette in her hair was coming loose. "Oh, look! Here, let me help." I gingerly pulled it out and reclipped it, making my face appear as doting and motherly as possible. Just at that moment the guards stormed past, on their way up the stairs.

I glanced over my shoulder to ensure the guards were well away, gave the girl a flash of a smile, and then continued descending as fast as I could.

Several flights before the bottom, Ethan suddenly appeared on the staircase, coming up.

"Where did you come from?" I hissed.

"I took the east elevator, then ran over here. I had to sneak ahead through that lineup. Okay, here, take my arm."

He stuffed my coat under his jacket and handed me a pair of

sunglasses and a tube of bright red lipstick. He'd come prepared. I casually shook out my hair, knowing that I looked completely different now, and together we slowed right down to the same pace as the tourists.

At that moment Hendrickx and the guards arrived at the landing just above us, charging down. I grabbed Ethan's camera and snapped a photo of him against the backdrop of the Champ de Mars while the search party ripped past us, clearly looking for someone who was fleeing.

Truth be told, it's often the best strategy for escaping a pursuit. To stop fleeing and simply blend in.

Ethan and I became part of the crowd. At the bottom stair, we stepped off the staircase arm in arm, snuggling and gazing into each other's eyes.

The guards' glances at the bottom of the staircase slid off us. We walked away from the tower, forcing ourselves to walk slowly and not run. I hazarded one glance over Ethan's shoulder just before we slipped behind the bushes. I could see Hendrickx having a heated argument with the guards, the whole group of them fanning out and looking with bewilderment and frustration at the hordes surrounding the tower.

We were away. I'd made it. We walked the few blocks to the Metro entrance and descended the concrete staircase.

"So, I hope you got some useful information after all that," said Ethan as we stepped onto the train.

"Sure did," I said, patting my bag. "Schematics. And Lafayette told me all about the vault underground, where they keep the Hope at night."

"Oh?" His eyes flashed with excitement as we gripped onto chrome grab bars and the train accelerated away from the platform.

"Don't get too excited," I said. "It's a perfect replica of the Geneva Freeport."

He stopped. "Are you serious? But that's completely impenetrable."

"I know."

* * *

That evening I went back to my hotel alone, planning to sit down and pore over the schematics. But there was a package waiting for me at the front desk. A small box roughly the size of a shoe box.

I signed for it and took it up to my room, wondering what it could be. Was it intel from Gladys? A piece of equipment from Lucas, my tech guy? Of course I'd love it if there was an actual pair of *shoes* inside that shoe box–size box. . . .

I poured myself a glass of wine, then sliced through the packing tape and folded open the box flaps. I recoiled in horror.

Inside was a severed hand cradled on a blue velvet cloth.

I squeezed my eyes shut and looked away as a chill of terror scudded through my body. I stayed there, frozen like that, for a long time. After a minute, I cracked my eyes and peered back inside the box. This time, I saw a small envelope inside the box, beside the hand.

It took me a long time before I gathered the nerve to grab the envelope. But eventually, my need to know overcame my repulsion. I reached in and grabbed it and scuttled away from the dreadfulness of the box.

Just thought you might appreciate a little extra motivation, in case you found yours flagging.

> *With love,*
> *Albert Faulkner III*

P.S. You may have your extra week. No longer.

Chapter 29

Seattle

The sky had gone black many hours ago, and Jack was still at his desk at FBI headquarters. The offices were otherwise deserted as he pored over a stack of files, routine paperwork that was taking an agonizing length of time. Mostly because he just didn't give a shit. He took a sip of stale coffee, then pushed it away with disgust. Then he glanced up and looked around, realizing for the first time just how alone he was.

He rubbed the back of his head and weighed the pros and cons of the idea that had just occurred to him. Victoria Sullivan would give birth to an ostrich if she knew, but Jack couldn't resist the urge to do a little unauthorized digging in some of the inner files.

If he could just figure out the identity of the Gargoyle—something neither Interpol nor the FBI had done yet—he'd be golden. He'd be back on the case then, surely. He'd certainly have sway with Hendrickx, and he'd probably be able to convince his ball-breaker supervisor that he was capable of handling this investigation, to boot.

Jack considered jumping on the computer of his desk mate, poor trusting bugger who'd given Jack his password a few days ago. Jack was halfway over to the guy's workstation when he changed his mind. No, he couldn't be responsible for someone else getting in trouble. If there was heat to come, Jack would have to take it.

He started opening folders in the system, going into restricted areas. He had the security clearance, sure. He just knew Special Agent Sullivan had forbidden him from investigating this case.

Jack sifted through files of known heads of organized crime. Which one of these was the Gargoyle? Or was it someone else entirely?

He thought about Hendrickx over in Paris and wondered how far he was getting in the investigation. The Paris connection still bothered Jack when he thought about Cat. Was there any chance she was wrapped up in this?

No. That was crazy. Besides, Hendrickx was investigating the Louvre itself as the potential target of a theft, and that was ridiculous. There was no way Cat would be involved in a theft that major. She was still on probation with AB&T, surely.

It had to be a coincidence. Only trouble was, Jack didn't believe in coincidences. He ignored the gnawing discomfort and pushed forward.

Hendrickx had told Jack they'd be following up on a lead about a corrupt security guard—someone who had helped, and then backstabbed, major thieves in the past. Maybe he'd lead them to the Gargoyle? It was the only thing Jack knew about the Paris investigation.

And it sounded pretty weak to him.

Snyder had a much stronger connection to the Gargoyle. He was the only solid lead. There must be something they'd missed. Had they explored everything about the man? Jack pulled up some new files, the surveillance on Snyder, tracking his prior movements over the past few weeks.

There was a notation about Snyder being in Washington, D.C. Nothing weird about that. Close to Philadelphia, where he lived. Jack opened a file with a list of the places he'd been tracked to: the bowling alley, a strip club, Walmart.

And then the Smithsonian.

Now, that was weird. What would a lowlife be doing at a museum? It was the one location that didn't fit. Jack moved the cursor over to the surveillance files. He hesitated, finger hovering over the mouse button. This was definitely not allowed. Victoria Sullivan would kill him, put him on probation, string him up, whatever.

But he couldn't just leave it now.

He clicked and opened the files. He scrolled through CCTV shots of Snyder in the Smithsonian.

Unfortunately, the files contained only still shots, spread apart by five minutes. That was all the FBI had saved, not the full videos. Trying to save storage space, no doubt—more efficiency measures from their Special Agent in charge. Jack frowned.

Still, maybe there was information to be had. Jack scrutinized the shots of Snyder lingering around the main foyer of the National Museum of Natural History, as if waiting. But for what?

Next, segments showed Snyder looking at a piece of paper and selecting the second bench beside the gift shop. Then checking his watch. Like he was there for a rendezvous.

Jack cracked his knuckles.

The next shot, after an interval of five minutes, showed Snyder leaving the museum through the front door.

Jack stared at the screen. But what about a meeting? Had the still shots missed it? If it had been a brief conversation, it could have happened between the five-minute slices.

But that person must have been in the shot somewhere, either before or after.

Jack scrolled back through the frames to see if he recognized anyone in the vicinity. Tourists with their heads buried in guidebooks. A small group of students, appearing bored. A couple of important higher-ups, like the Smithsonian's security director, Jim Haversham, strolling across the foyer. And the director of the museum, Madeleine York.

Not helpful. He sat back in his chair with frustration.

Then Jack had a brain wave. He lunged forward to his keyboard and set the computer to scan all the faces in the shots before and after Snyder leaving. He specified a cross-check to highlight any persons with a criminal record.

And one name came up: Albert Faulkner III. The computer high-lighted his face in the still shot. He'd been hovering by the gift shop when Snyder first sat down on the bench.

Jack minimized that screen and looked up Faulkner in the data-base.

A huge file scrolled up on-screen, including details of all manner of suspected and accused activity. Embezzlement. Tax evasion. Conspiracies and the like. Organized crime. Extortion. The guy was basically a walking catalog of white-collar criminal activity.

But none of the charges had ever stuck. He'd never been convicted. He had a long list of suspected associates. The guy had a huge network, clearly a deep layer of protection.

Jack sat back and folded his arms. Could Albert Faulkner be the Gargoyle?

He picked up his phone and called Criminal Justice Information Services, the FBI division that tracked people of interest and their movements.

"Special Agent Jack Barlow here. Looking for the last known location of Albert Faulkner the Third," Jack said to the woman who answered the phone.

"Just a moment, please." He could hear the woman punching a keyboard, searching the database.

"He has a private jet," she said. "It took off a few days ago."

"Destination?"

There was more clicking as the woman muttered softly about flight manifests . . . and then she got it. "Looks like they landed in Paris."

Paris? Jack closed his eyes and rubbed his face. It seemed he'd found his Gargoyle.

Question was, what to do about it?

Chapter 30

Paris

Brooke and I strolled into the lobby of the Mercure Hotel, chatting like old friends. Old friends who just so happened to be scrutinizing everyone in the lobby out of the corners of their eyes, old friends who had their pockets stuffed with lock picks and micro-cameras, old friends who were about to break into the hotel room of an Interpol officer.

I tried to ignore the churning discomfort deep in my belly. Brooke had talked me into this, and I still wasn't sure it was the right way to go.

She'd called me about twenty minutes ago, saying it was urgent. She'd had drinks with the Interpol officer Hendrickx, and she'd successfully charmed him. Specifically, this meant she had learned which hotel he was staying in, then had stolen his hotel key card.

Unfortunately, she hadn't gleaned any information about the case.

"It was too awkward a subject to raise," she said as we casually walked into the elevator of the Mercure. "I tried a couple of times, but he was very closed about it. Highly suspicious."

"So how do we know he's not coming back to his hotel room right now?"

"He invited me to the theater, and we planned to meet there. I told him I needed to go home and freshen up first. But the performance started ten minutes ago. Obviously, I'm not going to show, but he'll wait awhile, then either leave or just stay for the whole performance.

Best-case scenario, we get two hours. Worst, twenty minutes. But he'll definitely wait until the first intermission for me."

"How can you be sure?"

She gave me an impatient look. "Please, Cat. I can read that much about a man."

It was an opportunity we couldn't pass up. And as long as we were in and out in twenty, we should be fine.

But *should be* was never a very reassuring pair of words in my world. I tightened my fists as the elevator carried us up to the seventh floor.

Just outside the elevator, we heard a couple of people coming down the corridor, around the corner. We did not want to be seen, so we ducked into the staircase and waited until they were gone.

This was not the most modern of hotels, either. Disadvantage: the faint unpleasant smells of stale smoke and mildew. Advantage: no CCTV.

Still, we didn't want any witnesses.

We strolled along the corridor, like we were coming back from a shopping trip. Then we stopped outside Hendrickx's room. Brooke slid the key card in while I kept lookout.

The handle light went green with a faint click. She opened the door, and we both slipped in like a pair of Siamese cats.

Time was ticking. My stomach churned, and I prayed I didn't have a panic attack. I had work to do.

We fanned out. Brooke went straight for the desk drawers, and I targeted the safe inside the closet. Brooke found very little in the drawers. He was very careful, obviously.

But not so careful that he didn't trust the safe. I cracked it in no time at all. It was a very cheap, outdated safe; it would take me longer to get through the knots in my hair after a long drive in a convertible.

What I found was some money, his passport, and a notebook. I opened the small leather-bound notebook and scanned through the pages. He kept fairly scanty notes, likely committing the rest to memory. Probably smart.

But nonetheless, there was some useful information to be gleaned. I held my breath as I read his notes.

Meeting with Lafayette. Female. Thief? Black, curly hair, glasses.

He didn't know my identity. He didn't even have a very good description, as my disguise had clearly sucked him in.

This was good news.

Brooke walked over to where I sat on the bed, and she read over my shoulder. She snapped photos with her micro-camera while I inspected the pages for further clues. Halfway down a page I read,

Monitor Louvre.

I chewed a fingernail. He'd realized the Louvre was a target.

This was bad news.

It was okay, though—this wasn't exactly revolutionary. The Louvre was always a target. I just hoped he didn't know which *part* of the Louvre was my target. The next page read:

Phone call, April 23. Barlow convinced he has discovered the Gargoyle's identity. Barlow to investigate this lead.

Barlow. Did he mean Jack Barlow? I knew Gladys had provided Jack with Hendrickx's name, but now they were working together?

This was very bad news.

Chapter 31

Ethan and I were in the Gare de Lyon station, waiting for the train that would take us the three-hour journey to Geneva. Sounds of luggage being wheeled across a polished concrete floor echoed under the vaulted ceiling. Tour operators hawked their services, hoping to be heard over the din of squealing train wheels and crackly PA announcements. Light filtered into the station from windows high above.

After learning from Lafayette that the Louvre vault was modeled after the Geneva Freeport, we had been mightily discouraged at first. And then we started to see the advantage.

"Well, although there's no way in hell you're getting anywhere near the Louvre vault—unless you're an employee or something—you *might* have a chance to check out the Geneva Freeport," Ethan had pointed out.

Say you're a billionaire looking for somewhere to store your vintage collection of antique Louis Vuitton steamer trunks. The Geneva Freeport would be more than happy to court your business by opening the door and inviting you to tour their facilities and decide if you'd be satisfied with their layers of security.

It was brilliant.

"Okay, now for the fun part," Ethan had said. "Thinking up our covers."

"Our?"

"Yes, I'm coming with you, obviously. I can be a pretty convincing art collector. And billionaire."

I had looked at Ethan carefully. I had no doubt he could.

I was torn. On one hand, it made me feel safer that he would be coming with me. And our cover would be much more plausible. Between Ethan's knowledge of art and mine of sparkly things, posing as a couple with plenty of precious belongings should be no problem.

On the other hand, there was still that niggling guilt at the base of my brain. Was I betraying Jack? How would he feel knowing I was going on a weekend jaunt with Ethan?

But it wasn't a holiday. It was work. I had to keep that firmly in mind.

So I would have one main goal for the trip: to get a good look at the vault, gather as much intel as possible, and figure out how to break into it.

But a secondary goal was to keep things with Ethan on a strictly professional level. Okay, so, yes, we were headed out of town on a trip together. And yes, we would be posing as a married couple.

That didn't necessarily mean anything inappropriate. Right?

I glanced up at the huge boards with flipping numbers of train platforms and destinations. The air was filled with the smells of french fries from the fast-food stands and warm buttery croissants from the cafés. People in business suits strode by our bench, holding paper-wrapped baguette sandwiches.

We had about fifteen minutes to wait. I reached for the newspaper that rested on the bench beside me and glanced at a headline. In French, it said:

LOUVRE SECURITY OFFICER DIES FROM ANAPHYLACTIC SHOCK IN
BISTRO: IS THE CURSE OF THE HOPE DIAMOND REAL?

My eyes popped. I scanned the article quickly for more details. It seemed one of the staff from the Louvre was having dinner in a Beaubourg neighborhood bistro and developed a severe allergic reaction because the waiter accidentally served him the wrong kind of soup, a lobster bisque instead of cream of mushroom. It took only one spoonful. He had a known seafood allergy, so he carried an

EpiPen, but apparently, it malfunctioned. An ambulance was called, but according to local reports, an unusual clog of traffic prevented the ambulance from getting to him soon enough.

"Holy shit," I said. "Ethan, look at this."

His eyes went equally wide at the headline. We read the rest of the page together.

The article made special mention of the fact that this guard was involved in the transport of the Hope Diamond to the Louvre and, in fact, was the last person to touch it before it was installed in the museum display case. Chills went up my arms. The man's dining companion, whose identity was unknown at this point, could not be reached for comment.

According to the article, the instant fear and question on everyone's mind was whether this tragedy had been caused by the Hope Diamond curse.

I looked at the photograph, a grainy image of a middle-aged man with a mustache. Nobody I recognized. I immediately thought of Sophie. What would she think when she caught wind of this?

More importantly, what did I think?

"Think it's a coincidence?" Ethan asked.

I frowned. "It has to be. People die of anaphylactic shock, right?" In itself, it wasn't that weird. It was a tragic set of circumstances, to be sure, but nothing that couldn't have happened to anyone. No, there was no curse. It was not the sort of thing grown-ups believed in.

Right?

Ethan took the newspaper from my hands and stared at it closely. "Curse, maybe not. Suspicious death? Definitely."

I narrowed my eyes at the page as I gazed at it over his shoulder. He was right. But why would anyone want to kill an off-duty guard? Had he known something?

There was no making sense of it. And a few minutes later we boarded the train. I decided to put the incident out of my mind for now.

We stepped from the romantic, belle epoque aesthetic of the station onto a thoroughly modern train. It was all sleek lines and had a clean, updated interior, complete with huge picture windows and a new train smell. My feet made soft, muffled footfalls on the carpeted interior. My ears vibrated with the sound of air circulating through ventilation fans.

We trundled our way out of Paris and soon began flying through the French countryside. The city views of town houses and monuments gave way to rolling green pastures and old stone farmhouses. Now and then we zoomed past tiny villages, mere clusters of buildings, little more than a market, a tobacco shop, and a bakery.

Ethan gazed out the window. "They'd be beautiful villages to explore," he said. "A little wine tasting. A few nights in a charming bed-and-breakfast . . ."

I nodded, sighing. "Another lifetime maybe." I got an immediate visual of taking that kind of trip. With a companion . . . who turned, in my imagination, to gaze at me—and his face looked an awful lot like Ethan's. *Wait.* Shouldn't that be Jack?

I frowned, turning my face to the window to hide my distress.

And then a reminder to pay my Visa bill bleeped on my phone. I was thankful for the distraction. I smiled at this little system I'd developed. I was pretty good these days at staying on top of these things—not traditionally a forte of mine. But I'd made some changes after a disaster last year with the IRS—several years of unpaid back taxes—that almost landed me, à la Capone, in prison.

I pulled up the statement on my iPhone and scanned through it before paying.

Hold up.

Three hundred ninety-eight dollars at Coach? I drew a total blank. I had no memory of buying anything at Coach, certainly not for that amount. I looked at the date, April 13. And the location, Baltimore.

Huh? That didn't make sense. I hadn't been to Baltimore anytime recently.

I scanned down. There were several charges made in Baltimore. Including a gas station charge. And . . . a car rental?

Obviously, my card had been compromised. It happened all the time. I fished out my wallet from my purse. The card was still there, exactly where I'd left it. So it hadn't been stolen, just compromised electronically. Which—believe me—was quite easy to do.

The irony of a professional thief being robbed was not lost on me.

But it would be easily fixed. I made a quick call to Visa, informed them of what had happened, and after much waiting and repeating myself, they were satisfied the charges weren't mine.

Good. Problem solved.

We soon arrived in Geneva. On the cab drive from the station to the Freeport—located at the airport—I caught glimpses of the city, elegant and cosmopolitan, clustered around a shining lake with the Alps looming spectacularly in the background.

We checked into a sleek hotel by the airport and got ourselves cleaned up. Well, a bit more than that, because we needed to step up our game beyond merely clean. We dressed in Tory Burch and Ralph Lauren and Gucci. We adorned ourselves with a Tiffany necklace for me, a Rolex for him.

We were in disguise, too, of course. I wore a glossy dark brown wig and makeup that granted me an exotic olive-toned appearance. Ethan instant-colored his hair to a distinguished salt and pepper and inserted dark brown contact lenses to cover those striking green eyes of his.

We needed to look every inch the jet-setting couple, and I had to admit, we did a pretty good job. Ethan came to stand beside me in the mirror to straighten his cuff links, and I applied a final layer of lipstick. I caught a glimpse of the two of us in the bathroom mirror. We cut a good image. Today we were Michael and Veronica Channing.

I thought about the task at hand. Psychotic butterflies were flinging themselves around in my stomach like they were in a mosh pit. I really needed my nerves to hold out. This was not the time for a panic attack. Besides, there was no real danger here. I wasn't trying to steal anything, after all. This was a recon mission only. We needed to get in, tour around, take some surreptitious photographs, observe the locks and security systems, then walk out, all smiles and handshakes.

It's just . . . well, I wondered how they dealt with people who faked their identities, lied, and gained unauthorized access to the Freeport. Likely, the Swiss did not look upon such activity favorably.

I peeked into my clutch purse, catching a glimpse of the tarot card, which I had tucked inside. I snapped it shut and took a deep breath.

We arrived at the Freeport in time for our appointment. Ethan had called ahead to make arrangements, and our passports and documentation had been faxed ahead. Forged passports, I should say.

When we arrived, the security guard seated in the small hut at the front gate checked our passports, comparing them to the ones in his database. He scrutinized us with a serious, blank expression and then pushed a button. The gate lifted with a buzz, and we drove through in our rented black Mercedes.

We walked into the main office through a slick foyer of concrete, glass, and steel.

A man came out to the waiting room to meet us. He was short but had broader shoulders and a stronger build than typical Swiss men, who—like most Europeans—tended toward lean. He wore a gray flannel Oscar de la Renta suit with lapels so sharp you could shave a man's face with them.

"Monsieur et Madame Channing," he said. *"Bienvenue."* He introduced himself as Monsieur Claude Gurtmann, and he spoke in French, the predominant language of this part of Switzerland.

He wore a smile that did not reach his eyes; his gaze was formal, searching. His hair was combed so precisely, I suspected he accounted for each and every strand.

This was not going to be quite the cakewalk we were hoping for.

His employers would have hired him specifically to screen out undesirables and allow only the most appropriate clients into the Freeport.

Still, all we needed was a bit of a tour. To see the facility, specifically the vaults. And then we could be gone. We didn't need him to deem us appropriate clients, just to let us have a little peek.

After introductions were made, he led us through to his private office. The austere space appeared as though it had barely been used. Not a paper clip was out of place.

"So what brings you to the Geneva Freeport, Mr. Channing?" he asked in clipped French, his Swiss accent barely perceptible.

"We like the model of the others, like the Singapore Freeport," Ethan said, "but we believe the Geneva Freeport is the superior choice. Your facility is the best. And we like the best." He turned to me and put a hand on my knee. "Don't we, darling?"

I smiled at Ethan and turned to look at Monsieur Gurtmann. "We settle for nothing less," I said.

"What is it, exactly, that you are looking to store in the Geneva Freeport?" he asked.

I blinked. This was not a question I had expected—the whole idea of the Freeport was to have complete privacy.

He smiled and bowed his head. "It is not my intention to pry into your affairs, but what I mean is, do you have particular storage needs? For instance, we have climate-controlled cellars specifically designed for wine storage. And areas optimized for automobiles."

"Art storage," Ethan said, "is what we're interested in."

After interviewing us for a few minutes, Monsieur Gurtmann was apparently satisfied and asked us if we were interested in a tour.

We most definitely were.

Monsieur Gurtmann rose. "Please, I must ask that you leave any electronics here. Phones and the like. They will be quite safe, I assure you."

My stomach pinched. I'd hoped he wouldn't say this, but it wasn't unanticipated. We had made contingency plans.

As we stood, I retrieved my lipstick, applied a quick touch-up, and tucked the lipstick back in my purse. The fact that this is perfectly acceptable behavior in public, particularly in Europe, is a great advantage for women. Especially for those women whose lipstick tubes happen to contain tiny audio recorders that can be surreptitiously turned on while twisting the tube.

Now our conversation would be recorded, so I could capture all the tidbits I might miss the first time around. It was all part of doing good recon.

The instant we walked through the door, I had begun taking

mental notes on the windows, doors, and other escape options. On the guards, the CCTV.

The three of us walked through the first layers of security.

"Do you mind if I take a few notes?" I asked, withdrawing my pen and a tiny notepad. The pen, of course, was a very special Montblanc, fitted with a micro-camera. I hoped this request wasn't odd. I hoped it synced with the Swiss ideal of precision and attention to detail.

"Of course not."

As we approached the vault doors, I snapped pictures with the Montblanc. I took photographs of the steel bar doors, the keys, the biometric entry pads.

As we walked, Monsieur Gurtmann pointed out the various security features, which was supremely helpful. We punctuated his monologue with various sounds of approval and pleasure—thrilled that our valuables would be well cared for. With each flattering noise and murmur, Monsieur Gurtmann appeared to relax. Infinitesimally.

We approached the secure viewing rooms and the private access floors. I knew behind these walls were untold treasures—billions of dollars of art and valuables. My fingers twitched. I glanced sidelong at Ethan. From the glint in his eye, I could tell he was thinking the exact same thing.

We made it to the foyer outside the inner vault. I knew this was the part that was replicated in the Louvre. This was what Lafayette had been talking about.

I tried to memorize everything. I looked carefully at the locking system. It was one I'd never seen before. I took several surreptitious photographs and looked at it as closely as I dared without seeming unreasonably interested.

Monsieur Gurtmann was quite proud of it. "This vault is what truly elevates our Freeport above the average storage facility. It is our pride and joy." He gazed at it like a father at a graduation ceremony. "But this is as far as we can go. This vault door stays closed for visitors."

I had no idea if it was crackable. Frankly, it looked impossible.

But all I could do was record as much information as possible, and we'd study everything later.

As we turned, making our way back to our starting point, I felt almost light-headed with success—we'd accomplished what we'd come here for. I could tell Ethan was feeling the same; he was working hard at suppressing a grin.

When Monsieur Gurtmann walked ahead a couple of paces, Ethan dropped back and said to me in a low voice, "Have I mentioned how utterly fabulous you look today?"

Heat prickled up my neck. Ethan stared into my eyes, and for just a moment, I felt momentarily dazed. High-tech secure vault? What high-tech secure vault?

Monsieur Gurtmann cleared his throat discreetly. "So, Mr. Channing, you might be interested to note our electronic door locks at all entry points. Virtually impenetrable."

"Virtually, yes," Ethan said. His gaze was still on mine, his focus a little softer than usual. "It takes the lightest touch. Only a few people have quite the right touch, know to use just the right twist—"

Ethan broke off when he realized what he was saying.

It was like all the air got sucked out of the room. I froze, wondering if Monsieur Gurtmann had heard what Ethan had said. Ethan was not supposed to know that. And was certainly not supposed to sound like a burglar when he said it.

Monsieur Gurtmann's face twitched. Just slightly. He blinked and stared more closely at Ethan and then at me. His mouth went into a thin line, and he kept walking.

My heart was in my throat. He suspected. He had to. He suspected we were lying, and now he would test us.

We walked a little farther in silence. I would have been surprised if Monsieur Gurtmann could not hear my heart thumping. We grew inexorably closer to the exit, but I knew we were still very deep within the facility.

"So where did you say your collection is stored currently?" Monsieur Gurtmann asked.

"A private security facility in Paris," Ethan answered smoothly. He was back on the job now, professional as ever. But was it too late?

"Really?" Monsieur Gurtmann asked. "Which one? I know most of the facilities in Paris. I did an extensive tour there last year."

"It's Granville-Beaufort Fine Art Storage."

"Ah yes, of course. I know that one. Is Damien Favre still in charge over there? I remember Damien was always very personally involved with all of Granville-Beaufort's clients."

"Yes, of course. We met Damien once or twice. Didn't we, my dear?" he said, looking at me. "Very nice gentleman."

Monsieur Gurtmann stopped. "Damien Favre is a woman."

Shit.

I jumped in. "Oh, darling, you must be thinking of Denis, one of her assistants," I said quickly and turned to Monsieur Gurtmann. "You'll have to forgive my husband. He's terrible with names." I tried for a smile.

Monsieur Gurtmann's mouth went into an even thinner line.

We passed through a locked, barred doorway, which he opened with a key. But at the last moment, Monsieur Gurtmann stepped back through the doorway. "Oh dear," he said, slipping back. "I appear to have forgotten a set of keys. Please wait here a moment. I will return right away." The bars closed behind him.

With that, he disappeared around a corner, leaving us trapped in a locked corridor.

Oh, crap.

Chapter 32

Well, that did it. He knew, absolutely. Next would come the security officers, the police, and a jaunt in a Swiss prison. Swiss prisons held a reputation for being quite clean and civilized. Surprisingly, that didn't sway me one bit. The prospect held zero appeal for me.

I looked at Ethan. He was clearly thinking the exact same thing.

There was only one thing to do, and it certainly wasn't going to include waiting here. I gritted my teeth. We were going to have to escape.

Problem the first: we had little equipment. Our phones and Ethan's briefcase, with our most useful pieces of technology—glass cutters and jam shots to blow the locks off doors—were back at the front office. I had my purse, and our passports were inside. Much good they were to us now. Those images would likely be splashed on TV even if we did make it out of here.

Problem the second: we were inside an extremely high-tech secure facility. Their entire existence was to stop people exactly like us.

Although, to be fair, their emphasis was on stopping people like us from getting in. We didn't want to get in. We wanted to get out.

Problem the third: this place was drowning in security cameras. The instant we started to make a move, we would be seen. And then the artifice would be over, and they would simply send in a team to retrieve us. We needed to maintain the charade as long as we could.

And then get the hell out as fast as possible.

I assessed the situation while trying to slow my breathing. Three security cameras pointed at our exact location. The corridor was solid concrete, and the barred door was secured with a steel lock. How sensitive were the microphones on the security cameras? Would they pick up every word? We had to assume so. That was good; I could use that.

"Darling, I have to pee," I said in a stage whisper to Ethan. I clamped my knees together and did a ladylike impression of someone desperate to go to the washroom. "Do you think there's a restroom around here somewhere?"

I glanced at the CCTV and estimated the blind spot. I saw Ethan doing the same. Simultaneously, we made our way to the same location.

And then Ethan glanced at his Rolex. He pushed a couple of buttons, and I saw the briefest flash of red in the CCTV cameras and knew they were jammed. The feed would now show just an empty corridor.

I knew this would quickly become suspicious in itself, and that it was just a matter of time before we would hear alarms wailing. So we needed to move fast. But we also needed to move smart.

We had to get back through the locked door in front of us. I whipped off my four-inch black patent Louboutins and pulled a lock pick out of the left heel. In a matter of seconds we were through that door. As we moved through the building, Ethan scanned for CCTVs and jammed them just before we came into view. The longer we could keep up the charade, the closer we could get to the exit. And freedom.

Throughout this, images of Swiss prisons keep flashing in my brain. We made it through the next layers of lockdown. Hope burned in my chest—we just might get out of here.

And then the alarm sounded.

It blared, piercing and ripping through the air. For a thief, there is no sound quite so horror inducing as the sound of a burglar alarm puncturing the silence.

I froze. Suddenly, I didn't know what I needed to do next.

It was Ethan who basically dragged me into a run. There was

nothing else we could do—we had to get out of there, and sprinting was the only way.

The siren continued to scream as we ran at top speed through the stark corridors. I knew the guards were armed, and I knew they would not hesitate to use those weapons. We could hear them shouting. They were close, hunting us down like a pack of dogs.

We tucked into an alcove, hiding from the guards. "How are we going to get out of here?" I whispered. My heart was beating like a subwoofer in a teenager's pimped-out Honda.

Ethan peered out, monitoring for guards. He looked back at me. "I don't know."

"How about the loading bays?"

Ethan thought a beat, then nodded. "That might work. I think it's our only chance."

We needed to get down through the elevator shaft. But the only way to do that, and not get crushed by a descending elevator car, would be to lock it.

I hit the fire alarm on the wall next to the elevator. The screech of the alarm merely added to the din already coming from the intruder siren. Ethan prized the outer elevator doors open, then released the inner door restrictors and forced them apart.

Ethan clambered through first, going over the edge and hugging the wall of the elevator shaft to climb down it, and then I followed. I climbed out, fingers gripping the edge as I lowered myself down. I tried to slow my breathing. I attempted to focus on my contracting muscles and ignore the screaming that was happening in my head as I began my descent.

The elevator shaft was dark, with just a few glimmering linear lights marking each of the floors. Black cables hung around us like jungle vines, and my nose filled with the smell of grease. The elevator car was just above, locked up because of the alarm. The shaft dropped down into the darkness.

We climbed down the shaft, descending three levels to the bottom floor. When we reached the bottom floor, Ethan forced the doors open just a crack.

I peeked through. No guards were immediately visible. But, in contrast to the elevator shaft, there were plenty of CCTV cameras down here. Before climbing out, Ethan jammed those feeds with his Rolex.

As Ethan opened the elevator doors fully, I could see the muscles in his forearms working. We crawled out into the corridor of loading bays.

Dim emergency lights lined the corridor, illuminating painted cinder-block walls and a polished concrete floor. The air was warm, compared to the elevator shaft, and smelled of industrial cleaner and floor polish. I tasted blood in my mouth and realized I must have bitten my tongue during the descent. The adrenaline flooding my veins had dulled the pain.

There had to be guards down here somewhere. Most of their manpower would have been dispatched to guard the exit points on the main floor. But as I crept forward, I peered around a dark corner. Business was still operating as usual. Workers were loading crates from the loading bays into the trucks and unloading others from the trucks. Typical. The Swiss would never want their clients to know anything was amiss.

My eyes slid to the left. Two guards were stationed by the loading bays.

My stomach tightened. How were we going to take out the guards? We had no weapons. And Swiss guards were extremely well trained. They protected the Pope, for Christ's sake.

We needed something to draw out one of the guards. Both, ideally, but we could work with one. If we could get it down to one man and one weapon, we'd have a chance. Two people could maybe take on one man with an SG 550. And hopefully, nobody would get shot.

We huddled in an alcove and patched together a whispered plan. It was an old maneuver, but a classic, because it worked.

I waited until the workers were back in their trucks, out of view, and then I slipped back around a corner and placed my watch on the floor. With the watch's alarm set to go off in thirty seconds, there was enough time for me to get back into position.

I got back to Ethan just before the beeping started. The guards stiffened and went into full alert mode, which is a distinct disadvantage with this maneuver. Then they wordlessly decided how to respond. Disappointingly, only one of them left his post.

Once he'd disappeared, we had a matter of seconds to deal with the remaining guard.

"Remember the partner *shinobi* ambush maneuver we learned at that in-service over the winter?" Ethan whispered.

"Open triangle with a phoenix twist?" I asked, chewing my lip.

He nodded. "That's the one." He hesitated and fixed me with a steady gaze. "You got this, Montgomery?"

I nodded. I looked at the semiautomatic assault rifle the guard held, and swallowed. But there was no other way. This man was standing between me and freedom. He represented being locked up in a Swiss prison. Not to mention being shot. I did not want to die here, in this cold concrete building beside Geneva International Airport.

I had to get through him.

At Ethan's signal, we executed the ambush like a pair of ninjas. Before the guard had a chance to fire even once, we had taken him down.

But there was no time to celebrate. I heard the bootfalls of the first guard thundering back down the corridor.

Ethan quickly moved to a new position, and the instant the guard turned the corner, Ethan took him down with a maneuver so fast and physical, I hardly even saw it.

He stood over the unconscious guard, breathing heavily, stance broad, fists tight.

In spite of myself, my heart gave a schoolgirl quiver at the sight of him like that. "You know, Ethan, you still haven't told me how you became so well trained in combat techniques," I said.

"I'd be happy to, Montgomery, but I'm thinking now isn't exactly the best time."

"Probably right."

At the far end of the exit bay, two trucks were being loaded. The drivers showed no sign of noticing the scuffle that had happened on our end, and the fire alarm was being thoroughly ignored. No surprise there. Everybody always ignored fire alarms.

Now the rolling aluminum door was the only thing standing in the way of freedom. We were almost out.

"We'll have to sneak into a truck. Let them drive us out of here, unseen," Ethan said. "We wait until the one at the end has loaded everything. Then we'll sneak in and hide under the canvas packing."

We slipped along on the exact route we had mapped out, tucked out of view of both the camera feeds and the truck drivers. When the drivers lit up a cigarette each and stood chatting by the cabs of their vehicles, that was our moment. We snuck onto the back of one of the trucks and hid ourselves under canvas.

After another minute, the back door of the truck slammed shut, plunging us into even more darkness.

The greasy canvas was heavy and rough and smelled like old boots. The floor of the truck vibrated as the engine suddenly started up. My left side heated up with the warmth of Ethan's proximity.

I felt the truck drive up the ramp, exit the gate, and then drive forward to the security checkpoint. We paused at the exit. I heard muffled chatter and held my breath. Would they stop to look in the back?

I prayed they hadn't yet figured out that we had gone down to the loading bays. Could they still be chasing our shadows on the upper floors?

I squeezed my fists tightly. A crack of light allowed me to glimpse Ethan, crouched beside me under the canvas. I could see the tension in his every muscle from the position he held. He turned, and we locked eyes. We were utterly trapped. All we could do was wait.

Chapter 33

Ethan felt like the wait would never end. If they came back here—if someone checked the back of the truck—what would he do? He glanced at Montgomery, felt her tension as she huddled there beside him. She was nervous, obviously, but he could also tell she was ready to go. Ready to deal with whatever came through the back of the truck next.

She'd been battling fear since he'd found her in Paris, but Ethan could see she still had all the tools, all the tenacity she needed. The way she'd handled herself during their escape had shown him. If only she could grasp that.

Still, Ethan felt an overpowering urge to protect her. And right now he did not like his chances of being able to do that. He was blind, had no idea how many guards were outside, if they were armed, and if they had sniffed out the two fugitives making their escape in the truck.

The wait dragged on.

And then, after what felt like an eternity, the brakes released with a hiss. The truck started moving again with a shudder and a bump. Ethan breathed as the truck continued rolling forward.

The vehicle trundled along the road for a few minutes, and then the driver stopped for gas. Ethan could hear other vehicles at the station, smell the gasoline.

When the gas tank door on the truck snapped shut and the driver went in to pay, that was when Ethan and Cat snuck out the back.

It was over. They were out.

They hailed a cab back to the train station. It was time to return to Paris.

Less than an hour later, Ethan helped Cat climb onto the train at Gare de Cornavin in Geneva. Not that she needed it; the girl was more than capable. Somehow, she just stirred his chivalrous side.

They made their way through the lounge car with its rows of red fabric-covered seats. Ethan pulled hard on the heavy suctioned door, and they entered a first-class car. They squeezed through a narrow corridor, looking for an unoccupied compartment.

Ethan checked the time on the cheap flip phone he'd bought in the train station, the replacement for the phone he'd been forced to leave behind in Monsieur Gurtmann's office. They'd be back in Paris by early evening.

After what they'd just been through, Ethan was looking forward to this train ride back to Paris. A little quality time with his favorite crook was just what his soul needed. The chemistry between them was undeniable. Montgomery had to know it, too.

They found an empty berth and flopped down on the smooth bench seats, opposite each other. He looked at her, thinking about the details of their escape.

"You were amazing, by the way," Ethan said to Cat. "Back there."

She shrugged and rolled her eyes. "Hardly." Ethan enjoyed the way she blushed a little as she said that.

"I'm serious," he said. "The way you picked that lock in the Freeport corridor . . . You're like lightning. You know that, right?"

At that point, the food cart arrived with sandwiches and coffee. They ate and drank and chatted companionably.

They were a good team. He knew it. She had to feel it, too, right?

If only there wasn't that damn FBI agent in the picture. Ethan knew Cat was still emotionally attached to Jack and on paper they were still a couple. But it didn't make sense. A thief and a cop? It couldn't work. She'd see that soon enough.

But why was he even thinking along these lines? The last thing

Ethan wanted was a serious relationship that was going to give him a hassle and tie him down. Wasn't it?

Ethan stared out the window at the passing countryside, the rolling vineyards of the Burgundy region, leafy and pastoral under a late afternoon sun.

Cat pulled out a tablet from the backpack they'd stashed at the train station upon first arriving in Geneva. She'd downloaded photos from her micro-camera and was reviewing the images. Her small notepad, with the notes she'd gathered in the freeport, rested on the table beside her.

"Breaking into that vault is going to be tricky," Ethan said. "Do you see a way?"

Cat was frowning as she pored over their data. "They've got pretty much every security measure imaginable. I need a loophole somewhere. . . ." She flipped through more photos. "Here," she said. "These are the photographs of the vault itself. Take a look."

She moved across the seats and slid in beside him so they could both look at the tablet screen. Her hair smelled great. How was that even possible after all they'd been through?

Ethan tried hard to focus on the photographs. And then he saw something interesting. "There. Can you zoom in on that?" he said.

"What? Here?" Cat zoomed in on a part of the vault door.

As she pulled her fingers across the screen and the photo zoomed in some more, they both froze. The magnification had revealed an inscribed name on the vault door. The name of the manufacturer: Stratford & Black.

"Oh, shit. That's not good," Ethan said.

"No, it's definitely not," Cat said.

The problem with Stratford & Black was that their combination locks were among the most challenging to manipulate. They had an incredibly annoying tendency to use serrated wheels with false tumbler notches.

Cracking that safe would be an absolute bitch.

Cat flopped back in her seat. "I think I need a new approach. I don't know if I can get to it that way," she said. "And then there's that flooding thing Lafayette mentioned. . . ."

Ethan looked at her sharply. "Do you believe that?"

Cat shrugged. "I don't know. But if it *is* true?" She frowned.

"Right. You know what we need?" Ethan said, standing up. "A distraction. And a real drink. Something a little stiffer than coffee."

They made their way to the lounge car, and for a few minutes, Cat seemed to be enjoying herself. She laughed as Ethan relayed some of his adventures in Rome. They had a heated discussion about the various ways to overcome infrared security systems.

"But the thing is, Montgomery, all that high-tech security stuff . . . that's not really what being a thief is about," Ethan said, taking a sip of his frosty Heineken. "I mean, you have to take care of that stuff. Like eating your veggies. But it's just about making a level playing field. Then, once you've canceled out the high-tech stuff, the rest is down to finesse. The rest is up to you and your skills. That's what being a thief is really about. It's an art. Way more than a science."

She was looking at him with a strange expression. "I couldn't put it better myself. That's exactly what I think, too."

He smiled. "Like I've said before, babe, we're the same."

The train sped through a town, and Cat turned her face to the window. Tile-roofed stone houses, embroidered with vines, clustered together beside the tracks. Cat frowned, lost in thought again.

Ethan put his hand on hers. "You okay? Are you thinking about the job again? Never mind, Montgomery. We'll figure it out." He flagged down the waiter. "Here, have another drink with me."

Ethan could see the struggle on her face. "I—I think I just need to get some rest," she said. "I'm going to go back to the compartment and lie down. You don't mind, do you?"

Ethan looked at her carefully. Was this a proposition? Did she want company?

Ethan had spent a lot of time in his life analyzing the actions and language of women. This could go one of two ways. On paper, this could easily be a proposition. He was meant to follow. Or it could be the opposite.

But everything about her body language, her tone of voice suggested that there was nothing to read between the lines here. She wasn't interested in having company in that private car. She genuinely just wanted a nap.

"Of course I don't mind," Ethan said, covering his disappointment. "You need rest. Go ahead. I'll wake you before we get there, okay?"

She looked at him with unmistakable gratitude for not making things difficult. She'd experienced her fair share of come-ons, Ethan was willing to bet.

After Cat left, Ethan sat back in his chair and drank another Heineken. He stared out the window. The scenery was spectacular, but Ethan hardly noticed it. He was too much in his head. Maybe he should just give up. Cat was clearly committed to Jack. Why was he even bothering?

After five minutes of brooding, Ethan sensed someone by his table. He looked up to see a stranger standing there. A beautiful female stranger, a blonde with crystal-blue eyes and arched brows.

"Do you have a mobile phone I can use?" she asked with a faint German accent. "My battery just died, and I need to make a call."

Ethan reached into his pocket. "Sure. Here you go. Please, have a seat," he said graciously, indicating the empty seat across from him.

She sat down, explaining with an apology that she needed to ring the friend who was picking her up in Paris. She made her call, speaking in quick, passionate German, while Ethan watched her with great interest.

She hung up, eyes flashing with annoyance, and handed his phone back to him.

Ethan raised an eyebrow. "You look like you could use a drink," he said, then called the waiter over. "This woman needs a martini. Three olives. And the good gin, please. None of that Gordon's stuff. Hendrick's, if you have it."

The woman smiled, charmed.

It was just so damn easy.

As they chatted, Ethan sipped his beer and she, her martini. She laughed with abandon as he told a story about encountering a band of gypsies outside Bucharest, Romania. She started looking at him under coy eyelashes, and her face grew a little more flushed.

After the gypsy story, she mentioned in passing that she could read palms. He held out his upturned hand to her, accepting the challenge. She took it in her cool hands and started tracing the lines with her fingertip.

Ethan knew exactly where this could go if he wanted it to.

But did he want it to? It would be fun. And diverting. But could he get Cat out of his head long enough to enjoy himself?

Damn that little thief for working her way under his skin.

He had vaguely heard the woman make some reference to her private car and was about to politely give her a story about being in a serious relationship when, just at that moment, Cat arrived at the table. She looked vaguely rumpled, like she'd been tossing and turning. It was an unbelievably cute look for her.

Ethan pulled his hand away from the woman's and quickly erased the look of guilt on his face. Because it was ridiculous. He didn't owe Cat anything.

Cat stared at Ethan, at the table with their empty rounds of drinks, at the woman with her bare feet curled up under her. . . .

"Oh," Cat said. "Um, my apologies for interrupting. I just thought of something I was going to say, Ethan, but it can wait—"

"No, it's fine," Ethan said quickly. "We were just talking. Montgomery, this is—" And at that moment, something happened that had never happened to Ethan before. He forgot the woman's name. He stumbled and stuttered for a minute. Cat rolled her eyes. Worse was the look growing on the woman's face.

"It's *Galiena*," she said, angrily packing up her things. "Thank you for the drinks, *Ethan*," she said through her teeth. So now he was the asshole. Why did it always revert to that?

Ethan watched her go and didn't try to stop her. It was pointless. He looked at Cat's face. Her arms were crossed, and she looked vaguely disgusted.

Shit. Two women pissed off at him during one short train ride across the Swiss-French border. It had to be a record for him.

"Well, that didn't take long," Cat said.

"What? Me, offending a woman?"

She stared at him frostily. "No, you meeting someone. Chatting them up. Sorry I messed things up for you."

"No. Believe me, it doesn't matter." Ethan drained the last of his beer. "So? What was it? The thing you wanted to say?"

Cat glanced at him uncertainly. "Well, I had an idea." She seemed to be struggling over whether to stay annoyed with him or just dive into her story. Judging from the gleam in her eye, whatever her idea was, it was a big one.

"Okay, let's hear it. Have a seat," he said.

She did and leaned forward. "Well, I was thinking. We need to come up with a new plan. Because cracking that vault is going to be impossible. And I thought, what is the only other option available to us?" She paused, giving him a chance to come up with it on his own, barely able to contain her excitement now.

He waited. "I don't know, Montgomery. You're killing me. Just tell me."

She took a breath. "We steal it directly from the display case."

"What? While it's out on the floor? While everyone is looking?"

"I know it sounds crazy. But there's one time it's going to come out of the display case."

Ethan raised an eyebrow. "I'm listening."

"During the gala. On the last night of the exhibit, before the Hope goes back to Washington. Three people are going to win the privilege of wearing the Hope. They're going to take it out then and put it around the neck of each contest winner. Just for a few minutes."

Ethan got chills. "Now, *that's* interesting."

Cat's face grew even more animated. "I know. And I was thinking if *I* were one of those people . . . well, maybe that could be my chance."

Ethan narrowed his eyes. "Okay, but let's just say for a sec that you could actually finagle things to be one of the winners. How are you going to take it in front of everyone like that?"

She frowned slightly. "I'm not sure, exactly, but if there was some kind of distraction . . . I have pretty good sleight of hand. I could step it up with practice. . . . You know, stage magicians do this kind of thing all the time."

Cat went on to tell him that she'd done it before. In the Harlequin job, she had stolen the jewel from a display case during a party. But it was a much lesser gem and hadn't had as much security.

Ethan rubbed his jaw, thinking. "You know what? I think you may have it, Montgomery."

She beamed.

He leaned forward, toward her. "We need to hammer out some details. You're going to need a lot of practice, and we'll have to get tickets to the gala. And figure out a way to fix you as the winner." His gears were locking on now, rotating faster.

She nodded. "And one other big thing," she said, nibbling a fingernail.

"What?"

"We're going to need a really good fake Hope Diamond."

Chapter 34

After our train pulled into Gare de Lyon in Paris, Ethan headed back to his hotel and I went to mine. Although it was mildly inconvenient to be staying in separate hotels, I was somewhat thankful. The lines were getting blurred enough, and things were confusing enough, thank you very much, without adding hotel coziness to the mix.

Plus, I was exhausted. I had visions of a hot shower and a long sleep.

But when I returned to my hotel, there was a surprise waiting for me. I walked into the lobby, and sitting there in an armchair, reading a newspaper, with a small carry-on suitcase, was Jack.

I blinked and halted in my steps. "Jack! Oh my God, you're here. What are you doing here?"

In the back of my mind, there hovered a very relieved woman who was counting her lucky stars that Ethan was not staying in this hotel. We could have easily been strolling into this lobby together. And that would have been difficult to explain.

I dropped my bag and rushed over to him. But as I did so, I noticed his face looked somewhat less than pleased.

"Oh, have you been here . . . a long time?" I asked hesitantly when I reached him.

I wanted to embrace him. Standing this close, I suddenly craved the feeling of his body. He looked amazing. Black T-shirt and jeans, hair a little rumpled from the flight maybe, and a bit of scruffiness . . . but he didn't seem in quite the right mood to be touched.

"If you consider six hours a long time," he replied, looking up at me.

Ah.

He put his newspaper down with a snap. "Where the hell were you, Cat? Nobody here knew where you'd gone, and you weren't answering your cell."

I sat down in the armchair beside him. "Jack, you know I can't always tell you where I'm going or what I'm doing."

He stared at me, tightening and releasing his jaw. He knew I was right. It didn't make it any easier, though.

I put a hand on his leg; I could feel the muscles underneath his jeans. "Why don't we go upstairs? We can keep talking there, if you like. And order room service maybe?"

With a whole lot of silent treatment, we took the elevator up to my suite. He carried both bags.

I had a ton of questions. I wanted to know how long he could stay in Paris, what had changed his mind about coming, how the flight had been . . . everything. But his body language was about as open as a bank on Sunday, and he clearly had a bunch of pent-up annoyance from waiting in a hotel lobby all day, wondering if I was dead in a ditch somewhere. So I left him stewing in front of the TV, watching tennis, while I ordered some food to be brought up.

"I'm just going to hop in the shower," I called from the bedroom. No response. I padded into the marble bathroom.

The hot water felt like a miracle. It washed off all the remaining stress and exhaustion of my day. What a crazy day that had been. Images of our narrow escape flashed through my head as the steam surrounded me.

Then the bathroom door flung open. I jumped, and the shampoo bottle went flying.

"It's just . . . I *worry* about you," Jack said in a sudden outburst, striding into the bathroom. "I know you have to keep the details to yourself. *I know,* okay? But at the same time, I just need to know you're safe."

Jack pulled the steamy shower door open, practically ripping it off the hinges. He had more to say.

He stood in the bathroom, in front of the open shower door, his face full of anger and passion. "I've spent the past six hours imagining all kinds of horrendous things happening to you. You could have been injured, trapped, dead somewhere. I can't stand it. I just . . . I want to protect you at all times."

"Um—"

"I know it's not an answerable problem," he continued, barreling on. "Lord knows, I am well aware of that." He scrubbed a hand through his hair. My initial shock had passed now, and my face softened as I watched him struggle for words, and struggle with his emotions. "But . . ."

He trailed off here, and then his eyes focused on me in a different way. And suddenly he was climbing into the shower with me, clothes and all, and reaching for my face to kiss me with desperate, hungry kisses. His hands were all over me, and then I was tearing at his soaking clothes, and the hot water just kept running over our bare skin.

I think a while later room service knocked on the door, but food was the very last thing on either of our minds.

The next morning, I woke up with a smile, Jack sleeping peacefully beside me between the cool sheets of the giant hotel bed.

I stretched and luxuriated there for a minute, and then I remembered. I had important things that had to get done today. Ethan and I had put together a detailed plan of action yesterday. He was going to be working on securing blueprints and schematics, and I had my own mission.

I climbed out of bed to get started, tiptoeing quietly away. Jack could keep sleeping; there was no need to wake him.

I opened my laptop to confirm a couple of things with Gladys and began getting dressed at the same time. I had a lot of work to do. When I was partway through an e-mail with her, Jack walked out of the bedroom. He looked unbelievably sexy in the hotel robe, rubbing the remnants of sleepiness off of his face.

"How is it possible that you look so awake . . . and you haven't even had coffee yet?" he said, voice gravelly from sleep.

"Ah, but that's where you're wrong." I rolled the desk chair out of his line of view, revealing the tray of breakfast pastries and fruit and hot coffee that I'd had brought up. "Ta-da."

He beamed and reached for the food.

While he ate, I finished composing my e-mail to Gladys and sent it. And then I sat back, frowning slightly. Today was going to require some fancy footwork.

Getting me listed as the contest winner was easy enough. Gladys was already on it. And of course, we could get our names on the gala guest list the same way, but there was a problem with doing it like that. I knew that when we turned up in front of the security guards, we would need to produce the actual printed invitations.

So Gladys had hacked into Louvre e-mail and had learned that the gala invitations were being taken to the museum today. The events coordinator's assistant was picking them up at the print shop and was due to arrive at the Louvre later this morning. Somehow, I needed to liberate three. One for me, one for Ethan, and one for Brooke.

I didn't actually know yet if Brooke would be willing to come along as an extra pair of eyes, but I hoped I could convince her. And bribe her with a ticket.

So today my plan was to go and wait outside the Louvre, by the Porte des Lions entrance, for the assistant to arrive with the invitations.

But there was a problem. I chewed my lip and turned slightly to look sideways at Jack, who was contentedly biting into a croissant and flipping the pages of *Le Monde.*

"Jack, you know, you still haven't explained why you decided to come to Paris, after all," I said with a light tone.

He looked up from the paper. "Well, the idea of us being in Paris together was just too good to resist," he said. Then he grinned. "Besides, I know how Frenchmen are. I couldn't leave you to fend them off alone."

I laughed, but I couldn't help wondering, did he really mean Frenchmen? Or Ethan?

And then I studied him carefully. I knew he was involved in an investigation with the Interpol agent Hendrickx. Was that the real reason for his arrival in Paris? But the FBI had no official jurisdiction here. So what was he doing?

Problem was, I really needed to get to the Louvre and intercept those gala invitations. But Jack had flown all the way over here. I couldn't just abandon him. After everything that had happened lately, I had to do some damage control on my relationship.

But maybe I could do both.

And then I got an idea. *Bicycles.* Paris has little stations for renting bikes all over the city. We could borrow bicycles—nice and romantic—and go to the Tuileries together. It was a nice day, so we could lounge in the gardens . . . and then casually make our way over to the part of the Tuileries adjacent to the Louvre. I could stake out the Porte des Lions entrance and canoodle with Jack at the same time.

I proposed the plan and had to feign extreme enthusiasm to get Jack on board. He was all for spending the day in bed together with coffee and croissants as our sole nourishment.

Eventually, he agreed.

An hour later we were lounging in the lush greenery of the Tuileries Garden. I had positioned myself so I had a clear view of the Porte des Lions doorway—a grand arched door flanked by two green-copper lions. This was not the public entrance under the pyramid; it was the entrance used by staff and VIPs, among others.

The plan: I'd knock her down with my bicycle. I wasn't going to hurt her, of course, but I did expect the box to go flying. Then I could help her pick it up and would palm three invitations in the process.

I knew the box would be only loosely closed—one of the instructions in the e-mail was for her to check the invitations before leaving the shop, to make sure they were printed properly.

It was an overcast day, typical for spring in Paris. A fresh breeze moved gray clouds across the sky. It wasn't raining yet, but that probably wasn't far off. The air carried a metallic scent, the ozone smell of sparks that heralded rain.

The threatening weather didn't seem to discourage tourists. I glanced over my shoulder and watched people trundling toward the Louvre's main entrance, heading in and out of the museum like honeybees in a hive.

Mostly, I kept my gaze fastened on the Porte des Lions door. And so far, I hadn't seen anyone who matched the description of the assistant. But that was okay. I just had to be patient—

"Cat, are you listening to me?" Jack said, his voice slicing into my thoughts. "Did you hear what I just said?"

"Yes, of course," I said with a smile. "I just . . . I just got distracted by the traffic over there. . . ."

He nodded but looked somewhat skeptical.

"French drivers are insane, aren't they?" I said halfheartedly, with a short laugh. I had to work harder at paying attention to the conversation with Jack. But I couldn't ignore the entrance.

I asked him about his flight overseas, how long he had managed to get off for vacation, that sort of thing. All the while keeping half an eye on my objective.

Then he stopped talking again. "Cat, why are we here, really?" he asked abruptly.

I didn't like the sound of that. "What do you mean?" I kept my tone breezy.

"Well, is it really a coincidence that we're here, right across from the Louvre? I mean, maybe you've forgotten I work for the FBI."

I tried to laugh, but it came out rather brittle. "Oh, Jack, you're so suspicious. I guess that's part of the job, huh?" I was sure he noticed I didn't deny his accusation. "Anyway, tell me more about what you were just saying. You had an idea for what we should do tonight? A boat cruise on the Seine?"

One eyebrow rose as he looked at me sideways. "Cat. That's not what I was saying. Now I know you weren't listening."

Crap.

And I was about to lob another recovery when I saw somebody who looked a lot like the assistant emerge from the gardens and start walking in the direction of the Porte des Lions. *Damn.* This needed my full attention. I flicked my eyes back to Jack. He had leaned back against a low stone wall, sipping his water bottle.

"It's fine, Cat," he said. "Do whatever you need to do. I'll be sitting right here whenever you're ready."

I couldn't tell if he was pissed or amused. Or a little of column A, a little of column B.

The girl got closer. She was definitely headed toward the lions. Now I could see her better, and she looked exactly like the photograph: flame-red hair, tortoiseshell glasses, round, sweet face. And she carried a box.

I had to make my move. "I'll be right back, Jack. I, um—" But I didn't have any time to offer an explanation.

I hopped on my bike and headed down a gravel path, straight for the girl. To make it appear like an accident, I looked down at my phone, pretending to be distracted.

"Watch where you're going!" came the shriek in French as I veered away from her at the last second.

My reflexes were much faster than hers, but she made an attempt at lunging out of the way of my bicycle. Which sent her flying and tripping and sprawling on the pathway.

The box also went flying, as predicted. But, distinctly not as predicted, it rolled on the ground intact. The top remained tightly sealed with packing tape.

Damn. I picked up the box and for a brief second considered running away with the whole thing. But that wasn't going to work. Stealing the invitations would raise an alarm. Then they'd be vigilant with the guest list, and getting into the gala would become a big hassle. No, I really needed to get three invitations out of the box in a subtle manner.

At that moment, I heard Jack's voice.

"Oh, madam, that was a nasty fall. . . ."

I turned around. Jack had arrived at the girl's side.

"Stay sitting, please," he was saying. "I'm a doctor. I need to check you for head injuries." He was speaking in English. In spite of the language, the girl seemed to understand.

She made an attempt at standing, uttering an embarrassed "*Non, non . . .*"

But Jack placed a hand on her shoulder and gazed gently into her eyes. His face was full of concern. I recognized the look he was giving her. It was one that had frequently turned my own knees to jelly.

I knew how French people felt about Americans. They weren't exactly fans. But an American doctor who looked exactly like a professional athlete would, perhaps, be an exception.

The woman nodded. "*D'accord . . . ,*" she said faintly.

Jack looked over his shoulder at me. "Mademoiselle," he said to me, "please guard her belongings, will you?"

I nodded. I realized what was happening, of course. Jack was helping me. He was giving me a chance to do what I needed to do.

I had no time to question why. I grabbed the opportunity; I'd deal with the confusion later.

While he "checked her for head injuries," I turned slightly away, holding the box tight with one hand. With the other hand, I slipped two fingers into my purse and withdrew a lock pick—something I always carried—and sliced open the tape. I slid my hand inside the box and grabbed three invitations.

"That should do it," Jack was saying. "I think you're going to be just fine."

I tucked the invitations in my purse, then turned back around. I handed her the box with an apologetic smile. "I'm afraid the box tape may have opened a little when it fell," I said, hoping she wasn't sharp enough to question this.

She looked at me for a minute, hesitating, then said, "Oh, thank you. *Merci.*"

I exhaled. It was okay. She was still a little dazed from the fall, and from her close encounter with a handsome American doctor.

Mission accomplished.

Unfortunately, I now had to figure out what to do about Jack. Because suddenly I had an FBI agent who was not merely investigating my work, but getting *involved in it.*

Chapter 35

"No, no, no," Brooke was saying to me. "You need more misdirecting flourishes with your left hand. Okay, no, that's too much." She sighed with exasperation.

We were in Ethan's hotel suite at the Ritz, lavish rooms appointed with damask curtains and tufted furniture. Room service had brought up a tray of steaming coffee and pastries for us. I glanced over and my stomach groaned, but I wasn't stopping until I had mastered this.

Jack, surprisingly, had let me off the hook after the invitation incident. He had refrained from asking me any questions and had simply nodded when I said I had some work to do.

Or maybe it wasn't such a surprise, given our unspoken agreement.

Things were falling into place for the Louvre job. We had tickets to the gala. Gladys had finagled it so I would be one of the winners. But it would be all for nothing if I couldn't learn to seamlessly swap the jewel.

As a professional thief, you have to possess good sleight of hand. It's part of the job. But in this situation, "good" was not going to be good enough. My preferred modus operandi had always been to sneak in, snatch the target, and sneak out. Nobody sees me, I don't see anyone. It's all very covert, and the jewels just disappear like magic.

But this job was going to flex my skills in a whole new way.

"We're going to need some kind of distraction," Brooke said.

"Hmm . . . How much of a distraction?" Ethan asked, munching on a Danish pastry. He'd been watching and coaching me through this along with Brooke.

"Not much," said Brooke. "Couple of seconds, really. Something brief, something plausible." She looked at me. "If we can get the focus off you even for a microsecond, you'll be able to do it."

"What about a loud noise?" Ethan suggested. "A siren? A fire alarm? The band?"

"The fire alarm, I think," Brooke said, nodding. "It's so cliché, it's almost fresh."

I shook my head. "Nobody ever gets excited about smoke alarms going off," I said. "If we're expecting people to go running and screaming, leaving me alone with the Hope Diamond, we're going to need to think again."

"That's not what I envision," Brooke said. "All you need is a moment. The instant the alarm goes off, people's attention will be pulled away, and that includes all the guards. It'll just be a second, but that's all you're going to need to swap the Hope for a fake."

It sounded about as possible as achieving a salon-quality blowout at home. I looked at her dubiously.

"Here's how you're going to do it," she continued. We had made a mock-up display case, and we had two fake necklaces—a red and a blue one, trinkets we'd bought at a flea market—for practice.

She took the red necklace and tucked it up her sleeve. The blue one she clasped around her neck. She kept her arms up, as if she was fiddling with the clasp.

"Okay, Ethan, cough or something," she said.

Ethan coughed right at the moment Brooke took a step forward and kind of stumbled a little, letting her hair drop down in front of her a bit. All I saw was a twitch and a flourish, and then she straightened up. The necklaces had been switched. The red necklace was now around her neck, and there was no sign of the blue one.

I blinked. "Wow. That was amazing."

"Where did you put it?" Ethan asked.

She beamed at us. "I let it drop right down my top." She removed the red necklace, then reached into her top and pulled out the blue one. "That's how it's done, Cat. And that's how you're going to do it."

On one hand, it was exciting to see that it was actually possible. On the other hand, it was terrifying. Could I really pull it off? Brooke had executed it, but maybe she was the only one who could do it. Were my skills up to the task?

"You're going to need practice," Brooke said. "A lot of practice. And we're going to have to time it perfectly. You'll have to know the instant before the alarm sounds."

"That's no problem," Ethan said. "We'll be connected via ear-pieces."

Brooke handed me the necklaces, and I gave it another try. *Okay . . . you can do this, Cat. You own this . . .*

The necklaces dropped to the floor with a loud clatter. Both of them.

Ethan winced, then quickly recovered. "It's cool, Montgomery," he said. "You got this. You just need to work on it a bit."

Brooke showed me again. I watched her do it a few times. She slowed it down, did it in slow motion until I saw how she actually did it. Where she put her hands, how she moved the two necklaces back and forth, going from visible to invisible, and vice versa. "Got it?"

I tried again.

The necklace got tangled in my hair.

I sighed. "Brooke, maybe you could just do this for me? It would be a piece of cake for you."

"No can do, sugarplum. LNY would fire me. Kill me first and then fire me." Her tone indicated the matter was nonnegotiable.

It was no good looking at Ethan, either. There were no men in the contest to wear the Hope Diamond. Nope, it would have to be me.

Fine. I could do this.

"Don't get discouraged, babe," Ethan said. "You just need more practice. I've seen you pickpocket, and you're flawless at that. You can totally do this."

So I practiced. Over and over. But as I worked at it, a niggling little concern came into play.

I would be up on the stage, surrounded by Louvre guards. Louvre guards carried semiautomatic weapons. If I made a mistake . . .

Just thinking about it, I felt my heart start picking up pace. What if . . . what if I had a panic attack while I was up there?

I nibbled a fingernail and looked at Brooke and Ethan. I didn't particularly want to admit this fear to either of them right then.

But Ethan seemed to be reading my mind. "You don't have to worry, Montgomery. Magicians go onstage to do this in front of everyone all the time."

"I know," I said. "But if *they* make a mistake, they're not going to get shot. Or thrown in prison."

He shrugged. "True. But it would be the end of their professional careers."

Just like it would be for mine. And then some.

Chapter 36

Later that afternoon Brooke and I went to Les Puces, the flea market at Porte de Clignancourt. We had a very particular goal: to find a replica Hope Diamond. And it couldn't be just any old fake. We needed one that was virtually flawless.

It was exactly the sort of thing that would slip through official cracks, though, forgotten in somebody's attic for years, then turn up with the rest of their estate at a flea market.

Brooke wrinkled her nose in distaste as we climbed out of our cab just outside the market. Les Puces is in a rather undesirable neighborhood of Paris, and clustered around the outside of the flea market was an infestation of stalls filled with cheap clothing and replica football shirts. The air smelled of frying onions and falafel and sausages on food trucks and carts. I thought it smelled delicious, actually, but we didn't have time to stop for a bite.

Inside the enormous central pavilion of the flea market, however, the atmosphere changed. The air was powdery with the old-fashioned smells of perfume and talc and mildew. And the bargaining in here was less raucous. More of the cajoling variety, almost genteel. Music floated through the two-storied antiques market, a scratchy recording on a phonograph.

Still, I was on the lookout for cutpurses and con men. It would be a huge irony to be pickpocketed in here. And this sort of place was a pickpocket's office.

In fact, I witnessed a couple of street thieves operating as we wove our way through the stalls outside. It was fascinating, really, to see them in operation. It made me wonder how other people didn't see what was so plainly in front of them.

On the second level of the market, Brooke was rifling through a display of old locks, and I was studying a table of antique costume jewelry. Flea markets are wonderful places for a criminal to pick up supplies. For one thing, there's no record of sale. And you can find many interesting things that aren't available through traditional merchants. Old lock picks, for example, and grappling hooks and varied other bric-a-brac. People collect these things as curiosities.

We were finding many things, but none of them was a replica Hope.

I looked up from the jewelry table then and saw a sign for a fortune-teller. I peered into the alcove, and the face of the fortune-teller I'd seen in Montmartre stared back at me.

There was no mistaking Esmerelda as she stood at the entrance, tucked beside a heavy curtain: petite, masses of curly brown hair, and that faint scar on her left cheekbone.

Why she was here, I had no idea. Maybe she was helping out a friend. Or branching out. Her shop, perhaps, had burned down. Who knew? Regardless, here she was.

The minute I saw the fortune-teller, I knew I had to talk to her. Not because I wanted to know my fortune, but because my previous encounter with her had caused such a loss of sleep, I needed to re-assure myself somehow that it was a bunch of baloney. That it was parlor trickery.

I glanced over at Brooke and saw that she was engrossed in ne-gotiations with a stall merchant. I would slip into the fortune-teller's shop for only a few minutes. I didn't need to tell Brooke. Truthfully, I felt foolish, and I wasn't in the mood for merciless teasing from her just now.

When I stepped into the alcove, the fortune-teller recognized me instantly—I could tell by the way her eyes came alive.

"Sit. Please," she said, pointing to a scarf-covered stool. The alcove smelled the same as fortune-tellers' stalls the world over: faintly smoky, fragrant with incense.

"You think it is a coincidence we happen to be here at the same time," she said. "Let me assure you, it is not a coincidence."

I took a seat.

"This was intended," she continued. "By the fates and by the stars."

I ignored all this. I didn't have a lot of time. "I need to know if I have anything to, um . . ." I didn't know which words to choose. I wanted to know if I had anything to fear, if the curse of the Hope Diamond was at all, well, *real*. But I felt ridiculous even uttering the phrase.

The fortune-teller wasn't concerned about my unfinished question. She gave me an impenetrable look, and then one smooth, cool hand grasped mine.

She spent a lot of time looking at my hand and then my face. Was she reading my reactions? My aura? *What?*

"You are concerned about a curse," she said. "Are you not?"

A shiver slid down my spine. I nodded.

She pulled out her old tarot deck. "The answer is in the cards."

She turned over six cards one by one and placed them in a cross pattern. I recognized some of the cards she turned over—some were the same as the ones from before, in Montmartre. I had no idea if that was unusual. How many cards were in a tarot deck, anyway?

And then the fortune-teller turned over two more cards. I stared at them. The Knight. And the *Bateleur.* The Trickster.

I swallowed. "What about those cards? What do they mean?"

"You have two men in your life. You will have to make a choice."

She had said the very same thing in Montmartre. I still didn't understand how she could know. She had to just be saying things that would be universally true for anyone sitting in front of her. Right? Anybody's "fortune" could be shaped and massaged to suit the circumstances. I forced myself to believe that.

But I struggled. I felt pulled under by the convincingness of it all.

"How can I make that choice?" I asked in a low voice.

She gazed at me. "You need to look into your heart."

I looked at the cards spread in front of her. Two more cards were still unturned. I glanced at my watch. My time was up. Brooke's haggling was probably over by now. I didn't relish the idea of explaining all this to her. I wanted to wrap this up and get out of here. But the unturned cards were impossible to resist.

I pointed at them. "What about those?"

She raised an eyebrow, then reached for the remaining cards and turned them over.

The Queen of Diamonds. And *La Mort,* Death.

My mouth went dry. I blinked at the pair of cards, trying to hide my reaction.

"These images scare you," she said. Evidently, I was not doing a good job.

"What do they mean?" I asked, my voice little more than a whisper.

"Within the most precious things always lies a heart of danger. And whenever humans become tangled with such things, strife will always follow. Strife and death. This much has always been true, and will always be true."

Of course this was true. The race to possess, the desperation for riches . . . Human history is full of bloody incidents caused by that desperation. Especially when it comes to diamonds, with their unique strength, designed by nature to endure beyond human will. You can try to destroy them, but more likely, they will destroy you.

"You are afraid," she said. "I can see that. And fear can cloud judgment. So *what* do you fear?"

"I-I don't know. The same things most people fear. Pain. Death. Dying."

The fortune-teller gazed at me with that penetrating stare again. Her eye color was peculiar—hazel, with green rims.

"You are in danger," she said simply.

"But I'm in grave danger if I stop," I said hoarsely. More to myself than to her. I couldn't back out of the Hope job, because Faulkner would take his retribution.

She nodded solemnly. "There is no easy choice."

"Can you tell me what I should do?" I knew I sounded ridiculous, like a pathetic, gullible idiot. But I couldn't help it.

Then, behind me, someone cleared her throat. "Well, I never figured you as the believing type."

I turned. Brooke stood behind me, her mouth twisted in a wry smile. I cringed.

But then I looked past her and saw someone else I recognized. My heart stopped for a second as I shrank back out of view and pulled Brooke with me. In the stall across the corridor, looking down at something on a table, was Sean Reilly, the other thief who was going after the Hope.

I peered around the fortune-teller's curtain, watching Reilly for several seconds. There was no sign he was aware of my presence. He was thumbing through some old books, not trying to hide or be furtive. He glanced at his watch.

I had to accept the possibility he had followed me to the flea market. But nothing about his body language was consistent with that: he didn't seem vigilant enough, didn't seem particularly aware of anyone else's activity.

And then I realized this could be my chance. I could follow him and see what he was up to. Where he lived, what his story was.

"Care to fill me in?" Brooke asked, crossing her arms.

I turned to look at her, and at the fortune-teller seated behind her. I smiled and lowered my voice.

"See that guy over there?" I said to Brooke. "At the bookstall?"

"Short? Dark hair? Looks like that guy who played Henry the Eighth in *The Tudors?*"

I nodded. "Exactly. He's a thief. And he's going after the Hope, too."

Brooke's eyes opened wide, and she turned her head to give him an appraising look. Then she frowned. "You know, I think I recognize him."

The thieving world was not huge, so I wasn't surprised at this. "I want to follow him," I said. "Are you up for it?"

She gave me her best Cheshire smile.

This was good. A two-person follow is always more effective

than one. We didn't have time to discuss it any further, because Reilly was leaving the bookstall. Brooke and I switched into business mode.

Now, I may not be able to make a pot of rice without it coming out either mushy or crunchy, but I sure can tail a person without being detected. It's a skill I honed long ago.

Successful tailing requires being in sync with the person you're following. If possible, you need to know their habits, their behavior. . . . You need a *feel* for your mark. You've got to be intuitive, patient, smart. And, above all, invisible.

Most people are oblivious to being followed. They're too absorbed in what they're doing and where they're going to observe the signs. However, Reilly was probably different from most. Being a criminal, he would have a sizable degree of paranoia. Which would keep him vigilant.

Reilly left the flea market and turned left into the surrounding streets. This was a nasty part of Paris. Yes, believe it or not, there are nasty parts of Paris. It was entirely concrete, ugly, and run-down, containing all manner of criminal element. Even I didn't like it, and I was a criminal myself.

Fortunately, Reilly strode to a taxi stand.

Brooke and I split up and approached the taxi stand from different angles. This was a key feature of a two-person follow. Shake up the image of us as a pair and keep changing things around. As with jazz and comedy, the timing has to be impeccable when shadowing someone like this.

A taxi pulled up, and Reilly climbed in the back, looking around him before he did so.

I zipped into the next one waiting in line, careful to keep my face hidden in case Reilly glanced out the back of his vehicle. I instructed the driver to follow the taxi in front of us. Maybe he heard this line regularly, because he didn't flinch. And he didn't laugh at my cheesy cop-show cliché.

We pulled up a few feet, and I instructed the driver to stop. Brooke hopped in. Then the driver continued following the taxi in front for a couple of minutes.

Brooke said to me in a low voice, "How do you know he's going after the Hope, anyway?"

"I saw him casing it."

"How do you know he wasn't just admiring it? People do that, you know."

"A few days later he followed me and cornered me in an alley. And then he kind of threatened me."

"Oh."

Our taxi took a sharp turn as the one in front of us did the same.

"Do you know who he's working for?" Brooke asked.

"No. I had Templeton run a background check on him. He's a rare rogue, works for himself. Somebody must have hired him, but I don't know who."

Brooke's eyebrows went up. "Ah, a free agent. So . . . ballsy, bold, and slightly psychopathic? Must have been kicked out of an agency. Doesn't play well with others."

"Probably a pretty accurate profile."

Our driver stopped. Up on the block ahead, Reilly's taxi had pulled over to the side. He was getting out and paying the fare.

I knotted a scarf around my head and slipped out of the taxi, while Brooke stayed behind to pay the driver.

We were back in the center of the city now, on the right bank in the Marais, the Third Arrondissement. Reilly walked farther into the village, a cobbled pedestrian area of shops and restaurants. I smelled roasting lamb coming from the bistro we passed, and pop music pumped out from a nearby boutique.

I continued following him on foot, staying just far enough behind. Not for the first time, I experienced second thoughts about this. If he detected me, it could get ugly. Reilly was creepier than the strange guy who lurked at the back of every city bus. And probably way more dangerous. Was this worth the risk?

He was moving quickly, striding with purpose, but I caught him checking window reflections as he went. I had to keep back, well out of sight.

Brooke, I saw, was now following on the other side of the square. Heavy rain clouds started to gather, and a breeze picked up. I dropped back and let her take the lead for a few blocks.

I needed an outfit change, somehow. I hurriedly grabbed a hat from a rack in a market, and a cheap pair of sunglasses, thrusting several euros at the seller. I noted that Brooke had done the same with a cheap hooded coat.

This was proving to be a long, meandering journey. Which meant one thing. He was clearly trying to protect against a tail. I wondered why. Where was he going, exactly?

I had to admit, the harder he tried to shake potential shadows, the more I wanted to know exactly what he was up to.

We followed Reilly onto the Metro and all the way to his final destination, the Palais Garnier, the Paris opera house.

The Palais Garnier was an opulent building adorned with gilded statues and sweeping carriage ramps, topped with a grand copper dome. Guests had gathered on the staircase outside. Evidently, there was a matinee performance. I glanced down at my outfit, jeans and a sweater. Not exactly opera material, but it would have to do.

Reilly climbed the steps, and we lingered at the bottom. He reached into his jacket pocket and pulled out a ticket.

This could be a problem. We didn't have tickets.

Could we steal some? Often at a theatre entrance, people struggled with umbrellas or jackets, couples argued, and women applied final swipes of lipstick . . . various opportunities for pickpocketing.

I scanned the crowd and couldn't see any such openings. We moved to Plan B.

We darted around the outside of the enormous theater and ducked in close to the back, then picked the lock and snuck in through the backstage door. Once inside, we moved quickly to the lobby, where the sounds of clinking champagne glasses mixed with the general hum and press of people waiting for the performance to start. I glanced at Brooke, who was frowning at the crowd. She turned to me and gave a slight shrug, bewildered. Reilly wasn't anywhere to be seen.

"Let's split up and search," I said.

Moving freely through a theater, looking for someone, is often tricky. There's always a helpful usher hanging about, offering to help you find your seat, asking to see your ticket. I needed to steer clear of this type.

As I slipped through the crowd, I passed a middle-aged woman with a pair of opera glasses dangling from her purse. On impulse, I surreptitiously snatched them and kept walking through the crowd.

I climbed a staircase to the mezzanine level and ducked into a private box. From here I had a clear view of the entire theater. Strains of the orchestra warming their instruments floated upward.

I scanned the seats and balconies through my pilfered opera glasses. I bit my lip, worried we'd lost Reilly for good.

And then I spotted him. Across the theater, he had just entered a private box. And he wasn't alone—there was a woman seated there, evidently waiting for him. It was difficult to make her out, however, as her face was partially obscured by a red velvet curtain. I needed to get a better view. I sent Brooke a text.

Private box—second gallery, stage left.

I sharpened the focus on the opera glasses as I stared at the woman. She was speaking to Reilly. A waiter entered the box to take their drinks order. The woman shifted to speak to the waiter, and her face came more clearly into view.

My mouth dropped open. This was the woman I'd sat beside on the flight to Paris—Madeleine York, the director of the Smithsonian's National Museum of Natural History.

Chapter 37

My brain tilted with confusion, like my head was taking a ride on the Zipper. What was Sean Reilly doing meeting Madeleine York? Maybe it was his cover, working for the Smithsonian. Maybe he had tricked her and was gathering intel. Maybe they were having an affair.

But it was no good guessing. I had to know. I needed to listen to their conversation.

I scanned the galleries surrounding theirs. A box sat open to their left. I judged the distance. It should be close enough.

I slipped out and made my way around to the other side of the theater. In the mezzanine corridor, I passed Brooke, who fell into step beside me. She followed my lead, unquestioning.

We strolled into the private box, owning it, looking to all the world like this was exactly where our seats were located. A carved wall separated this box from Reilly's. I sat in the chair nearest the wall, while Brooke kept watch by the entrance to our box. I switched on my phone.

If you think your phone has a lot of nifty apps, just imagine all the possibilities for those of us in the underworld. Lucas, my tech guy, had installed all manner of sneaky tools in mine. Including one of my favorites, an eavesdropping microphone. I switched it on, popped the earbud into my ear, and aimed the phone at the conversation I wanted to hear. Brooke did the same thing, her phone similarly outfitted.

There was brief crackling, and then the microphone connected and sharpened on Reilly's and Madeleine's voices.

"Yes, it can be terribly unpredictable in Paris this time of year. Rain one moment, sunshine the next," Madeleine was saying.

"I've noticed," Reilly said. "But it's better than home. In Killarney we get rain one moment, rain the next."

They were talking weather? I shifted and kept listening.

There was silence for several moments. Then Madeleine said, "I need to know if you anticipate any trouble. I cannot afford any screwups."

"Well, it's a tight system at the Louvre," Reilly said. "But I think it can be done, if that's what you want."

"What do you mean, if that's what I want?" Madeleine said, her voice flinty. "You know there's no choice here. I need it, and I must have it. If you're not up to the job, I will find someone else."

"Relax," Reilly said. "I didn't say I couldn't do it. But the Hope isn't some grandmother's pearls. It takes a little planning."

I could hardly believe what I was hearing. I looked at Brooke, and her face showed as much shock as I'm sure mine did. Reilly was working for Madeleine? It was Madeleine herself who had commissioned the theft of the Hope?

"Fine. It's a tricky job," Madeleine said. "Of course it is. Are you saying it can't be done?"

"No, I'm not saying that. But I have another idea."

"What is it?" Her voice was sharp with impatience.

"I could take it while it's on the way back to the Smithsonian from the Louvre."

There was a pause. "Now, that's interesting," she said. "Tell me how that would work."

"Well, it would be an easier thing to do, to trash the security measures while the stone is in transit. We could have one inside man, right?" he asked.

"Yes. I could probably arrange that."

"Then all we have to do is be sure nobody else steals it in the meantime."

"Shouldn't be a problem," Madeleine said.

"I wouldn't be so sure. You remember the thief I told you about?"

"The Montgomery girl?"

"Proving a little more resilient than I'd thought."

"Hmm. So is she any good, as a thief, I mean? Does she actually have a chance?"

Reilly paused. I could hear him exhale. "She's good. Very good."

At this, I felt a ridiculous flush of pride.

"But probably not *that* good," he added, deflating my balloon with a barb.

Madeleine paused, perhaps thinking. "Even so, it sounds like we're going to have to take care of her," she said. "I cannot have her interfering with my plans."

Alarm bells clanged in my ears. What did she mean, take care of her? I didn't like the sound of that one bit.

"And you don't think the Pont des Arts thing will be enough?" Reilly said.

"Probably not."

What the hell were they talking about? I looked to Brooke for some form of clarity, but she shrugged her shoulders. The Pont des Arts was one of the bridges that spanned the Seine, a pedestrian bridge, specifically. But I had no idea what that had to do with anything.

Whatever it was, I didn't like the direction this conversation was taking. A creepy feeling of dread traced my limbs, and I suddenly felt very uncomfortable and vulnerable.

"Failure here is not an option," Madeleine was saying. "You understand that, yes, Reilly?"

"Of course."

"My buyers are getting antsy. They each want their piece of the Hope, and they do not want to be kept waiting."

"So you're planning to break it up?"

"Of course," Madeleine said dismissively. "The Hope itself, intact, would be next to impossible to move on the black market. Entirely too recognizable. But if we break it up, it'll be harder to identify officially, and many more underground collectors can have a piece of it. Plus, because of the notoriety, they'll be willing to pay close to what the Hope is worth as a whole. Especially with all this recent talk about the curse."

I cringed. How could she break up the Hope Diamond? It was a sacred thing. The Hope, with its history through the ages . . . just broken up for money. It was unthinkable.

So now I had something else at stake. If I didn't succeed, the Hope itself would be destroyed. It struck me as more than a little ironic that now stealing the Hope Diamond for a psychopathic collector like Faulkner was a bid to save the stone itself.

I had five days to go before the Hope left the Louvre. It was time to get down to business. But first, before I did anything else, there was somebody I desperately needed to talk to.

When you overhear people speaking about you in the terms Reilly and Madeleine were tossing about, and your brain starts imagining how you might be unceremoniously *taken care of* . . . who do you call to learn how to protect yourself?

A trained assassin, that's who.

Luckily, I happened to know one of those.

Chapter 38

"So, Atworthy, question for you. Say someone, hypothetically, of course, is trying to kill you. How would you defend against that?"

Silence on the other end of the phone line.

"Catherine, are you in trouble?"

"Well," I said, chuckling lightly, "I'm always in trouble. I'm a professional crook, you may be aware. . . ."

"Catherine," he interjected sharply.

I sighed. "Yes. I'm concerned that some of the other interested parties may be a little *too* interested in seeing me out of the race." I was walking back to my hotel from the opera, under my umbrella. A light rain had started, but I didn't care. The fresh air felt soothing, and the walk was good for my mental state. Besides, I wanted to talk to Atworthy about this as soon as possible.

"I see. Well, do you have any idea how they might attempt to harm you?"

"Nope. I heard something about the Pont des Arts, but I don't know if they were still talking about me at that point."

I could hear Atworthy shutting the door to his office and settling back into his desk chair at the university. "It's not going to be easy to describe these things over the phone, you realize. It would be much better to show you—"

"Not an option. And it really can't wait."

He sighed. "Okay, here's what you need to know. Whatever you do, don't let yourself get captured. . . ."

For the next thirty minutes he recounted all manner of counter-assassination tactics, from room surveillance to bomb detection.

Some of it I knew, of course. I already had the basics down, like being able to recognize when I was being followed and never sitting with my back to the entry point of any room. Still, it was a good review.

The stuff I didn't know was fantastic. I walked and did my best to commit it all to memory.

"It would be exceedingly helpful if you knew the method they might use," Atworthy said hopefully.

"You're right. It would," I said. "But I don't."

Another sigh from Atworthy.

We discussed methods of breaking out of a choke hold, if someone decided to attempt to strangle me. We discussed how to prevent being thrown out of a building or off a bridge.

I was particularly interested in the bridge tips.

We discussed poisons—the kind you can taste and the kind you can't.

"Should I carry poison antidotes with me, do you think?" I asked.

"It would be impossible for you to carry the antidote to every known poison. There are too many. However, having a supply of charcoal wouldn't be a bad idea."

"Charcoal?"

"That's how you treat most orally given poisons in an emergency. Charcoal binds with the poison and flushes it from the digestive tract. Of course, that's not going to help you if it's an injected poison. Remember that case many years ago . . . of that Bulgarian dissident injected with ricin through the tip of an umbrella on a London street? Beautiful job, that. Truly elegant work—"

"Atworthy? Focus, please."

"Right. Where was I?"

He moved on from poisons to sniper attacks. A tricky thing to prevent in the best of circumstances, but I took his suggestions to heart. Never sit near open windows, stay close to crowds, that sort of thing.

He poured as much wisdom into that conversation as he could, and I gobbled it down.

I hung up the phone and scraped a hand through my hair. Would his advice be enough to keep me safe?

Chapter 39

I returned to my hotel. I needed to think. I had some figuring to do about this job. But when I got back, Jack was there with files and papers spread out on the desk, working on his case.

"Hey, hon. I just ordered room service. Are you hungry?"

I shrugged. "I could eat, I guess." Truth was, all this talk of assassination methods and my life under threat had somewhat killed my appetite. But I couldn't get into that with Jack.

I gave him a quick kiss and went where I could do some solitary thinking and clear my head: the shower. As hot water poured down on my head, sending up goose bumps on the rest of my skin, I re-played everything I'd heard. Reilly thought it was possible to take the Hope from the Louvre. And yet he wasn't going to attempt it.

Was I crazy to attempt it?

I was just getting out of the shower when my phone, which was sitting on the bathroom counter, bleeped with a waiting message. I wrapped a fluffy towel around my torso, picked up the phone, and scrolled through the screen. There it was, a message from Faulkner.

Respond at your earliest convenience.

Which meant right fucking now.

I hesitated for a moment, though. And then there was a knock on the door to the suite. *Perfect. Room service.* I was hungrier now.

A little food first, and then I'd make the call. I tucked in the towel edges and left the steamy bathroom.

I walked out just as Jack reached the suite door and opened it.

But it wasn't room service. It was Ethan, standing in the hallway, holding a bottle of wine.

At the sight of Jack, Ethan's eyes went wide and his mouth opened just slightly. "Jack! What a . . . *surprise*. When, er, when did you get to town?"

I winced. I had been so distracted in the past twenty-four hours with planning this job, I'd completely forgotten to tell Ethan that Jack was in Paris.

The look of shock on Ethan's face was matched by Jack's own stunned expression. Which was quickly replaced by a look of open contempt.

"What are you doing here, Jones?" His voice was low, vaguely threatening.

Ethan hesitated. He appeared unsure about what to say, about how much he actually could say. He glanced at me. "Well, there's some planning Cat and I need to do. For a job, if you have to know."

"With wine?"

Ethan looked at the bottle of wine, as if he'd forgotten he was holding it. "Well, sure. Everything is better with wine, isn't it?"

"I think you'd better leave," Jack said. His right hand curled around the door frame.

I frowned. On one level, of course, I understood Jack's point of view. On the other hand, he was demonstrating some fairly unappealing qualities just then.

Plus, he was interfering with my ability to do my job. "Jack, just hang on," I said, placing my hand on Jack's chest in a gesture intended to soothe. Rather like how you'd calm a wild horse. "Ethan *is* helping me with this job."

"I'm sure he is," Jack said with tight control.

Ethan, wisely, stayed quiet throughout this. I looked at him apologetically. "Maybe we can do this a little later?" I said.

Ethan shrugged. "Sure. Give me a call."

The door closed firmly.

Jack turned to face me. His mouth was hard. "So much time spent together . . . Is it really all about work? And why was he surprised I was here? Maybe I'm right. Maybe there *is* something going on."

I could tell then that Jack and I were headed down a very ugly path. Where we would reemerge on the other side, I didn't know.

Chapter 40

Jack maneuvered into position; he had a clear view of the Seine and the motor yacht that belonged to Faulkner, which was moored along the riverbank. Amber streetlights lining the bridge of Pont Neuf shone against the dusky sky of twilight. The river waters shifted, creating fractal patterns of reflected light.

He stretched his neck and settled into a crouch. Finally, it looked like there was a development in his case. Which was good. Because if something didn't happen soon, Jack was going to be in a mess of trouble.

It was not that he hadn't tried to go through official channels. Before coming to Paris, he'd gone to Victoria Sullivan, his supervisor, with his suspicions about Faulkner. He'd shown her the surveillance tapes from the Smithsonian. He'd thought, just maybe she might be impressed.

Victoria, in no uncertain terms, had shut him down. In fact, she was so furious that Jack had done his own investigating, using his own hacker and everything, that she'd insisted Jack take a little time off, unpaid.

Which had supremely pissed him off.

Except once he started thinking about it, he'd realized this could work to his advantage. His schedule was clear. What was stopping him from going to Paris and continuing his investigation on the sly? In fact, it might be his only chance to save his job.

He'd booked a flight that very day.

So here he was, no backup, no official position. If only he could get some proof that would bring down the Gargoyle. And save his career in the process. Because right now it was not looking good. His record was terrible. His performance reports were going to be poor, he was sure.

In Jack's previous department within the FBI, his supervisor had valued intuition, hunches, and ballsy decisions. Things Jack specialized in.

Victoria Sullivan, in contrast, valued doing things by the book, following rules, and documenting everything in triplicate. Things Jack . . . well, needed to work on.

And if Jack didn't soon get a solid lead, some ironclad evidence that could be used, he might need to start looking for another career. Especially if his supervisor got wind of the fact he was in Paris. Would she believe Jack wasn't doing an illicit investigation?

The trouble was, so far he'd come up totally empty-handed. Until yesterday. While Cat had been in the shower, he'd received a message from his network of eyes and ears: Faulkner was having a meeting tonight on his boat.

Thinking about that incident in the hotel, though, set Jack's teeth on edge. *Fucking Jones.* The guy made his blood boil like nobody else. But also, Jack hadn't liked the way Cat had defended Ethan and his transparent offering of a bottle of wine. It didn't sit well with him, not at all.

But he couldn't think about that right now. He needed to focus. He repositioned himself and ignored the cramp in his thigh. Jack had been waiting a long time; maybe this was a false alarm.

As Jack waited, his mind spiraled away again. He wondered what was going on with the Fabergé egg quest. What was Wesley doing now? Maybe Jack shouldn't be here, chasing this weak lead. Maybe he should be with Wesley, doing something of significance.

No. This was where he belonged. On the right side of the law. The good side. Not that his position was officially endorsed by his superiors, of course, but he was still looking to uphold law and order. Right?

He frowned and cracked his knuckles.

Of course, Wesley was also trying to do the right thing. Just . . . through illicit channels. Finding the Fabergé egg and attempting to steal it . . . He was doing it for all the right reasons.

Jack felt a familiar tugging sensation. The familiar temptation flickered in view, like a shiny object in the corner of his eye.

No, just stay where you are. Keep the goal in sight. You are on this earth to stop criminals like the Gargoyle. Not to become a criminal yourself.

But then, on the riverbank, everything changed. Something was happening. A figure was approaching Faulkner's boat. The henchmen inside the yacht were taking up positions. This must be the person Faulkner had arranged to meet. Jack shifted, sharpening the focus on his binoculars.

And almost dropped them in the river.

It was Cat.

Chapter 41

I drew near Faulkner's boat, walking cautiously down the cobblestone ramp to the edge of the Seine. My palms were sweaty; it was dusk, and I was leaving the safety of the bustling streets for the shadowy water's edge. This was a meeting Faulkner had requested. And the use of the word *request* here is rather polite.

I didn't know what to expect. I certainly didn't like that it was on a boat. Too many variables, not enough escape options for my comfort level, altogether too much water. But even though it had been Faulkner who'd summoned this rendezvous, I had a very specific agenda.

I needed money. Specifically so I could buy a Hope replica. We hadn't found one yet, but we knew the sticker price would not be pretty when we did.

So I was going to ask him for funding, and then I was going to get the hell off his boat as fast as possible.

As I climbed aboard and felt the slight wobble of the deck, I could tell they were making preparations to leave. A late-night cruise along the Seine perhaps? I took stock of my surroundings and started assessing my exit strategy.

It was a beautiful yacht—trimmed in rich wood, sparkling clean and shipshape, open terrace on the top and a covered area underneath with lounge chairs and tables, like a richly appointed conservatory. That just happened to be on a boat.

For now, we were moored and not yet ready for departure. I knew plenty about boats. Sailing was the hobby my father and I had shared for years. I experienced a brief pang in my chest at that thought.

"Miss Montgomery," said Faulkner when I arrived at the lounge at the stern of the yacht. His tone was flat.

He was seated at a table, eating escargots, scooping the shells up with tongs and deftly forking the little creatures dripping with garlic and butter. He didn't offer me anything. This was not a social call, clearly. I tried to keep my hands still at my sides and to keep my face smooth.

At the same time, I started counting the weapons in the lounge.

"We have a couple of problems, you and I," Faulkner said.

"Oh?"

"For one, I am concerned. The Hope Diamond will be in Paris for only another five nights before it is returned to America. You know this, and I know this."

I nodded.

"I am concerned you may not be taking this seriously. I am concerned you will not be able to accomplish your goal. And I have started wondering if you are not sufficiently motivated."

My mouth became cottony. Was he going to do something to me, hurt me in some way? I prepared to defend myself, trying to remember Atworthy's advice.

But nobody made any sign of moving.

"Additionally," continued Faulkner, "it appears I have attracted the attention, unfortunately, of a certain FBI agent. I believe you know him. Jack Barlow?"

My eyes went wide. I couldn't help it. Jack was investigating *Faulkner?*

"How do you know? What is Jack doing?" I blurted out.

"Mr. Barlow is sniffing around. He appears to be investigating my activities. He is here in Paris, and I know you know this. Now, was it you who set him on me?" His voice had a snarling edge to it.

"Me? No! Of course not. I wouldn't—"

"Enough," he said sharply.

I swallowed and tried to think of what I would say next.

But Faulkner kept talking. "This displeases me highly. I'd been certain I'd told you not to involve him. And that if you did . . . what? What would happen?"

Did he want an answer here? Was this a rhetorical question? I stayed quiet, feeling this was the safest option. In my peripheral vision I could see two henchmen blocking the way I'd come onto the boat. There had to be another way off. The back of my neck felt clammy.

I started maneuvering myself toward the stern railing, standing with my back to the water, ready to attempt a quick exit if necessary.

"I believe you," said Faulkner. "That Barlow's involvement was not your doing. But this is what you can do now. *Get him off me.*"

How was I going to get Jack to stop investigating Faulkner without incriminating myself, and without further arousing Jack's suspicion? Could I come clean and tell him what I was doing? Tell him exactly what was at stake? Would that make him stop investigating? Or would he investigate all the more?

I knew Jack. If I told him the full story, it would only strengthen his resolve to investigate more deeply. And the more he did that, the more he was going to anger Faulkner. And the more danger I would be in.

Faulkner swallowed his mouthful of escargots, and his expression turned thoughtful. "The thing that bothers me is that I think you are close to procuring the Hope. I do believe that. I can feel it. And, quite frankly, that's the most important thing to me right now."

"I *am* close to finishing the job," I said, keeping my breathing even. "It's all in place. I have just about everything I need." I clenched and unclenched my hands, trying to relax. This was my moment to ask for the money I needed. "There's just one piece of, er, equipment that I need. It's very expensive." I swallowed, my throat dry as chalk. "I wonder—"

"You want to know if I can front you the money?" Faulkner said, his eyes narrowing.

I nodded.

He ate another escargot, staring at me as he chewed it thoroughly. I had previously quite liked escargots. The very thought of them now turned my stomach.

"That, my dear, is entirely out of the question."

I opened my mouth to protest, but he held up a hand to stop me. "Do not ask again. You will regret it."

I hated being so toothless. If I were in a less vulnerable spot, I would demand what I needed. But the semiautomatic weapons lingering by the exits did not help me feel I was in a power position.

"So here's what we're going to do. You are going to get Mr. Barlow off my case. Immediately. And you are going to step up your efforts and be absolutely certain that you are going to get the Hope for me. And to be sure that we are on the same page, in terms of motivation for these tasks, I'm providing a little incentive. It's something I should have done originally. I don't know why I let myself get talked out of it."

My heart rate sped up. What was he talking about?

"I was wrong," he said, nodding, almost talking to himself at this point. "I can admit that. I was wrong to think I could sufficiently motivate you by threatening you. I forgot all about the power of fear for someone you love. But I am not above admitting when I am wrong and taking steps to correct my mistake."

My chest tightened as I waited for whatever was coming next.

"Which is why it is important for you to see this," he said. One of his executive assistants handed him an envelope. From it, he pulled a sheaf of photographs and passed them to me.

I held the thick, slippery photography paper and looked at the first picture. It was my mother, outside in her garden. Then my father, at the boatyard. And my friends, at a café in Seattle. They were surveillance photographs. My loved ones were unharmed, but clearly, someone had been following them and photographing them.

Terror surged through my every nerve at seeing those images.

Faulkner took them back from my trembling hands. He gazed at them, flipped through them, smiling affectionately. Like he was looking at a prized collection. "Hmm," he said, frowning slightly. "No siblings? Tsk, tsk. That's a shame. People are often highly motivated to protect a younger brother or sister."

This brought up fresh memories of my sister, Penny. My alarm mixed with anger as heat flushed up my neck. But I couldn't lose my temper here. I had to do whatever it took to keep my family and friends safe. "What are you going to do?" I said in a low, clear voice.

At that moment the boat deck rumbled beneath my feet as the engines fired up.

"Nothing. Hopefully," Faulkner said. "If everything goes according to plan, your family will be fine. I can't say the same, however, if things do not work out between us. If anything goes wrong with the Hope job or if I get hassle from Mr. Barlow or the FBI or Interpol . . . well, you can use your imagination."

My fists clenched at my sides ineffectually. What could I do? "Yes," I said in a hoarse whisper, nodding. "I understand."

Faulkner looked at me with that pinchy, penetrating bird-of-prey look. And then nodded at the henchman nearest me.

The man reached forward and pushed me straight off the stern of the boat, right into the Seine. The cold water sent shocks through my brain and stole my breath.

As I surfaced, coughing, I became vaguely aware of Faulkner's boat pulling away from the bank and moving quickly downriver. I was left in the freezing water, head spinning.

Suddenly there was a strong hand around my arm. And then another. I heard gruff male voices through my waterlogged eardrums.

I looked up, straight into Jack's face. I blinked. No, it was Ethan's face.

No. It was both of them.

Chapter 42

Ethan had been watching Cat at her meeting on the boat. When she'd sent him the message, he'd headed down to the riverbank right away. He'd watched as she spoke to Faulkner. And when they'd pushed her off the boat, a cold hand of panic clutched his heart. He had been in motion immediately.

Ethan knew Cat was a good swimmer. She'd be okay. That was what he told himself as he raced down to the water's edge. He saw Cat reach the riverbank and cling on to the edge like a kitten in a bathtub.

In the corner of his eye he saw a figure sprinting down to the same spot. A bystander coming to help.

But as Ethan got closer, he realized this was no bystander. It was Jack Barlow.

And Jack got to Cat first, just a second ahead of Ethan. Maybe Ethan should have left it to Jack to fish her out. But, damn it, Ethan cared about her, too. And it was not in his nature to sit back.

"I got you," Ethan said, grasping her arms, looking into her eyes.

"What are you talking about? I have her," Jack said, pushing Ethan aside. "I can handle this."

"Right. Yes, you're handling it beautifully so far. I guess that's why she's in the river—"

"Would you two stop!" Cat choked out, slapping both their hands away. "Get your hands off me. I can crawl out on my own, thank you. Give me some room. You're both going to end up drowning me."

Both men stepped back. Jack refused to look at Ethan. Ethan was fine with that.

When Cat had managed to pull herself up and out of the water, with no help from either of them, Jack quickly wrapped his coat around Cat, and Ethan helped remove her sopping shoes.

Jack was shooting poison arrows at Ethan the whole time, but Ethan didn't give a shit. He wasn't going anywhere. He was going to help Cat. And he was going to find out what the hell had happened with Faulkner.

Ethan also had something important to tell her. He'd learned where they could get a superb replica of the Hope, at a very affordable price. But they would have to go there in person. And it wasn't around the corner.

But he'd save that for later. Now was not exactly the time.

Cat was shivering. Jack turned to Ethan. "Why don't you do something useful and go hail a cab?"

Ethan remained there, crouching by Cat. The last thing he wanted to do was take orders from Jack. But it was a good idea. Somebody needed to do it, anyway. He stood and looked at Cat, huddled in Barlow's jacket. At that instant, she looked up into Jack's face. And her face was full of gratitude for his safe, warm embrace. At least, that was how it looked to Ethan. And, to his chagrin, Ethan noticed his chest tightening.

Fuck. It was official. He had totally fallen for Cat.

And now he was in the extremely annoying position of being second goddamned fiddle. He suddenly felt extraneous. A third wheel. And whatever other cliché you wanted to throw into it.

The trouble was, Ethan simply could not shake the feeling that they belonged together. But what was he going to do? Give up? Or fight for her?

Cat's shivering grew more violent. She needed to get somewhere warm.

Ethan flexed his jaw. "Just stay here. I'll be right back."

* * *

I watched Ethan stride up the ramp to street level to hail a cab. My chattering teeth were so loud, rattling my head, I was having a hard time concentrating.

But this was important. I needed to come clean with Jack. And I needed to find a way to make him stop investigating Faulkner. I knew Jack, though. The more I tried to put him off doing something, the more he was going to want to do it.

He beat me to the subject, however. "Why were you meeting with Albert Faulkner?" Jack demanded. His brow furrowed with concern.

"He's just . . . It's nothing. He's just a jewel collector."

"A jewel collector who pushes you off the back of a boat?"

I pressed my lips together. "I'm doing a job for him, if you must know."

"What job?"

"Jack, you know I can't tell you that."

"This has to do with the Louvre, right?"

Ugh.

He was just way too close to all this, way too wrapped up in all the stuff I also happened to be wrapped up in.

"Jack, you don't want to get involved in all this. I'm too involved. And you and I . . . well, we need to keep our professional lives separate, don't we?"

I could see the struggle on his face. He knew I was right. He was wrestling with his professional obligations and his personal obligations to me. It was the sort of conflict we had worked so hard to avoid.

"It's too late," he said. "I'm involved."

I closed my eyes. This was not good. We were not going to be able to get this toothpaste back in the tube.

"But here's what I think," he continued. "You need to get out of this. Faulkner is bad news. He's dangerous. He's a major criminal, and he's violent."

No kidding. I wished I could talk to Jack about it, but my old instinct to protect him, to keep him in the dark, kicked in. "It's fine.

Faulkner is just an old man who's a lot of talk," I said. I hoped my voice came out more confident than I felt.

"Cat, stop. You don't understand—"

"No, listen." I needed to find a way to get him off the trail. I had to figure out a way. If I could just give him something else to sink his teeth into.

And then I had it. Reilly and Madeleine. A little corruption within the Smithsonian. That should prove interesting to an FBI agent.

"If you really want to investigate someone, take a look at Madeleine York. She's the director of the Smithsonian National Museum of Natural History, but she's actually working behind the scenes with a thief to steal . . ."

I stopped there, not particularly keen for Jack to know what was being stolen. The last thing I wanted was increased security around the Hope, making my job that much more difficult.

I reconsidered. Maybe this was a bad idea.

"Okay, never mind that," I said quickly. "That's not really your department, anyway. Just trust me. Albert Faulkner is nothing to worry about. He's just an old, somewhat fanatic jewel collector."

I looked sideways at Jack and tried for a smile. His face was flat with skepticism. He was not buying it for a second.

"I want to get you out of Paris," Jack said. "I'm worried about you and this job."

At that moment Ethan returned. "Cab is waiting. Let's go."

Jack turned to him then and said, "There's a lot I don't like about you, Jones, but I believe we do share a concern for Cat. I just told her I wanted her to get out of Paris. Are you gonna back me up on that?"

First, they were fighting over helping me, and now they were teaming up against me?

Ethan's expression was odd, unreadable. Almost like there was something funny. "Actually, I think you're right," he said. "I think that's the best idea you've had, Barlow."

"What?" I said disbelievingly.

"In fact, I know just the place you should go," Ethan said. "Where *we* should go, I should say. How do you feel about Thai food?"

Chapter 43

Bangkok, Thailand

Ethan and I walked down tourist-filled Khao San Road, sweating under the hot late afternoon sun. The tropical air clung to me like a wet blanket; we hadn't been there for long, and I already felt sticky. Awnings lurched out from walls at varying angles, and colorful strings of flags spanned the street. This street, the center of the universe for backpackers, positively throbbed with life.

We strolled through spicy clouds that smelled of lemongrass and peanut aromas. I glanced at a food stall and saw roasted meat skewers of some kind lying in the sun and attracting flies, waiting for sunburned backpackers to buy them and gleefully eat them.

We were looking for a very specific shop: a bespoke tailor and haberdashery owned and operated by a tailor who happened to have a side business in replica gem creation.

He was the best, or so we'd been told. He also had a perfect replica of the Hope that he was willing to sell. Which had all better be true. Getting here had not exactly been a walk in the park.

Specifically, flying out of Paris had not been fun.

At Charles de Gaulle the security staff carry semiautomatic weapons, with their fingers quite literally on the trigger. This is a fairly freaky sight for someone who has recently developed a terror of being killed.

Ethan had tried to coach me through it. "You're just going to have to forget about them, completely put them out of your head," he'd said as we made our way through the terminal.

I had said nothing, had just stared grimly ahead.

"You could handle yourself if you needed to," he'd continued. "You know that's true. That hasn't changed. The fear is the only new thing. And you can't let it own you."

He was right, of course. But it was easier said than done.

In spite of my fears, the journey here had gone smoothly. And today, as long as we were able to locate the tailor, we'd be on the next plane out of here, back to Paris, and back to Jack. As long as he was still waiting for me.

When Ethan had explained why we needed to go to Bangkok, I knew there wasn't a choice involved. I had to do it. And Ethan had to come, too, because it was his contact who'd set it up, and that was the arrangement.

When I'd told Jack I needed to go, I'd expected him to argue. To respond with heated anger over the very idea. Instead, he had been quiet and had gazed out the window of our hotel bedroom, making things even worse. Anger I could handle, but this cold detachment was another matter.

I knew why it was hard for him to accept me going away with Ethan. But there was nothing I could do about it. But then again, why *should* I do anything about it? Ethan was a colleague, and we were working on a project together. There was nothing wrong with that.

As Ethan and I wove our way along bustling Khao San Road, we kept a sharp eye out. But all we could see were endless stalls and shops bursting with batik-printed skirts and knockoff Ray-Bans and fake Louis Vuitton purses.

And then we found it. The shop had three rather ugly suits on display in the storefront window and a crummy little sign that read SUPREME CLOTHIERS: LADIES & GENTS CUSTOM TAILOR.

Unfortunately, there was also a sign that said CLOSED. PLEASE COME AGAIN.

"They're closed?" I said disbelievingly. "How can they be closed?"

Ethan pulled out his phone and made a call. He spoke angrily to whoever his contact was and then punched the END CALL button with annoyance.

"Looks like we're going to have to keep ourselves entertained for the night," he said. "Tailor doesn't open again until the morning."

Damn. I squeezed my eyes tight with frustration.

"Hey, it's no big deal," Ethan said. "We'll just lay low for the evening and come back first thing."

I nodded. He was right; it wasn't the end of the world. First, though, we needed to find somewhere to stay for the night. Ethan led the way to a crummy hostel in the Banglamphu neighborhood, not far from Khao San Road. I cringed as we walked through the door, but the low-rent digs were for a good reason. Ethan had been in Bangkok a while ago for a job. And, unfortunately, during his getaway they'd captured a photo of half his face. He was a wanted man here in Bangkok. We would need to maintain a low profile.

At the check-in desk there was a moment of supreme awkwardness when they asked about the number of beds we would need.

I firmly requested two separate beds. Exactly like I'd told Jack I would if this came up.

Once the desk clerk gave us a few key instructions—like "Do not drink the tap water," "If you see a lizard, ignore it, unless it's got a red stripe, of course, and then, by God, come get help," and, finally, "Pay no attention if a fire alarm goes off, because it's been acting up all week"—we were handed a key. As we climbed the stairs, I wondered how we were to know if there was an *actual* fire. And what the hell did the red-striped lizards do, exactly?

I put these trifles out of my mind when we arrived in the room and flopped our backpacks on the very separate saggy single beds. It was stifling. An antique air conditioner rattled away in the window, but I wasn't confident it was producing more than the faintest wisp of mildly cool air.

"You know, Montgomery, I think we need to go somewhere for a cold drink," Ethan suggested, gazing with suspicion at the air conditioner.

I wasn't sure. I thought maybe I should just sleep off the jet lag and be ready to go at daybreak. "I don't know, Ethan. . . ."

"Come on," he cajoled. "There's nothing we can do about the tailor right now. But we're here, and we might as well have a little fun. What do you say?"

He was making a certain amount of sense. Besides, I could barely breathe in this stuffy room. After another minute of considering, I agreed.

We found a patio just down the road, a colorful place strung with bright flags and populated by a large crowd of hipsters and backpackers drinking and laughing and getting high.

We sat and ordered Singhas.

"See?" said Ethan, clinking my glass. "There's no reason we can't enjoy ourselves a little while we're here."

The sun was beginning to set now, and the air felt marginally cooler and fresher. Above us, the southern constellations were just beginning to prick the twilit sky. We sat and talked and ordered another round of Singhas. And then another.

I noticed a trio of women thoroughly checking Ethan out as they walked by on their way to the bar, and I felt an irrational surge of pride. He was a superb specimen, that was for sure. And he was with me. At least, I knew that was how it looked.

And my inner self had to admit, *That's how it feels.*

As the sky grew darker, they turned on the string of glowing lanterns that surrounded the patio. In the glowing light, Ethan's face looked even more handsome, if that was possible. His hair ruffled slightly in the warm breeze. As if reading my mind, he gazed intently at me at that moment. Everything surrounding us disappeared into the background.

"Montgomery, I know I shouldn't be saying this, but I just have to. You are a very fine woman."

I said nothing, but my stomach did a backflip or two.

He continued talking. "I'm not trying to come on to you. I'm just stating a fact." He sipped his drink, pondering. "But that's not even the thing I like best about you."

Relaxed by the booze, I couldn't help raising an eyebrow, playing along. "No?"

"Nope. What I like best is how well we work together. You can't deny it—this whole Bonnie and Clyde thing we've got going on."

I couldn't deny it. And that was the whole problem.

"In many ways, you're such a good girl," he said, leaning forward and lowering his voice to a soft rumble. "But in this one significant way, you're bad through and through. And I find that irresistible."

A sudden warmth surged through my body. It was difficult to look away from his smoldering gaze, but it was his words that pulled me in more than anything. It wasn't lost on me that he was talking about the exact thing Jack would change about me, if he could.

Ethan was about to order another round when I stopped him. "Ethan, we gotta get back. It's late, and we can't miss our meeting in the morning."

"You sure?"

I nodded. Ethan shrugged and paid the waitress, and we walked back to the hostel in the marvelously comfortable evening air.

Walking now, I realized just how uneven this pavement was. Possibly it had something to do with how many Singhas I'd consumed. Either way, Ethan caught me as I stumbled to the side, and then held me with his arm the rest of the journey.

Which felt nice. In a very wrong way.

We returned to the hostel, and strangely, our room didn't look half so horrible in the evening light as it had in the full glare of the day. I went to the windows and unlatched the heavy shutters, which we'd kept closed against the heat of the sun, flinging them open to let the cool night air in. I gasped as I looked out. There was a tiny balcony and, beyond that, an incredible view of the Chao Phraya River. Lights shimmered from a Buddhist temple on the riverbank, and two boats slowly passed each other on the wide, dark waterway. How had we not noticed this view before? I stepped out on the balcony.

Ethan walked over and stood behind me. "Well, that's pretty incredible." He placed a hand on the balcony railing. He was very close; I could feel his body heat. In spite of the fresh air, I was finding it rather difficult to breathe.

My inhibitions had been dissolved by three drinks. Had my conscience, too? This was going in completely the wrong direction. I had to stop this.

Ethan brushed my hair to the side and bent his head to my neck. His lips barely touched my skin, but it sent a shiver through my whole body. I stood very still while a war waged within me. He felt so amazing. What we could have would be incredible. And yet how could I do it to Jack? Ethan took my shoulders gently and began to turn me toward him. I could feel my resolve crumbling.

And then a smoke detector pealed out, slicing into the quiet.

We both startled and jumped apart. I looked for an immediate exit—always my impulse on hearing an alarm.

"What the hell—" said Ethan, going quickly to the door of the room to check the hallway.

And then I remembered. *The fire alarm has been acting up all week. . . .*

It was a false alarm. Sure enough, after two minutes of sirens, the fire alarm shut off abruptly. The cicadas resumed their chirping.

But I did not resume my spot on the balcony. The spell was broken—thank God—and it was time for me to be a sober grown-up who did not do things to betray her perfect, trusting boyfriend.

"Ethan," I said. "I, um, I'm just going to go to sleep."

He said nothing, just nodded without argument. He went downstairs to check with the front desk about the fire alarm.

And I quickly climbed into my bed, alone, and turned off the light.

Jack ran a hand through his hair. He was exhausted. And when was the last time he'd eaten, anyway? He was alone in his hotel room, restlessly pacing. Even the spectacular view of the Eiffel Tower from the window failed to capture his attention.

His purpose in Paris was becoming increasingly muddy. The Gargoyle was proving to be incredibly difficult to nail. And the one solid lead he'd come up with happened to involve his girlfriend, whom he'd sworn not to betray.

Except what was she doing right at this minute? Jack scowled at the thought.

To her credit, Cat had been completely forthcoming about the trip to Bangkok. She'd explained that she needed to go for work. The exact purpose had been left unsaid, however, as per their arrangement. Which didn't bother Jack much.

She'd also been totally up front about the fact that Ethan was going, too. Which bothered Jack a great deal.

She had sworn on her sister's grave that he had nothing to worry about. It was strictly a business trip.

And he wanted to believe her. But he couldn't help wondering, was he being an idiot, trusting her?

No. He had to have faith. Cat and Ethan were just colleagues. Jack felt like a jerk, giving her such a hard time over working with another thief—someone who might be able to help her get out of the mess she was clearly in.

Jack frowned, thinking about that. Cat was in way over her head. He worried she was in serious bodily danger. Or, at the very least, major legal danger.

How could she be involved with Faulkner? *Goddamn it.* That was going to make his job much more difficult. Because he'd promised her long ago that he wouldn't compromise her.

But if he could just nail Faulkner, he'd be able to liberate Cat from his choke hold. She clearly wanted Jack to back off the investigation, but instead, he was even more firmly resolved that he was going to get this guy.

He needed to know more about how this all connected to the Louvre. What were they after? Since Cat had made it clear she wouldn't be telling him any more about this job, who could he talk to instead?

One name sprang to mind.

* * *

Later that evening Jack sat in Bar Hemingway at the Ritz. Piano jazz music mixed with the sounds of chatter and clinking dishware. He sipped his whiskey and gazed over the rim of his glass at his companion at the bar.

"So, Brooke, tell me," he said. "How's the job going, the one you and Cat are working on here in Paris?"

Brooke laughed. "Well, full points for trying, Jack. But did you think I'd just spell it out?" She swirled her drink, a sidecar, a Jazz Age cocktail made famous at the Ritz. He had to give her credit for style.

Jack knew plenty about Brooke. He knew she and Cat had been long-standing rivals. He also knew they worked together from time to time. And that Brooke had once, many years ago, been Cat's mentor. He was taking a gamble here that Brooke was helping Cat again this time around.

It hadn't been difficult to locate her. Brooke's activities had been monitored to a certain degree by Interpol and the FBI ever since her prison stint for theft last year. He'd known she was in Paris. Getting a message to her through his underground network had taken a mere couple of hours.

"You know I'm just worried about Cat," Jack said. "You can understand that, right? I'm not even here on official business. I have no jurisdiction here. But it's a big job she's doing."

"Don't worry about Cat. She's got it well in hand." Brooke smiled knowingly. "I mean, I'm sure I would do a better job, of course. But that's neither here nor there."

This wasn't getting him anywhere.

"Why *aren't* you doing the job, then?" Jack asked. *That's the ticket,* he thought. *Work away on the ego.* Jack knew hers was substantial. Sooner or later she had to slip.

Brooke sipped her sidecar, tension in her mouth. "It's not official business. And my agency has been pretty clear. No moonlighting."

"Didn't have you pegged as a rule follower, Brooke."

She shrugged.

"Anyway, a big job like this?" he said, pretending he knew much more than he did. "I'm surprised your agency wouldn't want you to make a play for it. I'm surprised Cat's agency is letting her do it."

Brooke placed her martini glass on the bar. "They're not. The *Hope?* Do you really think her agency has the cojones to take on that kind of job? It's too big. That kind of heist would always be below the table. That's why it's coming from outside."

Jack tried to keep his face blank. He covered his expression by sipping his whiskey. The Hope Diamond? That was what Cat was going after? Was she fucking insane?

Brooke finished the last of her drink. "Listen, Jack, this is lovely and all. But . . . maybe you'd be interested in continuing this conversation somewhere a little more private? My hotel is just around the corner."

She reached over and squeezed his knee.

He laughed lightly. "Yeah, I don't think so, Brooke."

He stood then. But she stood, too. And moved closer. "You're very tall, aren't you?" she said. "How tall are you?"

"Six-three. Thanks for noticing."

Jack looked at Brooke. She was a beautiful woman. Very sexy and very confident. She smelled good—her perfume was spicy, exotic.

"You know, Jack, you look a little tense. Maybe you need some way of relaxing, hmm? I can help you with that."

Jack smiled. "I don't think so, Brooke. But . . . I appreciate the offer."

She shrugged and gave a mock pout. "Can't blame a girl for trying."

Jack laughed. Brooke would be a temptation for any man. Any man who didn't have Cat as a girlfriend, that is.

Jack pulled out his wallet and put down enough money to cover the bill. "It's been fun, Brooke, as always."

"You're a good man, Jack," she said. "Which is probably your problem, and why it will never work out with you and Cat. But there it is." She shrugged again and glanced in a polished chrome banister to check her lipstick and sweep the hair out of her eyes.

Jack walked out to the Paris streets, to the sounds of traffic and the lush smells of the flower stand outside the hotel. Well, that had been fruitful, sort of. Trouble was, he was coming out of there with more questions than answers.

He dismissed Brooke's comments about things not working out with Cat. That was old territory. He'd been over it a thousand times in his head. He knew exactly how he felt about it.

But, he wondered, did Cat feel the same? Or right now was she doubting that a criminal and a cop could find long-lasting happiness?

At least he knew now what Faulkner was up to, and what he'd hired Cat to do. It was a huge job. There was great potential for failure, which would—possibly—mean they could nab the Gargoyle.

But wouldn't that mean arresting Cat?

Fuck.

There had to be a way to nail Faulkner without screwing Cat. But damned if Jack knew what it was.

As he walked toward the Metro entrance, Jack's phone rang.

Wesley's voice came through the line. "We've got it, Jack. We know exactly where it is." He sounded keyed up.

Jack stopped walking. "Okay. Where?"

"A private villa in Monaco."

Jack said nothing. Monaco was close. Less than a two-hour flight from Paris.

Wesley went on, speaking quickly. "It's all planned. I know how we're going to get it. I just need another guy—a partner, someone I can trust. That person is still you, Jack. You're still my first choice. You don't need to bring anything. I'll brief you on the job when you get here."

Jack remained silent, standing at the top of the steps that would lead down to the Metro.

"And Jack?" Wesley continued. "This'll be my last request. If you say no, I won't bother you anymore."

Jack was doing nothing in Paris. All his leads were drying up. He had no idea what his next step was, and he had no clue how to catch the Gargoyle without hurting Cat in the process.

But this request from Wesley—this was something real. It was a real difference he could make.

Of course, it meant getting tangled up with the criminal side again. Whatever the details of Wesley's plan, it undoubtedly involved full-on illegal activity.

After weeks of indecision, weeks of wrestling with this same old struggle, Jack suddenly knew what he was going to do.

He hung up the phone and hailed a cab.

"Charles de Gaulle Airport," he told the driver.

In the glare of the next morning, the awkwardness was palpable. As was the headache from those Singhas. But there was no time to feel sorry for myself, because we had a job to do.

We left our things at the hostel and made our way back to the tailor's shop. A cheerful OPEN FOR BUSINESS sign greeted us at the front door, and I breathed a sigh of relief.

Inside the haberdashery were bits and scraps of fabric, partially finished garments, and industrial-size spools of thread in every color. It carried a deep-fryer smell from the take-out stand right outside. It was quiet, with only the whir of a sewing machine and the hiss of a steam iron coming from somewhere in the back.

A plump Thai woman stood at the counter, filling out a ledger. I walked up to the counter, while Ethan hung back, and, with a perfectly straight face, said, "Hello. Do you happen to make tuxedo shirts? I need three. One bib front, one pleated front, and one with French cuffs."

The woman smiled, just as all Thai people did in virtually every situation, and bustled to the back, stepping behind a cheap curtain.

A few minutes later she returned and beckoned us to the back through a door and then down a flight of stairs to a basement.

The basement was dark and had a damp, mushroomy smell. As we crept down the stairs, I wondered if this replica was going to live up to its billing. And I worried about how much the tailor was going to demand in payment.

I had spent just about everything I had on this job. Between flights, hotels, all my travel expenses, equipment, and now this fake diamond . . . it was cleaning me out. But what choice did I have?

At the bottom of the stairs we found ourselves standing in a small cellar. A short man sat at a high table at the back of the room, a very tall cabinet looming behind him. Spread out on the table were gems and jewels in varying degrees of polish and completion. They sparkled like pieces of candy under the man's bright work light.

The tailor was a tiny creature with protruding ears. Perched on a stool, he wore a work apron and a jeweler's loupe, and he looked like a figure out of an old-fashioned fable.

The tailor looked up and smiled at us.

"We're here for the replica," I said. "Of the Hope Diamond."

The tailor nodded. He took a key and unlocked a drawer. He gazed inside at rows of small packages wrapped in tissue paper. He selected a package and pulled it out.

He turned and laid the package on the counter, opening the layers of wrapping. He turned on another desk lamp so we could inspect it.

The reproduction was incredible. It was almost unrecognizable as a fake. I looked closely. It was the same size as the Hope, the same deep blue. The surrounding ring of white diamonds glittered like a constellation. The sparkles, the internal fire—they were all there, beautifully re-created.

Ethan looked over my shoulder. "That should do, I'd say." I could tell from his tone he was as impressed as I was.

I nodded.

The tailor said, "You pay me three thousand dollar." He continued smiling as he wrapped up the package.

Ethan stiffened. "That is not the price we agreed upon," he said sharply.

The tailor kept on smiling and nodding. "Yes, yes. This is price."

"No. It is not," Ethan insisted.

I dug my nails into my palms. This could deteriorate to a conversation better suited for four-year-olds, but that wasn't going to get us anywhere.

I didn't have any more money. I had brought only twelve hundred with me, and there was no way I could scrape together more. Our first mistake, obviously, was showing openly how pleased we were with the replica.

"We can offer you one thousand. That's it. No more," Ethan said.

The tailor didn't budge.

It was time to start bluffing. "Okay, Ethan, I guess we're done here."

Ethan looked at me appraisingly, then nodded. And said, "Yep, we're done." We both moved to the staircase.

The thing about bluffing is you really have to believe it. It's like method acting. Or crashing a party.

We got a lot farther up the stairs than I thought we'd get. And then laughter chimed behind us. "Yes, okay, yes, yes . . . ," the tailor said. I turned and saw that his smile had changed in quality. There was an edge of worry to it now.

"What do you mean by *yes?*" Ethan asked.

"Your price. It is good."

We left the tailor's shop with Ethan carrying an extremely innocent-looking brown paper–wrapped package. Unless you held it, in which case you might find it to be a little heavy and lumpy for a simple cotton dress shirt.

Outside we were immediately beset by locals offering guided tours of the Grand Palace, cheap hotel rooms, and trips to various islands.

But it didn't bother me. We were mission accomplished. Now back to the airport. And back to Paris.

Now that we had the fake Hope Diamond in our hands, we could not be caught in any way. It would be incredibly suspicious to have a flawless replica of such a priceless thing. Particularly if your face was that of a wanted thief's.

In our crummy little hostel, we packed our bags and prepared to head back to the airport. I wouldn't miss this room, with its rattling air conditioner and sagging mattresses. I tried to keep the moment on the balcony firmly out of my mind.

It was late afternoon by now, and it was becoming unbearably hot and sticky. I went down to the lobby to get a Coke from the vending machine while Ethan was assembling our backpacks. I was in the back stairwell when I heard the voices in the lobby.

The walls were thin; I could hear everything.

In an instant, I recognized the voice of a man who was speaking in English. It was Hendrickx, the Interpol agent. In spite of the smoldering heat, my every molecule froze.

Chapter 44

I opened the door a crack. I had to see what was going on.

Hendrickx was standing at the front desk. I quickly scanned the rest of the lobby. Fans blew at top speed, flipping a sheaf of papers on the old, worn desk. Two Thai police officers leaned against the threadbare armchairs in the waiting area. Beyond them, in the street outside, I could make out at least one police car. Hendrickx was giving a curt description of two people. "Woman about five-two, light brown hair, slim, attractive. Man about five-eleven, strong build, blond. Looks like a film star."

The desk clerk, unconcerned, told him that yes, we were staying there, but he couldn't give him our room number.

This didn't give me much relief. They would find out soon enough, I was sure. We had to get out of there. The justice system in Thailand was not renowned for its fairness. There were all kinds of rumors of people languishing in prison for years with nary a charge or official arrest.

I silently slipped back from the door and raced the four flights up the staircase, heart thundering. I thoroughly scanned the corridor before entering it from the stairwell. It was clear. I sprinted to our room and darted inside, closing the door as quietly as possible.

Ethan was just zipping up his backpack. Mine sat on the bed, already closed.

"Hendrickx is here," I said in a harsh whisper.

"What?" His head snapped in my direction, eyes wide.

I nodded. "Downstairs. With the Thai police."

"We have to get out of here."

There was only one staircase and one lobby. We couldn't go that way. The only way out was the window.

We strapped on our backpacks—luckily, they were small—and clambered out our fourth-floor window.

We flew down the fire escape as quietly as we could, but the metal clanged with every step. Dropping down onto the grimy street below, we found ourselves in a back alley. The garbage bins emanated smells that made my eyes water. A handful of stray cats scattered at our arrival, and a rat slithered out of view behind a bin.

Just as we started to slip out of the alley, a shout rang out behind us. I knew only the most basic Thai words, but I understood "Hey! Stop!"

My gut seized. We kept moving, without stopping or looking behind us.

I spotted a tuk-tuk, one of the three-wheeled vehicles that zipped all over the streets of Bangkok. It was little more than a golf cart, brightly painted and covered with canvas. We leaped in.

"Go!" Ethan shouted to the driver.

The driver didn't miss a beat. I turned to see if anyone was giving chase. Sure enough, a car veered away from the hostel, wheeling fast into traffic.

"So? Where you like to go?" he asked us, chatting companionably, as we flew at a mad rate down the streets. The tuk-tuk careened through traffic and crowds and passed through a small market filled with bright scarves and loudly clucking chickens. Hot air whipped in my face.

"We need to go fast," I said to the driver.

"Yes, yes," he said.

"No. I mean really fast," I said.

"We are trying to get away from some bad men, okay?" Ethan said.

The driver nodded and smiled, then swung out from our lane and zipped between cars at a hair-raising speed. Of course, there were no seat belts, which made everything that much more terrifying. But less terrifying than getting caught by Interpol.

The driver slipped out of traffic and turned sharply down a shanty lane. The lane was lined with small huts, aluminum lean-tos with smoky fires burning. Families of grubby children and exhausted-looking mothers watched as we sped by. Strings of laundry flapped overhead.

In the tuk-tuk, Ethan turned to me. "How did they find us? How did they know? Has Hendrickx been following us this whole time?"

"I don't know. He must have followed us to Bangkok, though. How else could he have gotten here so fast? So that means someone in Paris tipped him off. Or someone might have spotted our arrival last night."

The tuk-tuk gave a sputtering sound. The driver looked down at his gauges. "Uh-oh, we are low on petrol. I must stop here at the service station."

"Here?" I said, shrieking.

The driver simply smiled that infuriatingly ubiquitous smile. I turned around. The cops were just turning down the lane, heading toward us.

Ethan and I leaped out, he tossed a handful of baht onto the seat beside the driver, and then we ran toward the river.

Clusters of long-tail boats sat at a dock on the Chao Phraya River. We had no time to ask permission.

I turned to Ethan. "We have to split up."

"No. I'm not leaving you," he said firmly.

"You know it's the best way. You know it's much easier to make a getaway solo. And we can divide them this way. And if one of us is going to get caught, there's no sense in both of us getting caught."

"How about neither of us getting caught?"

"Yeah, well, that's my goal, too."

In spite of his protests, I could tell he knew I was right.

"Okay, you take a boat," Ethan said. "I'll find another way. We'll meet at the airport, but not Suvarnabhumi. The private charter terminal at Don Mueang. Okay?"

I nodded and leaped aboard the closest boat. I hot-wired it in a second, and it rumbled to life. I'd never operated a long-tail before, but how hard could it be? Boats were my comfort level. Sailboats mostly, but I could manage this.

I punched the engine and roared out into the river. The churning water kicked up possibly the worst smell ever, a combination of garbage and raw sewage and bacteria. On the riverbank someone dumped something into the water. Within seconds, dozens of fish roiled the water's surface, splashing and gulping at whatever scum remained.

I started to get the hang of maneuvering the boat and tried not to think about all the muck spraying in my face. I glanced behind me, just in time to see Hendrickx and one of the police officers leaping onto another long-tail boat.

Which had to mean that Ethan had one person on him. There had been three of them in the hostel lobby.

Fine. I could handle it.

I turned the boat as sharply as I could down a side canal, trying to lose myself in the smaller waterways. I wondered how fast this boat could go. The more twists and turns I could make, the better I could shake them.

Nobody else on this river was moving as fast as I was. People were trolling the waters at a leisurely pace; many boats were being paddled or rowed. Shanty huts and shacks clustered along the banks among lush palm trees and grasses, and little docks on rickety stilts protruded doubtfully over the water.

I took another turn at a fork in the canal. I glanced back and couldn't see any pursuers. Could I have lost them? The canal took a bend, and once I rounded it, I saw a glut of boats ahead of me. The floating market.

There was no way through. Stationary floating boats filled the entire waterway. I looked behind me. Okay, I'd just turn the boat around and—

I saw Hendrickx's boat rounding the bend, heading fast toward me. I was trapped.

My heart flip-flopped in my chest like a fish. I continued speeding toward the market, thinking hard, trying to keep the panic down.

I killed the engine and pulled up beside a clutter of boats. When my boat bumped gently into a boat full of cabbages, I stepped across. I made my way through the market, moving from one boat to the next. One was full of chickens, and the next contained coconuts and bags of rice. The merchants were cooking food in these boats—I had no idea how that was even possible.

From one boat I casually grabbed a discarded straw sun hat, the cone-shaped kind all the sellers wore, and pulled it on my head. I kept going, stepping and leaping from one wobbly boat to the next. I needed to put some distance between myself and Hendrickx. I ignored clucking chickens and squawking sellers and kept moving forward.

Then I jumped out and joined the crowds on land, slipping into the throng.

It's always an internal tug-of-war when trying to escape. How long do you continue fleeing at top speed, and when do you slow right down and blend? Running gives you distance but attracts attention. The timing is an art form that requires a lot of finesse.

I disappeared into the darkness of the shaded, covered food market adjacent to the floating market. Here I passed stalls that sold grilled baby chicks on a stick, buckets of frog legs, and other horrible sights. The fish smell was overpowering, and everywhere there were bits of slimy fish on the ground. I had to watch out. If I stepped on one of those, I would slip for sure.

I needed some way to get out of here, fast. If I got lost in the labyrinth of food stalls, could they possibly find me?

I strolled more slowly through the market, exchanging my straw hat for a navy baseball cap in a souvenir stall and pulling a gray pashmina on over my shirt. And then I noticed in the street just outside the market a line of green buses. They were filling with people and pulling away. There was no sign of my pursuers. I darted from the shadows and stepped onto one of the buses as casually and as swiftly as possible.

I paid the overweight, sweating driver in bhat and walked to the middle of the bus. I slid into an empty seat and waited. I willed the bus driver to close the door and start moving.

Then I saw Hendrickx emerge from the market. There was no sign of his partner.

I sweated it out, keeping my cap low, slumping down in the seat, trying to keep an eye on Hendrickx.

Drive, damn it. Drive. My eyes bore holes into the back of the bus driver's head as he chatted and laughed with a woman who'd just walked on the bus. I focused on the roll of flesh at the base of his skull and tried to access the part of my brain that controlled telepathy.

I hazarded a glimpse out the window. Hendrickx was looking back and around, searching the crowds. And then I saw his eyes go to the buses. He locked on to the one in front of mine and strode toward it. I sweltered under the impossible heat, head prickling inside this damn cap.

I flicked a glance around the bus. What was my exit route from here? I shifted in the seat and looked behind me. There was an emergency exit back there, but it was blocked by a family with a tower of trunks. Some of the windows were open; others appeared to be crusted shut. But they opened only at the top. I judged the space. Would I fit through the gap? I wasn't sure I could.

The front door was the only way off the bus.

My mouth lost all moisture. I had trapped myself good and tight on this bus. If Hendrickx walked on after searching the bus in front, I would be caught.

Sweat trickled down my temples. Time ticked agonizingly. I could barely hear the buzz of conversation and flies around me. My gaze fixed on the bus in front of ours. Hendrickx hadn't emerged from it yet.

And then our driver released the brake with a loud hiss. The bus began to roll forward. I hunched down low in my seat as we passed the other bus. The moment we rumbled by, I saw Hendrickx emerge, look up, and see that our bus was leaving. At the same moment, Hendrickx's partner, the Thai cop, emerged from the market.

My chest constricted. Would they flag us down? Just when I was so close—

Then the bus shifted into a higher gear and smoothly began gaining speed. I glanced behind us. Both cops stood there, looking bewildered, shaking their heads. They had no idea where I was.

It was over.

I wanted to kiss the big, sweaty bus driver. Relief flooded into me in waves, better than the first sip of coffee on a six a.m. flight, better than a negative pregnancy test when you're two weeks late. The hot breeze washed over me, and I took off my cap. The wind ruffled my damp head.

Now, to get to the airport. I wasn't clear yet. I still had to get out of this country.

Chapter 45

Monaco

Underneath a velvety night sky, the villa was perched on a cliff overlooking the Monte Carlo harbor. Yachts and casinos glittered far below, a sparkling fringe to the wine-dark Mediterranean.

The view was spectacular. But Jack wasn't there to admire the view.

"So whose house is this?" Jack asked Wesley as they skulked along outside the villa. Dressed all in black, carrying night-vision binoculars, they slipped past palm trees and exotic gardens.

They paused to duck behind an elaborate fountain, eyes pinned on the villa beyond. "Apparently, it belongs to someone in the DOA," Wesley said. "Name of Franco DeAngelis."

They stayed immobile, watching the doors carefully.

"The advantage we have," continued Wesley, "is that the DOA is functioning under a false illusion of security. They think nobody knows the Fabergé is here."

Jack understood the urgency. It wouldn't be long before other people discovered its location, too. One group in particular simply couldn't get its hands on the Fabergé. Jack and Wesley didn't mention Caliga Rapio often, but they didn't need to. Caliga was always the unspoken threat in the shadows.

Except this time, Jack and Wesley had the jump on them.

Wesley kept his gaze locked on the villa. Seconds and minutes stretched by.

This wasn't the first time Jack had staked out and broken into a house with Wesley. They worked well together. It probably had something to do with the fact that Jack trusted him completely. Which was an interesting contrast to working with Hendrickx.

The rest of Wesley's team was stationed around the villa complex, covering them with a web of surveillance.

Jack shifted. "So what are we waiting for, exactly?" he asked.

Wesley stared through his binoculars. And then nodded. "That," he said.

A silver Ferrari pulled out of the garage and drove up the driveway. It disappeared along the curving cliffside road with a gentle roar.

They scanned the villa again. There were no signs of life—no lights, no movement through any of the multitude of windows. Wesley got the all clear from the rest of his field team. He and Jack began to move, slipping around the back of the villa.

Jack knew his role here. He was Wesley's backup. "It's an enormous house," Wesley had explained when they were planning the job. "We'll go in once we think it's deserted of all personnel, but we won't be a hundred percent sure."

So while Wesley picked the locks and hacked into the security, Jack watched his back. For a moment, he thought of how much he wished he could do this for another thief in his life, someone else whose safety was always a concern of his. There would be something highly fulfilling about being Cat's personal security. Her bodyguard. They could be a great team.

But no. He had to stop thinking along those lines, because that could never happen. This job with Wesley was a one-off. He was going back to his own side immediately afterward.

"Well, that was easy," Wesley said, disabling the security system.

Jack's head snapped up. "What do you mean, *easy?*"

"It just turned off. No sweat."

Jack frowned.

"Hey, don't look a gift horse in the mouth, Barlow," Wesley said.

But gift horses were exactly the sort of thing that set Jack's alarm bells jangling. On Jack's insistence, Wesley double-checked everything before they crossed the threshold into the villa. Jack himself did a thorough sweep of the front hallway and adjacent rooms. Nothing suspicious, nothing out of keeping.

They kept moving forward.

Wesley knew exactly where they were headed, and he'd shown Jack the blueprints before they'd gone in. They passed through opulent rooms full of antiques and lavish furnishings and made their way to the basement, to the safe.

In spite of everything going smoothly, Jack experienced a growing sense of creeping concern. Something was wrong.

But then he reminded himself he was breaking into a house without a warrant. For a Fed, that was plenty of reason to feel uneasy. He schooled his warring instincts and kept moving forward. Several minutes later they arrived at the basement safe.

Jack smelled the blood before he saw it.

In the center of the room, a man lay motionless on the floor, an impossible amount of blood pooling underneath his body. He was clearly dead.

Jack's weapon was out in a second. He crouched into ready position, taking in the room in an instant. There was no movement; the space was otherwise empty. It was clear, no threats. And there were no corners in which to hide.

Whoever had been there was long gone.

Wesley went to the dead body and looked down into the staring face. "This is Franco DeAngelis, the owner of this house."

"Then in the Ferrari . . . ," began Jack.

"The man who killed DeAngelis," Wesley said, nodding. "And made off with the contents of the safe."

They both looked up at the safe on the wall. The door was hanging slightly off kilter. Blown with a jam shot probably.

A crude job. No finesse whatsoever. Jack looked at the dead guy. "Looks like he refused to give up the combination."

Wesley briefed the field team, and they retraced their steps out of the house, vigilant for an ambush, but nothing happened. When they returned to the main security panel, Wesley stared at it, thinking.

"Now it makes sense. The security wires must have been cut," Wesley said. "That's why it was so easy to turn off the security. It wasn't on in the first place."

They retreated quickly from the villa, slipping back down the hillside to the car they'd stashed partway up. Jack knew he couldn't do anything about this crime. He'd have to arrange an anonymous tip somehow, but even that was risky. He was never supposed to have been there.

When they climbed back in the car, Jack looked over at Wesley. The other man's shoulders were slumped in defeat, and frown lines had formed on his forehead. Just like that, the egg was gone again. And with it, the Gifts.

"Who do you think did all that?" Jack asked, tasting bitter disappointment and frustration.

"Give you one guess."

Jack didn't need to say it. They both knew.

Caliga.

Chapter 46

I settled into the luxurious leather seat of the private jet that was lifting off the Bangkok runway, winging us back to Paris, and tried not to smile outwardly at the con we had pulled off to make this happen. I looked over at Ethan; he was wearing his trademark grin.

See, Ethan's look was a little bit Brad Pitt, a little bit Chris Pine, with a dash of Bradley Cooper for good measure. All it took was a pair of aviator Ray-Bans, a man scarf, and me posing as a harried personal assistant who insisted we had chartered the jet and surely they must have lost our reservation and "*Kindly* recheck your system, because my employer, who absolutely *must* remain incognito, is late for his premiere in Paris. . . ."

This scam would never have worked at home in the United States, but overseas it was a different story. In fact, Ethan had told me he'd pulled it off once before, in Zambia.

The sun beamed through the airplane windows, reflecting off the glittering crystal of our glasses. A dish of warm almonds rested on a tray in front of me, and Frank Sinatra crooned softly through the speakers. All we had to do now was let the pilot steer us back to France.

Except there was something that didn't sit well with me.

"How did Interpol know we were in Bangkok?" I asked.

Ethan looked at me and rubbed his jaw. "You're not going to like this. But have you considered maybe it was Jack?"

"What are you talking about? Jack would never betray me."

Ethan looked at me seriously. "Montgomery, he's FBI. When push comes to shove, he's gonna have to choose a side."

A queasy, raw-eggs-for-breakfast feeling developed in my stomach. But I denounced the thought. There was no way Jack would betray me like that.

There was more, though. Why, exactly, was Hendrickx coming after us so hard? I knew he suspected we were involved in a potential theft in Paris, but why would he be trying to arrest me before the crime? There had to be something else. I just couldn't put my finger on what it was.

I circled the problem in my mind over and over, until I began to develop a headache. Never mind. Maybe a little distraction was in order. I turned on the TV in front of me and selected an entertainment feed, a sitcom. One commercial, a brief news update, and then the show would start.

I was only half paying attention to the news when I heard the words *death* and *Paris*. I sat up sharply and paid attention.

A trench coat–clad reporter was speaking into a microphone, with a drizzly shot of Paris in the background.

"Two nights ago a man fell over a bridge in central Paris and died, drowning in the river Seine below. There were very few witnesses of the tragedy. But the reason for the interest is this. It was the third death in recent weeks that is connected to the Hope Diamond. The man was said to be one of the jewelers who had examined the Hope when it arrived in Paris last week. After three such deaths, people are starting to raise the alarm now. Is the curse of the Hope back? After so many years of good luck for the Smithsonian and the American people . . . is the Hope Diamond going back to her old ways?"

The image in the background was of a bridge, black iron. Underneath, its name appeared in small letters: Pont des Arts.

Instantly, a connection clicked in place. Reilly and Madeleine York had mentioned the Pont des Arts. At the time, I hadn't known what they were talking about. But it must have been about the murder. They were behind it. They were probably behind *all* the deaths. The hairs on my arms stood up.

"Madeleine and Reilly have been killing people," I said, piecing it all together. "Oh my God, I just figured it out."

Ethan looked sharply at me. "What? How can you be sure?"

"I can't be sure. But think about it. That seafood allergy incident in Paris—that could have easily been a murder made to look like an accident. And now, this incident at the bridge . . ."

"What about the other one? The car accident in the States?" Ethan said.

I nodded. "Yes, that one, too, I bet. That happened while Madeleine was still in the U.S. I can't believe I didn't see it before."

"Okay, so let's say hypothetically they're behind it. *Why?*"

I thought for a minute, chewing on a fingernail.

"People who are getting in their way?" Ethan suggested. "People who know what they're planning and are in a position to interfere or stop them? People who know too much?"

That made sense. I looked out the airplane window, deep in thought. We were flying above a landscape of sculpted clouds. The plane drew closer to Paris with every passing minute.

"There's another explanation," I said, still rolling it over in my mind.

Ethan looked at me, waiting.

"All this talk about the curse has increased the gemstone's value. It said so at the end of that news segment," I said. "What if—"

"That's all part of the plan?" Ethan said, finishing my sentence.

I nodded. I closed my eyes. Oh my God, that was it. The whole purpose of the murders was to revitalize the fears of the curse. To increase the value of the Hope right before they stole it. That way, Madeleine would get top dollar when she broke it up and sold it off piece by piece.

It was devilish. It was evil. It was murder for the basest reason. People's lives were taken to improve profit.

That had to be the explanation. But if true, it meant we were in even more danger than I'd thought. Madeleine and Reilly were even more ruthless than we'd realized.

I gritted my teeth with renewed conviction. More than ever, I needed to stop Madeleine. I could not let this succeed.

And the best way for me to do that was to steal the Hope before she and Reilly did.

Chapter 47

Back in Paris, Ethan and I took a cab into town. I dropped Ethan at his hotel and continued to mine. As the leafy boulevards slid by in a blur, my thoughts turned to Jack. I wondered what he'd been up to while I was gone, and I started craving his embrace.

But I wouldn't be able to tell him anything about the harrowing experiences I'd just lived through in Bangkok. He would never know what I'd gone through, and more than that, he would neither be able to soothe my nerves nor share in the victory of my narrow escape.

And then, as if merely thinking about him had summoned him bodily, I saw him standing on the sidewalk outside a hotel.

"Pull over here," I said to the driver.

I grabbed my backpack and leaped out of the cab. The civilized chaos of the street hit me right away. The smell of good coffee and fresh pastries from a nearby café curled around me like a favorite sweater. I'd missed the Parisian streets. Maybe Jack and I could go to that café, linger over drinks for the afternoon. . . .

I approached the hotel front where Jack was standing. A woman came out of the lobby and walked up beside Jack. He turned to her.

"Here Jack. You forgot this upstairs," she said, handing him his jacket. She was slender, blond, in her early twenties, with a heart-shaped face and a red, pouty mouth. "That was great, Jack. Thank you again. I'll call you."

My chest constricted.

Could this be anything other than *exactly* what it looked like? I thought about turning and running away. I thought about ducking behind a parked car at the valet stand, hiding, eavesdropping some more. But I just couldn't stomach it.

I walked straight over to them. "Hello, Jack," I said. I waited for an introduction while various shades of red flashed before my eyes.

Jack's mouth opened with surprise. "Cat . . . you're back? When did you get back from Bangkok?"

This startled response, this faux innocence, this hand-in-the-cookie-jar expression, well, they made me want to vomit. And gouge something.

I ignored Jack and turned to the woman. "I'm sorry. You are?" I said with an arsenic tone.

She smiled and thrust out her hand. "Taylor," she said. "And you?"

Jack jumped in and said, "Taylor, this is Cat, my girlfriend."

For a long time I let her stand there with her ridiculous hand outstretched. Then a small doubt crept in. Maybe this wasn't what it looked like.

I darted my hand out, hedging my bets, and briskly shook her hand.

"Cat, Taylor is a tech consultant," Jack said. "She's helping me with my case."

I nodded stiffly. It actually sounded viable. Taylor left after a polite interval, striding away down the sidewalk, leaving me and Jack standing there, staring at each other.

I turned on him with narrowed eyes. Now I would get the truth. "Why did she thank you?" I demanded, my voice dripping with accusation. "Why did she say, 'That was great,' if she's helping *you* on a case?"

Jack just stared at me. "Are you serious?" He looked genuinely taken aback. Then his frown deepened. "You know, you're acting crazy. If anyone should be suspicious, it's me. You spend day and night with Ethan Jones—"

I turned and walked away, crossing the street to the Seine riverbank, darting between speeding cars and ignoring their furious honks. I couldn't stand it anymore. He was evading the question.

Which, in my mind, was basically the same thing as admitting he'd been cheating. I wanted to throw up.

A nasty tangle of emotions twisted around me, though. Who was evading *whose* questions? Was he right? Was I doing the same thing?

Jack caught up with me on the other side of the road. "Stop," he said, reaching for my arm. "Just stop, Cat. Taylor was thanking me because I was helping her with her career. Gladys—your hacker—gave me Taylor's name because she is here in Paris and is trying to amass experience and referrals. The more jobs she gets, the more she moves up in the hierarchy." He looked really angry now.

Okay, that sounded plausible.

I stood there quietly beside the green *bouquiniste* stalls of antique books and old prints. I didn't know what to say.

Below us, the *bateaux mouches* plied their way slowly upriver, serving lunch and sending up faint notes of music on the breeze. People rode their bicycles past us, along the promenade that lined the river.

Jack set his jaw. "You know, I'm not sure this is going to work."

"What are you talking about?" I said. But I knew what he meant.

"You don't trust me. I don't trust you. Things are broken between us. And I'm not sure it's fixable."

My heart crushed inward. I looked down at my feet.

We stood there in silence for another minute. A family strolled by, carrying ice cream cones and a bouncing red balloon.

Then I said, "I know. I think you're right."

It was over.

Chapter 48

Later that afternoon, Jack sat by himself at a sidewalk café. He'd already packed up his things in the suite he'd been sharing with Cat, and checked into the Hôtel de Crillon several blocks away.

He'd brought case folders with him to the café. Being left alone with his thoughts was not a good idea; it would be much better to plunge into work. He reached into his bag and pulled out a file, the stuff he'd been working on with Taylor.

The Fabergé trail had gone cold again. After Monaco, Jack had flown back to Paris. To avoid going insane from wondering what had happened to the Fabergé, he'd dug straight back into the Gargoyle case. What he'd told Cat about getting a local hacker's name from Gladys was true.

The information she'd helped him unearth was useful. So Jack had pushed all thoughts of the Fabergé away—Wesley could handle it—and instead had focused on the new lead in the case. Specifically, the deaths linked with the Hope Diamond.

He'd asked Taylor to dig up all the information about the victims and the circumstances surrounding their deaths. Since he was FBI, Jack's sixth sense had been triggered by the rash of events. There had to be a connection between the Gargoyle, the Hope, and the recent murders.

Truth be told, the whole thing smacked of organized crime. And that was Jack's department. If he could get to the bottom of it, he'd go a long way toward forging a return to his previous status with the

FBI. At this point, his digging around in this case had nothing to do with helping Cat or liberating her from Faulkner. That was over. It was dead. It was just about him now. At least, that was what he was telling himself.

It pissed him to no end that he had to go through underground channels to get this information, but he knew his supervisor would not support an aboveboard investigation. He thumbed through the pages Taylor had unearthed and copied. Confidential files and e-mails and the like. There was a lot of chatter about the curse.

He certainly didn't believe in a curse. When there were coincidences—especially when those coincidences resulted in people dying—there was usually someone behind them. He just needed to figure out who.

His first thought, of course, was Faulkner. All the evidence Jack had found so far pointed to Faulkner being the Gargoyle. But even still, there was something about this case that didn't make sense. Jack couldn't quite put his finger on it.

He pored over the evidence again, trying to make some connections. There was the local police file on the case in the United States and a Police Nationale file on the incidents in France. But nobody appeared to be investigating a connection between the cases, as far as Jack could see. Not yet, anyway.

He pawed through the pages, looking for discrepancies, searching for links. A peal of laughter burst out from kids climbing on a nearby statue, sending a flock of pigeons up to the sky in alarm.

Then something caught his eye. It was in the photograph of the restaurant in Paris where the man had died from a seafood allergy. Jack's heart skipped a beat. He urgently flipped to the other files, reading the witness statements more closely.

No. How could this be?

The ground dropped out from under him as he made the connection and realized, once the FBI and Interpol made the same connection—any minute now, probably—who they would be going after. Who they might already be targeting.

Chapter 49

I strode along the path beside the Seine, eyes stinging with hot tears, throat tight. I'd been walking the city for an hour, ever since leaving Jack. I couldn't concentrate on anything else.

And then my phone rang in my pocket.

My heart leaped. Was it Jack? Maybe he was calling me to apologize, to tell me in soothing tones that we would work it out, that he missed me already—

I pulled out my phone and glanced at the call display. *Ethan Jones.*

Disappointment mingled with a faint ripple of happiness. Maybe talking to Ethan would make me feel a little better. It would be a distraction, at least.

"Hi, Ethan. What's up?"

"Where are you? I thought we were going to meet to review the final details? I'm at Chez Christophe right now, staring at a very lonely glass of Syrah."

I pressed my lips together. I'd forgotten.

Wallowing, over. Time to get back to business, princess. "I'll be there in fifteen minutes. Just hopping on the Metro right now."

When I arrived at Chez Christophe, I walked straight over to Ethan. He was nestled in a dark red upholstered booth near the polished brass bar. Smells of roast lamb, garlic, and buttery potatoes made my stomach groan with hunger. When was the last time I'd eaten, anyway? I pressed my personal issues to the back of my mind.

Ethan turned to me under dim, rosy lights and smiled. He wore an oxford striped shirt, open at the neck and rolled up at the sleeves. It was like he'd gone lengths to look extra hot right at that moment. Did he know somehow that Jack and I had just broken up?

"Hey, gorgeous," he said, flashing a grin.

I slid into the booth and tried to sit tall with a smile on my face. I really didn't want him to detect that anything was wrong, as I wasn't interested in getting into a whole conversation about Jack.

A waiter brought food. "I took the liberty of ordering a little something for us," Ethan said. The waiter set down a platter of foie gras, olives, and crackly fresh bread.

"Where's Brooke?" I asked, digging into the foie gras with a silver-plated knife.

Ethan shrugged. "Said she'd be here. She's probably on her way."

He was probably right, but I couldn't help the small worm of worry that began burrowing into my brain. I was counting on Brooke for a lot here. What if she let me down?

Ethan pulled out his notebook. We reviewed our plans, going over every step. Just about everything was in place.

And as long as I managed to avoid having a panic attack, I just might be able to pull this off. The thought of that, of course, started freaking me out. I dug into the food again, distracting myself with the mouthwatering flavors.

The waiter then brought two bowls of steaming onion soup with a thick layer of melted cheese and croutons on top. It was Jack's favorite. I closed my eyes briefly and tried to wipe him from my mind. I did not want to get stuck thinking about him right now.

"So, Montgomery, are you going to tell me?" Ethan asked. I looked up to see him gazing at me steadily.

"Tell you what?"

"What's up with you? You are a million miles away. Did something happen?"

I opened my mouth to make up some excuse, to claim that everything was fine. But I just couldn't do it. "Jack and I broke up."

He watched me carefully. "You okay?"

I shrugged and took a sip of my wine. I didn't trust myself to speak.

"I get it, Montgomery. We don't have to talk about it." He reached across the table and placed a hand on mine. "You're gonna be fine. You're a survivor."

I nodded. My hand felt warm where he was touching it. The warmth spread through the rest of me, and I looked up at Ethan with soft eyes.

And immediately felt a cramp of guilt in my chest.

What was I doing, taking comfort in Ethan's arms? Well, not his arms, exactly, but close enough. This was precisely why Jack and I had broken up. Ethan was clearly not out of my system. Maybe Jack had been right to cut me loose.

At that moment, Brooke walked into the bistro. I exhaled with relief. I knew she wouldn't have left me in the lurch.

Ethan followed my line of sight and turned to see her walking over. "Oh, good. There you are."

Brooke strode toward us with purpose, her face bright and hopeful. Did she have a new idea for the job? A new development?

"Right on time," Ethan said when she arrived at our table. "We were just getting to your bit."

"Well, belay that," she said. "Because I have to tell you both that, unfortunately, I'm not going to be able to do it."

My mouth went slack. "What? What are you talking about?"

"Um, what I just said. No can do. Sorry."

Silence followed as she plucked a piece of lint from her black merino wool skirt. I waited for her to make her meaning clear. But a further explanation was not forthcoming.

"Are you going to elaborate on that?" Ethan demanded.

She sighed. "Listen, I got an offer that I can't refuse. LNY contacted me, and a very big job has come up in New York. They say enough time has elapsed from my previous job, the heat is off, and I can go back and start getting prepped for this new job. It's the Star of India Sapphire, in New York. A big opportunity, something I've been wanting for a long time."

I stared at her in the way I typically stare at my credit card bill after Christmas. Stunned. Speechless.

"I'm flying back right away," Brooke said. "This afternoon, actually. I'm on my way to Charles de Gaulle right now."

I looked at Ethan. His reaction was much the same as mine.

"Listen, it's nothing personal," Brooke continued. "You knew I was just biding my time until I could go back, of course."

"Brooke, I don't see how we can do this job without you," Ethan said.

She flashed him a bright smile. "Oh, Ethan, darling, flattery is not going to help you here."

"It has nothing to do with flattery," I said through my teeth. "You're a key part of the plan. You can't just abandon us now. Can't you stay a couple of days?" I knew I was begging, and I hated myself for it.

How could I have been so stupid? This was the old Brooke I knew and loved. How could I have trusted her?

She laughed lightly. "Of course I can't stay. This job is waiting for me back home. Now."

Ethan put down his glass. "Brooke, you have totally fucked us," he said.

She scowled at him and folded her arms, tapping her finger on her forearm with annoyance. "This has nothing to do with either of you. If I stay here, I'll be screwing myself. I'd be messing with my own career. I'm not going to do that. You guys will be fine. You'll figure it out."

With that, she walked out. Leaving me staring at Ethan in disbelief, wondering what the hell I was going to do now.

Chapter 50

I gazed out the cab window at the lights of Paris as they slid by in an amber blur. Ethan and I were taking a taxi back to our respective hotels. My brain was churning. Brooke had abandoned me. What was I going to do now? How was I going to pull off the Hope job without her?

Her role had been crucial. She was going to be the one to take Reilly out of the equation on the night of the gala. We knew both Madeleine and Reilly would be at the Louvre on the night of the gala. And part of Ethan's job would be to distract Madeleine. It wouldn't be a problem for Ethan. He'd be able to charm the pants off her.

But I had been equally worried about Reilly.

"Reilly will see through the disguise. He's seen me enough," I'd said to Brooke. "Do you think you can distract him sufficiently?"

Brooke had smiled her wickedest grin. "I think I can handle that."

But now that she'd bailed, who was going to deal with Reilly? I couldn't just leave him to watch everything and interfere, but Ethan was going to be busy dealing with Madeleine.

We needed to find someone else to substitute. We needed another accomplice. In the cab, Ethan tried to call in a couple of favors with people he knew in town. But he kept coming up empty.

And then my phone rang. I picked it up and, to my shock, heard Jack's voice. "Cat, where are you now?" he asked urgently.

I frowned with confusion and could only mutter, "Uh, why—"

He cut me off. "You need to get somewhere safe. I need to talk to you. Is Ethan with you?"

I hesitated. "Um, yes . . ."

"Good. Bring him, too."

"Where?"

"It has to be somewhere very private. Safe." There was a pause on the line as he was thinking. "Can you meet me at the Père Lachaise Cemetery?"

"Now?"

"Yes. Be there in twenty minutes. At Oscar Wilde's grave, okay?"

I hung up and stared at the phone in my lap. What did Jack want? He hadn't sounded angry on the phone. More . . . *concerned*. But why?

Did he want to reconcile? Had he changed his mind? The timing was terrible. I was alone with Ethan. This was going to confirm everything Jack suspected. But then again, he seemed to expect me to be with Ethan. And he sounded more relieved than anything else.

I instructed the cabdriver to take us to Père Lachaise Cemetery.

The driver seemed unconcerned at the change of destination. Ethan not so much. "What are we doing, going to a cemetery?" he demanded. "Who was that on the phone?"

"It was Jack. And I'm not really sure why we're going to the cemetery. But that's where he wants to meet us."

"Us?" Ethan looked at me uneasily. "Montgomery, he's not likely to flip into a full-blown psychotic, jealous ex, is he? I really don't feel like dealing with that tonight. . . ."

I laughed. Jack was many things, but psychotic? Never.

A small niggling doubt hooked into my thoughts, though: He *was* FBI. Was there any chance this could be . . . some kind of a trap?

No. It was impossible. This was Jack. Yet somehow my churning, fluttering stomach wasn't entirely reassured by that.

A short while later we pulled up to the cemetery and got out of the cab. We approached tall stone gates and walked through into the hushed, darkened cemetery. A crushed stone pathway led us into the center, toward Oscar Wilde's tomb.

A chill rose on my arms. A cemetery was a disturbing place to go at night, particularly for someone who had recently developed a terror of death. But it was a good clandestine meeting spot. I had to hand that to Jack.

When we arrived at the tomb, Jack was already there, waiting for us. My skin crawled with the supreme awkwardness of this moment. Jack glanced at Ethan, and I caught only the briefest glimmer of emotion—anger or sadness or something—before Jack rearranged his face into a neutral mask.

He then proceeded to ignore Ethan and instead turned to me. "Cat, I have to talk to you about something. It has to do with the Hope Diamond. More specifically, about the curse. And the recent deaths."

Any thoughts I might have had about reconciliation quickly crumbled and blew away. And were immediately replaced by the cringing awareness that he knew the Hope Diamond was my target.

"For starters, I want you to know I think you're insane. You know that, right?"

I gave a weak smile.

"But it gets worse than that. Because there's now an investigation into these deaths," Jack said.

"The ones that have to do with the Hope?"

Jack nodded. "Interpol, the FBI, and the Police Nationale are working on it."

"Okay. And?"

"And you are the prime suspect."

I uttered a strangled, choking sound. "What? Me? Why would they suspect me?" I reached out and leaned back on a headstone for support. It felt cold and rough under my hand.

"They have evidence."

"What evidence could they possibly have? I had nothing to do with it!"

I became aware that Jack was watching me very closely, watching my reaction.

"You believe me, right? Jesus Christ, Jack, I may be a thief, but I'm no murderer. You have to know that."

He was silent for several seconds, during which my entire body turned inside out. Would he believe me? Was he here to arrest me?

"I know, Cat," he said in a low, calm voice. "I know you're not a murderer. Of course I believe you."

My heart resumed beating.

"But they are not going to believe you," he continued. "This is a big problem. They're already looking for you. I'm sure of it."

"What am I going to do? What sort of evidence do they have?"

"An item of your clothing. Credit card charges that place you at the site of one of the murders. And a witness."

I shook my head. "*What*? How could that possibly be? It makes no sense."

"You're being framed," said Ethan, who'd been quiet through this whole thing so far.

"He's right," Jack said. "It's the only explanation."

The witness could be easily faked. Somebody could be black-mailed or paid off. But what about the other lines of evidence? *Credit card charges.* Oh my God, I remembered now—those faulty charges on my card that had originated from Baltimore. But what about the clothing?

"A cardigan of yours—confirmed with DNA testing—was found under the table at the restaurant where the victim died of anaphylaxis to seafood. Like it had slipped off the chair or something. Not suspicious enough by itself, but taken together with everything else . . ."

My missing cardigan. I felt a perverse vindication. I *knew* it had been taken.

A crisp breeze stirred suddenly, whispering through the leaves and fluttering my hair. The hairs on the back of my neck went up, and I felt cold. A storm was coming.

"Who is behind all this?" I asked.

"Who else?" Ethan said calmly. "Madeleine York."

"Madeleine York?" Jack said with surprise and confusion. "What about Faulkner?"

Ethan shook his head. "No, Faulkner wants Cat to succeed. It's Madeleine who wants to stop her. And it's Madeleine who was behind the murders in the first place. Framing Cat is probably just insurance for her."

Panicky, I looked between the two of them. "What should I do?"

Jack rubbed his face, frowning. "You should lay low. Ideally, you should get out of here."

I chewed the inside of my cheek. "I can't. The Hope gala is tomorrow night. That's when I'm taking it. I have to. If I don't, Faulkner will—"

"Cat, are you kidding?" Jack said. "There's no way you can risk it. You will be arrested on the spot." Jack put his hands on my shoulders and looked into my eyes with concern.

I knew what he was saying. It made sense. For my own sake, I had to get to safety. But I couldn't just abandon the quest. Images of those photographs in Faulkner's possession flipped before my eyes. For my family's safety, I had to do the job.

"Not if I'm in disguise. And not if I pull it off and don't get caught," I said.

"What does Faulkner have over you, Cat?" Jack demanded.

I explained then about Faulkner and the threat.

"Can't you just—and I can't believe I'm actually suggesting this—but can't you just take the Hope Diamond later, another time? Like when it gets back to the States? Does he really care when you get it for him?"

I shook my head. "Reilly is going to steal it while it's en route to Washington. They've already fixed it."

"Unless you think you could stop that theft," said Ethan to Jack.

I shook my head. "You won't be able to. They'll have several decoys flying back at the same time, and by the time you figure it out, it will be in Reilly's hands. Besides, they've got an inside man. I heard them saying that. You won't have a chance."

There was a somber silence then. Doing it myself was the only way. I couldn't risk losing the Hope.

"I have to do it," I said. "I have no choice." I turned to Jack. "I will be fine. I'll be in disguise. Nobody will know it's me."

He stared at my face then for a long time. I knew he knew I was determined. He'd seen the look before. At last he nodded. He knew I wasn't going to change my mind. "And then you'll get out of Paris, right?"

"Of course." If I was successful, that was.

He looked at me uncertainly. "Are you . . . are you going to be able to pull it off? Are you ready?"

I took a deep breath. "I thought we were. But—" I glanced at Ethan.

"But what? Cat, what's gone wrong?" Jack demanded. "Is there a problem?"

"It's nothing. I'll figure it out."

"Cat, tell me."

Reluctantly, I told him about Brooke abandoning me at the last minute. He looked supremely pissed off, but not terribly surprised at what she'd done. I shouldn't have been, either.

I was exhausted. I needed to rest. I had a big day tomorrow.

"You need to get some sleep," Ethan said, echoing my thoughts, looking at me with concern.

I nodded.

Jack scrubbed a hand through his hair. "There's something else," Jack said. "You can't go back to your hotel, Cat. They're already there. That was the first place I looked for you. The police were all over it."

Chapter 51

We were in Ethan's suite, getting ready for the gala. I was putting the finishing touches on my disguise and tucking things into my purse: a lock pick concealed within my lipstick, a mini UV wand embedded in a mascara tube. God, it was good to be a woman in this line of work. How did men even do it?

I glanced at Ethan as he finished shaving in front of the mirror. I had stayed in his suite last night. But I had slept on the sofa bed in the living room area. Nothing had happened between us. Which was good. I did not need any complicating factors just now.

I had panicked when Jack told me about my hotel, that I couldn't go back. I would have to abandon everything that was there. I frantically tried to think of what incriminating pieces of evidence I might have left behind. The good news was that all my equipment and gear were already at Ethan's hotel, because we'd been practicing here. That, and I tend not to want to keep incriminating tools in a room I'm sharing with an FBI agent.

The other good news was that I hadn't checked in under my real name, of course. I never did.

The bad news, however, was that it would just be a matter of time before they pulled photos of my face from the lobby CCTV. My photo would be all over Paris soon.

But it didn't change anything. I still had to go through with this job. It was why my disguise had to be flawless.

I adjusted my wig, a big helmet of mousy brown hair. My disguise was designed to create the net effect of a blowsy middle-aged woman: enormous glasses, a flouncy evening gown of peach chiffon. Theater makeup and a judicious use of costume latex plumped and aged my face nicely. I glanced at my reflection and barely recognized myself. Which helped with the anxiety.

A little.

I reminded myself to take slow, deep breaths and touched reflexively the Kevlar vest underneath my gown. And when Ethan wasn't looking, I tucked the tarot card into the waistband of my panty hose. I breathed a little easier with those two items on my person.

The other disappointment, however, was Gladys. Her plane had been delayed getting here, rerouted to Frankfurt due to fog. But it was okay. Her role wasn't critical. I'd really just wanted her there for backup. This wasn't a high-tech job, for once; this one was all down to me and my skills.

No pressure.

I moved to the desk and grabbed the two necklaces and practiced doing the swap a few more times. In the middle of the third runthrough, Ethan emerged from the bathroom.

"Are you sure you want to wear the Kevlar?" he asked, patting his face with a towel. "I can see it makes your movements just a little trickier. You know that, right?"

"You've seen the weapons those Louvre guards carry, haven't you?" I said, finishing the last flourish in the sequence, completing the switch. "Besides, if it makes me feel safer, that'll help to prevent a panic attack, right?"

Ethan looked at me closely and folded his arms over his chest. "You know what I think? I think that kind of thing is actually prolonging this little problem of yours."

"What are you talking about?"

"You didn't used to wear Kevlar," he said. "You never needed it before. Just go back to that."

"I wish it were that easy, Ethan."

"Nobody said anything about *easy*, Montgomery," he said. "I know it'll be hard. But I think what you need to do is embrace the fear. And . . . you have to go completely unprotected. No flak jacket, no talisman-type things, like . . . oh, I don't know, a tarot card?"

I blushed. "How did you know about the tarot card?"

He raised an eyebrow. "Please, Montgomery."

I pouted and continued practicing.

When I was done, he said, "You're ready, babe. You are."

"I wish I felt that."

"I'm serious about the Kevlar, though. Trapeze artists and tightrope walkers do their best work when there's no safety net, right? Listen to the immortal words of Mark Twain. 'So throw off the bowlines. Sail away from the safe harbor.'"

I chewed a thumbnail. I just didn't think I could.

"Listen, Ethan, let's just get on with it, shall we?"

He shrugged. "Sure thing, buttercup." Ethan disappeared into the bedroom to finish getting ready. After a few minutes he emerged, looking unreasonably good in a tuxedo, as usual. Then there was a knock on the door.

Standing in the hallway was Jack. Dressed in a tux.

I blinked. "What are you doing, Jack?"

"Going to a gala event at the Louvre," he said casually.

I hesitated a beat. "Why?"

"A friend needs help."

I closed my eyes. "No, Jack. You can't do this. I'm in a ton of trouble as it is. I don't want you caught up in that, too."

"Cat, you don't have much of a choice, as far as I can see it. Brooke abandoned you, and you need an extra set of eyes and hands. I'm not going to do anything illegal, exactly. I'll just be there to back you up."

Everything about Jack—his tone, his posture—suggested he was totally decided. But I knew Jack. I knew his layers, and I knew the way he portrayed himself. I could see a hint of uncertainty in his eyes.

"Jack, you really don't have to—"

"Cat, I'm doing it," he said firmly. He wasn't budging. "It's not how I would prefer this to go down. But the most important thing to me is your safety. And the more of us there to help secure that, the better." His eyes flicked to Ethan, who was standing behind me.

At last I nodded. "Okay, Jack. Thank you." I stood there awkwardly, not knowing what to do with my hands. Should I hug him? Shake his hand? I settled with opening the door more fully and stepping aside as he entered the room.

As he walked in, the tension between Jack and Ethan was Spanx caliber. I knew how this looked. I knew it appeared as though Ethan and I were a couple and Jack was the tossed-aside ex-boyfriend. But that was not how it was. I hadn't chosen Ethan over Jack.

In fact, if I did have the choice, who would I choose? I frowned, lost in that for a minute. I quickly shook it off. I needed to get my head in the game.

We reviewed the plan, the three of us. And then we prepared to leave.

As we rode the elevator downstairs, Jack said, "By the way, I've sent Hendrickx off on a wild-goose chase for the evening. I told him you'd been spotted at the airport again. So he'll be chasing that shadow for a couple of hours, anyway."

I didn't know what to say. Jack was really going out on a limb for me.

Outside, Jack crossed the street and climbed into a car he had parked there. We would each be traveling to the Louvre alone. Ethan and I climbed into separate cabs.

And I tried my best not to throw up. It was beginning.

Chapter 52

Jack walked from his parked car into the Louvre through the Passage Richelieu entrance, showing his invitation as he did so. Small signs led him to the covered sculpture courtyard, the main venue for the gala.

The enormous space had been transformed for the evening with candles and twinkle lights. Trays of champagne adorned every surface, and white flowers spilled from a hundred crystal vases. A chamber orchestra played atop a small platform, filling the courtyard with baroque melodies.

As Jack walked through, he had yet another moment of doubt. What the hell was he doing here? Was it too late to back out now?

Cat needed help, clearly; she was in big-league trouble. She'd been abandoned by Brooke, and Jack didn't trust Ethan as far as he could throw him. He worried that Ethan would do the same—bail on Cat if the pressure got too high.

Well, Jack wasn't going to abandon Cat. Even though they had just ended their relationship—what, twelve hours ago?—he still cared about her. Even if they couldn't be together, he suspected that would always be the case.

A waiter approached, offering Jack a flute of champagne. Jack accepted graciously and strolled away, holding the glass. But there was no way in hell he was going to drink it. He needed to be sharp as a switchblade.

Jack started scouting for Interpol and the French police. Almost undoubtedly, they would be there. And just as undoubtedly, they would be looking for Cat.

Fortunately, Cat's disguise rendered her virtually unrecognizable. If she hadn't answered the door to Ethan's hotel suite, he wasn't sure he'd have known who she was.

Jack breathed a sigh of relief at that. It would give her a small cushion of safety. But not much more than that.

He scanned the courtyard, looking for undercover Interpol and French police officers. For the average person, they often blended in. For the trained eye of an FBI agent, this was like a gardener spotting weeds.

"Undercover agent by the chamber orchestra," he said quietly, knowing his words would be picked up by his invisible earpiece and heard by both Cat and Ethan, who each had their own earpieces. He continued surveying the courtyard, his gaze sliding over the marble fountain, where silvery water splashed and sparkled in the candle-light. "Another one between the bar and the fountain."

There was also, of course, a handful of uniformed security guards in the courtyard, but Jack was less concerned about them. Yes, they were the ones with the weapons—in plain view, at least—but they were lower on the totem pole and inherently less skillful.

Most problematic, to Jack's eye, was the undercover agent hover-ing close to the black velvet–edged stage. This was where Cat would be doing her thing, switching the necklaces when she was up on-stage, so it would be particularly important for this guy not to be standing right there.

Jack would have to prioritize—it would be impossible to eliminate the presence of all the hostiles in the courtyard. The one by the stage was the one he'd have to deal with.

It would have to be well timed. But Jack was ready. He had what he needed.

Jack smiled a little, in spite of himself. And then recoiled at that reaction. Was he actually *enjoying* himself? To his chagrin, he had to admit doing this illicit stuff was actually a bit of a . . . rush.

That, he would have to think about later. In therapy perhaps. For now he still had a lot of work to do. Next up: locate and neutralize Sean Reilly.

This had been Brooke's primary role in this operation, to take Reilly out of the equation. So now that job was up to Jack. Before leaving the hotel, they'd briefed him on Brooke's strategy: to attract Reilly's attention and seduce him if necessary in order to distract him, at worst, or to entice him right out of the courtyard, at best.

Possibly Jack would need to employ a different strategy than Brooke had planned.

He strolled through the courtyard and soon spotted Reilly over by a large potted fern. He was watching the proceedings silently, taking it all in. The guy might be an excellent thief, but he wasn't all that terrific at remaining incognito.

It was a skill Cat had in spades. He felt an unaccountable flush of pride at that. Which was ridiculous.

Besides, she wasn't his anymore.

Jack closed his eyes for a second, resetting his focus. He needed to think. How was he going to deal with Reilly?

He hated using his badge for crooked purposes. But this time, he wouldn't be doing anything wrong, per se, just calling attention to a potential thief.

He didn't have a lot of time. He'd need to report Reilly, get him taken care of, then set his sights on the undercover agent if he was going to deal with him before Cat's moment.

"I've got Reilly," Jack said in a low voice. "I'm making a move to clear him out."

Jack sized up the security guards and approached the one who looked the sharpest, standing by the entrance doorway. He needed someone with enough authority, enough decisiveness, to deal efficiently with a problem. Jack showed the man his FBI badge, hoping the guard would recognize it, more or less.

"Do you speak English?" Jack asked.

"A little," the guard said in heavily accented English. "But Michel is much better. . . ." He indicated another guard.

Jack frowned slightly but turned to the other guard, Michel. "I'm

FBI," Jack said, showing his badge again. "I'm not here on business, and I have no jurisdiction here . . . but I'm concerned, because I can see you have a thief here tonight. It's someone I recognize. You probably want to take him upstairs for questioning."

The guard's eyes lit up. Jack hoped the guard was interested in gaining brownie points with his superiors.

"Show me," the guard said.

Jack pointed to Reilly's location. "We have a file on him," Jack said. "I can't do anything. I'm just here on vacation. But you should handle it before he steals something."

The guard nodded. "Thank you. I'll contact my supervisor. Wait here, please."

What? No, he was just supposed to take Jack's information, pull Reilly off the floor for questioning, and let Jack carry on his way. There were still undercover agents to be dealt with.

The security guard spoke into his walkie-talkie, presumably to the supervisor, and then he turned to Jack. "Please come with me."

Jack blinked. *Damn.* But what could he do? "Sure thing," Jack said and followed the guard to the security office.

Chapter 53

Ethan strolled into the Louvre gala alone, taking a deep breath as he surveyed the courtyard. Everyone here was dressed like fashion was a competitive sport: Armani here, Versace there. He adjusted the cuffs on his shirt, enjoying the sensation of the tux on his body—as comfortable as pajamas. He smiled.

This is gonna be good.

Now, to locate Madeleine York. The timing was perfect. He'd arrived about thirty minutes before they would be presenting the necklace to the winners, which should give him just enough time for some prescription-grade charm.

Ethan couldn't be more in his element if he tried. The only black streak on his mood was his concern for Cat. Would she be able to pull it off? She was more than capable, if only she could get out of her own head long enough.

"I'm in, you guys. Looking good, Barlow." He'd spotted Jack over by the chamber orchestra. The man looked casual, relaxed, and very professional. He could tell Jack was scanning the room, but only because Ethan was aware of his mission. For a second, he experienced a twinge of something—a little like admiration, a little like a feeling of inadequacy. At that moment he understood why Cat found Jack so compelling. Why she felt safe around him. He definitely had the hero thing down. It was something Ethan had spent the past several years trying to resist.

"I'm almost in," Cat said. "Just at the coat check now."

"Welcome aboard, Montgomery," Ethan responded.

"Undercover agent by the chamber orchestra," Jack said. He was starting to pick them out. "Another one between the bar and the fountain." Jack continued describing the operatives he'd spotted, including the uniformed guards.

Shit. There were more of them than they'd counted on.

"That many?" Cat said, with a note of trepidation.

Ethan cracked his knuckles. "Montgomery, I'm just gonna ask you once more. *You sure?*"

Silence stretched for a moment. Then, "I'm sure."

Ethan nodded. Okay, well, the girl had tenacity, that was for sure. Ethan took a glass of champagne from the bar and began strolling the ballroom, searching for Madeleine. He held her image firmly in his mind. But he couldn't see her.

"Still looking for Madeleine. Anyone pick her up?" Ethan said quietly.

"I'm at the seating plan in the foyer," Cat said. "You're on here, Ethan, under the name Gladys entered, Rafael Augustin. You're at table twenty-one. Madeleine is at table five."

"Okay, table five. I'm heading right there," Ethan said. "Montgomery, can you handle the name switch?" he asked Cat.

"Already on it," she said.

En route to table five, however, he heard Jack cut in urgently. "Problem," he said. "I've been asked to go to the security office, to talk to the supervisor about Reilly. I don't know how long I'll be stuck there, but I can't get away to take care of the undercover agent. Ethan, can you do it?"

Ethan paused mid-stride and checked the time. "Okay. But I need a waiter's uniform. And the stuff." The plan they'd concocted was this: Jack would dress as a waiter and slip a fast-acting laxative into the operative's drink. He was already wearing a waiter's vest under his own tux.

"One step ahead of you," Jack said. "I'm making a quick stop in the men's room on the way to the security office. I'll drop the vest in the far stall. The vial is in the pocket."

Ethan headed to the men's room, arriving within three minutes. He went immediately to the far stall. Unfortunately, someone else was in there. As he waited, he tried not to pace or otherwise betray his impatience. But time was perishing.

At last the toilet flushed. When the door opened, an old man emerged, holding a black vest and looking at it with confusion.

Ethan smoothly intercepted him. "Oh, that's mine," he said. "I left it in there. Thanks."

He took the vest with a smile, and once the man left, Ethan slipped into a stall to change into it. There was also a pair of glasses in the pocket, and a long black waiter's apron.

He made a quick stop at the bar to grab a tray with two drinks: one without alcohol, one with. An agent on the job would probably want a nonalcoholic beverage. But . . . this was France. You never knew.

Ethan tucked himself into a small alcove, out of sight, and hesitated a moment over which drink to spike. He made a quick decision, poured the powder into the liquid, and stirred.

"Okay, I'm good to go," Ethan said quietly. "Now, who's my target, exactly?"

"Undercover guy by the stage." Jack described him in crystal detail: flat face, eyes too close together, blackish-brown hair.

As soon as Ethan walked toward the stage, he spotted the man. "Sir, some refreshment?" Ethan said with a knowing smile, holding the tray out to him. The agent took the drink containing alcohol.

Ethan walked away, smiling to himself. Good thing he'd doctored them both.

Circuiting back, Ethan returned to the service hallway and deposited the tray on the bar, dumping the nonalcoholic drink down the drain. He removed the waiter's vest and returned to the men's room to lose the glasses, vest, and apron.

"Montgomery, you got the table fixed up? Am I official?" he asked.

"Yep, you're at table five. Green light."

Ethan reentered the ballroom and strolled toward Madeleine's table. He approached the table, holding a card that read TABLE 5 and had his alias printed on it. In his pocket rested thirty-five similar cards, each with a different table number on it.

"Well, this is me," Ethan said in French, arriving at table five.

He introduced himself to two other table guests before turning to Madeleine. "Bonjour, madame," he said, sitting down beside her. He flashed her his most glittering smile—the kind he knew made his green eyes sing.

Madeleine raised an eyebrow. Her face couldn't possibly be colder, even if it had been chipped out of ice.

But Ethan didn't let that stop him. He poured himself a glass of Bordeaux from the table. But not before pouring one for Madeleine. "Please forgive me for saying this," he said to her, "but has anyone ever told you how much you look like Anne Bancroft?"

Madeleine pierced him with a steely gaze that was sharp enough to draw blood. "In fact, I *have* heard that before." And then a twitch about the mouth, "Usually from young, excessively slick men trying to get something from me—like money." She turned away frostily, clearly unimpressed.

Hmm. This was going to be a little trickier than he'd anticipated.

Chapter 54

I entered the Louvre sculpture courtyard in my floor-length, peach chiffon ball gown, my hair a news anchor helmet circa 1989. Not my style, not by a long shot, but that was the point.

My stomach flipped and spun like pizza dough being tossed into the air. This was it. This was go time. No excuses, no backing out.

I touched the back of my gown at my waistband, where I had tucked the tarot card. It made me breathe infinitesimally easier.

The chamber orchestra filled the vast, airy space with lush string music. Through the glass ceiling high above, the sky glowed a dusky purple. The room vibrated with people in Alexander McQueen and Marchesa, Harry Winston and Tiffany. Gardenias and Chanel No. 5 gave the evening a blue-blooded fragrance.

The centerpiece, of course, was the Hope Diamond. It rested in a display case up onstage. But I couldn't get a good look. There was no getting close to it before the ceremony.

But that was okay. If all went according to plan, I'd have an up close and personal experience very soon.

First, I had one little errand to take care of. I needed to stash my change of disguise. Rule number one of every professional thief: always have more than one getaway option. Gladys had "ordered" a security guard's uniform in the Louvre's system last week—my size, complete with badge and walkie-talkie. I just needed to retrieve it and stow it somewhere that was easily accessible.

Because all the security staff were out on the job, it was a piece of cake for me to slip into the security locker room, find my uniform in its shrink-wrapped package, and grab it. I snuck down the corridor and stashed it in the utility closet in the Sully wing, stuffed behind a mop and bucket. I took a pack of cigarettes out of my purse and tucked it underneath the uniform; it might come in handy later, for verisimilitude.

I returned to my assigned table in the ballroom and focused on making pleasant small talk with my tablemates, playing the role of a wealthy widow.

I glanced over at Ethan and Madeleine's table, hoping to see him charming her utterly. But her body language didn't say she was exactly *taken* with him.

I frowned. This sort of thing was usually a waltz for him, but Madeleine was looking rather . . . *wintry.*

Ethan's skills in this department were substantial, I reassured myself. He just needed a little more time. At that, my thoughts on Ethan's skills spiraled away. Had he been using those skills on *me?* Had he been working me like a target? Was it a game for him?

I shook my head, rattling it back to focus. What the hell was I doing? The last thing I had time for at this particular moment was thinking about my love life.

I glanced at the security guards with their semiautomatics. My stomach did a double pike with a half twist. I touched the edge of my Kevlar vest, tucked under the layers of chiffon. Touching it softened the edge of my anxiety.

The ceremony was scheduled to take place while we were served dinner. The first course came out—endive salad. But I barely tasted it as my mind was so singularly focused on the task ahead of me.

I continued polite conversation on autopilot and nibbled my salad.

And then, up onstage, they announced the first winner: Sophie DeHavilland. A wisp of a woman with a thin ribbon of long silvery blond hair stood and floated to the stage. She was guided by security guards to the side, where a black velvet curtain swallowed her up as she stepped backstage. My gut twisted. That was where I'd be going soon.

* * *

Jack cooled his heels in the security director's office, trying to crush the urge to pace. Appearing impatient would send the wrong message, but this was taking too long. He clenched and unclenched his fists. On the far side of the room was a bank of CCTV screens, which he surreptitiously studied.

He watched as the first winner, an elfish-looking woman with white-blond hair, made her way backstage. And then he watched as a security guard frisked her.

Fuck. That was unexpected. Were they going to do that to all the winners? What were they going to do if they found the fake Hope on Cat?

"Did you two know they were going to frisk the winners?" he said quietly. Jack kept his gaze fastened on the screen. They were doing a pretty thorough job, to his eye.

There was a pause. "Are you serious?" Cat hissed.

"Oh, shit," Ethan said.

"Okay, well, is everything else in place? Has Reilly been taken out yet?" Cat asked.

"No," Jack said. "Not yet. I'm just waiting in the security director's office now."

"Ethan, have you got Madeleine? Can you get her out of there?" Cat asked.

There was silence, and then a mumbled "Not quite. Working on it."

Jack looked at the CCTV image showing the front of the stage. The undercover guard placed there was holding steady; there was no sign of the drug Ethan had given him taking effect yet.

Was *anything* going according to plan?

Then Cat spoke again. "Wait a sec, Jack. Did you just say you were in Severin's office? The security director?"

Jack looked at the plaque on the inner door. "Yes, Pierre Severin. Why?"

There was silence for a moment. And then, "Any chance you could get his left thumbprint?"

"What?"

"I can't explain right now. Just get the thumbprint, if you can."

The first winner was onstage now, and they were removing the

Hope Diamond from its display case and carefully placing it around her neck. Jack watched, mesmerized.

They took her photograph while she smiled and glowed, and the Hope sparkled about her throat. In the security office, Jack shifted in the uncomfortable chair.

Where was the goddamned director? He had to get Reilly out of there.

After two brief minutes, the chief curator removed the Hope from the first winner's neck and returned it to its display case. The elfin woman made her way offstage. And then they called the second winner's name.

Cat was going to have to back out, Jack thought.

But just as he was about to say this, Jack heard Ethan excuse himself from his table to get a drink and then, more urgently, say, "Montgomery, you can't go through with it. You have to get out of here. They can't find you with the replica."

There was no response.

Jack said "Cat? He's right."

Cat's voice came through quietly. "I understand your concern, you two, but I can't back out. Maybe they won't feel my sleeve." Jack knew that was where she'd stashed the Hope replica.

"Even if they don't feel your sleeve, what about your earpiece?" said Ethan, his voice tight with concern. "And the Kevlar? They'll feel that. Don't you think they'll think it's suspicious?"

Cat was wearing a flak jacket? That was out of character. Jack felt a ripple of discomfort. There was a lot he didn't know about Cat's emotional state right now.

Jack watched on-screen as the second winner made her way to the stage. She was an older woman with steely gray hair in a short, asymmetric cut. She looked every inch Parisian glamour, old money. The only thing missing was a tiny dog at her side.

Jack glanced at the clock, which loomed large in the room. They had only a few minutes to sort this out.

On another screen he saw the guard frisking the second winner. Jack squeezed his fists.

At last, a man emerged from the inner security office. He wore a suit, had a tiny mustache, and smelled heavily of cologne. He approached Jack and introduced himself in heavily accented French as Pierre Severin, director of security. He then said, "So who is your suspect?"

Jack pulled his phone out of his pocket and scrolled through his secure folder of images. He found the photograph of Reilly and handed Severin the phone. "He was over by the piano . . . there." Jack pointed at the CCTV screens. "Right there."

The director held Jack's phone and studied the photograph of Reilly. He inspected Jack's badge. Then he peered at the CCTV screens and back at the phone.

Jack looked down at Severin's hands as he held his phone. Severin was enlarging the image with his right hand, holding the device in his left. Most importantly, his left thumb rested on the smooth acrylic case.

While Jack had been waiting for Severin, he'd surreptitiously wiped his phone completely clean.

He had the thumbprint. Whatever use it was to Cat.

Jack flicked his glance to the main stage. They were just removing the Hope from the Parisian woman's neck. How had that happened so fast?

Severin grunted and said, "We need to speak to this man." He then got on the radio and dispatched his guards to collect Reilly. Jack watched on the screens as the guards moved surprisingly quickly to approach Reilly and asked him to come away quietly. He was then hastily, discreetly, marched away.

Next thing he knew, the emcee was announcing the name of the third and final winner. "And the final winner of tonight's honor, Christiane Beaulieu." Jack knew that to be Cat's alias for tonight. His stomach clenched. He watched Cat as she stood, smiling and blushing, and then started to walk backstage.

Shit. She was going through with it.

Jack needed to do something to help her. "I'm going to have to leave," he said quickly to the director of security. "As you know, I have no jurisdiction here, and my supervisors would be truly pissed if I broke that mandate and was involved in questioning a suspect."

The director narrowed his eyes, then nodded. "You're right. Thank you." He handed Jack his phone.

Jack casually strolled out. And then, as soon as he was out of sight, he broke into a run. He had a very sketchy plan. "Slow down, Cat," he hissed into the receiver. "Take your time getting there." He sprinted all the way to the main stage.

Chapter 55

Ethan slugged back more of his drink. He was trying everything he could think of to woo Madeleine. But she was proving to be an incredibly tough nut to crack. If he couldn't get Madeleine out of there, it could ruin the whole thing.

He reached for the bottle of wine on the table and filled her glass, then his. "One of the things I like best about a fine wine is how it gets better with age," Ethan said smoothly. "More sophisticated, more layered, more interesting." He gave Madeleine a glance that was laced with meaning. "But maybe that's just me. Perhaps you prefer your wine on the young side—vigorous and bold?"

He got nothing back. Madeleine met his gaze, sipped her wine, and looked away.

Then the emcee onstage called out, "And the final winner of tonight's honor, Christiane Beaulieu!"

Ethan tightened his fists. He had to do it now, with his very next line.

It was a risky one, but he had to give it a try. He leaned in and said in a low voice, "There's a balcony off the Napoleon III apartments. I hear there's an incredible view of the pyramid right at sunset. Right now, in fact. I'm not sure it's allowed, going out there, but shall we try to sneak out and see it, anyway?"

This was probably coming on way too strong. He would be lucky if she didn't slap his face. But he had to try.

Madeleine turned slightly in her chair to glance at him over her shoulder. She gave him an appraising look. "Yes, Mr. Augustin, I believe we shall."

It was all he could do not to fall off his chair with surprise. But he didn't miss a beat when standing and holding her hand as she rose. As Madeleine paused to retrieve her clutch, Ethan took a moment to watch Cat, to assess how she was doing.

And she did not look good. Not at all. There was full-blown panic in her eyes as she made her way to the stage.

Ethan placed his hand on Madeleine's lower back as they walked from the room. There was nothing more he could do for Cat at the moment. Although maybe this was the time to start praying.

The moment before they called me up onstage, I saw two security guards arrive and quietly take Reilly away. Jack must have done his part.

Then the emcee announced my name, and everything went into blur mode.

I glanced over and saw that Ethan had finally managed to capture Madeleine's attention. They were standing, heading out of the room.

I stood, trying to calm my quaking knees. What about the undercover agents? Were they still on point, or had Ethan and Jack managed to take care of them?

Then, as I approached the stage, a man just in front of the platform suddenly clutched his abdomen and dashed in the direction of the men's room. *Yes.* It was the undercover agent Ethan had furnished with our handcrafted cocktail. The superfast laxative had worked like a charm.

My way was clear. Of the dangers they could help me with, anyway. Now I just needed to do my bit.

There was applause as I walked up to the stage. Of course, I couldn't hear it over the rushing blood in my ears. I could tell only because I saw people's hands moving rapidly, clapping together.

A panic attack was brewing. I could feel it.

This was very bad. Anything less than laser focus wouldn't work.

"Babe, either you're doing your best impersonation of a housewife panicking under the spotlight . . . or you're starting to lose it," Ethan said quietly in my ear. I could see he'd let Madeleine walk ahead of him a little, out of earshot. "Just breathe, Montgomery. Slow it down."

I wobbled a little on my heels as I approached the steps to the stage. I touched the lower edge of my Kevlar vest. I didn't want to, but I couldn't stop myself.

It helped fractionally.

In my ear, Jack hissed, "Slow down, Cat. Take your time. I need a few more seconds to get there. . . ."

I was able to calm myself just enough to see straight. But I was miles away from the person I usually was in these situations. And miles away from the person I wanted to be.

Somehow, I was just going to have to dig deep and do this. I commanded myself not to look at the guards. Or their Walther P99s.

I found myself walking backstage. Just a few feet away from me was the display case, laid open onstage. The Hope was there, staring at me. I experienced an irrational urge to just grab it and run. To dispense with all the pretense and the show and the sleight of hand plan . . . and just take it. It was like that sick, irrational urge to step off a cliff edge when you got too close.

Oh my God, I was losing it.

My breathing was loud, like a wind tunnel, and everything looked like a tight-focus, wobbly scene in a movie. I knew what I had to do. I tried hard to keep that in mind.

But first, I needed to figure out what to do about this frisking issue. I walked closer to the stage and saw that I was, essentially, walking into the embrace of a security officer.

Could I refuse it? Could I claim some kind of harassment thing? Just as I was formulating a plan, I heard the footsteps of someone coming briskly up the back steps. The security guard was about to start frisking me when Jack tapped him on the shoulder.

"Hey, man," Jack said in rough French. "FBI." He flashed his badge. "We're working with Interpol, and we're taking over from here. You're on break as of now." He held out a cigarette and lighter for the man. I had no idea if the guard smoked or if Jack knew this, either.

But the guard simply stared, not backing down.

"Check with your superiors," Jack said impatiently. "I was just there, in the security office."

The guard held his walkie-talkie to his mouth, keeping his gaze latched on Jack. "I have a Jack Barlow here, FBI or Interpol or something. . . ."

There was crackling on the line. And then, "Yeah, he was just up here. Talking with Severin about a suspect. What about him?"

The guard shrugged. He accepted the cigarette from Jack and said, "All yours," indicating me. He walked away, and Jack stepped in. I tried to school the smile that was threatening to take over my face.

Jack's expression didn't crack. He was a pro, and he was all in. Just like I needed to be. And if I *could* get it together . . . well, I just might pull this off.

At that moment I was led out onstage.

Ethan's voice chimed in my ear. "Montgomery, I'm here," he said. "Just for a minute. I left Madeleine on the balcony for a second. Hang in. You can do it."

I looked out to see Ethan standing in the ballroom by the bar, gazing in my direction. Then I spotted Jack striding across the room, heading toward the restrooms, and I knew he was getting in position to pull the smoke alarm. Jack and Ethan were doing their part. Now it was my turn.

At that moment, I became dimly aware of the person holding up the Hope necklace. It glimmered in front of my dazed eyes. I fought to focus on it, but it was like one of those hypnotizing pocket watches in cartoons.

I felt for the replacement in my sleeve, and it was there, a hard lump in the folds of fabric. Everything was ready.

And then, suddenly, it was around my neck. Heavy and cold. Wait. The *real Hope Diamond* was around my neck. Panicky flashes of the curse spun through my head. I needed to get it together here. I could feel myself on the paper edge of a full-blown panic attack.

Escape, was all I could think. I needed to escape. But I couldn't run now, not with the Hope. It was like a handcuff for my neck. A collar that dogs in training wear, one that administers electric shocks.

I posed for photographs and had no idea if I appeared happy or terrified.

"*Smile,* Montgomery," Ethan said in my earpiece. "And breathe. You're almost there, kiddo. Just wait for the alarm and then do your thing. You got this."

My hands went up and around the back of the necklace. I knew what I had to do. I knew how the clasp worked. I'd practiced a thousand times. I took a step away from the host so he wouldn't reach out for me or interfere with my swap. My heart was beating like it was going to explode.

And then Jack's voice sliced into my consciousness. "Cat, you ready? Here we go."

The smoke alarm wailed with a sudden, unexpected piercing. Everyone looked up, around, and most importantly, away from me.

At that instant I pretended to stumble. My pashmina swept across my throat. My hands unclasped the necklace and let it drop down the front of my gown, concealed by the pashmina. The replica slid out of my sleeve, and I brought it up, clasping it at the back of my neck.

I stood up straight once more and swept the pashmina back and away. I gazed at the crowd as confusion about the smoke alarm settled and people turned back to the stage again. I scanned the faces. All it would take was for one person to have spotted the swap. Was anyone frowning with suspicion? With conviction or outrage? Had anyone seen what I'd done?

In my mind it was the clumsiest swap I'd ever done. The worst one since I'd started practicing. Worse than my first attempt. I was sure in a matter of seconds the guards would be upon me. It was over.

And then I heard Ethan say, "Perfection, Montgomery. Your best ever. Now, smile. You're almost done."

Perfection?

The panic attack was still surging through my nerves. I wanted to vomit. There was a strong possibility I still would—all over the shoes of the emcee.

I felt the curator undo the clasp behind my neck, raise up the fake Hope necklace, and place it back in the display case.

"You got it, Montgomery. Now, *get off* that stage."

"But go slow," Jack added. I could see him strolling back to the table.

I had it. It was in my gown. The Hope Diamond. I could feel it, snug inside the bodice of my gown.

Someone turned off the smoke alarm, and everyone relaxed again.

On wobbly legs, I stepped toward the edge of the stage and walked down the stairs, still forcing a smile. I knew what was in my gown. I had visual images of it dropping straight through, falling to the floor by my feet, appearing under my ball gown. And me, caught red-handed and frozen, like a deer in headlights, as camera light-bulbs flashed.

Somehow I got off the stage and back to my table.

"Breathe, Cat," Jack said.

The crowd's attention went back to the front of the ballroom as the emcee continued speaking, announcing dessert and dancing. And pointing out that the champagne bar was still open.

I think. It was all very Charlie Brown's teacher to my ears.

"Take three more breaths, Montgomery, and then get moving," Ethan said.

If I didn't have these two coaching me through this, what would I have done?

I had the Hope. I had it. Still, there was a big part of this that felt like a failure. I was a shadow of my former self. The old Cat would have gone up there easily, totally under control. And more than that, she would have had fun.

Right then, I knew my career as a thief was over. I'd lost it. I couldn't do it anymore. I wanted to hide and cry and run.

And I would have done all those things. Except I still had to complete this job.

I took the three slow breaths Ethan had instructed me to take, then calmly stood and walked out of the ballroom and toward the restroom. I chose the restroom that was far away from the ballroom and down a long dark hallway, the Richelieu wing, well away from security or anybody else. And I was happy to have the walk to help settle me down.

Once there, safely locked inside a stall, I set to work. I needed to switch the location of the Hope, to put it somewhere more secure. I plucked the Hope from my bodice and stared at it a moment.

It was gorgeous. Sparkling. And . . . *Oh no.*

What I held in my hand was a fake Hope Diamond.

Chapter 56

I couldn't believe it. Bitterness flooded my veins. This was a massive fail.

The fake was a good one. Very good. Not quite as good as the one I'd swapped it for, however, the one we'd procured in Bangkok. But only a trained eye would recognize the difference. And my eye was very trained. Now that I looked carefully, though, it was obvious from the degree of reflection, the quality of the sparkles and the interior fire. It lacked luster. It lacked that magical quality. The white diamonds that collared it were fake, too. The whole thing was a replica.

I couldn't help thinking, if I had been of clearer mind up onstage, would I have noticed earlier and saved myself this whole heartache and risk?

I was out of time. I clutched onto the cold metal bar inside the toilet stall for support. *Faulkner.* I couldn't let him find out. Not yet. I needed time—enough to make an escape.

But what about everyone else he'd threatened? Would he really go through with the punishment?

My mind was a churning fury of gears and pistons. One question pressed forward. Where the hell was the real Hope Diamond?

I immediately thought of Madeleine and Reilly. Had they already snatched it, replacing it with this fake?

No, that made no sense whatsoever. Madeleine's plan depended on a very public theft. She needed the world to know the Hope had been stolen. Taking it subtly and replacing it with a fake did not suit that plan at all.

Was it possible this had been the jewel in the Louvre all along? And I was only now noticing it was a fake? No, there was no way. I would have recognized it. When I came to see the Hope in the Louvre that first day, that was the real one. I was sure of it. This was a replacement. So where was the real one?

And then I remembered something: *the underground vault.*

That was where Lafayette had said they stored the Hope at night. Maybe they'd kept it there for the gala, too, using a replica during the high-risk time of the gala, when strangers, members of the general public, would be wearing it?

Could it possibly mean . . . Was the real Hope still in the vault downstairs?

"Cat, you there?" came Jack's voice in my ear.

I had forgotten Jack and Ethan; they were waiting for me to give them a report. I exhaled and closed my eyes and said, "You're not going to believe this."

"What?" Ethan said.

"It's not real."

"What's not real?" Jack said.

"The Hope."

A suspended silence hung on the line. Then Ethan said, "Are you sure, Montgomery?"

"I'm sure."

Ethan swore in response.

"What now?" Jack asked.

"Now I need to get out of here. After that, I don't know. I can't even think about it yet. I'll meet you guys in the ballroom."

I tucked the fake Hope into my bodice and slipped into the corridor, making my way back to the ballroom. Rows of looming carved columns cast eerie shadows in the darkened hallway. Nobody else was here as I walked. My shoes echoed eerily on the marble, and the skin at the back of my neck prickled.

And then a cold blade went to my throat.

"Hello, princess," a familiar voice hissed in my ear. "You seem to be lost."

Jack heard the voice through his earpiece, then a muffled shout from Cat, then nothing. He immediately bolted into action. Cold terror surged through his body when he heard a loud crackle on the line, then nothing more from Cat or the man. He started running to the Richelieu wing.

"Barlow! Do you see her?" Ethan was hollering through the line. "Do you see her? Can you get to her?"

"No! I'm on my way, but I can't see anything yet," Jack barked. "*Respond,* Cat. Are you there?" But there was nothing from her. The line was dead. He refused to consider the possibility that Cat was in the same state. He just kept moving forward. "Jones, who the hell was that?" he demanded. "Do you know?"

But there was almost nothing from Ethan—some heavy breathing only. He was on the move, too.

Jack sprinted through the dark corridor, his heart pounding in his ears. He was not concerned that he had left the party so abruptly. Not concerned about the Hope Diamond. One thing alone concerned him right then: getting to Cat.

He rounded the corner at a sprint to the Richelieu wing. On the floor he spotted something. One of Cat's shoes. And beside it, a crushed earpiece. But there was no sign of them otherwise.

She'd been taken.

Jack spun on the spot, trying to judge which way they'd gone. Then he heard shouting in his earpiece. It was Ethan.

"Jack! She's here. He's taken her to the courtyard!"

Jack covered his ear to hear better. "Where? Jones, where are you?"

"In the Cour Carrée, the square courtyard! The west wing—"

Jack sprinted like a cheetah to get to that spot. He knew exactly where Ethan meant. It was a fully enclosed, large courtyard at the back of the Louvre, where few people went. He could hear Ethan gasping for breath. And then something that sounded unbelievably loud, like a motor.

Jack burst into the courtyard just in time to see a helicopter lifting off the ground.

The instant Ethan heard the voice, he'd known exactly who it was. Sean Reilly. Thief, probable murderer, all-round son of a bitch.

He'd started running immediately. But not to where Cat had been. Instead, he'd cut a course to where he figured Reilly would take her. Ethan knew her approximate location in the Richelieu wing, and he figured Reilly would want to get her out of the building and away to a more secure location. This was the fastest route out of the building. It was smart. It would take Louvre security a few minutes to lock on this location and mobilize people back here.

The chopper was still on the ground as Ethan emerged from the building. He raced for it, not stopping to think. What was he going to do? Jump in? Hang on?

He saw Cat inside through the windows. She was sitting very still, with a knife against her throat. He barked into his receiver, "Jack! She's here. He's taken her to the courtyard!"

Ethan was a full-throttle locomotive. He had to get to her across the courtyard. He ignored the erupting terror of what would happen to her and focused on his determination to stop it.

The sound of the helicopter was deafening, the wind like a hurricane as he got closer. But as he sprinted, muscles burning, the helicopter lifted up. Panic clutched Ethan's throat.

Ethan looked around frantically. Cars were parked on the far side of the courtyard, valet parking for the most exclusive clients at the gala. He would need something that moved fast. He jumped into the first one in line, a black Aston Martin.

He hot-wired it in a second, trying to keep an eye on the helicopter. The engine came alive with a vibrating roar. He pressed his foot to the floor.

He knew it was ridiculous. How was he going to keep track of a helicopter and drive at the same time? Then Jack exploded into the courtyard. Ethan steered the car to him, swinging open the door.

"Get in!" Ethan barked. Jack didn't ask questions as he leaped in the passenger's side.

"Keep your eye on that helicopter," Ethan said. They flew underneath the archway leading out of the courtyard and into the streets.

"Jones, there's no way we can follow a helicopter in a car. Not even this one."

"We have to try," Ethan said. He despised the fact that his voice cracked just then. Who the hell had he become? "Even if we just see what direction they take her in."

Jack kept a firm eye on the helicopter, and Ethan drove like a madman. He did his best to keep up as Jack snarled directions.

"Faster!" yelled Jack. "You're losing them."

Ethan gamely swerved through traffic. But after a few seconds, he knew it was going to be futile. There was no way they could keep pace with a helicopter in Paris traffic. In a matter of seconds the helicopter was too far away to catch. After several more seconds it was out of sight entirely.

They had lost her.

Ethan's chest crushed with defeat. He pulled the car over, into a bus pullout beside the Seine, and both men climbed out. They stared into the sky in the direction the chopper had disappeared.

Ethan needed to think. Where could they have taken her?

"Who was it? Who grabbed her?" Jack demanded.

"It was Reilly." Ethan rubbed his face. "I recognized the voice. Then I saw him in the helicopter."

Jack stared at Ethan with bewilderment. "I thought I'd dealt with him. He was supposed to be detained by security."

"I guess he got out of it somehow, *Jack,*" Ethan said with a cutting tone. "He must have doubled back."

Jack was clearly frustrated; he looked like he might bite through sheet metal. "Why did they *take* her, exactly?" Jack demanded. "Why not just seize the Hope? Knock her out or—" Jack stopped abruptly, and Ethan gave him a sharp look. There would be no mention made of anyone killing Cat.

Jack nodded, both men in silent agreement over this. Ethan raked a hand through his hair, thinking hard.

Jack interrupted his thoughts. "So how did you get this car, Jones?"

"You don't wanna know."

Ethan looked sideways at the FBI agent, who clearly knew it was stolen and didn't seem to care. Surprising.

"Okay, what now?" Ethan asked. "Any ideas where they would've gone?"

Jack worked his hands, cracking his knuckles. "None."

They both stood staring off in the distance, in the direction in which the helicopter had disappeared, somewhere over the Left Bank.

"Fuck," Jack spat, echoing Ethan's thoughts exactly.

Chapter 57

Okay, breathe. Stay calm, Cat. I had to keep my head. Being dragged out of the Louvre and stuffed into a helicopter had been terrifying and bewildering. As the helicopter's churning blades roared in my ears, I frantically tried to get my bearings. I needed to figure out which way we were going and, more importantly, find an opportunity to get away.

My stomach swooped as the pilot dipped the helicopter to the side in a tight turn. The world tilted, and I struggled to stay oriented.

My arms were tied behind my back with a rough rope. I strained and tested it. There was no give whatsoever. I had attempted to get out of the knife hold Reilly had pulled on me in the Louvre, but he had anticipated my moves. It was the rare person who did that. Men tended to underestimate me when they attacked me. Something that happened with alarming frequency.

I knew they weren't going to kill me right away. Otherwise Reilly would have done that in the Louvre when he had a blade against my throat. But what did they want with me? What did they need me for?

After several minutes the pilot brought us down for a landing in a broad parking lot. Reilly and another man—bigger, stronger—hustled me out with rough hands, and I almost lost my balance stepping down. Falling would be bad with my hands behind my back: my face would be the cushion for my fall. I recruited every muscle I had in an effort to stay on my feet.

They pulled me upright and forced me to walk forward. I tried to look around and get my bearings, but this was a part of Paris I didn't recognize. It was a quieter arrondissement, farther out from the city center.

Then came the window of opportunity. Reilly paused to answer his bleeping phone. The big man still held me, but I had to try.

I made a play. Executing an arm loop maneuver in a brief flash, I kicked back into the big man's left knee and he dropped. I took two steps, seeing freedom . . . and then Reilly caught me with a lunge and a grab of my elbow.

Disappointment tasted bitter in my mouth. A worse sensation immediately followed, however, as Reilly delivered a sharp blow to my nose.

Stars exploded in my vision. It wasn't a hard enough smash to break the nasal bones, just enough to make my nose bleed like a stab wound. They did not offer me a Kleenex.

Next thing I knew, they had opened a hatch in the ground and were stuffing me into it. I was forced down a rickety iron ladder into the darkness.

Even through the blood pooling in my nose, I could smell the foul odors of sewage and mildew. The air was cold and clammy, like fingers on your skin. Apart from the eerie sounds of drips echoing in the darkness, it was quiet and muffled down here, in contrast to the upper world. The only source of light came from the headlamps Reilly and his assistant wore.

I jumped down and found myself in a tunnel. And then it dawned on me. I knew where we were.

The catacombs.

Underneath Paris lay miles and miles of uncharted passageways. They dated back hundreds of years, and only a small portion of them was open to the public. Entry to all the other passageways and underground caverns was forbidden. Which meant they were the subject of many rumors and secrets.

They forced me to start walking. Within moments I realized how much of a problem this was going to be: this was a one-way journey. I was not going to find my way out of this maze.

Be smart, Cat. I needed a plan.

How did Theseus escape the labyrinth? How did Hansel and Gretel find their way out of the forest? Well, they each had outside help. Ariadne gave Theseus a thread to help him get out. Hansel and Gretel had those damn bread crumbs.

Memo to self:

Bring bread crumbs on next abduction experience.

And then I had a thought. *My nosebleed.* Blood was still dripping from my nose, running down my face. I leaned forward, letting blood drop on the ground. I breathed heavily through my nose to get more blood flowing. Blood could be my bread crumbs. Now I just needed a chance to escape.

We walked for a long time through endless twists, turns, and forks in the path. Sometimes the pathways were paved with dirt, sometimes gravel. At one point we trod on ancient cobblestones, worn and forgotten.

At last we arrived in a cavern. I went in first, followed by Reilly, while the other man stayed outside, presumably to guard the entrance. At first glance I thought the cavern was hewn from stone, the bedrock underneath Paris. As my vision focused, I saw that the walls were made of bones. Hundreds of human bones, skulls and femurs and ribs, stacked and jigsawed together like macabre interlocking bricks.

It was one of the ancient burial crypts of the catacombs. Every horror-movie torture scene was flashing before my eyes, and I shuddered, struggling to hold on to my nerves. A panic attack was just in the edges of my consciousness. It took everything in me to fight it.

I focused on the fire that burned on the floor of the cavern, a small campfire-esque heap of wood and charcoal surrounded by stones, flickering and smoking off to one side of the space.

And then someone moved in a corner of the dark cavern. A figure came forward, out of the shadows, dragging a metal chair and a length of rope.

As the person emerged into the circle of light cast by the head-lamps, I saw her. Madeleine York.

Of course.

Reilly shoved me down onto the chair and tied me to it. Madeleine then reached into the bodice of my gown and ripped out the Hope Diamond. Her eyes flashed with victory. And then changed.

"It's a fake," I said dully, verbalizing what she'd just realized.

"No!" Madeleine screamed, her face twisted with rage.

Reilly stayed silent, but his mouth went into a tight, thin line and his nostrils flared. He ripped my purse away and tore through it, dumping the contents. He looked up at Madeleine. "Nothing," he said. "Where the hell is it?" he demanded, turning on me.

"How would I know? Obviously, I was sucked in by the fake just like you two were." I was striving for a casual tone, but I was think-ing as hard as I could. I needed a way out of here.

Madeleine, meanwhile, was composing herself with several deep breaths. "That ridiculous man, Severin," she muttered. "He'd said he wanted to use a decoy and keep the real one in the vault. Never mind that nobody else agreed. He must have gone ahead and done it, anyway." She straightened her shoulders, looked at me, and quietly said, "Well, we still have you."

My mouth went dry. I didn't know what she meant by that, exactly, and I was truly hoping I would get out of here before I found out.

"I'm willing to extend a very generous offer to you, Catherine Montgomery. I'm giving you a choice. And a chance. *Join us.*"

It didn't sound much like a choice to me; it struck me more as a command.

"Why would I do that?" I said.

"Because if you don't, you'll die down here," Reilly said with an unpleasant curve to his lip.

"This is your only chance, my dear," Madeleine said. "If you do not join us, we have no further use for you. But you appear to be capable. And you have skills I can use. I would prefer if those did not go to waste."

I looked at Madeleine carefully. There was something about the way she was speaking, the way she seemed to be . . . *recruiting* me. It was like she had a bigger operation than just she and Reilly working together. And this concept tickled my brain in an unpleasant way, but I wasn't entirely sure why. It was like there was something I was supposed to remember, but I couldn't just then.

"If you don't choose to join us, you'll be in good company, of course." Madeleine glanced around the cavern and gestured, taking in the wall ornamentation.

I kept my gaze firmly away from the bones and skulls. "Why would you want me working for you?" I said.

"We could use your skills."

"Why?" I had to keep her talking. I had to come up with a plan.

She shrugged. "I have the need for a reliable roster of thieves. Assassins, too, but I think it works well when people's skills are specialized."

"Oh, assassins, right," I said, subtly testing the ropes that tied me to the chair. "That's how you killed those people connected with the Hope."

Instead of looking angry, Madeleine smiled with devilish delight. The hairs on my arms went up.

"The notoriety of the Hope has been declining ever since it landed in the Smithsonian's possession. People used to be truly afraid of the curse. In recent years, people have forgotten about it and just think of it as a curious but charming story. What we did changed all that." She pulled her shoulders back and stood tall, seemingly proud of her accomplishment.

"Who is *we?*" I asked. "Just you two? Plus that guy outside, I guess? Or do you have a full-blown organization of some kind?"

"A lot of questions from the one tied to a chair." Madeleine's eyes flashed with annoyance. "But since you're curious, in fact, yes, I do happen to have something of an organization."

I could tell she was understating this. She was a master puppeteer of some kind, and she was collecting people to work for her . . . like you'd recruit assets if you were running a spy ring. . . .

Oh my God. Madeleine is the Gargoyle. Could it possibly be true?

It was all I could do not to show my shock outwardly at this revelation. Jack had been looking for someone, a master engineer with his or her fingers in all kinds of illicit operations. He'd suspected Faulkner. But I now saw that it could be Madeleine York.

This was not a good development.

Madeleine sighed with impatience. "I should advise you, if you're having fantasies of escape, forget them. People have lost their way and died down here. What was that story I was telling you about, Reilly?" she asked pleasantly, looking up at him. "That guy who was missing down here for four years or something?"

Reilly nodded.

"They found him eventually. Dead just a few meters from the exit," Madeleine said.

"This isn't like a labyrinth. It *is* a labyrinth," Reilly said.

"Complete with Minotaur?" I asked, looking at Madeleine.

She shrugged. "There are maps. But, um, you don't have one of those, do you? I didn't think so." Madeleine brushed some dust from her skirt. "Besides, it wouldn't do you any good if you were to escape. You must know by now that everyone is looking for you as the prime suspect in the Hope Diamond murders."

I raised my chin, hoping I looked braver than I felt. The steady trickle of blood from my nose had slowed.

Madeleine smiled a small, tight smile. "A tidy little situation. When they find you, weeks from now probably, they'll assume you came down here to hide from the law. And that you got lost and died. They'll say you were a thief who planned to steal the diamond, that you tried to increase the notoriety of it beforehand by bumping off a few people, but all plans backfired. Case closed."

"How does that help your cause about the Hope curse?" I jumped on this loophole.

She laughed. "Oh, the public will still believe the Hope curse exists. Now that it's been planted in their consciousness. They'll think you were another victim. And that's what matters."

"And what about the Hope itself? The real one? What are you going to do?" I asked.

"We're still going to take it," she said with a self-satisfied smile. "Everything's in place for the theft tomorrow, while it's in transit back to Washington." She glanced at Reilly. "Am I correct?"

He nodded.

I shifted in the cold metal seat; it squeaked under my weight. Maybe I would be left alone to consider their offer. Maybe they'd go off for a bit to do some other nefarious work.

That's what they would do in the movies, anyway. But I didn't seem to have any such luck.

"So what's your answer?" Reilly was standing over me.

Madeleine narrowed her eyes, studying me closely. Then she turned to Reilly. "Get the girl some water. So she can speak."

Reilly gave me a bottle of water and held it to my mouth. I drank it heartily as water dribbled down my chin and neck. I was so thirsty, and my tongue was so dry.

I swallowed. I knew as soon as I refused them, they would leave me down here to rot. But I was not going to be trapped in this labyrinth. As soon as I got the chance, I was going to get out of here.

Hope floated up like a bottle at sea as I thought of the drops of blood on the pathway. I had my bread crumbs. I'd be able to find my way out. Now I just needed to wait for them to leave me to wither and waste and die down here . . . and then I'd set to following the path.

They watched me. Then Madeleine said, "So, have you decided?"

I looked at them defiantly. "Thank you for your kind offer. But I'm going to have to decline."

They stared at me a moment. Then Reilly nodded and Madeleine lifted her chin.

"Yes, that's just what we thought you'd say," she said.

"Good call," Reilly said to Madeleine, inclining his head to the water bottle, which lay discarded on the ground as he began packing up their gear.

"Yes, well, it was a bit of a wager," Madeleine said, shrugging. "But we'd have been able to take care of the consequences had things gone the other way."

It was like they were speaking in Armenian suddenly. I frowned with confusion. They were talking like I wasn't even there anymore.

And then the horrible truth sank in to me. I looked down at the water bottle. *Oh my God.*

Poison.

Chapter 58

My head started spinning. Whether from the actual poison or the sudden panic, I couldn't be sure.

"What did you give me?" I gasped, staring at them with wide open, frenzied eyes.

Reilly looked back at me, cold, detached. "It won't take long, Miss Montgomery. And it won't be painful. Well, actually, that part's not completely true."

I tried to retch it up. But hardly anything came up. I strained against the bonds, and I could feel them starting to loosen. But would that happen quickly enough?

Madeleine straightened to her full height and glared down at me with contempt. "Farewell. It's a shame we weren't able to come to more of an agreement, Ms. Montgomery."

At that, they left the cavern. I thrashed against the ropes around my wrists, frantically scanning my mind for what I knew about poison, any fragments Atworthy had told me. But I couldn't grasp a single thing. I strained against the bonds—the ropes were unraveling, but so was my mind.

The cavern started swimming before my eyes. A black claw tightened around my throat. Screams ricocheted inside my head. Possibly outside my head, too. Maybe that was why my throat felt ragged. Or maybe that was the poison.

I wanted to live. I did not want to die down here in the cold and the damp. Alone. Terrified. I had too many things to live for. I wanted to see my family again. I wanted to see Jack and Ethan. I was too young. This was impossible.

I was teetering on the edge of a black abyss, and at this rate, my mind was going to go down before my body did. But my fear of death was too strong. . . .

I struggled in the chair to loosen the ropes further and felt a sharpish edge in the small of my back. The tarot card.

The fortune-teller. What had she told me about fear?

She'd said I did not need to fight my fear of death. The fear was a good thing: I was afraid of death because I had so much to live for. Someone who was not afraid would not have the fight in them that I had in me.

Without a fear of death, you could go peacefully. And that was the opposite of what I wanted to do. I wasn't going to go peacefully, because I wasn't going to go at all. It was not my time.

So I embraced the fear. I ran toward it like a long-lost lover.

And a chink of light appeared. I started to gain control. Atworthy's words about poison came filtering back to me.

That stuff had not tasted like anything. There also had been no odor or color.

What was that? Arsenic? Sarin?

I couldn't be sure. It maybe didn't matter at this stage, because just then, I remembered one key thing. *Charcoal.*

Charcoal would bind the poison in my system. How could I get charcoal?

My eyes slid to the small fire in the corner. I ripped the last of the ropes off my wrists and crawled toward the fire. I scrabbled at the embers and grabbed at the cooler chunks on the periphery.

I did not hesitate about eating the charcoal. I stuffed it in my mouth, as much as I could. It cracked and crumbled and tasted of burnt ash.

I held on to my fear tightly, like the terror itself was my life preserver.

I intended to be alive at the end of this day. And that was why I was scrabbling through the remnants of the fire, chewing charcoal.

Then I started vomiting.

It was nasty, driving down to the depths of my being. My throat burned; my stomach heaved and cramped. Adrenaline rushed through my system, bringing out a cold sweat and forcing my heart to beat at a rapid rate. But it was still beating.

I had done as much as I could. I needed to get out now. I spotted my purse lying on the ground, discarded where Reilly had tossed it after not finding the Hope. My phone was inside. My phone had GPS. Was there any way it would work down here? I pulled it out with desperate hope. It was smashed, probably by Reilly's shoe.

Okay, back to bread crumbs. I could see the faint drops of blood leading away.

I wrapped my purse around me and lit a torch using a strip of fabric from my gown and a stick from the fire. I stumbled down the pathway, doing my best to be silent. I had no idea who else was around these corners, but I had to weigh that against my urgent need to get out of the catacombs as fast as humanly possible. Still, I suspected there were some highly unsavory types down here.

As I went, walking, stumbling, sometimes crawling, I couldn't help noticing the drops of blood were getting fainter and more difficult to pick out.

The blood was drying. I had a very weak light, and the ground was dark. It was getting harder to see the splotches. My heart squeezed.

It wasn't long before the traces of blood dwindled to imperceptibility. And at that point, I came to a fork in the pathway, with three different choices.

Shit. Which way to go? I just didn't know.

Could I make a compass of some kind? Well, I could, probably, if I'd been a Girl Scout. Which I hadn't.

I needed a map or something. Or someone who knew the way. Should I just wait for someone to come by? There were other people down here. I knew that much. But they could be anywhere. And, most likely, they were the kind of people I did not want to encounter.

I scrabbled around in the dirt to find any sign of blood. But it was invisible. I knew the blood drops were there. I just couldn't see them.

I leaned against the wall. Nausea flooded over me, possibly from the traces of poison in my system, possibly from terror. Hopelessness followed, and despair pressed down all around.

This was where I was going to die. This was it.

Wait. I groped in my purse, my mind wild with the possibility. Not daring to get too excited . . .

My hand closed around the thing I wanted, and I pulled out my mini UV wand. I flicked it on and shone it around. For a moment, I thought it wasn't going to work. But it had to work. Blood and body fluids showed up under UV light—even trace amounts that were impossible to see with the naked eye. I held my breath.

And then I saw them. Dark smudges made black and obvious by the UV light. Leading the way out of the far left tunnel.

I exhaled. I had a chance.

After crawling through the tunnel for a long time, fumbling about on the ground at every cross-path to discern the blood drops, I noticed the path finally leading upward. There was a short ladder in front of me. I climbed out the manhole above.

The fresh Paris night air hit me like the first day of spring. I had faced death. And I had won.

But my feeling of victory was short lived. I still needed help.

I took stock of my situation. About the best I could say for myself was that I was alive. Did I need medical attention? Definitely. Did I have time for that? No. Also, going to a hospital would be a poor idea, swarming as hospitals were with officials and police and such.

I needed a phone. I started walking. It didn't take long before I was in a neighborhood I recognized: a small village on the outskirts, in a largely residential area.

I walked through the streets while people sat in cafés, talking and smiling. Live music wafted on the night air—the trumpets and guitars of a jazz band. The air was unseasonably warm for a spring-time night. I moved quickly, avoiding the gaze of anyone who might think to rush to the aid of a woman in obvious distress.

I would have loved to change into something more comfortable and more suitable. This peach chiffon gown just wasn't doing it for me anymore. Not to mention the fact that it was covered in blood, charcoal, and vomit.

I glanced at a clock in the bar I was passing. It was pushing close to midnight, but there was a music festival happening in this part of town and many people were still out. I chose a particularly busy café and strolled right in, trying not to think too much about my appearance.

I wove my way through the mingling crowd, scanning for an unattended phone. You know, dangling out of a purse, protruding from a back pocket.

Then I saw one. Just sitting on a table. Its owner had stood up and turned to greet someone who'd just arrived. The hug was my cue to sweep by, snatch the phone, and simply keep walking.

I walked straight out of the bar, down the street, and directly up the steps into a church as though I was going to admire the frescoes and the stained glass. I needed someplace safe, someplace quiet. I had a very pressing issue to address, namely, the poison antidote.

I flicked on the phone and called the person I needed the most: Templeton. Mercifully, he answered.

"Templeton, don't panic. But let's just say hypothetically that you were in Paris and you were poisoned with something . . . arsenic maybe. Where would you go to get medical attention?"

There was silence for a moment. I could hear polite chatter and the clinking of glassware in the background. I glanced at my watch. Templeton must be having guests over for afternoon tea.

"Good *God,* Catherine. Are you okay?"

"Well, I will be if you can give me the name of a very discreet clinic in Paris, something AB&T uses or recommends?"

I could hear him rummaging in desk drawers. "Yes. Here we are." Then he spoke as though he was reading from something. "Nineteen rue Thibaud, in the Fourteenth. You go to the back door. They will take care of you."

"Thank you, Templeton. And please don't worry."

"Arsenic, hmm? An old-fashioned remedy to an old-fashioned problem. Well, at least it has style."

I smiled a wry smile as I disconnected and immediately started in the direction of the Fourteenth Arrondissement.

As I walked along damp cobblestones and past cafés filled with live bands and people on their final glass of Pernod liqueur, I was thinking hard. And one conclusion came to mind. I was going to have to go after the Hope. The real one. In the vault far beneath the Louvre.

And I was going to have to do it tonight.

Chapter 59

The physician at the back-door clinic gave me the antidote. He attached me to a monitor and took some blood to ensure the effects of the poison had been fully reversed.

While I lay there, waiting for everything to be okay, I picked up my phone. And hesitated. Who did I want to call first? Jack or Ethan?

I decided and dialed the number. But the phone rang and rang without a response. The call went to voice mail. I hung up before leaving a message. I dialed the second number. But again, there was no answer. This time, however, I left a message. "It's me. I'm okay. Call me when you can."

I lay back, churning everything through in my mind. The Hope was going to be shipped out of the Louvre first thing in the morning. Reilly would be stealing it en route home. It was all arranged; I wouldn't be able to interfere with that theft. The only thing I could do was grab it first.

I shifted on the gurney and stared at the bottles of liquid and the clear jars of cotton swabs and tongue depressors as my mind worked the problem over and over.

Admittedly, I had the advantage of surprise. Reilly and Madeleine wouldn't be trying to stop me now—they would assume I was dead.

This would be my only chance.

I thought about attempting to contact Faulkner. I thought about attempting to renegotiate with him and telling him what happened. But I knew the response I would get, and it terrified me. He was not a man to negotiate with. He'd made it clear many times prior to tonight that failure was not an option. Well, not an option without dire consequences.

No, I really only had one way to go.

My phone rang. It was Ethan calling me back. "Montgomery! Holy shit! You're alive," he breathed when I answered the phone. "Are you okay? Where are you? I'm here with Jack. We've been going out of our goddamned minds over here."

I told him to meet me at the clinic. And I asked him to bring everything.

"What do you mean by *everything?*"

"Rappel harness, glass cutter . . . everything," I said.

It didn't take Jack and Ethan long to get to me. They burst in, concerned looks on their faces. Jack's eyes raked over the IV the physician was detaching and the bottles of pills on the table, and Ethan came directly over to me, wincing at the sight of my bruised nose.

"I'm fine. Everything is fine," I said, knowing I would need to repeat this, at minimum, twenty more times.

I told them what had happened in the catacombs. As I described the situation, I watched Jack's face cloud over into a rather homicidal expression. Ethan's face grew dark and uncharacteristically serious.

"And, Jack, there's something else you need to know," I said. "Madeleine is the Gargoyle."

Jack's mouth opened, and then his eyes grew wide as all the pieces dropped into place.

I looked between them both. "So here's the situation. I need your help, because I've got one last chance," I said.

Jack's eyes narrowed. "What are you talking about, Cat?" he said. "It's over. You have to let this go. There's no way. Contact Faulkner. Maybe he'll understand."

But, of course, there was no way Faulkner would understand. They knew that, and I knew that.

I shook my head. "I have to try again. I have to go in and get the

Hope before they take it tomorrow morning. It's in the vault. It has to be."

There was silence for a moment. "You're not serious, Montgomery," Ethan said. "We already considered that. It's an undoable job. There's no way."

"Cat, you're in no condition—"

"I'm fine."

The ultra-discreet doctor, at this point, left us alone to discuss things.

"Forgive me," Ethan said, "but even for a thief at the top of her game, that vault is impenetrable. And . . . well, I'm not sure you've been at the top of your game lately. You know what I mean?"

I knew exactly what he meant.

But I could do it. The past few weeks I'd lost faith in myself, in my abilities, because I thought fear was my problem. I now knew it was the opposite.

"I can do it," I said firmly. After what had happened in the catacombs, I knew a fear of death didn't own me anymore. I owned *it*.

Jack rubbed his chin, and Ethan folded his arms, looking down at me doubtfully.

I kept talking. "I can't assume you guys are still in. If you don't want anything to do with this, I totally understand. But I'm going to do it. And if you want to help me, that would . . . Well, it would mean a lot."

Jack furrowed his eyebrows, clearly agonizing. "I have to raise it again. Why don't I try to stop them tomorrow? I could talk to Hendrickx. . . ."

I sighed. "Well, that would certainly help the Hope, but it wouldn't help me. I still won't have fulfilled my command from Faulkner. You know he'll hurt my family, Jack." I lowered my voice. "You know it's true."

"Montgomery," Ethan said after a while, "why don't I do this? You were just poisoned, for Christ's sake. You're not going to be able to concentrate. Let me do it."

"No, Ethan, I have to do it. This is my job. My responsibility." I attempted a smile. "Besides, I've got something else I need you to do. And only you can do it."

Ethan watched me carefully for a moment. "You know I think you're crazy, Montgomery. But . . . I'm in."

I looked at Jack reluctantly. He stood there a long time, saying nothing. Finally, he closed his eyes and said, "After this, no more."

In short order, Ethan pulled out the blueprints and we got down to work. What we needed was a kick-ass plan. And that was what we started creating.

And while we were in the thick of that, I received a message, a response to one I'd sent, and it made me smile with eager anticipation. We just might be able to pull this off.

Chapter 60

I slipped silently along the shadows of the Louvre courtyard, making my way to the far Denon wing. I checked the time. Six minutes to complete this part of the operation.

The cobblestones were slick—there had been a brief rain shower just after midnight, two hours ago. My breathing was heavy, but I controlled it. I tried not to think about the armed guards who patrolled outside the Louvre, wearing fatigues accessorized with semiautomatic weapons.

I knew Ethan was also moving toward his target entry point, approaching from a different direction. We had split up for safety, as a precaution.

"You there, Gladys?" I said quietly, knowing it would be picked up by my earpiece.

"Yes, dear. All set," Gladys answered.

This was the good news I'd received at the clinic. While Gladys had not been able to be there to help us during the gala, because her plane had been delayed, that delay meant she'd arrived just in time for this attempt on the vault.

She was positioned in a crepe truck outfitted with all the equipment she needed, and parked just outside the Louvre gates, courtesy of Jack and his Parisian hacker contact, Taylor. This fact, of course, gave me a cramp of guilt in my chest, which I tried hard to dislodge and ignore.

Having my hacker on-site was definitely a boon. Everyone was doing his or her part; now I just needed to do mine.

And my first task was breaking in. This is always a tricky maneuver in the best of circumstances, but it was especially true in this case because the Louvre was a fortress.

Except for one spot: the roof.

Being a former palace, the Louvre contained grand rooms with ceilings that soared high above. And many of those ceilings were made of glass.

That would be my way in.

I was wearing my black Lycra. It felt good to be moving easily again after spending so much time in that peach chiffon. The other thing that made me feel more free was the fact that I wasn't wearing a Kevlar vest.

Ethan had held it out as I was getting ready. I had stared at it and shaken my head.

His eyebrows had gone up. "You sure?"

I'd nodded. "I'm sure."

The tarot card, however, was a different story. I had it tucked in my bra. I suppose this meant I wasn't entirely able to let everything go, but that was okay. Once this was all over, I'd get therapy or something. For now, I was solid enough to do this job.

I hoped.

The rest of my equipment was tucked into a sack wrapped around my body. I had a glass cutter, a CCTV jammer, a rappel harness, a magnet, and two lengths of rope. Plus a small, portable scuba tank. Just in case.

I approached my target area, and after glancing around to be sure there were no guards in sight, I began scaling the wall. My fingers, gloved, worked their magic, and the muscles in my legs and shoulders burned as I crawled ever upward. I paused briefly to readjust my positioning and took a fleeting look down. The ground was incredibly far away.

But I wasn't scared. I mean, I was nervous and apprehensive, but

I wasn't terrified. It wasn't stopping me from doing what needed to be done. There was no panic attack hovering offstage in the wings.

I silently prayed that it would last.

I reached the roof and levered myself onto it. I slithered the rest of the way and stayed low, moving over the glass like it was a frozen pond until I reached my objective. I shone a flashlight into the dark cavern to locate just the right spot.

Far below, I knew these floors contained movement sensors. There was an override panel in this wing, and I needed to drop down and disable it.

I cut the ceiling panel with my glass cutter. It sliced like a dress-maker's shears through silk, making a faint scraping sound that gave me shivers. I cut a hole just big enough to fit through and anchored the rope from my rappel harness to the far edge of the panels, right where the glass met the stone of the roof.

I licked my lips, took a deep breath, and clambered through the hole. I eased my weight onto the rope holding me, then gingerly dropped down. With that, I was committed.

Jesus, what the hell was I doing?

Breaking into the Louvre, that's what.

I paused for a moment as the full insanity of it hit me like a falling piano. *Surely* they must know what I was about to do. They were probably just waiting for me to break in and grab the Hope. They'd all have a good laugh. Of course that was what they were doing. This was the goddamned Hope Diamond, after all.

And then I reminded myself that this was the Louvre. There were countless treasures in here. The museum itself was over six hundred thousand square feet, and every inch was covered in priceless objects. And the fact was, the French guards were much more concerned with protecting, say, the *Mona Lisa* than the Hope Diamond. The *Mona Lisa* was a national treasure. The Hope was just on loan from the cursed Yanks.

There just weren't enough guards to protect it all. And that was why this was going to work. Why it *had* to work.

"Do you have a fix on the patrol locations?" I whispered to Gladys.

I knew guards patrolled inside. I did not know exactly when the next one would be approaching my area. That was where Gladys came in handy, and her ability to hack into the CCTV system.

"There's a patrol in the east part of the Denon wing, but they're not coming your way just yet. You've got time, my dear." Breaking into this system had also allowed her to block out the feed from the CCTV for the immediate area in which I was operating.

But she had no control over the floor sensors—they were strictly manual access. I needed to disable the panel, and I needed to do it fast. I was hanging here like a fish on a hook. I pulled myself horizontal and set to work, hacking in.

There was a fingerprint scanner. I grinned, pulling out latex replicas of Severin's fingerprints—now a complete set including the left thumbprint, courtesy of a certain FBI agent.

But then I noticed beside the fingerprint scanner, there was also a combination code touch pad. *Damn.*

I carefully applied the latex fingerprints, and the panel emitted a soft beep. But it remained activated. I squared my shoulders and set to work on the combination code. My mini UV wand illuminated fingerprints on four different buttons of the touch pad: two, three, seven, and eight. That gave several possible combinations. I just needed a little time to find the right one.

The last time I'd done this, I was trying to break out of the Westin in Seattle, and I was in full-blown panic mode. Things were very different now.

I tried a few combinations, with no success. I methodically went through the sequences, substituting and swapping numbers. I wasn't worried. I would get the right combination eventually.

I was about to enter my sixth attempt when my earpiece crackled. "Cat, dear," came Gladys's voice. "The floor patrol changed direction, and they're now starting to come your way. Two guards."

I entered a seventh attempt. Nothing.

"How much time do I have?"

"Judging from their speed and route, I'd say about one minute."

Okay, that was still enough time. If I hit on the combination soon.

I kept trying. No luck. I bit the inside of my cheek hard. This panel was proving to be a real son of a bitch.

"Cat, you've got about thirty seconds now."

If I could just disable the floor sensors and hide in the alcove beside the door, the guards would simply stroll by without seeing anything amiss. If I was still dangling on this rope, however . . .

"I'm going to have to retract back up and wait on the roof and then try again," I whispered.

"Okay," began Gladys. And then, "*Wait.* Don't go back up right now. The guards doing the perimeter sweep are just outside your wing. They'll see you if you pop up on the roof right now."

The air left my lungs. I couldn't go back up, and I couldn't stay here. My only option was to disable the sensors and hide. But I had to do it *now.*

I sped up my attempts, still trying to keep the numbers straight in my head.

"Ten seconds."

I had fifteen combinations to go. And then, suddenly, I thought, *Three, seven, eight, two.* I just realized what that sequence of numbers could mean. It was Severin's home address, his street address in Saint-Germain-des-Prés.

I punched in that combination. There was a pause, then a soft beep. The panel illuminated, showing the word *désactivé.* Disabled. Then it clicked off.

"Five seconds."

In an instant, I unclipped myself and dropped down to the floor of the gallery. No alarm sounded. I pushed AUTO-RETRACT on the rappel rope and watched it zip up to the open ceiling glass high above. My heart was in my throat as I slipped into a dark alcove right beside the iron gate that blocked the gallery entrance. I pressed myself back into it, standing stock-still.

The guards approached, talking about the soccer match from last night and bemoaning the dismal performance of the Paris team against the Marseille team.

My heart pounded in my ears. It was almost a surprise that they couldn't hear it. My hand went reflexively to the spot where there would be a lower edge of my Kevlar vest. If I had been wearing one, which I wasn't.

Their boot steps stopped outside the gate, right beside my hiding spot. Their flashlights shone through the gallery, and I held my breath.

Then they continued talking and walked on. They'd seen nothing amiss.

I exhaled with relief. I held my position for several more seconds and then moved out. For the time being, I was safe.

I now had the small issue of my retracted rope. I turned my face up to the ceiling thirty feet above, my one and only getaway route. My plan had been to tuck the rope away somewhere that was easily accessible, not to get rid of it altogether. Now I'd have to find another way out.

But I couldn't worry about that just now. One way or another, I was going to need a new exit strategy. But I'd be damned if I was going to do it without the Hope Diamond.

I focused on the next phase of the operation: descending to the underground area where the vault was. Elevator shafts were familiar territory for me. Sometimes it felt like I spent half my life in spots like that. But it was just part of the job description. Some people's offices were cubicles and meeting rooms. Mine were elevator shafts and air vents.

I had my harness and the spare rope, but I'd lost my favorite carabiner—it was sitting on the ceiling right now. I'd have to use a knot instead, which was more dangerous but still doable. I tightened my jaw as I tied the rope. It would have to do.

My stomach flipped as I began the descent. I moved smoothly, my muscles remembering these maneuvers. The dark elevator shaft smelled of cable grease and rubber and steel. A faint light clipped on my belt illuminated my immediate surroundings without throwing too much light around. There was something beautiful about sailing down, like an explorer descending into a diamond mine.

I reached the bottom and touched down on the ground level of the shaft. I arrived in the foyer right outside the vault chamber. It looked exactly like the one in the Geneva Freeport.

Except the foyer was hewn out of stone. And that stone was somewhat damp.

It certainly lent credence to the rumor that we were right next to the Seine, and that a small switch could trip a mechanism that would fill the chamber with water in a matter of seconds. I clutched my portable scuba tank, feeling the cylindrical outline in my fabric sack for reassurance.

I turned and studied the chamber door. This was the second to last layer of security before the vault itself, my next obstacle. I put all thoughts of water-filled chambers out of my head. The lock on the door could be opened with an electronic key card. This was something I didn't have. But what I did have was a magnet, and the lightest of touches.

After several seconds and a few attempts, I disabled it with little difficulty.

But I didn't open the door. Not just yet. I needed to hold off until I got the go-ahead. I looked around at the stone walls, the steel door . . . and waited.

Chapter 61

Ethan was skulking through the corridors of the Louvre, schooling his breathing, keeping his peripheral vision wide. The corridors in this wing were ornately carved, every inch of them decorated. They smelled of old art and floor polish. His heart was beating fast—as much from excitement as nerves. This was a pure thrill for an art thief. The Louvre was the holy grail.

Too bad he wasn't able to enjoy it more. Ethan's concern for Cat was overshadowing much of his exhilaration.

He had climbed in through the roof, just like Cat, only in an entirely different wing. Ethan had a very specific goal. He was here to steal a Rembrandt, *Bathsheba at Her Bath,* in particular.

And botch the job. Just enough to trigger the alarm and get out.

One of the beauties of doing a job at the Louvre—and what they were using to their advantage—was the sheer number of treasures contained here. The security staff didn't know at any given time what someone would try to steal.

The door to the wing he'd wanted to enter was controlled by an electronic key-card panel. Getting through that had been virtually a nonissue. Now he was close to the inner gallery containing the Rembrandt, and it was guarded by much tighter security: there was a simple door, but once he opened it, he'd be in a zone monitored by infrared.

And as soon as he entered the zone, tripping the infrared sensor, his little jaunt in the Louvre would be over.

When Ethan was a lifeguard in high school, he'd learned a crucial concept, and it was this: not to abandon the rest of the pool just because one person over in a corner of the deep end was drowning.

Here the concept was the same. Once the alarm sounded because of his attempted theft, Louvre security would suddenly become very busy. And busy meant distracted.

The distraction alone might be enough to give Cat a chance. But she actually needed more than that.

"Thing is," she'd explained when they were planning the heist at the clinic, "it was too expensive for the Louvre to install completely independent infrared systems. So they're all connected. Once the system has been breached, they'll have to turn it off, clear the area, and allow the sensor to recalibrate. So that will give me time to get into the vault, steal the Hope, and get out."

The whole thing had been Cat's idea, but after she'd described what she wanted Ethan to do, she'd looked at him with concern. "I'm worried, though, because of the risk. What if you get caught?"

"Montgomery, that is not going to be a problem," he'd assured her. "I'm not going to get caught."

Jack had stood there, arms crossed, as he listened to the plan. "Ethan, the second you enter that room, the system will go off. You won't have time to do much. Just grab the closest painting and get out. Doesn't matter if it's the Rembrandt." He'd nodded, looking at the blueprint. "It's a good plan. It can work."

Ethan had raised an eyebrow at Jack, wondering about the man's motivations. Did he really think it could work? Or was it a matter of not caring if Ethan got caught?

Either way, here he was, ready to breach the door.

And this was where the finesse of his part of the job ended. Something that just about killed Ethan. He reminded himself he was doing it for Cat.

Even so, before he entered the gallery—just for a second—he allowed himself a momentary pause to savor the moment. To relish the fact that he was here in the middle of the Louvre itself. Then he readied himself to hear a deafening alarm and pushed open the door.

But there was nothing. Silence.

Ethan stood there for a second, confused. "Are you fucking *kidding* me?" he said under his breath.

Unbelievable. Here he was inside the Louvre, poised to steal something, and he actually needed the alarm to go off. But it didn't.

And now the trouble was, he could take the Rembrandt if he wanted to. Get off completely free, because he hadn't been detected. But that wasn't the idea.

Shit.

For a moment he felt sorely tempted. But he couldn't do it to Cat. He couldn't leave her hanging like that. She was waiting for the alarm to sound and then the infrared to go off-line before she could get into the vault.

So with a curse to the patron saint of art thieves, he set his mind to getting caught. Somehow.

He was going to need a little help. "If you can bloody well believe it, the alarm didn't go off," he said in a low voice to the others on the line.

"*What?* Oh God. Can you do something else to set off an alarm?" Cat said.

Everything Ethan could think of was riskier, with too many variables, not as firmly under his control.

"Don't the paintings have sensors on them? Will an alarm go off if you just grab one?" Jack said.

There was only one way to find out. Ethan grabbed the Rembrandt, pulling it off the wall. He flipped over the frame, checking for a sensor. Nothing.

And then, as he stood there, he made a decision. He detached the canvas from the frame, rolled it, slid it into the mailing tube he'd brought with him, and strapped the tube to his back.

He still had the problem of setting off the alarm, however.

"What about the window? The window foils?" Cat suggested.

Yes. Good idea. Ethan raced to the window. All he had to do was smash it, and the entry alarm would go off. But then he checked the window's perimeter. No foils. He remembered why: this was the third floor. They had window foils only on the ground floor. Presumably, this was because they didn't expect anyone to scale and break into the third floor. Or out.

Okay. Next idea? He couldn't just trip the alarm in any old room, because it wouldn't necessarily set off the infrared.

"Where's the next area with infrared?" Ethan demanded. "The closest one to here? I'll have to trip that alarm. Gladys?"

"Give me a moment . . . ," said Gladys. "Ah. Here we are. The Denon wing. First floor, room six."

"I'm sorry. Did you say what I think you said?"

"Yes."

"Jesus, *really?* All right. I guess that's my only option."

Room six in the Denon wing was otherwise known as the Mona Lisa Room. Because that was exactly what it contained.

Ethan had a floor map on his phone of the inside of the Louvre, so he turned it on and quickly planned his route. The danger now was getting busted in some other way before he managed to make it to the Mona Lisa Room.

As he moved, he pondered another problem. His getaway motorcycle was waiting outside the Rembrandt gallery. He would have to trip the alarm, then get back to the previous room and escape out that way.

He moved quickly through the corridors, staying ever vigilant. Encountering a patrolling guard at this point would be a bad development.

At last, Ethan stood outside room six. His fingers twitched, and his skin tingled. This would be the pinnacle job of his career—of the career of any art thief. And here he was, about to intentionally fuck it up.

He glanced at the electronic panel and wished he could hack into it and do this job properly. Instead, he simply opened the steel door. For a microsecond, time stood still as he stared at the *Mona Lisa* . . . and she stared back at him.

Then the alarm wailed like an air-raid siren.

"Another time, my dear. We shall meet again," Ethan said, heavy with regret. Then he turned and raced away from the room as fast as possible. He had to get back to the Rembrandt gallery now. He flew through the corridors, expecting to encounter a guard at any second. If he could just make it to the Rembrandt room, all he'd have to do was slip in, out the window, and down to his waiting motorcycle.

Except when he got there, the door he'd previously hacked and opened had automatically swung shut and sealed. He would have to re-pick the electronic lock.

Then he heard guards thundering up the staircase.

No time to work on the lock. He would have to get out through another window, as close to the motorcycle as he could. What about the gallery one floor above this one? It was a higher fall than he'd planned, but that was the only option.

Ethan leaped onto the staircase and climbed fast. Boot steps clattered below him, getting closer. At the next level up, he lunged into the room he needed—this gallery was not as secure, so no lock to pick or door to hack. He raced to the window and looked down. There it was, the Ducati he'd stashed there earlier. Way down there.

Ethan pulled his mask down, opened the window, and clambered out with no hesitation. He used window ledges and carvings as foot- and handholds and scrambled four levels down to the waiting motorcycle.

His identity was hidden by the mask. He knew the external CCTV would pick him up and security would spot him escaping. But that was what he wanted.

Now, he just had to hope his motorcycle would be faster than the gendarmes. Fast enough to lead them on a bit of a chase, anyway.

Chapter 62

Jack knew Hendrickx didn't sleep. That was what made it easy to call him at two in the morning.

"Hendrickx, it's Jack Barlow. I need to talk to you about the Gargoyle case. Can you meet me?" Jack said.

"Do you know what time it is?" Hendrickx said in a tight voice. He sounded even more pissed off and unpleasant than normal.

"It's two o'clock. I thought you didn't sleep," Jack said.

"I don't. But *you* do, don't you?"

Cat had insisted on this part of the plan, and it had been the thing Jack had struggled with the most. But he'd agreed in the end. She'd said she couldn't have somebody else going to prison because of her. So it was going to be Jack's job to finagle things, if necessary, so that didn't happen.

He just didn't know, when push came to shove, if he was going to be able to do it and help Ethan Jones.

"I want to show you something," Jack said. "I'll come pick you up in fifteen?"

Once Hendrickx got in the car, Jack checked the time. He knew Hendrickx carried a phone that gave APBs about significant events to Interpol and local police. Jack tried to avoid staring directly at it, and he also tried not to be obvious about checking his watch. But he knew that it should be any minute now.

"So?" Hendrickx grunted. "What is it?"

"I'll take you there. You'll see."

Jack started driving and realized he really didn't have anywhere specific to go. He'd have to bluff it while he waited for the call to come. But what was taking so long?

Jack started to sweat. He was going to need to fabricate something for Hendrickx. And while Jack prided himself on being a good FBI agent, he knew he was not a great liar. Something Cat could teach him. Or . . . *could have* taught him, he thought, correcting himself.

Hendrickx's phone rang. Jack could hear the recording on the other end of the line.

"All units . . . theft in progress . . . Louvre . . ."

Hendrickx turned to Jack and opened his mouth to start to speak.

"I got it," said Jack quickly, turning the wheel. "Just switch that thing to speaker so I can hear what's going on."

Hendrickx nodded.

The speakerphone crackled to life. "Suspect is on a black Ducati motorcycle. Headed west on Haussmann."

Jack did a 180 around the boulevard and sped off in the opposite direction. He flew along relatively empty Parisian roads, streetlights flashing by, following the barked sightings of the thief they were in pursuit of. It took some fancy footwork on Jack's part to appear as though he was in pursuit but just slightly missing a turn here, responding to a direction just a hair too slowly.

Hendrickx called in the description of Jack's vehicle, explaining he was with an FBI agent, so the local authorities would understand why this car was suddenly involved in the pursuit.

"East on Rivoli . . . ," came the announcement.

Jack's heart sped up. He could interfere with that. "We're close," he said. It was time to step things up.

Somewhere along rue de Rivoli, Jack spotted Ethan on his Ducati. He could see the other vehicles in pursuit, lights flashing and sirens screaming. Jack sped up, attempting to head him off. Then he pretended to miss the turn by a fraction. Which blocked the other pursuing vehicles.

"Let me drive!" Hendrickx shouted as Ethan flew far ahead.

"I can't pull over now!" Jack said. "We'll lose him completely."

Ethan's motorcycle drove up and onto the Pont des Arts, the pedestrian bridge of steel and wood glittering with the thousands of padlocks tourists had attached to it.

Jack's car came careening around the bend and screeched to a halt just beside the *pont,* unable to follow. This was good. Exactly as planned. This was how Ethan was to make his getaway, because the cars could never follow him onto this bridge. And any officers on the other side would be too slow. As soon as they heard he was on the Left Bank, he would be long gone.

The motorcycle bumped and roared across the planks. It stopped midway, and Ethan leaped off. Jack frowned. What the hell was he doing? He was supposed to keep going. He put something down on a bench in the middle of the bridge. Jack couldn't quite make out what it was.

Hendrickx was screaming for units on the Left Bank to come to their side of the bridge and cut off his retreat. Jack could see flashing lights flying along the quai d'Orsay, the road beside the opposite side of the river.

He quickly judged Ethan's chances. If Ethan got on his motorcycle right now, he'd make it off the bridge. Another second passed. Jack's abdomen tightened. It had to be *now.*

Hendrickx was hollering down the phone line. And then he was out of Jack's car, dropping his phone and running toward the bridge, reaching for his firearm.

At that instant Ethan leaped back on his motorcycle and sped off toward the far side of the bridge. Hendrickx continued running.

Jack stayed with the car. Hendrickx's phone lay on the passenger seat.

"Need a heading. The Left Bank team will pick him up. Can you confirm the suspect's direction . . . ?"

Ethan's bike flew off the end of the bridge, bumping down the steps on the other side. Jack could see the flashing lights of the Left Bank team just a few blocks away from Ethan and closing fast.

At that moment, Jack realized he was in a position to help them catch Ethan. He could fix things so they would actually get him on the other side of the bridge. Ethan headed straight off the bridge and up the road ahead.

If Jack gave them the correct heading, Ethan would be caught. He would be charged. He would go to prison.

It would solve a lot of problems for Jack. But it would be betraying Cat big-time.

Jack rubbed the back of his neck. He picked up the phone. "South on rue Mazarine," he said. "The suspect is going south on Mazarine."

Jack watched the gendarmes turn up the road he'd sent them on, as Ethan sped off in the opposite direction. Nobody was anywhere near him, and he disappeared into traffic.

He was gone. And Jack, an FBI agent, had just helped an art thief steal a Rembrandt.

Meanwhile, Hendrickx had reached the middle of the bridge. He bent down and plucked something off the bench in the center. It was a long cylinder. Hendrickx stared at it with bewilderment, then opened it up. As Hendrickx withdrew the contents, Jack could see what it was at last.

A canvas, tightly rolled.

Chapter 63

"Okay, Cat, dear, you have twenty minutes before the system is recalibrated," Gladys said in my earpiece.

I had been waiting for the go-ahead, worrying about Ethan and whether he would be able to get away, concerned about Jack and whether Hendrickx would figure out he was playing the role of double agent tonight.

But now there was no more time to think about anyone else's job. I just had to have faith that they would all be fine. And get down to my own task.

I set my stopwatch for twenty minutes. And then faced the door that led to the vault, the door I'd already unlocked. I knew the infrared was off, but still, I held my breath, terrified of a miscalculation or some other unexpected factor that would trip the system, fire the alarm, and fill this chamber with water.

I put my hand on the lever and opened the door.

Nothing happened. No water, no alarm, no drowning. Just blessed silence as the door swung open. I entered the vault chamber. First on my to-do list: apply a thick layer of hair spray over the infrared sensor in here. It was a precaution—in case it came back on sooner than I expected. The hair spray would stop the sensor from detecting any increase in body heat. I pulled out the strongest, firmest helmet-hair version of Aqua Net and did the job. It might buy me a few extra minutes, should I need them.

I breathed fractionally easier after that.

I faced the foot-thick steel door to the vault. With a combination lock right in the center and the small etched name in the right-hand corner: Stratford & Black.

It was going to have to be the safecracking job of my life to get in.

Surprisingly, I got past the first two tumblers with relative ease. And then I reached a problem. Something didn't feel right. I didn't know what it was, but something was definitely off about this vault.

I paused, breaking my rhythm, taking a wider view of the vault, trying to see what was different. But there was nothing. Maybe it was my imagination?

After checking my watch, I returned to the job. That momentary distraction had cost me several precious seconds.

I immediately reimmersed myself in the task. And quickly found my groove again. I paused only once more, to wipe the sweat from my forehead, and then, after several more minutes . . .

I was in.

I did it. I breached the combination. My heart burst open with triumph. I placed a hand on the vault handle to open the door, grinning as I did so. But then I noticed that the light hadn't turned green.

The door remained locked.

But I was through. I had gone through the combination. I was positive of that. So what was going on? I double-checked everything about the vault door. And then I noticed something that hadn't been on the Geneva vault door. A slot for a key card. On the very far side of the vault door.

They had doubled up the locking mechanism. A combination *and* a key card. But I didn't have a key card.

My stomach dropped into my knees. I had come so far, and now, to be thwarted by a key card.

"A key card. Oh my God, I need a key card. They added that," I said.

There was a faint crackling on the line and then a response. "Oh dear," said Gladys. "Are you sure?"

"Yes, I'm sure."

"Do you know how to get through a key-card lock?" Gladys asked.

I looked at my watch again. Eight minutes left.

"You can jumper it, Montgomery," came Ethan's voice, muffled by lots of background noise from the traffic and the motorcycle engine. He must be on the streets of Paris, enacting his getaway.

Yes, I could totally jumper it. I looked back at the key-card slot.

But how could I do that and open the door at the same time? The handle was on the other side of the vault door, farther away than my arm span could reach. Clearly, this was designed as a two-person open. Both mechanisms needed to be unlocked simultaneously for the door to open.

It was enough to make me gnash my teeth.

"Okay, I have some bad news," Gladys then said. "They're resetting the infrared already. It will be online in about thirty seconds. I don't know how they cleared things so fast, but they did. Do you have the hair-spray layer in place?"

"Yes," I said.

"Okay, that should hold and buy you a couple of minutes. But not much longer than that."

"You should get out, Cat," Jack said. In the background there were sirens and car engines and shouting. I was desperate to know how things were going on their end, but I had no time to ask.

I sized things up again. There had to be a way.

It could be done with a rope. I could tie a rope to the handle and open the door from a distance while I jumpered the key card. But I didn't have a rope—I'd left one on the ceiling, the other in the elevator shaft. I didn't have a wire or anything like that, either.

What I did have was my portable scuba tank. It contained a rubber hose. I pulled on the hose, testing its flexibility. It would work. It was strong and had only a little elasticity to it.

But I'd have to dismantle the scuba tank. Which would mean I wouldn't be able to use it if I got into trouble.

It took me a second to make the decision. It was the only way. I was not coming this far to give up now.

I ripped the hose off the scuba tank and wrapped it around the handle. Holding on tight, I moved to the other side of the door and, tucking the hose under my arm, used the magnet to begin jumpering the key-card lock.

My timing had to be perfect. I needed to open both mechanisms at the same time.

I took a deep breath. If the alarm went off, this would be the moment. At the instant I breached the key-card lock, I yanked on the hose with my other hand to pull on the vault handle. And the door to the vault swung open.

At last, I was inside. In front of me lay a jewelry case, a large, flat metal box like a safe-deposit box. I pressed my lips together and tasted sweat.

I opened the smooth, cold case. Inside, cradled in the velvet-lined interior, resting in a perfect circle, was the Hope Diamond necklace.

Ceiling lights inside the vault set the gem sparkling like it contained the North Star itself. I'd seen it before, of course, but up close and intimate like this was an altogether different experience.

"The system is back online," Gladys said. "Your hair-spray layer will hold for approximately two minutes, Cat." Her voice sounded extremely worried.

I shared her concern, to say the least. But this time, I needed to be sure this diamond was the real thing before doing anything else. It had the right degree of brilliance and fire, and the color was perfect. I stared at it as though hypnotized.

And then I suddenly felt as though the Hope Diamond was gazing at me as much as I was gazing at it. An unfamiliar image flashed in my mind, then a carved Indian goddess, beautiful, ornate. . . .

I blinked, and the vision disappeared. I stared at the Hope. It was the real deal. No question.

But I was out of time. I captured the necklace, stowed it inside the pocket sewn into my suit for just this purpose, and zipped it tight. I snapped the empty box shut.

I slipped from the vault and reset everything. I worked backward, moving quickly.

"Forty-five seconds," said Gladys.

If I could just make it into the elevator shaft.

The infrared was designed to sense a rise in temperature, not absolute temperature. Although the temperature of the vault would be warmer than it was before, when the system came back online, it would not sense any ongoing increase. As long as I was out.

I closed and locked the door to the vault chamber.

"Ten seconds," Gladys said.

I sprinted straight across the foyer and clambered into the elevator shaft. I had no time to reattach the rope to my harness, so instead I started free-climbing upward, desperate to put distance between the vault and myself.

"It's back on," Gladys said. "Are you out?"

"I'm out," I said breathlessly. I paused momentarily halfway up the shaft; there were no alarms, no signs anything had been breached.

A few minutes later, I emerged from the elevator shaft, two stories up. Exhilaration fizzled my every nerve. I had the Hope.

But I also had a problem: how the hell was I going to get out of the Louvre?

Chapter 64

I had no way of climbing back out the ceiling. Scrambling a few feet up an elevator shaft was one thing; getting myself to the middle of a glass ceiling thirty feet above in an enormous gallery was another.

I was inside the Louvre, with the Hope on me. And most of the security systems were in place again. Much like wearing lip gloss with your hair down on a windy day, this was a bad plan.

What the hell was I going to do? I needed to be able to walk out.

And then it occurred to me: there was only one class of person who could do that at this time of night. A security officer.

And I had an officer's uniform stashed in this building, because that had been my backup plan for the gala. Could I get to the utility closet where I'd hidden the guard's uniform? Could it possibly still be there?

"Gladys, is the CCTV still out?"

"Still frozen, yes. I am the only one receiving the correct images. You're free to move about. Where are you going?"

"To fight my way out of here."

I crept to the Richelieu wing, slipping silently through the hushed galleries and hallways, ever wary of encountering an unexpected security guard. Moonlight filtered in through the high leaded windows.

I reached the end of the Richelieu wing, the remote section containing the utility closet, and opened the closet door. The hinges gave a squeak, which sent a blast of adrenaline through my veins. I froze, waiting, but there was no sign I'd been heard. I clambered into the closet, reached back behind the mop and bucket, and—yes—the uniform was sitting there. I quickly pulled it on over my Lycra suit.

I experienced a moment of major doubt. Was this actually going to work? But I reminded myself there were more than a thousand security officers in the Louvre. There was no way any one individual could know them all.

Right?

I had to get moving. I had been good at covering my tracks thus far, but at any moment someone might discover there was an intruder. The hole in the ceiling, for one. The missing Hope, for another—if they happened to decide to take this moment to do an unscheduled spot check of the vault.

I exited the utility closet and quickly changed my gait. I was no longer a thief trying to stay hidden. I was a guard on patrol.

I managed to reach the atrium under the pyramid without encountering any guards, though, no small miracle. My heart was beating the rhythm of the headhunter tribe on *Gilligan's Island.* I tried not to think about what was zipped inside my suit, underneath this uniform. Equally, I tried to avoid thinking too deeply about what the real guards held themselves: semiautomatic weapons, handcuffs, nightsticks, and so on.

I stepped onto the escalator and rode it to the top of the pyramid entrance, and there two guards came into view. *Good, just two.* The rest of the team, I imagined, was still in the Denon wing, investigating Ethan's break-in.

I was hoping for a minimum of interaction. But I knew I wouldn't be able to get away with no interaction at all. I prepared myself for my most flawless French ever. "Evening, gentlemen," I said. "Just popping out for my break." I held up the pack of cigarettes I'd stashed in the pocket.

The first one, the taller of the two, looked at me with an expression as soft and warm as a sledgehammer. The other repositioned his hands on his AR-15.

"I haven't seen you before," said the taller one. He tilted his head like a bird of prey scrutinizing a field mouse.

"Yeah, I'm new. Just started last week. I was late for the start of shift tonight." I knew the guards on night duty started their shift at midnight, and they all would have seen each other in the locker rooms of the central security offices.

I left my explanation at that. The rule about lying was that you needed to give just enough details to make a thing sound plausible, but not so much that it smacked of overcompensating.

There were a few moments of silence as they studied me. Those few moments stretched out and felt like three hours. My mouth was stone dry. I needed to break the stalemate.

"Got a light? Either of you?" I asked, holding up a cigarette.

The hard mask softened infinitesimally on the taller guard. He nodded and fished a matchbox from his pocket. The other guard stepped to the side, out of my way.

I thanked them and walked forward, sidestepping the metal detectors, and out through the glass doors of the pyramid, into the cool night air. All around me the palace walls of the Louvre reached toward the sky, and dead ahead was the archway leading into the Tuileries Garden.

I forced myself to walk casually, to stroll away and light my cigarette. I needed to know they weren't watching me. I could tell through my peripheral vision that they hadn't turned away yet. But surely I would get boring soon. And once I did, I'd be off like a jackrabbit.

What if they changed their minds? What if the supervisor came back from his break and denounced me before I got out of view?

I kept strolling, heart thundering. And then they turned their gaze away from me and continued their conversation.

In an instant, I sprinted away. I stayed close to the shadows and moved as fast as my legs would spin. I felt the weight of the Hope cradled into my body.

A thrill ran through me—I was escaping with the Hope Diamond. The actual Hope Diamond. A bubbly, giggly sensation threatened to burst out of me.

I quashed it immediately. There was no reason to celebrate just yet. I was nowhere near the edge of the woods.

In the streets of Paris just outside the Louvre, I ducked down an alley and found the dark, quiet alcove where I'd stashed a change of clothes. I pulled on a dark hoodie and jeans and tucked the Hope in one pocket and the tarot card in another—a silly urge, but at that moment I was thankful for every bit of protection I could get. Then I sent a message to Faulkner on the encrypted line he'd given me.

My phone vibrated seconds later.

"I have it," was all I said when I picked up the call.

"Good," he replied. "Meet me at the Seine, underneath the Pont Alexandre III. Left Bank, right down by the river."

"I can be there in ten minutes."

"Good. And, Catherine, as a show of good faith, it will only be me there. But it also has to be only you."

I hesitated a second. And then I said, "Agreed."

I disconnected and started walking.

As I walked, I flicked on my micro earpiece again. "I'm on my way to rendezvous with Faulkner," I said quietly, hoping Ethan and Jack were both still on the line. "And I'm going alone."

"Just wait a little," Ethan said. "I've shaken the cops, but I'm on the other side of the city. Just gimme a few minutes. I want to be there, Montgomery."

"So do I, Cat. You do *not* want to meet him alone," Jack said, his voice lowered to a barely audible volume. "I'm still with Hendrickx, but I may be able to slip off in a minute or so."

"It's okay, both of you," I said. "I can do this. And it will be over in a matter of minutes. You don't need to come."

"Like hell I don't," Ethan said. "I'm seeing this through. Besides, I don't trust Faulkner."

"It kills me, but I have to say I agree with Ethan," Jack said.

I appreciated their concern. I really did. But I'd promised to come alone. And more than that, I just couldn't wait. I had to get this thing off me.

"I'll send you a message when it's all done." I clicked off my earpiece, pulled up my hood, and headed across the bridge.

Chapter 65

On the other side of the river, I hopped a cab.

Climbing into the backseat, I quickly scanned for the CCTV camera I knew was here somewhere. There, I spotted it—just below the headrest right in front of me. I surreptitiously blocked it out with a piece of chewing gum.

The cab sped along the Seine toward the Pont Alexandre III. I sat in the back, admiring the glimmering lights of Paris that flashed by, and tried to prepare for the one last step I had to take.

Then a brighter flash and a siren went flying by opposite us, in the direction of the Louvre. Had the theft been discovered? I swallowed. Then I heard more sirens. And more flashing lights zipped past at top speed.

Yes. It had to be the Louvre. I closed my eyes and took a deep breath.

Okay, time to get out of this cab. I did not relish being confined to a car in which I was not in control. Drivers received police bulletins on their feeds all the time, and I did not want to be in the car of some hero cabbie. I called forward to the driver and told him I had changed my mind, and could he please let me out right here?

He looked at me in the rearview mirror and narrowed his eyes just slightly.

Do not be memorable here, Cat. Be casual. Don't do anything weird that's going to be reported to a supervisor later.

The cabdriver shrugged in the classic French form and pulled over. I stuffed some euros into his hand and leaped out into the cool night air.

The rest of the journey would be on foot. Which was fine, since it wasn't too far away at this point. I walked briskly through the empty streets. Very few people were up at this hour—not even the street sweepers were out yet. It would still be another hour or two before the bakeries started warming up their ovens.

I was walking west in the Seventh Arrondissement and every so often caught glimpses of the Eiffel Tower through gaps in the tall, patrician buildings of creamy stone.

Then I heard another siren a few blocks away, coming closer. I pressed myself against a building wall as it passed. The sound changed pitch as the vehicle moved farther away, passing me by.

At last, I arrived at Pont Alexandre III, a beautiful ceremonial bridge with ornate lampposts and a single graceful arch. Even the long row of shining lampposts did little, though, to chase away the moody fog that hovered down by the Seine.

I spotted Faulkner sitting on a park bench at the river's edge with his back to the pathway, unconcerned about any dangers that lurked there. I wondered what that would be like—to be so sure of your own untouchability.

I scanned the area for others. I couldn't see anyone else, but I wanted to be sure. I descended the curving staircase to the river's edge, but I stayed concealed, deep in the shadows. It was creepy down here by the shifting waters of the Seine; all the hairs on my arms prickled upward.

I knew there was no CCTV down here, which was both good and bad. I began to have second thoughts about not waiting for Jack and Ethan, not letting them accompany me here.

"How close are you guys?" I whispered, flicking on my earpiece.

"I'll be there in fifteen," Ethan said.

"About seven," Jack said.

I chewed a fingernail. It was too long. I couldn't wait. This close to the Louvre was not a good place to be; my every fiber wanted to get out of here. So, I was on my own.

I stepped out of the shadows.

Chapter 66

I walked slowly toward Faulkner, and he turned his head.

"You have it?" he asked. "With you?" I could see he was trying to control his emotions. I could see the gleeful boy in him trying to get out.

I desperately wanted to hand the Hope over and get it out of my possession as fast as possible. And then get out of there. Alive, ideally.

But one thing I knew for sure: I was not giving up this diamond until I had his word it was over. That I would be released from his demands.

"You get nothing until you promise you will not harm my family," I said.

Faulkner stared at me. He blinked. "Of course. They are safe."

"And this is over now, with this. Once I give you the Hope, we're done. We're square. Yes?"

He smiled. "It is over." He held his hands out in a gesture of goodwill. "All right? And now?"

I reached into my pocket and pulled out the diamond. It filled my fist and felt cold in my hand. The chain of white diamonds clicked faintly as I held the necklace out. "Here."

His eyes lit up like Christmas morning.

I wondered if he knew how much of an illusion it was to possess a diamond. Jewels were here before us and will outlast us all. You can hold them in your hand, you can possess them for a while, but they will be here when you're gone.

Even still, Faulkner's adoration of this stone was evident. And, in a strange way, I felt like I was doing the right thing because of that.

Faulkner was a monster in many ways, but at least he respected the sanctity of the diamond. I knew it would be safe with him. He stood to face me and reached forward.

Suddenly, without warning, a shot rang out. Faulkner's face went blank. And he fell backward into the Seine with a robust splash. I knew instantly he was dead.

I dove to the ground reflexively, clutching the Hope tightly to my chest. I needed to get somewhere safe; I was so exposed.

And then out of the shadows of the bridge Reilly emerged, a Walther P99 leading the way. Just behind him, Madeleine appeared, also carrying a handgun. The pair walked slowly toward me.

"Stand up," Reilly said in a chillingly calm tone.

My brain was churning as I stood, still gripping the diamond. I knew the only reason they hadn't shot me yet was that they were concerned that if I followed Faulkner into the river, they would lose the Hope.

So to survive, I needed to do two things: hold tightly to the Hope and stay close to the river.

"Well, well," Madeleine said. "You *are* surprising, Cat Montgomery. I would love to hear how you got out of the catacombs. But I think that might have to wait."

The options ripped through my mind. I could run. And get shot in the back. I could jump into the Seine and swim away. But there was nowhere to go. They would just follow me downriver, shoot me at their leisure when I eventually climbed out.

I needed a weapon. Or a distraction.

I could feel the edges of despair start to creep in. There was no way out of this. Reilly was coming closer, the gun in his right hand. His left hand was out for me to hand the Hope to him.

But I knew the second I did that, he would shoot me.

Madeleine was standing behind Reilly, her Smith & Wesson trained on me.

"Looks like the Hope Diamond is going to be a curse for you, after all, Catherine Montgomery," Madeleine said. "Just like all the others. Thank you for playing along. So nice of you to help my cause. Your body will be found, and you will be known as the thief of the Hope. They'll try to find the diamond on the bottom of the Seine—

fruitlessly. It's perfect, really. Another mysterious, grisly death for someone who touched the Hope Diamond. I couldn't have planned it better myself. My buyers will be thrilled to have a piece of that."

My gaze shifted between Madeleine and Reilly. This was going to come down to a physical fight. My heart hammered. I knew I could take Madeleine, but I wasn't sure I could win a physical confrontation with Reilly.

Suddenly, a figure dressed entirely in black leaped down from the side of the staircase, taking Madeleine down.

Reilly turned, and that was my moment.

I lunged forward, dropping the Hope, and struck the hand holding the gun, cracking the back of his wrist. I kicked hard into the side of Reilly's knee. As Reilly fell, the gun fired before it flew from his hand and the bullet shot harmlessly across the water. The gun skittered across the ground. Reilly was up in a second, though, charging at me.

I dodged his advance, coming up beside him and kicking him off kilter. He recovered and spun, grabbing me in a choke hold. I dropped instantly, throwing him off balance. Then I lunged, tripped him, and pushed him forward. He went straight into the Seine.

I ran to Reilly's gun, grabbed it and the Hope, which was lying beside it, and straightened. A glance over my shoulder told me the figure in black had Madeleine subdued on the ground, handcuffed. The stranger turned to look at me, and I saw who it was.

It was the fortune-teller, Esmerelda, from Montmartre. She looked completely different, but nonetheless recognizable by her curly hair, now tied back, and the faint linear scar on her left cheek.

My mouth opened with bewilderment. "What are you doing here?" I demanded, breathing heavily. Movement by the river caught my attention. Reilly had reached the edge; he'd be climbing out any second.

"I'm French secret service," she said quickly. "I've called for backup. Should be here imminently—"

And she was right. Just as Reilly put his hands on the riverbank to climb out, agents descended, weapons trained on all of us. Hendrickx was leading the way.

It was over. But not just for Reilly and Madeleine—for me, also.

There was nowhere for me to go. Images of French prisons erupted in my head.

Madeleine's crystalline voice rang out. "But what on earth are you arresting *me* for? I'm just retrieving the Hope from this thief!" She pointed at me.

All eyes went to me, standing there, clutching the Hope as it burned a hole in my palm like a brand. There was silence.

At that moment, I could see Jack running down the cobblestone ramp that led down to the riverbank. He had just arrived. But what would he be able to do? He had no authority here.

And then the fortune-teller stepped forward between me and the line of fire.

"Not her," she said. "She's with me."

Hendrickx stepped forward. "What are you talking about?" He was flushed, and his eyes narrowed with anger.

"Madeleine York and Sean Reilly are the true culprits," Esmerelda said. "They killed a man, for one thing." Her head indicated the area on the Seine where Faulkner's body was floating. A police boat was already there, moving closer, getting ready to fish him out. "They're behind this whole thing. Madeleine just *thanked* Agent Montgomery for stealing it for her."

Hendrickx guffawed. "*Agent* Montgomery?"

"She has been working with me on this case," Esmerelda said. "She's a secret service asset."

Hendrickx narrowed his eyes. "This is something I'm meant to believe?"

And then Jack cleared his throat. "She's right. This was all a plan to smoke out Madeleine and Reilly," he said, picking up the thread. "If we didn't do it this way, they would have found another way to steal the Hope, and then it would have been lost forever. Hendrickx, *this* is the Gargoyle." He pointed at Madeleine. "I can show you all the evidence you need."

"Barlow, you are on dangerous ground—" Hendrickx began.

"Maybe this will help," Esmerelda interrupted. She produced a wire and a recording device, pulling them out of her vest. "Everything Madeleine York said in the past twenty-two minutes."

* * *

After Hendrickx and his agents had packed Madeleine and Reilly into the police truck and gone off with the evidence, I remained by the river with Esmerelda and Jack. We would have to go to the station eventually to make our statements, but we would make our own way there.

I took a deep breath. I had completed the circle by handing the Hope back to the authorities. It would be safe now.

Esmerelda turned to me and Jack. "So, there's something else I need to tell you both. When I said secret service, that's just a part of what I do. The more complete truth is that I work for the DOA."

Jack made a sound. "The Department of Antiquities?"

Esmerelda nodded.

I frowned, trying to figure out what on earth they were talking about. I felt like I'd missed an episode. That I'd gone to get popcorn partway through the movie and missed a bit. "Anyone care to explain what that is, exactly?"

Esmerelda looked at Jack with surprise. "You haven't told her?"

Jack glanced at me apologetically but let Esmerelda continue. "The Department of Antiquities is a covert organization that protects precious objects of historical significance."

"Like the Hope Diamond?" I asked.

"Exactly. And . . . like the Aurora egg."

I blinked. "The Fabergé that contains . . . the Gifts?" It was the Fabergé egg I'd been hunting last year. The one that had disappeared into the mists beneath Big Ben.

Jack cleared his throat. "Wesley Smith and I have been on the trail of that Fabergé for the past few weeks. We tracked it to Monaco, to a private villa owned by a member of the DOA. While you were in Bangkok, we made a play for it."

"But it had already been taken by Caliga," Esmerelda added.

I stared at them both. How had all this been happening without me being aware? "Why are you telling me everything now?"

"For one thing, you have a right to know the full truth," Esmerelda said. "For another, there's something you both need to be aware of."

I glanced at Jack, but he was watching her closely, waiting for what she would say next.

"Caliga has the egg now," she said. "And, indeed, they have disturbing plans for it."

I nodded. This I knew. I wasn't sure I believed any of the stuff that was said about the mysterious powers of the Gifts of the Magi. But it didn't matter, because the members of Caliga believed it, and they were prepared to do all kinds of unspeakable things in order to get at that power.

"However," Esmerelda continued, "as they will soon find out, the Gifts contained within the egg are incomplete."

Jack and I exchanged a look. "What do you mean?" I asked. "I saw all three—gold, frankincense, and myrrh. I tested them. I sent samples to the lab. They were dated to two thousand years ago."

Esmerelda nodded. "Yes, you sent samples of the two you didn't recognize to the lab. Frankincense and myrrh. The third, the gold, you took at face value."

Oh my God. She was right. I didn't specifically test the gold.

"The gold had been fashioned into a pelican," Jack protested. "And a pelican is a symbol of Jesus, isn't it?"

"It is," Esmerelda said, nodding. "And that's why the shape was chosen at a much later date, as a decoy."

A decoy. I felt simultaneously foolish and impressed.

"The real gold had been separated from the frankincense and myrrh long ago," she said. "Much farther back than the nineteenth century, when the Fabergé eggs were first made."

"Do you know where the real gold is?" Jack asked her.

She shook her head. "Nobody does, not yet. But . . . if we can find it, we can stop Caliga. They can't do anything with the Gifts until they have all three."

I closed my eyes and exhaled. After what I'd just gone through, I could barely think about all this. I opened my eyes and glanced at Jack. He had a faraway look on his face.

"Anyway, I thought you two needed to know," Esmerelda said. "We will be in touch . . . *soon*."

At that, she left us and walked back up the ramp, disappearing into the shadows of Paris.

Chapter 67

It was four thirty in the morning, still dark and chilly, with no sign of daylight yet. Paris was illuminated with thousands of lights that reflected off the water. Things had grown quiet, apart from the sound of the Seine lapping against the stone walls that contained it. Hulls of riverboats groaned faintly as they rubbed against the ancient stone. The Pont Alexandre III curved gracefully across the river from where we stood.

Jack turned to me and began to speak. "Cat, I—"

He stopped, interrupted by the rumble of a motorcycle. Ethan appeared on the bridge. He drove down the ramp beside the river, stopped on the cobbles, and swiftly climbed off the motorcycle, rushing to me.

"Montgomery, are you okay?" he asked, his face rife with concern as he looked me over. "I heard something about a shooting—"

"I'm fine," I said. "Physically, anyway."

It became obvious that it was just the three of us. Everyone else had melted away. My skin crawled with the awkwardness of the situation.

"Cat, let me check your hand." Jack moved in closer, examining my bleeding hand, which I must have scraped on the cobbles at some point.

"Don't crowd her, Barlow. Give the woman some space," Ethan said.

Jack spun and glared at Ethan. "Excuse me?" he said.

"Okay, you two," I said. "Just stand down a little." I took a deep breath and brushed a strand of hair out of my face.

We were all safe. It was over. But there was still one more Herculean task I needed to complete. I bit my lip; this was not going to be easy. But I knew what I had to do.

"Listen, I don't know if this is the right time . . . but I feel the need to clear the air about some things," I said.

I looked at the Parisian skyline, the Eiffel Tower spearing the sky. How things had changed since the last time I stood by a river with these two in the middle of the night. Months ago—a different river, a different city. And I was different, too. At least, my feelings were.

"You both mean a lot to me. In fact, I know I couldn't have made it through all this without either of you."

"Especially me," said Ethan without missing a beat. His mouth twisted in a wry smirk. I laughed a little.

"But the fact is, I think I need some time to be alone right now."

An awkward silence followed.

I looked carefully at them both. Ethan shoved his hands in his pockets and looked away.

Jack's jaw tightened. He looked at me for a few long moments. And then he nodded. "I think it's for the best. I think that's exactly what you need."

Ethan cleared his throat. "Can't change your mind?" he asked, raising an eyebrow.

I smiled weakly and shook my head.

He shrugged. "Well, *I* think you're making a mistake, Montgomery. A grave mistake." His voice carried a faint note of teasing. And then he grew serious again. "But if that's what you need, then I can respect that, too."

A lump stuck in my throat. I loved them both. How was that even possible? They were so different. So wonderful in their ways, but entirely incomparable. Like chocolate and pizza.

"I think I'm going to just walk for a little. Okay?" I said. There were no more dangers tonight. Nothing to be afraid of.

I could see Jack struggling with an urge to protect me, to take me home.

Instead, he nodded.

"Be careful," Ethan said to me. And with that, the two of them went their separate ways, Ethan climbing back on his motorcycle, Jack heading to his car.

I walked back along the Seine alone. The breeze ruffled my hair, and I gazed at the lights reflected in the river. A gust of wind carried the ever-present smell of bakeries just starting their day, impossibly early. I took a deep breath.

Paris was the City of Lights. A fabled city. Just like the diamond that had only minutes ago been in my possession. The cursed diamond that had saved my life.

I reached into my pocket, and my hand closed around something flat and smooth. I pulled out my tarot card: the Star. I stared at it for a few moments, then tossed it into the Seine.

I had conquered my fear, and I had faced my own mortality. Fear did not own me anymore, and death was not going to have me. Someday, of course, it would find my door. But that day was not yet.

Not just yet.

Acknowledgments

I would like to thank all the people whose lives were touched—for better or for worse—by the Hope Diamond: Jean-Baptiste Tavernier, Marie Antoinette, Louis-Francois Cartier, Evalyn MacLean, Harry Winston, and U.S. Postman James Todd. Their stories are more incredible than any fiction I could have dreamed up.

I want to thank my agent, Sandy Lu, my editor, Peter Senftleben, and the incredible team at Kensington Books.

A giant hug of gratitude goes to my critique partner Karma Brown, for making everything better. Heartfelt thanks go to Eileen Cook and Melissa Cutler for helping me navigate the bewildering waters of authorhood.

Thanks to the Surrey International Writers' Conference, and the SIWC community at large, for providing encouragement, a safe haven, and an annual writerly paradise that has encouraged this writer to dream impossible things.

Kisses to my boys for being patient with their mama when she needed to disappear under her laptop for just a few more minutes. Hugs to Disney Channel and Lego, for buying me extra slivers of writing time.

I will forever thank my partner in crime—my husband Ken—for supporting me right from the start.

And thank you to the city of Paris. No explanation required.

About the Author

Kim Foster is the author of the Agency of Burglary & Theft Series, a series of novels about a professional female jewel thief. Prior to writing thrillers about thieves and spies, Kim obtained her degree in medicine, and she has been a practicing family doctor for fifteen years. (Don't worry, it doesn't make much sense to her friends and family, either.) Online, you can find her blogging about her left-brain, right-brain mash up on *www.kimfoster.com*. Kim lives with her husband and their two young boys in Victoria, British Columbia, where she's hard at work on her next book. And drinking a ridiculous amount of coffee.